IGOR AND THE TWISTED TALES OF CASTLEMAINE

IGOR AND THE TWISTED TALES OF CASTLEMAINE

RICHARD L MARKWORTH
& IAN J WALLS

Copyright © 2022 Richard L Markworth & Ian J Walls
Cover artwork by Simon Pritchard

The moral right of the author has been asserted.

Apart from any fair dealing for the purposes of research or private study,
or criticism or review, as permitted under the Copyright, Designs and Patents
Act 1988, this publication may only be reproduced, stored or transmitted, in
any form or by any means, with the prior permission in writing of the
publishers, or in the case of reprographic reproduction in accordance with
the terms of licences issued by the Copyright Licensing Agency. Enquiries
concerning reproduction outside those terms should be sent to the publishers.

This is a work of fiction. Names, characters, businesses, places, events
and incidents are either the products of the author's imagination
or used in a fictitious manner. Any resemblance to actual persons,
living or dead, or actual events is purely coincidental.

Matador
Unit E2 Airfield Business Park,
Harrison Road, Market Harborough,
Leicestershire. LE16 7UL
Tel: 0116 2792299
Email: books@troubador.co.uk
Web: www.troubador.co.uk/matador
Twitter: @matadorbooks

ISBN 978 1803132 068

British Library Cataloguing in Publication Data.
A catalogue record for this book is available from the British Library.

Printed and bound in Great Britain by 4edge Limited
Typeset in 11pt Minion Pro by Troubador Publishing Ltd, Leicester, UK

Matador is an imprint of Troubador Publishing Ltd

For Jenni and Anne

In loving memory of Trevor Markworth

CONTENTS

Preface	ix
The Heads Up	1
Body Part I: Igor's Undertaking	24
Body Part II: The Nun, The Saint, And The Crypt o' Zoology	100
The Midriff	161
Body Part III: The Hyde Entity Crisis	166
Body Part IV: Medium At Large	217
Body Part V: The Graveyard Shift	276
The Tale End	326
Postface	330
Acknowledgements	332

PREFACE

The following is an extract from Roderick Sump's *The Saddle-Sore Traveller: My Life on the Road*, originally published in serialised form in the gentleman's quarterly *The Loafer's Gazette* (discontinued due to reader apathy).

There are dark places in this world.

Existing in the grey periphery of a so-called reality that educated man has convinced himself is the one and only truth, sinister enclaves lurk atop a mysterious nexus of interweaving doorways; doorways that lead from and to the unearthly supernatural plane.

These are bad places. They act as magnets to creatures of unimaginable darkness, to the criminal, the insane, the vice-ridden, and politicians. Amongst those poor denizens who attempt to eke out a living here and lead a normal, everyday existence dwell *others*; creatures of myth and legend to most, but here in these cursed domains, creatures that are all too real.

Such a place is the ancient settlement of Castlemaine. Nestled in the foothills of the Carpathians in the haunted land of Transylvania, it squats like a malignant, if slightly tatty, spider, surrounded by a web of deeply forested mountains, waiting, ever waiting for the unwary traveller.

The citizens of Castlemaine are mostly simple folk, low on teeth but stout of heart. And how they need to be to live and thrive in such an environment. A nagging sense of danger is an ever-present companion as they weave their way through the narrow alleyways and go about their business. Nonetheless, they take solace in their church, their families, and large quantities of ale.

Tarry not in this vicinity, fellow traveller, for here the night holds terrors. In Castlemaine, the vampire takes wing, the cutthroat lurks around every corner, the witch casts her spell and the dead travel fast. Well, some of them. Others tend to shamble a bit.

Castlemaine is not a place for the pure of heart; it is a village of the damned, although, to be fair, you can still get a tasty pie. Pass through if you must but make haste and, whatever your circumstances, be sure to have left its sinister grasp far behind before darkness falls. For if you linger, you may find yourself forever entwined in the deep and dreadful twisted tales of Castlemaine.

THE HEADS UP

'Two more jugs of ale, Basil, and look lively.' Hector Smallfoot, puffed up, self-important and all-round loathsome clerk to the Burgermeister of Castlemaine, shouted across the saloon bar of The Cadaver's Arms to its huge, one-eyed landlord.

Smallfoot and his two sniggering companions, Maurice Flatweight and Percival Stoat, were often to be seen conspiring drunkenly together at one of the inn's corner tables after work hours. The abhorrent trio were generally avoided by most of the other townsfolk on account of their penchant for tomfoolery and causing unnecessary suffering and embarrassment to the lower classes at every opportunity.

The three miscreants had just spent several minutes loudly berating an elderly man at the next table for smelling of wee and threatening to have his aged wife imprisoned for extreme ugliness and had, as a result, worked up a serious thirst.

Most other townsfolk knew better than to interfere on the grounds that Smallfoot had access to the town's land records and had been known to move a field boundary here or burn a deed of ownership there, whenever he felt slighted.

'Basil! Ale! Move it man!' shouted Smallfoot impatiently, before adding, 'You pathetic one-eyed bag of old flab,' under his breath. His two companions giggled noisily at what they thought was a subtly crafted and highly witty invective.

Angering Basil rarely did anyone's hopes of a long and happy life much good, but what Smallfoot lacked in common human decency, he more than made up for in cowardice. He always kept his voice low when casting insults at the bear-like landlord.

'Keep your wig on, you powdered prat,' muttered Basil as he fought to deliver five plates of something brown and steaming to a table of travelling pike sharpeners.

It was well known across much of Europe that Transylvania had trained the best pike sharpeners since the days of Vlad the Impaler. Impaling an enemy on the point of a blunt pike was seen as incredibly gauche and unsophisticated, and was generally frowned upon, not least by the person on the receiving end. It was a matter of great pride in the country to have their executed prisoners slide smoothly down the shaft of a well-honed pike rather than see them stick part way down and have to be tugged at in a most undignified manner. That sort of uncivilised behaviour could be left to those nasty foreigner types.

The pike sharpeners had arrived at the inn unannounced that afternoon on their way back from a highly successful pike-sharpening conference, somewhere north of the

Carpathian Mountains. Their unexpected arrival had upset Basil's delicate catering plans. Finding a supplier of sufficient steaming brown at this short notice was never an easy task.

Having deposited the plates, he swung back towards the bar to fulfil Master Smallfoot's order, gathering up empty mugs and jugs as he went.

Two of the inn's scrawny servants scuttled to and fro between bar and kitchen carrying various trays of filth and detritus, all the time keeping a wary eye out for a sweeping right-handed slap from their employer. Basil liked nothing more than to vent his perpetual seething anger at his hapless minions.

It was common knowledge locally that Basil seethed angrily most of the time. In fact, the only respite Basil had from angry-seething was the odd occasion when he upgraded his ire to a full-blown furious rage. This top-level lividity however was usually reserved for when the regional tax collectors came to visit. Basil's books were the best cooked in the area but still his cordon bleu accounting skills were no match for the blood-sucking talents of the Queen's top tax inspectors, all of whom descended from one or other of the region's ancient vampire families.

On those days, the servants usually wore their thickest woollen garments, layer upon layer as a pathetic form of armour that they somehow believed would soften or deflect the harsh thumping salvos that would randomly explode from their monstrous employer. It rarely did.

Of course, all this pent-up anger had a negative effect on Basil's blood pressure, which usually sat somewhere between throbbing eyeball and pulsating temple, but was known, on occasion, to hit the rarefied heights of 'run away, run away, he's going to blow'.

It was during a particularly difficult visit by the full entourage of Prince Wilderhelm, minor royal and well-known drunken roisterer, that a surge of blood pressure had finally caused Basil's left eye to burst out of his head, and fly directly into the Prince's gin cocktail. Prince Wilderhelm, a great one for jolly japes, and a total git to peasantry everywhere, had merely picked up the alcohol-soaked eyeball and proceeded to munch on it like a bloated and bloodshot olive.

Basil, slow as he was under normal circumstances to comprehend the wider consequences of his more violent actions, somehow managed to rein in his temper and thereby avoid being pricked to death on the expertly sharpened pikes of the Prince's guards.

The points of said weapons were, at the merest flicker of the Prince's eyebrow, aimed at the apoplectic innkeep's more delicate areas, provocatively but silently daring him to say something rude or out of turn so they could slice him into perfect juliennes of landlord.

Instead, knowing his place, and with a canny instinct for avoiding suicidal outbursts, Basil bowed meekly and shuffled backwards to the scullery door.

Once inside he gave the sweeping boy a fearsome look that turned the poor lad's knees to jelly, and his teeth pure white.

The eyeball incident had happened over twenty years previously, but it still gave Basil a great deal of pleasure to remember that the Prince had died several days after from a severe bout of gastro-conjunctivitis.

THE HEADS UP

Basil filled two great earthenware jugs with dark, frothy ale from a barrel behind the ancient, worm-ridden bar, and grasping one in each hand carried them to the inglenook where Master Smallfoot and his companions sat smoking and joking in a loud alcoholic haze.

'Top man, landlord,' blustered Stoat, a wiry youth sporting a short curly white powdered wig and a pair of cheap business hose above scuffed and dull-buckled square-toed shoes.

Basil mumbled something foul and uncomplimentary under his breath as he turned to attend his other duties. He was stopped suddenly by Smallfoot who placed a limp and clammy hand upon Basil's scarred and heavily tattooed forearm.

'I say, Basil, old chap. I don't suppose any of your charming serving wenches would be available to join our merry little party tonight, would they?'

Basil, always happy to fleece extra money from his customers by supplying a wide and interesting range of services, anything from buffet catering to contract killings, considered the options.

'Hmmm, well, it's Rachel's night off and Gilda had to go and visit her dying uncles over in Hertzberg.'

'Dying uncles? Plural?'

'That be so, yes.'

'Is there a pox among them?'

'No, they're being hanged in the morning on the orders of the bishop.'

'Ah, crimes against the Lord! Quite right they should swing. What exactly did they do?'

'Well,' explained Basil, scanning the room as he spoke as if imparting a deeply guarded secret, 'seems they took a jug of holy water from the font at Saint Augustine's church without asking permission. Something about cleansing the village of an evil, undead creature that's been roaming around in the night and causing the local sheep to walk funny.'

'That sounds like quite a noble action,' put in Flatweight. 'Not a hanging offence at all, surely?'

'Normally you'd be right,' replied the landlord, 'but the Bishop of Saint Augustine, as many in Castlemaine know to their cost, is a vain old sermoniser. He took umbrage at the brothers for cramping his ecclesiastical style. Said if anyone was going to exorcise undead spirits of the damned it'd be a properly trained member of the Catholic Church, and not some jumped-up peasant ghost blusterers.'

Basil removed a filthy, foul-smelling rag from his belt and began wiping the table with it, leaving dark, greasy smears where previously there had only been light greasy smears. With a furtive glance over his shoulder to ensure their talk was not being overheard, he continued. 'Well, you know what religious folk can be like. They enjoy nothing more than a good bit of killing in the name of the Lord. So, he had them arrested for practising witchcraft and sentenced to death without appeal.'

'Ah, of course,' declared Smallfoot knowingly. 'A bishop is perfectly entitled to use spiritual magic but if a layperson does the same then it's obviously witchcraft. If I wasn't so convinced of the divine purity and forthright benevolence of the Church and its ministers, I'd be inclined to suggest that it's a tad...' Smallfoot paused to consider his words, 'hypocritical? Don't you think?'

THE HEADS UP

'Mind what you say, Master Smallfoot,' replied Basil in low tones, once more checking the room with his remaining eye for anyone who might have overheard their exchange. 'There hasn't been an official witchfinder in these parts for many a year, but that doesn't mean there aren't still folk around willing to earn a few schillings by selling overheard whispers to the Church. Bishops still need to hit their hellfire and damnation quotas, however enlightened the times may be. And the Bishop of Saint Augustine's knows how to hold a grudge.' Basil raised his hands to illustrate his point, his palms upturned. 'Very, very firmly by the boll…'

'Hmmm, well, I see,' interrupted Smallfoot impatiently, 'that's all well and good and very entertaining I'm sure, Basil, but your lack of available wenches is certainly not encouraging. Have you nothing to offer us this night but cold mutton chops and filthy beer?'

Basil mumbled something noncommittal while his thinning brain cells worked on the problem. He could feel his chances of earning a few extra bob slipping away and made a mental note to have the rest of Gilda's relatives quietly murdered as soon as possible so she'd have no further reason to take time off.

'I see,' continued Smallfoot, pushing away his near-empty tankard of ale. 'Well, we shall just have to take our custom to the Butcher's Block down in Lower Flinching from now on.'

'Well, I suppose there's old Flossie,' mumbled Basil in desperation.

'What? That ancient, toothless old hag?' blurted Smallfoot, gurning his features into a rictus of disgust at the very thought. 'She must be, what? Forty-five at least.'

'Maybe so,' grumbled Basil defensively. 'But she knows more tricks than Merlin's dog, and you can have her company for the evening at… err… shall we say three silver schillings a piece?'

'Three silver… are you mad?'

'All right, two. But mind you buy her drinks. She has a nasty habit of cutting bits off folk when she's kept sober too long.'

'Oh, well all right,' complained the clerk. 'Any port in a storm, I suppose. Where is the old trollop?'

'I sent her out to fetch wood for the fire, should be back any moment.' So saying, Basil shuffled back across the saloon bar, giving an unlucky servant a hefty cuff on the forehead, for no particular reason.

*

Outside, the wind had picked up and rain was battering the nicotine-encrusted panes of the Cadaver's Arms. A sudden bolt of lightning rent the heavens. The gnarled and twisted shapes of ancient trees flickered into view before once again disappearing into darkness leaving nothing but a vague tree-shaped impression glowing ghost-like in the eye of the beholder. Not that there were any beholders around to behold anything quite so prosaic on such a filthy night as this. Except for one, perhaps, wrapped in a tattered cloak with her hood pulled tight against the stinging bite of the foul weather, slipping and staggering in the wet mud of the road with the large cumbersome load she carried bearing her down.

THE HEADS UP

Flossie cursed her aged bones as she struggled towards the scullery door, laden as she was with a shifting bundle of fallen branches gathered from the nearby woodland. Gone were the days when she had servants of her own to do this type of thing. She shuffled to the door and gave it a thump with her elbow, causing the uneven branches to cascade from her grip and land in a woody heap on the rain-sodden ground. She swore loudly and bent down to pick up her burden, just as Basil jerked open the door from within.

'What are you playing at there, you haggard old trout?' shouted Basil, caringly.

A short blade of steel caught the light from the scullery lantern as it flashed towards Basil's throat. For all her years, Flossie had the speed of a whipped mongoose and a look in her keen, green eyes that would make the devil himself think twice about swearing in front of his granny.

'Mind your tongue, Basil,' hissed Flossie as the point of her knife pressed into his sagging dewlap. 'And remember your place. Don't start believing our little charade is real or I'll have you buried… with the others.'

Basil swallowed nervously; his demeanour changed to one of cowering contrition.

'Apologies ma'am, I was just keeping up appearances, you know, in case… you know who… should overhear.'

Flossie released her grip on Basil's shirt collar and sheathed her knife in a swift and well-practised movement. At the same time, she seemed to shrivel back into an old worn-out sack of bones and disappointment.

'Next time I'll aim a lot lower and you'll lose another left one,' she murmured as she picked up her bundle and shuffled into the scullery. After dropping the wood near the stove, she sagged into a low chair beside the kitchen fireplace.

For several minutes Flossie didn't move. To a curious onlooker she could just as easily have been asleep or dead. She was neither, which is not important as there were no curious onlookers to worry about it anyway.

Slowly, Flossie shuffled herself upright and cast a keen glance around the room to satisfy herself once and for all on the question of curious onlookers. Having established their definitive absence, she put her hand inside her coat and gently pulled out an old and worn silver locket. With her thumbnail she prised it open, the two halves falling apart in her hands. The hinge had long ago given up the ghost and no longer fulfilled its one simple duty.

Inside one half of the locket was a miniature portrait of an attractive young woman, aged no more than twenty-four, with full, cherry-red lips, keen green eyes and a cascade of sumptuous auburn hair, which curled in an appealingly charming manner over her soft, sun-kissed shoulders. The other half of the locket bore the faded and mildewed image of a man. Neither young nor old, handsome nor unattractive. When Flossie looked at his picture, he appeared for all the world to be staring at something just over her left shoulder. She smiled as she remembered the events of that day, when the image had been painted, and what it was he had been so obsessed with behind her. In those far-off days pretty much everything had been possible. The world was a very different place then. She had been young, vigorous, and full of adventure; he had been a bright, if somewhat sarcastic and occasionally psychopathic, companion.

THE HEADS UP

Her reverie was shattered by the return of the bulbous landlord, back now in full character.

'There's a group in the saloon bar have paid for your company. Go, wench, and make sure they drink plenty.'

Flossie carefully closed the locket and tucked it back inside her tattered jacket. Raising her withered limbs from the chair she went to the mirror with the intention of juggling her aged and battered features into something resembling human. She sighed as she contemplated her reflection.

'Oh, well. Silk purse, pig's scrotum,' she mumbled as she made her way towards the bar.

*

Smallfoot and his two crapulous companions had finished the jugs of ale and were embarking on a bottle of rough gin when Flossie shuffled across to their table.

'Evening gents, what'll it be?' She smiled her best gap-toothed grin at the expectant trio. 'Harriet handy and her five little friends? Or shall I drink you all under the table, if you get my meaning?' she emphasised with a conspiratorial wink.

Flossie had always relied on her less-than-appealing looks to ensure that she'd never actually have to perform any such salacious acts. Her breath alone was normally sufficient to send any potential punters running for the chuck bucket. This was why she always waited until their blood alcohol level was at maximum before flashing her deflated cleavage in the direction of any randy revellers. She knew that if she timed it right, she could keep them upright just long enough to pocket the silver and watch as they keeled over into a fug of forgetfulness. She hoped and expected that these three losers would be no different and she could make a few silver pieces without having to overstretch herself, either emotionally or orally.

Tonight, however, Hector Smallfoot had decided that he was a man on a mission. After a hard day's clerking for the corpulent, cantankerous, and highly corrupt Burgermeister of Castlemaine, he was ready for some real man's fun. He'd ensured his comrades had outpaced him with the drink so he would be certain to be the last man standing, and by extension, the first man laying, and he was full ripe and ready to dip his quill into a very different kind of inkwell tonight.

'Here, wench,' he cried as he grabbed Flossie forcibly by the wrist and dragged her with a painful thump and clatter of broken pottery and bruised elbows over the table. It was to be a grave mistake; her finely honed defensive instincts kicked in instantly and produced a flash of steel that sent his earlobe spinning across the floor towards the startled pike sharpeners.

A shrill squeal emanated from the wounded clerk. Nimble as a pricked weasel, he spun Flossie around and forced her knife hand above her head, holding it in the tallow-smoked flame of the candle. Flossie screamed and let go of the knife, just as she brought her knee up into Smallfoot's unsuspecting dangly bits.

Smallfoot groaned and rolled into an agonised ball in the sawdust. By this time however his two accomplices had roused themselves from their drunken indolence and were just quick enough to pin Flossie back onto the table before she could stand up to finish the job.

Smallfoot staggered to his feet, a look of sheer hatred etched into his features. He picked up Flossie's knife and lunged towards her, intent on carving rude characters all over her already tortured face.

He was about to start cutting the first slice when Basil's huge hairy fist caught Smallfoot under the chin and lifted him several feet into the air and he went crashing backwards into the coat rack.

Basil immediately turned his attention to the other two miscreants, who rapidly hightailed it out the side door on seeing his huge bulk moving in their direction. With the other two gone, Basil cast a final glance towards Smallfoot, who was now clearly unconscious and quite satisfyingly impaled on a jagged coat hook, which protruded in a very pleasing manner from his right shoulder.

Most of the bar's other customers settled back to their drink and interrupted conversations, the night's entertainment seemingly over.

Flossie forced herself up and examined her bruised and battered limbs. Nothing broken at least. But she was angry that such a whelp as Smallfoot could have bested her. There was a time when his throat would have been yawning redly, cast open by her scything blade long before he'd got a hand on her. Age, it seemed, had finally caught up with her.

With a barely stifled groan she stood upright and started to clear away the damaged crockery when she suddenly realised that the rest of the room had gone utterly silent.

Looking around she saw that all of the inn's customers were staring at her with an air of surprise and wonder. One of the elderly pike sharpeners, an ancient master of the art, was holding something in the palms of his hands. Everyone was crowding around and craning their necks to catch a glimpse of the object.

The old pike sharpener looked at Flossie, his eyes moist with remembrance and recognition, two halves of a broken silver locket resting on his upturned hands.

'Esmerelda,' he said at last. 'Is… that… really… you?'

Flossie staggered backwards into the table, shocked at hearing herself called by the name Esmerelda after so many years. Her locket, having fallen free during the scuffle, was now being held by a man she didn't know, but who seemingly knew her, and her secret.

*

Esmerelda sat across from the old pike sharpener, the broken locket on the table between them. This, it seemed, was where the curious onlookers had been lurking all along, as a gaggle of them huddled around the table, always glad to hear anything with a whiff of gossip and scandal about it.

'How do you know that name?' she asked, trembling, unsure whether it was because of fear that her secret had been discovered after all this time, or of anger that her secret had been discovered after all this time. Unable to decide which, she determined to put the matter aside for consideration at a more suitable moment.

'Your picture, here, in this locket. I should have seen it the minute you came into the room. Nobody has eyes like Esmerelda of Castlemaine.'

'But who are you?' she asked softly, still taken aback by the sudden whirlwind of memories being awakened. Then, quick as a blade, her tone changed to one full of menacing grit and suspicion. 'And what do you want?'

'So, you still don't recognise me?' The old man smiled and laid his hand on hers.

'There is something familiar about you but I can't quite...'

'It's not surprising, I have changed much. But I wasn't always a master pike sharpener you know,' the old man confided. 'I was a... village priest once.'

'Father Price!' Recognition instantly flooded Esmerelda's vision as the years rolled away and she saw before her again the young novice priest who had been a part of so many of her youthful adventures. 'I can't believe it. I never thought I would see you again. But how...? Why...? Wh...? Why a pike sharpener?'

'It's a living,' replied the old man.

'But you were a priest, I thought you were all married to God for eternity or something.'

'Technically, yes, but I'm sure you remember the incident with the nun, Sister Vigilanta?'

'Oh yes,' replied Esmerelda. 'She was quite the unholy bitch.'

'Yes, well, the Bishop of Saint Augustine's had had it in for me for a very long time. Many years after the event, and having discovered nothing of the truth of Sister Vigilanta's "disappearance", he decided that I was to be held responsible,' said the priest. 'It had happened in my parish, on my watch. It was perfect for him. He needed a scapegoat to deflect any papal displeasure from his own doorstep, so he had me excommunicated. Would have had me imprisoned as accomplice to her murder too if I hadn't made a run for it.' The old man paused in remembrance of the events and fondled his pike, thoughtfully.

'But as far as anyone knows she's still alive out there, somewhere.' Esme waved her arm vaguely in the rough direction of somewhere.

'You and I know that, as did most of Castlemaine at the time, but the bishop refused to listen. He wanted my scalp. Anyway, I did what any self-respecting priest would do in such circumstances and legged it. After a few months travelling with no purpose in mind I happened across a group of itinerant pike sharpeners on the road and decided to stick with it. The hours are OK and the money's not bad, plus it's handy to have a trade to fall back on. Although, you don't really want to fall back on a sharpened pike… harrumphahaha.' He chuckled noisily at his own joke.

After a few moments of stony silence from his audience he gathered himself and continued.

'I keep up with the self-flagellation of course, just for the err… exercise.'

Esmerelda laughed.

'But you,' the old man enquired, 'why the false name and the deception? Your father owned this place, surely it should be you in charge now, not that lumbering ogre.'

'I do own it,' she admitted. 'Basil is my guard dog. More dangerous than a dozen Rottweilers, although admittedly he smells worse and isn't as bright, but he's good with a duster. After my father died, I inherited the inn and all that went with it, the good and the bad.'

Esmerelda turned away from the old man and looked ruefully through the filthy window. She made a mental note to get one of the servants to scrape off a few years' worth of nicotine build-up, brighten the place up a bit. A moment passed silently before she turned her gaze back to her old friend, quickly wiping her sleeve across her damp eyes.

'Things have changed here since you left,' she continued. 'All the magic has gone. All the spirit, all the fun. Chased away by cruel people with no love of the unknown and no sense of imagination. It's just a dark, cold, poverty-stricken hole like any other town in this dismal country.' A look of deep sadness shadowed Esmerelda's already gaunt face as she thought about those days long ago.

'When the old king died and his pious young daughter took the throne there was the purge, and all the old ways were destroyed. Anyone thought to have been involved was imprisoned or executed. I hid. The old Esmerelda had nothing to stay here for, so I left Basil in charge and disappeared. Went to spend some time with my mother's folk up in the mountains.' Esme studied the backs of her old and wrinkled hands.

'I came back as Flossie, to all intents and purposes a raggedy old scrubber. Most of the townsfolk had either moved on or forgotten me, thinking me dead or in prison. I'd changed a lot in the intervening years, so keeping up the pretence wasn't difficult. Until today.'

There was a long silence as the old man thought about the changes in her and how hard her life must have been since he last knew her.

'And what happened to…?' he began.

She cut him off abruptly. 'Finish your story, tell me, why was the pope so interested in the disappearance of a single, low-grade nun in some Transylvanian backwater?' asked Esmerelda.

'Ah, well, it turns out she was one of *his*.' The old man let the word hang in the air like a dying criminal.

'One of... his...?' she prompted.

'Yes, one of the Holy Father's elite demon hunters. Sent here to rid the country of the scourge of the undead and all other forms of manifest evil.'

'Well, she definitely had her work cut out here,' replied Esmerelda, smiling.

'Yes, and we all know why,' replied the former priest. 'You and Igor had quite a hand in events back in those days.'

Esmerelda winced at the reference.

'Where is... he... by the way?'

'Don't know,' replied Esmerelda, trying to hide the sudden dry croak from her voice.

The old man looked caringly at his old friend from many years ago and sighed.

*

'Igor! I remember that name,' said a rough voice from across the bar. 'A name of ill omen in these parts, so they say.'

The rough voice belonged to a weathered traveller with a long, tousled beard, worn leather boots, an ancient tricorn hat that sat low across his brow and a battered and stained travelling cloak, which he had cast onto the bench beside him. Until this moment, he had been sitting alone and unnoticed under the large bay window, silently watching the lightning tear up the night sky.

'Well, they say wrong,' replied Esmerelda fiercely.

'Do they indeed?' said the traveller, warming to his subject. 'I've been wandering these dark roads and forests for nigh on thirty years and I've heard a thing or two about old Igor in my time. Even now, men fear to speak his name too loudly within earshot of the boneyard after darkness. 'Tis said that he was dragged down into the fearsome sweaty pits of hell by the Devil hisself.'

'Cobblers!' shouted Esmerelda.

Another voice joined the conversation. 'I heard he ran off with a pack of rampant nuns on All Hallow's Eve, taking the gold cross from the altar and wearing a crown made from the holy relics of Saint Augustine,' suggested a small, barrel-shaped woman with an intense stare and a long bone pipe clenched between her uneven yellowed teeth.

'Absolute rubbish... he wasn't like that.'

'Came back from the dead and brought pestilence to the village, and a plague of ducks...' added another voice. 'Least, that's what I was told.'

Suddenly a cacophony of voices started shouting out snippets of half-heard legends and rumour that they'd picked up from very reliable and expert sources on the subject, usually in the alehouse after a long night imbibing copious flagons of Brother Percy's Rampant Smock Lifter.

'He turned the Burgermeister into a pig and spit-roasted him,' called a voice.

'Cut off his own head and played skittles with it,' suggested another.

'He lay with a cat.'

'Ate people's livers while they were asleep.'

'Drank the blood of virgins... well, not in Castlemaine, obviously.'

'Cavorted with witches and warlocks.'

'Taught Morris dancing.'

'NOW THAT'S ENOUGH!' shouted Esmerelda. 'I won't hear any more of these lies about...' she paused, trying desperately to hold her emotions together. She failed. 'About the man... I loved,' she ended, slumping down into her chair, and burying her face into her hands, tears leaking through old bony fingers.

The crowd, mumbling and abashed, settled back to their tables. Father Price put a caring arm across Esmerelda's shoulders.

The rough traveller threw back his head and laughed hard. As he did so a shower of food morsels dropped from their hiding places within his grizzled and twisted beard. He cared not a jot. His beard contained more decaying crumbs of bread and flakes of meat than the grocer's barrow and village midden pit combined. With a beard such as his, no man needs go hungry for long. It was said that travellers' beards were highly prized among the starving poor, who could sustain their families for many weeks on the edible remains contained within the longest and most tangled examples.

It was mainly for this reason that the bearded traveller was becoming so rare a sight these days, and was believed by many to have been pushed to the brink of extinction by hungry beard hunters. The traveller by the window was long in both tooth and beard and gave not a fig for such trivial dangers.

'She loved him!' he taunted quietly from his window seat. 'It's all lies, she says.' He spat onto the beer-soaked floor, improving it slightly. 'Good riddance to bad company I say,' cursed the traveller, rising to his feet. 'And this Igor, so the old folk tell it, was the darkest company you could ever fear to find yourself troubled with in those days. Brought evil and damnation to the land hereabouts, so he did. Are you all fools? Do you all not remember the dark tales of Igor?'

He sat down with a thump, scattering bits of cheese and cake across the table from deep within his bushy follicles.

Slowly, the pike-sharpening former priest stood up and cast a withering look around the hushed and sceptical gathering.

'I remember!' he proclaimed. 'I remember what Igor did for the people of this town all those years ago. He was no villain. He was no devil. He was no saint, I'll grant you. He was no murderer. Well, OK, maybe he was a bit of a murderer, but only when absolutely essential, and only ever for the greater good of the community. But those were indeed dark times, and Igor was a beacon of hope when all forms of law, order and authority had sought to beat us down. It was a time of vampires, of werewolves and lunatics. Of dangerous, mad scientists, necromancers, and ghastly demons. And worst of all,' the old man's voice fell to a whisper, 'nuns!'

An awed silence fell upon all those present as the former priest's sermon continued.

'When we'd all but given up the dream of ever finding peace in our tormented lives, it was Igor who came to Castlemaine and brought with him hope, and a means to fight back. Do you not remember *that*?' The old priest resumed his seat, wearied by the exertion and emotion.

'Thank you,' said Esmerelda, placing her gnarled old hand gently on his.

'Pisspots!' said the traveller.

'You knew him so well,' put in the pipe-smoking, swivel-eyed barrel woman. 'Tell us then. Tell us the truth about this "holier than thou" Igor of yours.'

Esmerelda felt her face getting hot and her eyes dampen as she fought back the tears of memory and loss.

'I can't,' she whispered weakly.

'Pfft! What did I tell you?' crowed the weathered traveller. ''Tis nothing but lies and mummery from those who would hide their own past crimes. There is nothing good to hear about that devil, Igor. Why, if she could tell us but one single piece of good that that man had done, then I'd happily shave off my beard, strap a full-grown badger to my naked buttocks and run from this place to spend the rest of my days in service to the sea-dwelling monks of St Olaf the Salty.'

Esmerelda slowly lifted herself upright, a steely look of resolution in her keen, green eyes as she stared down the traveller.

'All right then,' she said firmly, 'you're on.'

*

The storm outside raged noisily on as the inhabitants of the Cadaver's Arms crowded around Esmerelda and Father Price to hear the tales of Igor. Some gossiped among themselves and others joked freely as the two servants brought more jugs and bottles, along with trays full of edible dainties that Basil had quickly thrown together.

THE HEADS UP

As soon as the nibbles were set down, the hungry revellers fell upon them with gusto. Some of them were sweet, some of them were savoury. But in the main, most were highly unsavoury and in fact downright unpleasant. Complaints were muttered quietly about the sudden mysterious and suspicious disappearance of the weathered traveller and the high number of beard hairs curling out from the prawn vol-au-vents.

Basil, gently kicking an ancient tricorn hat under the seat by the bay window, averted his eyes innocently.

But all chatter stopped and those present sat rapt in a respectful silence as Esmerelda began.

BODY PART I

IGOR'S UNDERTAKING

Igor stood in his dank, smelly chamber and stared into a broken shard of mirror at his sorry reflection. Neither young nor old, handsome nor unattractive; anywhere else he could have passed as just a normal everyday man about town. Albeit one with a slightly twisted set of morals and a penchant for keeping spare human body parts about him on the off-chance they'd come in handy.

Another day of toil and drudgery was grinding slowly by. His reflection looked back at him with an air of resigned indifference as if to say, 'This is it boy, this is the life you wanted, what you spent all those years training for. You made your bed, now wallow in it!'

Bed! Igor hadn't seen a bed in years let alone slept in one. The closest thing to a bed he could actually remember sleeping in was a pile of cow dung when he was seven. The corners of his mouth twitched involuntarily upwards as he recalled the warm, blissful comfort of the fresh, steaming heap. His reflection glared back at him, unimpressed by this brief glimmer of emotion. It was not his place to be happy, not even for a split second. 'No mirth here, chummy,' whispered the voice inside his head that berated him constantly. 'You're not paid to smile.' Igor's brow furrowed; he couldn't remember being paid for anything at all.

Bed! The very thought reminded him of the long hours of toil he still had ahead of him before he could sink, ever so fleetingly, into the abyss of forgetful sleep. He slept in a bucket these days. A bucket in the mortuary toilet. The only concession to his existence as a real, living, breathing, caring, sensitive human being that had been afforded him by his psychopathic employer was a bucket in the mortuary toilet to call his own. It wasn't his own, of course, it still belonged to his master, but he chose to call it his own anyway. A Transylvanian's bucket is his castle, after all.

A chill wind blew into his chamber through an iron grate set high in the thick stone wall above, bringing the rain with it. His back hurt. In fact, pretty much most of him hurt pretty much most of the time. It was one of the many occupational hazards he had to contend with in his line of work.

Igor spat in his palm and ruffled up his hair. It didn't do to look too kempt in a job like his. Lab assistants were expected to be almost as crazy as the lunatics they worked for, and should never exhibit even the slightest intelligence or freedom of thought.

Those who dared to show enquiring minds, or worse, question their master's decisions, could easily find themselves reconsidering their life choices as they dropped speedily from the highest castle battlements onto some uncomfortable-looking rocks several thousand feet below.

This is exactly what had happened to Old Scrote, Igor's unfortunate predecessor, who had made the mistake of suggesting that a number-three scalpel might possibly be more effective at removing a particularly stubborn eyeball from a leathery old stiff, instead of the number-two scalpel his master had asked for.

Igor had been emptying buckets of rat entrails at the base of the castle wall when he heard the splash that Old Scrote made as his crumpled body liquified on the rocks nearby.

Still, every corpse has a silver lining, as the inspirational motto of the Lickspittle College for Unwanted Children reminded him, and it was due to Old Scrote's unfortunate and rather messy demise that Igor had finally received his chance for promotion. He determined early on that he would never make the same fateful mistake and had for many years now acted the part of the snivelling, dim-witted cur to a tee.

'Mmmm-me-me-me-me-me-me-me-meeeee.'

Igor began to work through his daily vocal exercises. It took serious training and a great deal of concentration for his voice to hit the right level of obsequious purr.

'La-la-la-la-la-la-la-la-la-la-la-la-la-laaaaa.'

The mummified body of a rat stared at him through its empty eye sockets from under a broken chair on the other side of the room.

'Come on Simon, join in. Ba-ba-ba-ba-ba-ba-ba-baaaa.'

The rat continued to stare back blankly, clearly unimpressed and with no intention of allowing itself to be drawn into the sad pantomime of Igor's sorry existence.

Simon, the dead rat, was Igor's only friend in the castle. He had been thoroughly loyal and kept all of Igor's secrets for nearly two years, ever since he'd wandered into the powerful spring trap that Igor had placed there for him.

Igor was grateful to have a friend like Simon with whom he could share all of his dreams and desires and to whom he could vent his ever-increasing frustrations at the tormented life of pain and drudgery he had to endure.

Life as the loyal, simpering sidekick to one of the region's top mad scientists hadn't turned out to be nearly as glamourous as he'd been led to believe during his time at Lickspittle College. Especially as his boss was the renowned Victor Frankenstein, the maddest crackpot in a region known the world over as the scientific equivalent of a box of frogs.

'Eeeee-eeeee-eeeee-eeeee,' continued Igor, grinning widely to ensure the correct enunciation.

According to his college lecturers, a career in Lickspitology was a great honour for any of the raggedy peasant children that found themselves abandoned on its doorstep virtually every day of the week. How else could they ever dream of a future that didn't involve a lifetime of scrabbling for decaying root vegetables in the compost heaps and cesspits of the world's better and more affluent folk?

Most of the children failed to make the grade and were either cast out in ignominy or, as was sometimes whispered, employed as the star attraction in one of the college's many dismemberment classes.

Those who managed to scrape through the exams learned all the vital skills that would one day see them elevated to the heady heights of subservient menial with a roof over their head and if they were really lucky, a bucket to sleep in.

'Oooh-oooh-oooh-oooh.   Aaah-aaah-aaah-aaah. Yeeeeeesssss maaaaasssteeerrrrrr.'

Igor had come top of his year in the fawning vocalisation classes. He was very proud of his servility skills and had honed them to a sharp point over the years.

But his heart just wasn't in it today. He sighed heavily and sat down on his bucket.

'It's not fair, Simon. I was never meant for this life. Not really.'

Igor saw the dead rat wink in sympathy to his moment of sadness as a small spider crawled into its blank eye socket.

'I know you'd help me if you could, old friend. It's just that I've been doing a lot of thinking lately and I feel I'm destined for so much more than this.' Igor glanced sadly at his sleeping bucket.

'I see people with real trades in the village and I really want to be part of that, you know? In the market, there are bakers and chandlers, greengrocers, and tinkers. Butchers! I could do that. I can cut up a body as well as any of them.'

Igor's face lit up as he spoke, his dreams of a better life among the normal folk of the world came alive before him. His misty eyes glazed over for a brief moment as he saw himself running a successful market stall, with housewives lined up around the block hoping to be on the receiving end of a sizeable portion of his meat.

Despite his rough upbringing and his long hours of menial servitude in the castle, Igor was no stranger to the ways of the wider world. He had travelled with his master on several occasions, when his brawn was required to help lug weighty corpses around the medical lecture circuit. Once in a very blue moon, Igor had managed to steal away into the night while his master was at some sumptuous dinner, or was busy entertaining the great and the good in an effort to secure backing for his latest crackpot scientific venture.

On those heady nights, when he was free, ever so fleetingly, to taste the pleasures of sin and debauchery like any normal person, Igor made sure to stuff everything humanly possible, as well as a few things morally questionable, into his moment of freedom. This usually consisted of a huge amount of alcohol and as much food as he could fit inside himself and his pockets. One time, he even entertained the company of a grim-looking lady of the night; which unfortunately left him with a nasty case of chaps in the morning.

All this fun was paid for by Igor's ability to filch purses from the oblivious hips of passing merchants, a trick he had learned long ago from an enterprising young girl at Lickspittle College who had taken him under her wing. Although how she had managed to keep those wings a secret from the other children was a total mystery to him.

Igor sighed as the images of a future where he was master of his own destiny danced before his eyes. Then, without warning, the vision flickered and faded as grim reality pushed its way back in once more.

'But no, Simon. I'm stuck here. It's so frustrating having to creep and fawn to that fruitcake physician up there. "Yeeesss masssteeer, Igooor looovveeess masssster",' said Igor sarcastically, rolling his eyes and bowing his head. 'It's so bloody demeaning.'

The spider ejected a trail of silk that shone silver in the candlelight, and looked just for a moment like a tear rolling over the rat's bony snout.

'No, don't upset yourself, dear Simon. I'm just a fool. What right have I got to feel sorry for myself, eh? It's not as if I have to live off rancid fish skins in the market gutters like old Claybark. He so nearly got the job in the acid bath house. If only he hadn't made such a fuss about the lack of PPE, he'd have been a shoo-in. And then there's Snudgepole. He got so desperate for food that he donated himself to the guild of body snatchers in return for a few silver schillings. Of course, he forgot to stipulate lead times. Got paid enough for one last meal of minced turnip and potatoes before he was clobbered from behind and taken away for dissection. I suppose that could have been me. Maybe I'm not so badly off after all.'

The spider forced its way into the dead rat's brain cavity and began nibbling on a nerve ending, causing Simon's parchment-like earlobe to twitch back and forth.

Igor immediately understood what his friend was saying.

'Of course, you're right Simon. Why shouldn't I have dreams, eh? Why can't I think of getting out, of bettering myself? I don't plan to end up as a stain on the mountainside like Old Scrote, and Old Toad before him. And Old Groveller before her. I'm so much better than them, I know I am.' Igor paced angrily around his grotty chamber, the swirling mixture of emotions making his head spin. Caring not a whit for the ironic symbolism, he kicked the bucket. 'I am so much better than… *this*.'

Igor's frustrations were building with all this pent-up self-reflection. He had come so far since his days as a gutter rat, passing through Lickspittle College and achieving more than he ever dared to dream in those far-off days. But as he grew, in stature and confidence, so had his ambitions. He knew he should be grateful for the opportunities he'd had, but that didn't stop the yearning within that just kept him wanting more and more out of life. He had buried his dreams of a better future deep but inside he knew he was capable of so much more than this miserable existence. One day he would strike out and make his way in the world. One day, the name of Igor would be known the world over, he'd be rich with servants, with a wife and family to call his own. He would be free.

A sudden flash of lightning scorched the sky outside the castle and the boom of thunder echoed long and deep within its walls.

The heat had gone from Igor's sudden burst of passion as quickly as it had arrived and he sagged visibly.

'No, Simon. I am who I am and I fear I will always be. Unless something serious changes, I expect to meet my end vertically as a wet smear on the unyielding granite below the castle. Thank you as always, my friend, for your sage counsel.'

The spider tugged on a desiccated remnant of the rat's spinal cord and Simon raised his paw in an apparent gesture of solidarity with his old friend's plight.

Igor smiled warmly.

'Well, better get back in character, I suppose.' He rose from his bucket and with a long-practised manoeuvre, he transformed his posture into the bent and twisted form he'd been taught to assume all those years ago in sycophancy class.

A bell rang somewhere deep in the castle.

'Commmiinnnnggg, maaaassssteeer,' he called into the darkness.

Igor picked up a tray of expensive-looking glass instruments and shuffled out into the winding corridors of Castle Frankenstein.

*

Laboratory A3, or the Edward Lionheart room as it was known, named in honour of a serial-killing thespian whose executed body had been put into specimen jars there, was dark. Dark, that is, save for a single flickering oil lamp standing at the edge of the surgeon's operating table. Thunder rumbled in the night sky and lightning tore great shreds out of the disgruntled heavens, as was so often the case in this part of the world. A place that God had turned away from in disgust so many ages ago.

It wasn't often that God threw up his hands and said, 'Sod it, I'm off,' but the lands around Castle Frankenstein had proved to be too unruly, too dark, and too evil even for Him to handle. Writing it off as a tax loss, God turned His attentions to other parts, and so created a new and purer land. A land of majestic mountains and wide deserts, verdant forests, and cold, clear rivers. And lo, he allowed this new land to be called 'America', and he looked down upon it and was glad, happy in the knowledge and sure expectation that nothing could possibly go wrong this time.

The dark, stormy atmosphere leant a good deal of gloomy ambience to the castle, which is, in fact, the main reason why the ancestors of the current owner had built it in the first place.

IGOR'S UNDERTAKING

The ancient stone edifice had stood with its roots embedded deep into the mountainside for more than six hundred years. Barely a day had gone by in all that time when the sky above the castle's vast roof and high turrets was not shrouded in brooding, menacing clouds.

Lightning had struck the castle so many times in its long and tortured life that the scarred spires and scorched battlements gave the appearance of having been whipped furiously throughout the ages by the devil's own fiery scourge.

In the gloom, the laboratory could have been a vast cavern with edges so distant that no quantity of lamps and candles could ever hope to pierce the infinite darkness. When the lightning outside blazed fiercely, for a brief instant it was possible to see just how close and confined the chamber really was.

Flash: there are the shelves, stuffed full of huge quantities of glass vessels, many containing organic specimens of unknown and dubious provenance.

Flash: there are the surgeon's tools, abandoned and bloodied in the cracked and dented bowl into which they had been roughly cast just moments before. Another frustratingly unsuccessful experiment had left its subject twitching and bleeding out its life essences in the night.

Flash: there sits the surgeon, fatigued beyond measure, weeping pitifully, a mixture of anger, weariness and desperation in his plaintive cries.

Flash: there stands a tall figure, watching, always watching.

Flash: it has gone.

IGOR AND THE TWISTED TALES OF CASTLEMAINE

*

Victor Frankenstein shifted slowly in his chair. His weariness shrouded him like a dark and heavy cloak. His head rested on his arms, cast down after the failure of yet another disastrous experiment. Why could he not replicate his masterpiece? Why could he not even reanimate the simplest of specimens?

It had been many months since he'd brought his creature back from the blackness of the abyss.

After a series of great successes in the preceding years, successes that had culminated in his greatest achievement, Victor's luck had turned sour and now everything he touched turned to grim decay.

A sudden thought sprang from nowhere and presented itself, clear and sharp, into the scientist's inner vision.

'Of course!' he exclaimed wildly, running his hands roughly through his long, grey, thinning and unpleasantly greasy hair, as his eyes beamed like two full moons. 'How could I have been so stupid?' As if from nowhere, Victor remembered that scrawled in the margin of his notebooks were the formulas he had copied down from ancient scrolls he'd once studied in Cairo. The scrolls had described the processes used to send the ancient pharaohs off into the afterlife and, more specifically, the methods used to bring them back once they arrived there. He remembered that it was one of those formulas that had been the key to the success of his ventures. Perhaps he had misremembered the combination of factors he had used before; the complex blend of exotic herbs and rare minerals was crucial, what if he'd got the quantities wrong and had upset the delicate formula? It's very possible that a slight imbalance of the vital salts and active components in the replacement spinal fluid would cause the lightning to pass through without triggering the spark of life into the inanimate flesh. Of course, that had to be it. He needed to rediscover the exact chemical proportions, he needed to go back to the very start and rebuild his work from scratch. He needed to find his notebooks.

With a renewed sense of urgency, Victor Frankenstein began thrashing about the room, searching frantically, swiping jars and books from the shelves to meet their ruin on the hard, unforgiving stone castle floor.

'Igor!' he yelled, summoning his assistant from whatever dark hole he grovelled in between experiments.

'IGOR!' he screeched again, still sweeping this way and that across desks and workbenches, desperately seeking the thing he believed would give him the answers he sought, and cure him of his recent wave of cursed bad luck.

'IGOR! Damn you, you pestilent turd. Where are you?'

The short, hunched, stooped and distorted figure, which Igor called his 'classic bootlicker pose', made its shuffling way through a dark doorway into the chaos of the laboratory.

Still carrying his tray precariously stacked with an array of flasks, test tubes and other precious equipment, Igor approached his master nervously, fearful of yet another harsh beating. He had taken so many painful beatings of late. Not through any fault of his own. Igor had always given first rate service to his master, observing his duties diligently and putting himself in harm's way whenever there was danger; taking the electric shocks, carrying the heavy corpses, sharpening and polishing the tools and instruments his master needed for his work.

But Victor had noticed none of this in his blind obsession. When the specimens died, it was Igor who bore the brunt of the scientist's fury. When the lightning failed to produce the current necessary to reanimate his subjects, it was Igor who took the full force of Victor's evil temper.

During his many years of faithful service, Igor had remained a diligent subservient, and through an inherent sense of professional pride had only ever wanted to please his master, to make him happy and, hopefully, one day, to stand in some dark, forgotten corner and bask in the merest sliver of light that made it through to him, from the reflected glory of his master's radiant brilliance.

'Yeees, maaasssteeer?' wheezed the decrepit creature, bowing low and avoiding eye contact with Victor at all costs.

'Where have you been, you odious little dreg? I've been calling for you!' Victor aimed a sharp, spiteful blow towards Igor's head. Igor carefully sidestepped the blow in a well-practised move, causing Victor to merely scuff the side of his cheek with just enough force to satisfy himself that he didn't need to follow up with another, more frustration-fuelled salvo.

The shift Igor made in his position was slight, but sufficient to start a tremor among the stacked piles of glass flasks and phials on his tray. They wobbled precariously for a few seconds, before Igor expertly brought the tremors under control and the pile steadied.

'Yeees, master, Igor came when he heard your sweeeeet, radiant voice rising over the fearsome tempest that rages without.' Igor's slow, snake-like voice was honed to give just the right amount of soothing grovel without overstepping into an all-out grating whine.

'Sweeeet, like an aaaangel in mourning,' he continued. 'Raaadiant as the fiery embers cast forth from a sombre pyre funereal. Igor is heeeere, master. Igor lives to seeerve, master!'

'Have you quite finished?' complained Victor unkindly. 'I don't need your simpering, sycophantic ravings you demented freak. What have you done with my notebooks? Eh? They were here not two hours ago!'

Igor carefully placed the precariously stacked tray of valuable glass items onto the laboratory table, in the certain knowledge that another harsh blow was coming his way. The last thing he needed was to have to clear up even more smashed equipment. Equipment that he knew he would have to pay for when it got damaged.

Victor made Igor pay for all breakages within the laboratory, whether Igor had been in the room at the time or not. And since Igor's pay was such a pittance, and didn't involve the handing over of any actual money, it would naturally take Igor more lifetimes than he expected to endure to pay back all that he owed to his master. Igor's only reward for all his years of servitude consisted of a bundle of rough woollen rags he called clothes, cold water to drink, from the stream at the foot of the castle wall, and all the rodents he could eat, assuming the castle's cat didn't get there first.

Still, it was a living.

'Notebooks, master?' enquired Igor, returning to the point.

'Yes, my notebooks, you gibbering troll. All my work. My formulas, my calculations, my measurements, my anatomical sketches. My sodding notebooks! Everything I need to replicate my greatest creation is in those books. AND YOU'VE BLOODY GOT THEM!'

Frankenstein lunged unexpectedly at Igor and caught his poor, long-suffering assistant by the throat before he was able to execute one of his classic dodge manoeuvres. The red mist upon him, Victor started to shake the bowed and weakened creature violently from side to side. Igor was quite used to this type of treatment and just went with it. He knew that if he endured it long enough then Victor would eventually tire and just satisfy himself with a few half-hearted kicks into Igor's groin.

Taking great care to steer himself and his raging boss away from the stacked tray of valuable equipment, Igor finally managed to croak out a response to his master's accusations.

'Nooo, master. Igor would never take master's notebooks. Igor wouldn't daaare.'

Victor's rage intensified and he bundled Igor viciously onto the floor, landing punches into any exposed parts he could reach.

'Of course you have them! Who else could it be, eh? You've always hated my creation. Ever since I brought him to life you've been behaving like a slapped dog. I see it all now!' Victor's rage was hitting a crescendo. 'You've stolen my notebooks to stop me making another one, haven't you? HAVEN'T YOU?'

'Nooo, master… Igor loves master's creation.'

Clearly now in a deranged frenzy, Frankenstein lifted Igor by the lapels of his torn and tattered lab coat and began slapping him hard about the face with a severed human foot that he'd grabbed from the operating table.

Igor tried to roll with the punches, or were they kicks? All the while keeping a close eye on the stacked tray of glass instruments, doing everything he could to guide the flurry of violence away in a safer direction.

The intense attack ended abruptly as Victor dropped Igor, and the foot, and stood panting heavily with his eyes wide, madness spinning in his expansive pupils.

'Or... wait a minute,' he exclaimed through deep, heaving breaths. A look of extreme anguish twisted the scientist's features as a new realisation hit him. 'You've stolen my notebooks to *sell*. That's it! You plan to sell my work to the students at the medical school, don't you? Or is it that pompous Professor Krempe who claims to be an expert in all things biological? He's nothing but a hapless child compared to me. Of course! He'd pay handsomely for just a sniff of my genius. He's bought you off, hasn't he? He's paid you to steal my work, you conniving little monkey's arse!'

A fresh wave of anger swept over Victor at the thought of all his years of progress and accomplishment in the hands of such simpletons and fools.

He reached over to the workbench and picked up a menacing-looking electric probe with a huge pointy end and dangerous-looking spiky bits protruding from under a shiny rim. Staring wildly, he advanced on the cowering Igor, intent on using this unforgiving tool on his last remaining soft bits.

Igor scrambled backwards towards the darkest corner of the room, issuing terrified squeals as he curled into the smallest space possible.

Victor advanced, brandishing his instrument of pain and destruction menacingly as he approached the cowering and terrified figure. Never before had Igor endured such vicious, undiluted hatred from his beloved master. Never before had he feared so deeply for his own pathetic, insignificant existence. All his years of faithful service, of sacrifice, of stifled ambition, of pretending to be something he wasn't for the sake of his career, a career that was built on lies and misinformation, false promises, and the belief that he wasn't worth the steam off Victor's... breath. All the rage, the fear, the torment. All of it focused into this single pivotal moment.

Something had to give.

*

'Bugger this,' roared Igor in a clear, strong voice, so unlike his usual snivelling tones that Victor was brought up dead in his tracks.

Igor stood up, uncurling his body and limbs from their crooked and cowering pose. He stood tall. Taller than Victor had ever seen him before. Gone was the hunched back and the crooked legs. Gone were the twisted features, the wide ugly mouth, the squinty eyes, and the dribbling nose. Gone was the cringing little creature that had haunted the depths of Castle Frankenstein for so many long winters. The true Igor was emerging before him, and Victor just wasn't prepared.

'Right, stop! That's it!' shouted the liberated Igor as he stretched his aching limbs back into a more regular human pattern, 'You can put that... that... thing away. I've taken just about all I can from you, you bloody psychopath, I quit!'

'Wait… what…?' Victor's immense brain was struggling to comprehend what was happening before him.

'You've finally gone completely bananas. Mad is what you are. All that electricity floating about the place has done for your thinning brain cells, you barmy old sod. You've cracked.' This new, confident Igor was on a roll.

'I've played my part as the faithful drudge. Played the snivelling, tormented, twisted underling to a tee, exactly as they taught us in Lickspittle College. "The perfect underling is a pathetic, humble creature with no mind of its own," they taught us. "Always be the best gibbering little cowardly cur you can be," they said. I did all that for you. I did everything you demanded of me. I've put up with your abuse for more years than I care to remember, but NO MORE!'

'Wha…?' Victor's brain had stalled and was still failing to engage a useable gear.

'In fact,' continued the now strident Igor, 'I've a mind to report you to the TGWU. The Transylvanian Ghoulish Workers' Union takes a very dim view of attempted murder in the workplace. Well, unless it's properly justified. And only then if the paperwork's all handled correctly. Or if it's a woman. But a dim view, nevertheless. Constructive dismissal this is. Breach of contract. I could get compensation.'

'Compen…' Victor's clutch was still slipping and his thought processes were grinding horribly.

'You've never appreciated me. I gave you the best years of my life, and… and…' Igor waved his hand towards the inhabited specimen jars on the shelf, '…and quite a few of other people's too; and all I get in return are insults, physical abuse and a small bucket in the mortuary toilet to sleep in. I've had it!'

Finally, the great scientist managed to rewire the thinking bits of his brain and was at last in a position to join the conversation in a meaningful manner.

'This is all about my creation, isn't it? You've never been happy since I gave him life. You're jealous!' exclaimed Victor triumphantly, thinking that at least he was living up to his name.

'Me? Jealous? Of that eight-foot simpleton?' cried Igor.

'Yes, I see it all now,' continued Victor, wearing his deluded self-importance almost as a badge. 'You want it back to how it was, just the two of us, together, night after night, alone in the lab. You want the great Victor Frankenstein all to yourself!'

Igor, incensed at the epic display of narcissism before him, struggled to find words.

Frankenstein's tirade continued: 'It was you who left the dungeon door open last week, wasn't it? You wanted him to escape. It took us three days to track him down. If he hadn't slipped inside Old Mother Shipton's coal chute, we may never have found him.'

'Don't I know it,' replied Igor, angrily. 'The screams from Old Mother Shipton as we pulled him out still haunt me.'

'Yes, she didn't want us to take him,' remembered Victor. 'Said he reminded her of Old Father Shipton, only warmer and more attractive. And with a much larger—'

'You didn't have to bury her though, did you?' interrupted Igor. 'She wouldn't have said anything.'

'Well, I couldn't take the chance. That reminds me, I must

go back and check if she's dead yet. Some useful spare parts there potentially.'

'You see, this is exactly what I mean. You're completely out of control with your disdain for the basic laws of nature, humanity, and the rights of your fellow man. Talk about a God complex! Exactly like your father. At least he had the decency to take those abominable character flaws where nobody would think twice about them, and went into politics. And don't think I haven't seen you swigging the alcohol from your specimen jars. No wonder all those strange little wriggly, wobbly things you collect keep going off. You're finished, Victor. I'm out!'

'But Igor,' cried the desperate scientist, pawing at his menial's hand and fawning unashamedly, 'you can't leave. Our work here is not finished. And…' Victor began to sob like a lost child, 'where are my notebooks?'

'I haven't got your festering notebooks,' said Igor firmly. 'You've probably sewn them inside one of your "experiments" for all I know. It's where we found the cat last winter if you remember.'

'But, Igor, please, I'm sorry, I'll make it up to you, I promise. I'll save you some of those nice soft fleshy bits you like to play with when the next body comes in.'

'Not this time, Victor,' said Igor finally. 'Goodbye.'

*

Despite all Victor's pleading and promises, Igor remained steadfast, now that his decision to strike out and find a new life away from Castle Frankenstein and years of back-breaking servitude had finally been made.

With a contemptuous look at his former boss, kneeling, snivelling and weeping on the hard stone laboratory floor, Igor went to the door that led towards the passage back to his room, to grab whatever he could for the uncertain road ahead.

Seconds later, he stormed back into Laboratory A3 and with a swift stroke he upturned the precariously stacked tray of precious and highly valuable flasks, test tubes and delicate instruments and watched as they shattered into a million tiny, satisfying fragments. Pausing only to flick a final V at the now recumbent Victor, he made for the door and a very uncertain future.

*

In a shadowy corner of the laboratory stood the silent, watchful figure of an eight-foot-tall, muscle-bound giant, with lustrous black hair and tight, yellowish skin. In his enormous hand, he held the screwed-up remains of the scientist's notebooks.

In the few short months of his existence, he had learned to think of Victor Frankenstein as his father. With the crooked little snivelling one now out of the way, he could command his father's full attention. No more distractions. No more experiments. It was finally playtime.

He turned and left the lab, the pathetic figure of his creator, the great Victor Frankenstein, still lying curled in a foetal position, weeping inconsolably on the floor. He would come back once the great scientist had pulled himself together. He chuckled at the suggestion. 'Pulled himself together.' With an effort, a huge smile began to force its way awkwardly across the creature's stiff, leathery face. He had it all 'sewn up'. He'd certainly 'stitched up' that Igor creature. Now, there's irony for you.

A deep, rumbling laugh rose slowly in the giant's chest. The sound of heavy footsteps shrank away down a long dark corridor, as the walls of the castle boomed and echoed with the deep resonant sound of the monster's laughter.

*

It was exactly three hours and nineteen minutes after leaving Castle Frankenstein for the final time that Igor began to wonder if he hadn't just made the most monumental blunder.

Having left the lab, he'd rushed back to his bucket in the morgue lavatory and retrieved his few meagre possessions. The most important item of all was the only thing of value he owned. Wrapped up inside a stinking rag, which was encased in muck, surrounded by a mouldy bread roll, and tucked inside an old fetid sock, was hidden the most beautiful and delicately wrought silver locket. Igor couldn't remember where he'd got it. As far as he knew, he'd always had it. It was with him when he was dumped on the steps of Lickspittle College for Unwanted Children as a mere toddler. He'd kept it safe, hidden away from the other children for eleven years, while he studied all the skills needed to become a successful underling to one of the region's many celebrated scientific psychopaths.

He took the treasured jewel with him when he was eventually handed over to a silent, grim-faced man in a tall stovepipe hat who took him to work as apprentice vermin chaser in the myriad vaults that lay beneath Castle Frankenstein. In those days you had to have a degree in dismemberment to go straight into lab work, so Igor was forced to start at the ground and work his way up. Well, in truth, to start a hundred and thirty feet underground in the dungeons and work his way up.

From those early days in the dank, dark depths of the dungeons, Igor had worked fastidiously, and in time had progressed to the position of head rat mangler. Then, one glorious day, the young master of the castle called all of his servants to assemble in the courtyard and from them chose Igor to be his new assistant.

Of course, Igor's foreknowledge of the demise of Old Scrote went a long way towards helping his master's choice; in that he had spent the night lacing all the other servants' water jugs with concentrated prune extract from the apothecary. He had thereby ensured they were all rather too busy attending to their unnaturally violent posterior explosions to heed their master's call, and had thus made certain that he himself would be the most suitable, if not the only, candidate in the courtyard that morning.

Promotion brought with it great rewards, and with joy in his eyes and a song in his heart, Igor was catapulted (literally catapulted, in a small trebuchet) up sixteen floors to his beloved bucket in the castle mortuary, just below ground level.

Now, a mere three hours and nineteen minutes after leaving it all behind, Igor was cold, wet, and very lost.

*

IGOR'S UNDERTAKING

Igor had said his fond farewells to Simon and made his way through the tortuous winding corridors, only stopping occasionally to stuff the odd item of value into his pockets as he went. He finally left the castle through a heavy wooden gate, which swung open reluctantly on ancient, rusted iron hinges. Once through the outer wall he was faced with a long, winding stone staircase which descended for hundreds of fathoms down the side of the mountain, towards a dense and foreboding forest that stretched for many leagues towards the horizon.

Still in the fervour of his recently discovered sense of purpose and with his self-confidence riding high, Igor had skipped down the first few thousand steps. But as the huge, familiar, comforting shape of the castle dwindled further and further behind, and with the dark, forbidding forest (known locally, and not very encouragingly, as the Forest of Grim Death) coming ever upwards to greet him, he began to have doubts.

Having at last scraped, scrambled and in places even tumbled his way to the bottom of the stone staircase, with the castle now lost in the swirling clouds above and the deep blackness of the trees ahead, Igor was seriously beginning to question his decision.

He considered how his life had changed since he was elevated to the position of Victor Frankenstein's lab assistant. He was initially delighted when his beloved master had anointed him with the full job title of 'Deputy Organic Reanimation Keyworker', until he finally realised that it was the initials part that was the problem.

He should have known there and then that his time with

the offensive, sarcastic, bullying psychopath wouldn't be his best work. But he'd stuck with it, hoping that things would improve as he settled in. They didn't. And it was the memory of all the rude names, all the blame and the beatings that hardened Igor's resolve once more as with a defiant 'Oh, bugger it!' he plunged headlong under the black and gloomy canopy of the grim and ominous forest.

As the twisted, damp, and creaking darkness of the trees closed in around him, Igor forced himself to think positive thoughts about the bright, sunlit uplands of his new liberated future. Free at last from the shackles of his former existence, Igor dared to believe that his dreams of a normal job in a normal town, with a normal wife and normal children, living a normal, workaday life would become his new normal.

Whether it was a sudden cold gust of wind which penetrated deep under his flapping smock, or the thought of all that terrifying normality that sent the chill up Igor's spine, he couldn't tell. He knew, deep in his inner core, that despite his fanciful whims, he could never really survive the turgid drudgery of eight point six children and a regular sixteen-hour-a-day job in some dull backwater village, with a rosy-cheeked wife making potato surprise for him every teatime. Every day, for the rest of his life? Wash, rinse, repeat (a catchy slogan Igor had once seen employed by a very smart chemical company who used it to double their sales of 'Bodywash corpse detergent' overnight).

Although the idea of being a 'family butcher' in a cosy little village still appealed to him, Igor couldn't be certain which of the two possible career options that job title described would be more fulfilling. Could he reform and settle into a life of domestic bliss, or would his past be forever tapping him on the shoulder and tempting him back to his old nefarious ways?

One thing he was certain about was that, whatever the future held, whatever lay ahead, it was infinitely better than what lay behind. Igor girded his loins with a well-polished girding action, stiffened his resolve (which was quite stiff anyway because of the cold wind penetrating his smock) and strode forward, a renewed sense of purpose, confidence and vigour completely failing to materialise in his brooding uncertainty.

The path through the trees was narrow and in places so overgrown that before he'd gone more than a few hundred paces, his legs were stinging with a myriad of scratches from the grasping thorns and brambles. Resolutely, Igor trudged on. In the far distance behind him he could just make out the sound of the bells from the castle tower striking three. It was the deepest pit of the night, and it had started raining.

Igor decided to stop for a rest and to see if he could get a fire going, but the brush and undergrowth were saturated, as the fat drops of rainwater plopped down around him from the dense canopy above.

It was three hours and nineteen minutes since Igor had left the castle. In desperation, he crawled inside the hollowed-out bole of an enormous old elm tree and, shivering, fell quickly into a fitful sleep.

*

The sound of the castle's distant bell tower striking eight roused Igor from his restless slumber. Rain was still falling heavily and though it was now morning, a gloomy twilight held sway under the shade of the thick foliage.

Igor was cold and very hungry. He looked about to see if there were any fruit trees he recognised. Alas, there were none. Nor were there any bread stalls, alehouses, hog roasts, pie shops, gingerbread houses, or magic porridge pots, but he looked for them anyway just in case.

His stomach grumbled loudly. He sniffed at a few of the more appetising-looking leaves but none smelled particularly good and all the mushrooms he could find were purple and leaked a blood-like ooze when he picked them.

Hungry, but resolute, Igor began to contemplate the road ahead. He would soon have to leave the relative comfort of the old elm tree and strike onwards. Instinctively, as he pondered his course, his hand went to the locket that he kept in its secure wrappings inside a fold of his undershirt.

Taking it out, he suddenly remembered that beneath the stinking, festering, fetid old sock, was a hard, desiccated, delicious mouldy bread roll. Tearing the rotten sock material away, Igor quickly removed the locket, scraped away most of the muck and with a feeling of total joy and satisfaction, sank his ravenous face into its piquant green crustiness.

With neither thought nor care for the future, Igor scoffed the lot. Thus revived, he felt ready for the day ahead and set off once more into the damp gloom under the trees.

*

The rain relented as the day wore on, and to Igor's great relief the path he was following opened out into a proper forest track after several miles. Here and there he began to hear the joyful chirruping of woodland birds, and he saw the occasional flash of a startled deer as he wound his way on through the forest. He almost entertained the notion of whistling a merry little walking song, but realised quickly that he hated merry little walking songs, so he decided to make up very rude walking songs instead. Chuckling to himself at his inventive crudity, Igor plodded on through the dappled sunlight.

Sadly, Igor's luck with the weather didn't hold for long as the grey, swirling clouds gathered overhead once more, and the sound of thunder echoed around the nearby mountains.

As dusk descended, Igor began to look about for somewhere to camp for the night. He was regretting his earlier decision to stuff his face with the entire mouldy roll in one sitting as his hunger raged once more.

Looking ahead through the gathering gloom, he could just make out what appeared to be an old wooden signpost standing beside the path. Hurrying forward, he discovered that it was in fact an old wooden signpost standing beside the path. There were five arms, each one bearing the destination of the tracks that merged at its base.

Along the route that Igor had taken, the signpost directed the traveller towards Castle Frankenstein. A cold shiver ran up Igor's spine at the thought of ever returning that way.

He walked slowly around the road sign and read off each destination.

To the left, it pointed towards a dark road which led to a place called 'Devil's Passage'. A flash of lightning ripped through the still air as Igor read the name. It sounded like a place of ill omen, so he quickly ruled out going that way.

The next arm pointed steeply downhill towards 'Dead Man's End'. Thunder cracked and a group of startled crows swooped and swirled noisily overhead. Igor dismissed that direction.

The arm pointing straight ahead was covered in lichens and very hard to read. He reached up to wipe away years of mossy growth and tried to make out the old and worn lettering beneath. B... E... L... What was it? Ah, it looked like 'Belgium'. A huge flash of lightning blinded Igor momentarily and the roar of thunder left him cowering and deafened. Definitely not that way.

Recovering his nerves, Igor turned towards the last track and regarded the sign. It read 'Castlemaine 8 miles'. Covering his ears, he looked towards the sky expectantly. Nothing.

Castlemaine. What madness would drive a man there? The very name of that cursed place should have struck terror into the depths of Igor's being. He had of course heard the dark, whispered tales of Castlemaine since his days at Lickspittle College when he had first learned of its reputation as an evil place that would blight the very soul of an unwary traveller.

Luckily, he had also heard that the pies were good, so he put aside any doubts and with a smile, patted his empty stomach.

'OK, Castlemaine it is then,' he said to himself, as with a renewed spring in his step, Igor turned onto the right-hand trackway and down the gently sloping valley towards the village of Castlemaine and, he hoped, a hot meal, a warm bed and a peaceful night's sleep.

Well, two out of three ain't bad.

IGOR'S UNDERTAKING

*

Igor stood on the brow of a hill looking down at the village of Castlemaine. Lights were on in most of the cottages. Smoke rose from the scattered chimneys, and away to his left, the spire of a small church stood out, silhouetted against the dark sky.

From his vantage point, he could hear the voices of villagers as they closed their businesses and bustled about preparing for the coming of night.

Towards the centre lay a large building with blazing lights and several chimneys pumping woodsmoke into the cold night air. The sounds of raucous laughter and the occasional bout of drunken singing could be heard from that direction, so Igor decided that must be the village inn, the perfect place for him to settle for a few days while he decided his next move.

He took the path that led down into the village and wound his way towards the inn. The few people that saw him as he threaded his way along the narrow, winding streets looked on suspiciously, always fearing the passage of strangers. Some spat as he passed, others made a sign against the evil eye behind their backs as they herded children indoors or tended their animals, locking them away in stable and barn against the coming of darkness.

Igor paid no heed; all he wanted was the comfort of a warm fire, something to eat and maybe a hot bath. It wasn't his birthday as far as he knew but, still, anything to help dispel the chill from his bones would be very welcome indeed.

After a few false turns, he finally arrived in the town's central square with the inn standing to the right-hand side.

It was a large three-storey building with a steep thatched roof and the light of many candles glowing behind cracked and filthy nicotine-stained windows.

Above the door was a faded sign which read, 'The Cadaver's Arms'. Below the name was a rough painting of two crossed, severed limbs.

Home from home, thought Igor as he pushed down on the latch and walked into the bright, smoky interior.

Silence erupted, instantly.

Igor stopped dead.

Still holding onto the door handle and with one foot raised in frozen perambulation, he slowly looked around and took in the scene.

Thirty or so villagers were sat, eating and drinking on long, low benches at trestle tables dotted around the crowded room. Others were standing by the large fireplace, warming their hands and behinds after a hard day in the fields. A few stood at the bar, sloshing mugs of frothy ale. A couple of scrawny servants carried trays with mugs of beer and plates of stew to expectant tables.

A rough-looking old man with a large belly covered by a long, stained cotton apron stood behind the bar. Beside him was a very attractive young woman with keen, green eyes and a flow of auburn hair which fell across her shoulders in what Igor considered to be a very eye-pleasing manner. Every face was turned with a cold, dead stare in his direction.

Igor raised his hand in gesture of greeting, every sinew poised and ready for him to bolt out into the night and leg it back up the hill if things went the wrong way. With what he deemed to be his most disarming smile moulded onto his face, he managed to utter a feeble 'evening' to the motionless gathering.

For several seconds, nothing happened. Igor took this as a positive sign and ventured to lower his foot and gently push the door closed behind him. Having thus committed himself, the villagers quickly relaxed and went on with their conversations as if nothing had occurred.

Cautiously, Igor made his way towards the bar. The innkeeper was busy filling jugs of beer. A large man wearing a coachman's livery was perched on a high bar stool and dozing drunkenly. 'I won't take 'em, not after dark,' he mumbled randomly before his head sagged forward and he resumed snoring quietly.

The attractive young woman looked Igor squarely in the face.

'Can I 'elp you 'andsome?' she asked flirtatiously.

Igor looked over his shoulder to see who she was talking to. When he saw there was nobody there, the penny dropped and he realised she had been talking to him.

'Um, yes, I'd like a brandy please, and some of that fine-looking stew if there's any going.'

'OK deary,' purred the bar girl. 'Coming right up.'

The girl's shapely form, soft lithe figure, smouldering eyes and her provocative off-the-shoulder dress all merged into a strange set of tingly feelings in places Igor hadn't had strange tingly feelings in for as long as he could remember. He had been out of circulation since, well, he'd never actually been in circulation where women were concerned, so he was a little disturbed to find himself affected by the attentions of this… he could only say stunningly gorgeous bar girl. He hadn't really thought of finding any women attractive before. His daydreams of another life in amongst the day-to-day folk of the world had only produced vague images of the sort of women Igor had met in the castle kitchens, mainly matronly, ruddy-faced older women with wandering hands, a paucity of teeth and a little too much facial hair. These feelings inside him were quite new and a little unnerving. He decided to leave it for the moment and maybe take up the thought again later, in the bath perhaps. Which reminded him, he needed to secure a place to sleep after his busy day tramping through the forest.

As the bar girl left to fetch his order, Igor called across to the innkeeper.

'Excuse me, I don't suppose you have any spare rooms for the night, do you?'

Silence instantly filled the bar for a second time as all faces turned once again to this mysterious stranger.

The innkeeper sidled quickly across to where Igor stood and whispered in confidential tones, 'You mustn't stay here, sir. It's not safe in Castlemaine. The murders, you see?'

'The murders?' replied Igor, much too loudly.

The villagers all gasped unanimously, looks of fear and hostility on their hardened faces.

'Aye, murders,' said one villager, pointing his pipe stem in Igor's direction. 'Bloody murders. More of 'em now than most can count, and no one knows who, or what, is responsible.'

'I know someone who knows,' added a second villager.

All faces turned towards him as they awaited his revelation.

'Who?' asked the first villager looking confused.

The second villager sighed heavily and replied as if talking to a small child, 'The murderer hisself!'

The other villagers mumbled in agreement with this sage deduction and went back to their beers.

'Aye, thirty-twelve murders,' continued the landlord, trying to count them on his fingers as he spoke. 'Much, much worse than the regular common-or-garden everyday clean and tidy civilised murders we normally get hereabouts, though. Thirty-twelve filthy, violent, messy murders. Lumps missing, blood, organs, and entrails everywhere. Onlookers puking their guts up in the street at the sheer hideous, grotesque, sloppy, gruesome red wetness of it all. Those kinds of murders.'

'Oh, those kinds of murders,' replied Igor, feeling his appetite for the impending bowl of stew more keenly than ever.

'Why not move on to Dead Man's End, sir? It'll be safer there.'

A crash of thunder boomed overhead at the mention of Dead Man's End.

'I understand the Cutthroat Razor is a fine establishment, sir. They do a passable meat pie. Eric here is the local coachman; he could get you there in no time.'

The landlord flicked his damp bar towel at the coachman who snored loudly and sat upright, bleary eyed.

'I'll not take 'em, not after dark,' he proclaimed firmly, before slumping back down into his drunken stupor.

A few moments later the attractive bar girl brought Igor's meal and rested it down on the bar. Her delicate finger brushed fleetingly against Igor's hand as she deposited the plate. A thrill like the passing of a small colony of bats fluttered in Igor's chest, before descending into his trousers, as his eyes met hers for the briefest instant.

A demure smile played across her lips as Igor, feeling his face reddening, forced his eyes back towards the bowl.

As he set about the hot food, the girl turned towards the innkeeper.

'Father, has Squire Kolchak come down for his supper yet?'

'He's the only guest that hasn't, Esme,' replied the landlord. 'I haven't set eyes on him since he asked for young Valerie to take a bottle of cognac up to his room this afternoon. He must still be resting.'

The landlord gestured towards a young serving girl who was flirting loudly with a group of admiring male guests.

'Valerie,' he shouted. 'Go upstairs and rouse Squire Kolchak, will you?'

'What again?' she whined. 'Might take some doing at his age!'

Valerie left the bar and went upstairs to find the missing squire.

Igor quickly finished his stew, mopping up the thin gravy with a chunk of fresh-ish bread, then turned his attention to the strong, warming brandy. He tried again with the innkeeper.

'Look, um, sorry, what's your name?'

'Folks around here call me Clam,' replied the landlord.

'Do they?' enquired Igor, his weariness starting to show a little.

'Aye, that being my name you see.'

'Ah, OK. Right. Look, Clam, I've had a terrible day. I'm tired, soaked through and I just want somewhere to put my head down. I've got money.'

He produced a large leather pouch with the initials VF stamped in gold lettering on the side. He'd picked it up on his way out of the castle in lieu of all the Christmas bonuses he'd never got. It jangled pleasantly in his palm as he gently squeezed the silver and gold coins nestled within.

'Oh, come on, Father. We can't send him out again on a night like this,' offered Esme, kindly.

'Well, I suppose...' began Clam with a worried look, but then stopped suddenly as a high-pitched scream pierced the air.

The girl Valerie burst into the room, screaming hysterically.

'Murder! Murder!' she cried, a look of sheer terror twisting her features. 'There's been another one.'

Esme rushed over to comfort the distraught servant, whose screaming hysteria was still gathering steam.

'Slap her!' suggested Clam, covering his ears against the shrill noise.

'That's a bit harsh, Father,' replied Esme. 'She's a bit over-friendly with the male guests sometimes I grant you, but—'

'No. I said SLAP. HER!'

One of the female villagers ran up and cuffed the hysterical Valerie across the face with perhaps a little too much glee, but that together with a proffered glass of brandy helped to calm the girl down sufficiently for her to recount what she had seen.

'There's nothing left of him,' whimpered Valerie, tears

streaming down her pale cheeks. 'Just a horrible stain on the bedsheets.'

'Urgh!' suggested several villagers at once.

'You do mean blood, I hope?' enquired the landlord.

Nervous villagers began chattering noisily, fear of yet another mysterious killing in their midst spreading panic among them. This was all too much. Who would be next?

'Someone call for Helsing!' cried a voice from within the throng.

'No need, I am already here,' boomed a loud, commanding voice from across the room.

The crowd parted to allow two figures through towards the trembling servant. Helsing, local magistrate and county witchfinder, was a tall, lean, officious-looking man. He wore a dark military-style uniform with lots of fiddly gold trimmings that shouted power and leadership. His boots and buttons gleamed fiercely, having been obsessively polished to within an inch of their lives every morning and evening by his own image-conscious perfectionist's hands.

However, despite his noble features, his military bearing and his finely honed, masterful persona, everyone knew that Helsing was thick as mince, totally incompetent and quite probably barking mad.

His companion, by comparison, was the absolute opposite. Short, squat, brutish and grim-looking, Hopkins perpetually tried to avoid being obscured by Helsing's wand-like shadow. Hated by almost everyone in the region, Hopkins was a total sneak. Someone who sold both his grandmothers for a speedy promotion and who was certainly not to be trusted further than you could spit an anvil.

The two men strode purposefully through the crowd, gazing this way and that, scanning every face, ready to point the finger and accuse anyone who looked remotely guilty.

Approaching the bar, Helsing's steely gaze fell immediately upon Igor. He stood tall in his best authoritative pose, his fists set firmly inside huge leather gauntlets, which in turn were set firmly on his hips, and his hawk-like nose set firmly and dangerously in Igor's direction.

'Well, well, well. A stranger!'

'No stranger than some!' replied Igor, swirling his brandy in the glass with an air of disrespectful nonchalance.

Helsing glowered at the impudent newcomer.

'Your name, sir?' he hissed through gritted teeth.

'Me, my name's Igor,' replied Igor tautologically, but quite truthfully, seeing no reason to do otherwise, 'and yes, I'm new in town. Just a weary traveller looking for bread and board. And who might you be?'

'I am Helsing!' crowed Helsing, desperate not to be outdone in the being-up-front-with-his-name department, 'magistrate, chief of police and...' He paused for dramatic effect.

'Witchfinder!' crowed Hopkins triumphantly, through the crook of Helsing's elbow.

'Witchfinder!' repeated Helsing, his bubble of pomposity deflating fast.

'I've told you not to do that!' hissed Helsing, rounding on his smug assistant. 'Keep silent, fool, or I shall have you back on cesspit inspections, do you understand me?'

'But sir...' Hopkins' protest got no further as Helsing raised a gauntleted warning finger.

'One more word, Hopkins, just one, and you'll be cleaning out my privy as well, and with your own toothbrush, am I making myself clear?'

Hopkins gave a mumbled, 'Yessir, s'pose so, sir,' and slumped his shoulders huffily like a chastised teenager.

'Witchfinder, eh?' mocked Igor, unimpressed by Helsing's puffed-up sense of self-importance. 'Ever found one?'

'My record is unsurpassed!' boomed the rattled magistrate, angry that this newcomer wasn't showing the right level of deference. A few chuckles and embarrassed coughs rippled through the crowd at Helsing's proud boast.

'Interest you in some lucky heather, deary?' A wizened old crone had approached unnoticed and was holding out a small bunch of limp, dried foliage towards Helsing's disapproving face.

'Thank you, no,' replied Helsing, politely but with an air of irritation clear in his voice.

The old woman straightened her pointy black hat and reached into a small bag attached to the end of a hazel twig broomstick.

'How about a nice love potion? Drive the ladies wild?'

'That is not something I require,' snapped Helsing indignantly.

Hopkins was pulling frantically on his boss's cloak, still too afraid to speak. Helsing chose to ignore him.

'Are you sure, deary?' persisted the old woman, stroking an evil-looking black cat on her shoulder. 'I brewed it up especially in my *cauldron* only last night.'

Helsing snapped. 'Madam! I am currently engaged in an important conversation. Will you kindly desist and leave me alone?'

The old woman smiled and winked at the sniggering villagers as she gathered up her belongings and gently swept the floor with her old, battered broomstick. As she made her way back to the door, the villagers' barely restrained hysterics burst noisily from behind their hands. Hopkins stared after her, his eyes bulging and face red with frustration, his frantic gesticulations towards Helsing completely ignored.

'As I was saying,' continued Helsing, rattled, cuffing the apoplectic Hopkins on the head for good measure, 'my record is unsurpassed. No witch shall escape justice in my village. Tell me, *Igor*, are YOU a witch?' Helsing all but shouted the last word in his most dramatic voice in an attempt to whip the villagers into a fervour of superstitious frenzy. The villagers looked on, blankly.

Igor raised himself to his full height, which was much higher than most in the room, but still not high enough to look Helsing directly in the eye.

'Certainly not,' he exclaimed indignantly. 'I happen to be a highly experienced medical assistant, currently taking a… sabbatical.'

'*Sabbat*-ical eh?' boomed Helsing accusingly. 'This sounds like the practice of… WITCHCRAFT!' Again, the dramatic effect; again the villagers failed to bite.

'Oh, for goodness' sake,' replied Igor hotly. 'It's a type of holiday. I'm between jobs at the moment.'

'And where was your last place of employ?'

'I worked at Frank…' Igor checked himself quickly, '…ly that's none of your business. Although I can tell you that I happened to be the trusted personal assistant of an eminent physician.'

'Don't you think it's a bit of a coincidence that we have a series of grisly murders in our village, then less than a month after they start, you show up?' Helsing stopped himself, his sluggish brain juggling with the notion that something in what he just said didn't quite sound right. He decided to worry about it later.

'There's something about you, sir, that I don't trust,' continued the witchfinder. 'Be about your business, but know this: I. Am. Watching. You.'

As Helsing strode pompously towards the guest rooms to begin his investigation into this most recent murder, Hopkins stepped forward and leaned menacingly towards Igor, unable to contain himself any longer. 'I'm watching you too!' he hissed through clenched teeth before scampering after his boss.

Helsing whispered angrily at his assistant. 'No one cares if you're watching! For the last time, I'm the important one. They care if *I'm* watching.'

'Well, they certainly know how to make a fellow feel welcome,' Igor smiled at the innkeeper and his daughter.

'Keep away from those two,' she advised. 'They're idiots, but they're powerful idiots. They'll be busy for a while now at least, what with another murder to fail to solve.' Esme looked pensively after the two retreating officials. 'Could do without it being so close to home though,' she added under her breath. Brightly, she turned back to Igor. 'We're not all so unfriendly here, you know. You probably heard already, but my name's Esme, short for Esmerelda.'

'Pleased to make your acquaintance, Miss Esme,' replied Igor with a slight bow. 'Is it always this interesting in Castlemaine on a weeknight?'

'We have our moments, sir,' Esme stood upright and held out her arms to indicate the charms of the establishment, then continued as if reciting a well-rehearsed sales pitch.

'We've got hot food, a warm hearth, plenty of ale, a supply of overdramatic serving girls, cheap comedy double acts in military uniforms and violent blood sports in the guest rooms, what more could you ask for?'

'I'm sold,' replied Igor, quaffing the last of his brandy. 'I might just hang about for a bit and see what the weekends are like.'

'Well, then,' smiled Esme warmly. 'Better get that room sorted for you.'

*

A short while before dawn the next morning, Igor was roused from his deep and weary sleep by a distant, but quite distinct thump. The thump was in turn followed by a muffled scraping noise. All of it seemed to be coming from somewhere below his room, and almost certainly inside the inn. He lay in the dark, listening, but was unable to work out what was causing the noise, or where exactly it was coming from.

After a few minutes, the sound disappeared. Igor pondered whether to get up and investigate or just drift back to sleep and let things sort themselves out. *This is Castlemaine*, he thought to himself. *Weird stuff happens here all the time if the legends are true.* Why should he get involved? This wasn't his town after all, and the people's problems were not his problems.

He reached across to the side table for the water jug. Finding it empty, he decided that he would go to the kitchen for a refill, and maybe just have a quick nosey about at the same time. He never could resist a good snoop, after all, plus he might be able to discover which room was Esmerelda's, in case just on the off-chance he might need that knowledge for any reason at some point in the future.

Lighting a candle, he opened the door, consciously pulling down the ragged hem of his smock, which threatened to reveal more than just his latent curiosity should anyone else be on the prowl. He crept along the landing to the back stairs that descended by several flights into the guests' passageway, which in turn led towards the bar at one end, and the kitchen at the other.

Every floorboard and stair he walked on gave out its own particular creak and squeak. Before he'd gone more than a few paces, he felt certain that his movements must have woken the entire household. Hearing no other movement but his own, he carried on cautiously, trying not to make too much noise as he went.

Carrying his empty jug, he went into the kitchen to look for the water pump. The sound of loud, heavy snoring could be heard through a closed door which led to an adjacent room. Igor hoped that was the innkeeper's room and not Esmerelda's.

Through an open door at the far end of the kitchen, he could see a dim, flickering light as if someone had left a candle burning. He went across to the door and saw that beyond it was a steep staircase that went down into the cellar.

Despite knowing that anybody watching him at this moment would be screaming at him not to go down there, he went down there. As his foot touched the bottom stair, an unexplained puff of wind blew out his candle. A light still flickered somewhere in the far depths of the cellar. Turning a corner, he entered a low, wide space stacked with huge wooden beer barrels and ancient furniture.

At the far end, with a candle on the floor beside him, was the hunched, labouring figure of Eric, the coachman. He appeared to be lifting something heavy into one of the empty barrels.

Is that…? Igor suspected he knew what was afoot, mainly due to a foot that was dangling over the rim of the barrel. *Yes, it absolutely must be, the lifeless body of the late Squire Kolchak, murdered in his bed the day before by persons unknown and removed from his room for reasons unknown before the hapless serving girl had discovered his sheets that were heavily stained with bodily fluids, the type of which were probably best left unknown.*

Delighted at having so easily discovered the culprit behind the spate of local murders, Igor gave out a confident 'Ah-ha! Got you!'

At the same moment, something hard and unforgiving introduced itself very firmly to the back of Igor's head. He spun round as he fell, in time to catch a fleeting glimpse of a heavy wooden mallet being held aloft, and a pair of keen, green eyes that shone in the glow of the flickering candle.

Then suddenly, all the lights went out.

*

The sun was groping its way with searching fingers through the raggedy old curtains of his room when Igor awoke. His head hurt, very badly. Actually, it hurt really well. As far as hurts went, this was one of the more polished and professional ones that had clearly practised every day until it could do its job to painful perfection.

He forced his eyes to focus on something solid. That something was Esmerelda, who was standing over him brandishing a tray of breakfast.

'Good morning,' she sang cheerily. 'I've made you some tea, toast and eggs. No, don't get up. I'll leave it here. Enjoy!' Turning swiftly, she danced out of the room, leaving Igor bewildered and wondering if the events of his late-night wanderings had been just a bad dream.

The throbbing lump on the back of his head suggested they hadn't.

Esme's scent clung to the air and he felt glad that whoever had put him back in bed last night had remembered to pull his blankets up.

Igor set about his breakfast, then after a quick wash, he pulled on his breeches, tucked in his tattered and frayed smock, and descended the stairs once more. Servants were toing and froing in the kitchen, so Igor decided that now was not the time to reopen his investigations in the cellar, and went instead towards the bar.

As he entered, he spotted Esme and Eric talking in animated fashion by the fireplace. On seeing Igor, Esme whispered something hurriedly in Eric's ear at which the coachman picked up his hat and hastily left the inn.

Igor wandered over to her table.

'What did you hit me for?' he asked, preferring the direct approach.

'Me? Hit you, deary?' said Esme in her best simple bar floozy voice. 'No, a bad dream surely, Master Igor. Too much cheese, perhaps?'

'Oh, come on,' complained Igor. 'The only cheese around here is that phoney bimbo act you've been putting on. You're a smart cookie and you're up to something, you and that coachman, or my name's not Ignatius Nigel De-Pfeffel Schicklgruber.'

Esme looked hard into Igor's eyes, pondering.

'How do I know you're not one of Helsing's spies?' she asked, reasonably.

'That preening prat from last night?' scoffed Igor. 'Give me some credit. He's got less brains than roadkill and only half the charm. Besides, if I was working for him why would I have lifted his purse?'

Igor handed Esme a leathern purse with a large and flamboyant 'H' embroidered in gold silk on the side. It was stuffed full of gold pieces.

Esme looked at the purse with wonder. 'Yep, that's his purse all right,' she said, squeezing the swollen bag firmly between her long, delicate fingers, 'I've been trying to steal that from him for years. How on earth did you manage it?'

'Oh, just a bit of good old-fashioned sleight of hand,' said Igor proudly. 'A light finger here, a light finger there.' He emptied a bag of severed fingers onto the table.

'And one or two dark ones,' said Esmerelda. 'Looks like they're going off a bit.'

'Yes, well my source has dried up of late.'

Esmerelda picked up one of the fingers and turned it around in her hands.

She sat quietly for a moment, thinking hard and staring at Igor as if to penetrate his mind with hers.

'Seems from your finger collection that you've had some dealings with the dead,' she mused, a deep, thoughtful look in her eye.

'Yes, I've seen my share of the dearly departed. It was all grist to the mill in my last job. That and being the lapdog to a psychopath with too much access to illicit, mind-buggering chemicals. Until recently,' he confided, glancing furtively round the room and lowering his voice to a whisper, 'I worked for... Victor Frankenstein.'

A bolt of lightning struck the nearby church tower and an ear-splitting crash of thunder shook the inn to its very foundations.

Esme and Igor looked through the open window into the clear blue morning sky.

Odd, they both thought simultaneously.

'Never heard of him,' declared Esme after a pause, and with a blank look that didn't surprise Igor very much at all. Victor rarely left the castle except on one of his lecture tours or money-raising jaunts. He'd certainly never stoop to visiting anywhere so grim as Castlemaine, and it was very unlikely that the villagers would have read about him in *New Mad Scientist*, if any of them *could* read, that is.

'He's a complete nutter,' explained Igor. 'A dangerous, wealthy, reckless, brilliant nutter. In truth, it was a bloody awful job. He treated me worse than one of his cast-off specimens. Still, I learned how to cook, I learned how to clean, I learned how to serve, I learned how to deal with the recently deceased. I learned how to make a stiff drink... even if he didn't want to.'

Esme pondered his words, still staring hard at Igor and trying to pierce his inner thoughts.

'I'm not sure…' she said quietly.

'Look, I know you're up to something,' said Igor, standing up and looking Esme straight in the eyes. 'That squire met his end while staying in your guest room and the fact you had Eric bundling him into a barrel in the cellar clearly means you know what's going on and are trying to cover it up.'

Igor paused and belched loudly, his breakfast eggs threatening to make an unwelcome, sulphurous reappearance. 'If it wasn't for all the blood and guts,' he winced, slapping himself in the sternum, 'I'd think you had a poisoner at work. The only positive thing anyone ever says about Castlemaine is that the pies are good, but that stuff you imaginatively call food in this establishment should come with a government health warning. That coq au vin I had last night tasted like the chef really had put his cock in it.'

Igor studied Esme's face intently. 'It won't take long even for those dimwit investigators to rumble you. You might as well spill the beans; it'd be far preferable to eating them.'

Esme sighed. 'Well, I suppose I have to trust you.' She paused for a few heartbeats before grabbing Igor's smock front and pulling him down so her mouth was next to his ear. His heart thrilled as he felt the sweet warmth of her breath on his cheek and saw right down her top. 'It's my dad,' she whispered sadly.

'What? Old Clam?' cried Igor, exclaiming his disbelief far too loudly.

'Shhh,' hissed Esme, 'keep your voice down.'

'Sorry,' replied Igor much more quietly, 'but really? Clam's doing the murders?'

'Yes, he's got an ism.'

'An ism?'

'Yes, an ism that makes him kill people.'

'What kind of an ism does that to a man?' asked Igor expectantly.

'Somnomicidalism.'

'What?'

'Somnomicidalism!' repeated Esme. 'You've heard of somnambulism? When people sleepwalk? Well, Dad's got somnomicidalism. He's a sleep murderer.'

'Well, I can understand why you'd want to keep that quiet,' said Igor. 'Definitely not good for the customer reviews that one. "Had a great time, welcome was warm, beer frothy, wenches earthy, lost one or two members of the group to the whims of the psychopathic host, but the chef's breakfast sausage was surprisingly hot and throbbing."'

'Yes, I know, but what can I do? He's my dad,' replied Esme, as a look of sadness trembled across her face.

'What? And he's been wandering around the village at night slashing up unsuspecting locals? I can't believe it. He seems such a quiet, mild-mannered chap.' Igor pondered Clam, the simple, kindly yokel he'd met the night before. 'Classic serial killer when you think about it. When did all this start?'

'A few weeks back,' replied Esme. 'We'd had some trouble with a band of travelling folk who'd pitched up their wagons in the village square. The men would come into the bar at night, tell ghost stories and read people's fortunes in exchange for ale. The womenfolk would swap herbal recipes and sell charms. All that was fine and for a few nights we had a bit of extra entertainment and the bar was full.'

Esme leaned forward and Igor entirely failed to resist glancing again at her cleavage.

'Then one night,' she continued, 'a game of cards got out of hand. One of the travellers accused a local of cheating, which to be fair, he almost certainly was. Things got ugly, insults were thrown, rapidly followed by numerous punches, a couple of chairs and a bewildered-looking Jack Russell terrier called Barry.

'Dad waded into the fray trying to separate the brawlers but just at that moment someone from among the travellers shouted a curse of fearsome death on the whole of Castlemaine, I mean, like that's ever gonna make any difference!

'Anyway, the curse caught Dad square between the shoulders. Knocked him flying. The travellers were chased from the village. Dad was laid up for a few days but appeared to make a full recovery.'

'What happened to the Jack Russell?' enquired Igor. He forced his eyes to meet Esme's.

'Got very drunk lapping up all the spilled ale,' she confirmed. 'Anyway, a few nights later there was a murder. Not something that would normally raise many eyebrows hereabouts, but this one was particularly messy. Blood up the walls, entrails and bits spread over a wide area. Had all the hallmarks of a werewolf attack. Except this wasn't on a full moon. Got the villagers a bit worried.'

'And how did you link that back to Clam?' asked Igor, fidgeting uncomfortably as Esme leaned in closer.

'It didn't take a genius to work it out,' she replied with a tear glistening in the corner of her eye. 'The morning after each murder we found Dad slumped on his bed in bloodstained clothes and mounds of unsavoury-looking offal bubbling away in the stock pot.'

Igor's stomach gave a lurch as he remembered the unpleasant stew from the previous night. He swallowed hard and forced himself to continue. 'And yet he doesn't know it's him?'

'Nope.'

'But what about all the mess? He must wonder why he wakes up drenched in other people's bodily fluids.'

'He says he spent the night hunting in the woods. Won't accept any other explanation. That must be what he's dreaming about when he's on one.'

'Hang on a minute,' said Igor. 'That squire who copped it yesterday died in the middle of the afternoon.'

'Yes,' said Esme, a pained look on her face. 'Dad went for a sit-down after the lunchtime rush and dozed off. It must have happened then. He was only out for about ten minutes but he can be quite nippy for a big bloke. It's uncontrollable and totally unpredictable. Is there anything you can think of to help? I can't talk to Dad, he has no idea he does it. Eric lends a hand but we're running out of ideas. Not to mention empty barrels.'

They sat silently for a few moments, each one glancing furtively at the other. Esme was still trying to discern whether Igor could be trusted, and Igor was still trying to cop another shifty down Esme's shirt front. Briefly, their eyes met and they both reddened before hastily looking away. Esme broke the silence.

'Anyway, old Helsing didn't find any clues in the squire's room yesterday. Luckily, a couple of the servants had got there before Valerie went in and moved the body. They were just about to go back and clean up when Dad sent Valerie to find the squire. The rest you know.' Esme bit the blackened nail on the severed finger she'd been holding, then realised what she was doing and tossed the desiccated digit back onto the table.

'So anyway, because the window was open and there was so much blood, Helsing has decided that the murders are vampire-related and has gone off scouring the countryside, looking for open tombs and bleeding virgins.'

'Well, we're all looking for—' began Igor, but Esme cut him off.

'Don't even think about it,' she said sternly. 'It looks like the snivelling sidekick Mister Hopkins is less sure, though; he's still snooping around so we have to be very careful.'

Igor sat thoughtfully for a few moments. He weighed up his desire not to get more intimately involved in the internal mysteries of the fabled dark village of Castlemaine, against his desire to get more intimately involved with the internal mysteries of the homicidal innkeeper's attractive daughter.

'All right, I happen to know a thing or two about repurposing the newly deceased. Do you have a lab?'

'A lab? No.'

'Oh,' replied Igor. 'How about an acid bath?'

'Err… no, I don't think so.'

'OK, what about a furnace?'

'We've got a barbecue out back,' offered Esmerelda helpfully.

'Hmmm… does your cook-cum-poisoner have a mincing machine?'

'Ah!' exclaimed Esmerelda. 'We tried that with one of the first ones. Cook made pies. People came from all over the parish to try them. But the owner of the Cutthroat Razor came in one day shouting blue murder. Said we were taking all her custom and if we didn't stop she'd get her boyfriend the barber to pay us a visit. Nasty bugger. Very sharp razor.'

'Right, so options are limited. Well, I suppose we'll just have to bury them then.'

'We can't just go digging random graves,' complained Esme. 'The priest for one will get suspicious and you know how interfering they can be.'

'Fear not,' said Igor with a conspiratorial wink. 'I think I've got an idea.'

*

Dusk had fallen. A lone barn owl screeched her plaintive cry into the face of the westerly wind then, turning, flew on silent wings into the fields to seek her prey.

Two dark figures flitted stealthily through the village. Making sure to stick to the deepest shadows, they flitted as stealthily as one can possibly flit while carrying the heavy, rigid corpse of an old squire, wrapped in a thick woollen blanket.

Creeping cautiously between barns and storehouses, shops and cottages, they made their way steadily towards the village churchyard, beyond which lay the dimly lit half-timber building that was their goal.

Part way across the churchyard they were forced to drop their burden and scurry for cover behind one of the large granite headstones, as the silhouette of the village priest came out of the south transept door and fumbled with a heavy set of ancient iron keys.

The key turned grudgingly in the old lock with a rusty scream. The priest looked about himself nervously, made the sign of the cross, then pulled up his collar against the chill night air and made his way hurriedly towards the safety and comfort of his own little cottage.

Father Price was a young novice priest who had only been in Castlemaine for a few months. He had been both surprised and excited when the bishop had awarded him his own parish at such a young age, but that was before he'd been told which parish it was. He'd later heard through whisperings in the seminary that he hadn't actually been the bishop's first choice for the post. According to popular rumour, the bishop had tried to appoint several older and more experienced priests to the parish, but despite his best efforts, which mainly comprised of bribes, blackmail and threats of excommunication, none of the other candidates could be persuaded to accept.

Price had originally dismissed these rumours as nothing more than jokes and stories, told by jealous young colleagues and those who would try to put the wind up him in advance of his arrival in the region, but as the weeks went by he soon came to realise that the stories were probably downplayed so as not to make him cast off his cassock and run screaming for the Foreign Legion.

Igor and Esmerelda watched silently as the priest made his nervous way across the dark churchyard and out of sight.

Swiftly, they gathered up their bundle and carried it

the last few hundred yards towards the home of the village undertaker.

*

It was fully dark outside by the time Esmerelda tapped lightly on the glass pane of the funeral parlour's front door. The glow of a few scattered candles could be seen through the windows. Igor dragged the squire's blanketed body to the side so as not to be seen the moment the undertaker opened his door.

A few tense seconds passed, then from within came the gentle sound of keys clanking in the lock. The door opened slightly and the craggy face of the undertaker appeared in the crack between door and frame.

'Hello, who's there? What do you want?' the old man's voice was wavering and nervous. It didn't do to open the door to strangers in Castlemaine after dark.

Esme stood full in the light that was escaping from inside the shop and puffed out her bosom in a sultry manor.

'Hello Hubert,' she purred in her most disarming voice. 'It's just me, come to pay you a visit. You did say I should come to pay you a visit sometime.'

Hubert Plank, the town's undertaker, had indeed said that Esme should come to pay him a visit some time, but he had been well in his cups in the bar at the Cadaver's Arms at the time. Never in his wildest imaginings did he truly think that such a lovely young creature as Esmerelda would be seen dead with him in his funeral parlour, then he checked himself as his choice of idioms was clearly getting away from him.

'Esmerelda, why yes, it's you,' said Hubert nervously. 'What a lovely surprise.'

A sudden sound to his left grabbed the undertaker's attention. He stuck his head out of the door and peered through the gloom in Igor's direction.

'Who's that with you?' he demanded, suddenly back on his guard.

'Oh, this is my... cousin, Igor. He's new to the village. He's looking for a job and I thought, as you are such a... *big* man hereabouts, that you'd be amenable to helping out a soul in need. I'd be ever so, *grateful*.' A shiver went up the old undertaker's spine as Esme whispered the last word close to his ear, her warm breath making the wiry hairs on his earlobe tingle with pleasure.

'Well, I'm not sure. I don't need any assistants at the moment,' replied Hubert, suspicion in his voice.

Igor suddenly sprang forward and, dragging the heavy blanketed bundle, he barged past the old man into the entrance hall.

'Perhaps we can come in and talk about it?'

'Well, this is highly irregular,' remonstrated the old undertaker.

Esme followed Igor as he dragged the body through the entrance hall and behind a long black curtain into the undertaker's workshop.

A number of coffins stood empty in various stages of construction around the room. Sheets of timber and a rack of tools took up one end of the workshop, while cans of varnish and boxes full of screws and brass handles were stacked on a table nearby.

Glass jars with labels such as Formaldehyde, Glutaraldehyde, Methanol and Mixed Humectants stared gloomily down from high shelves.

In the centre of the room was a trestle table upon which sat a completed coffin; completed that is by the presence of an elderly woman dressed in a black woollen smock with white lace trim. Her pinched and wrinkled features described a woman who'd died at a ripe old age after a long and burdensome life of much toil.

'I'm really sorry to trouble you with this, Hubert,' said Esme in her most calming voice, 'but I really need your help.'

'Well, if I can be of any assistance, of course, I'll do what I can,' replied the undertaker reasonably. 'But why all this urgency at this time of night, and who is this person?' The old man's eyes turned once again on Igor, a look of deep suspicion darkening his features.

'Like I said,' continued Esme in her most nonchalant, sing-song manner, 'he's my cousin and he's looking for a job. He's got experience in the death trade, so to speak. He knows his way around a cold body.'

'And I've even brought you a bit of trade here,' interrupted Igor. 'Look. I can demonstrate my skills if you like.' Not waiting for an answer, he began to fumble with the wrappings on the old squire's body.

'This is most irregular, Esmerelda,' repeated Hubert. 'I'm really not sure I can oblige on this occasion.'

By this time, Igor had lifted the squire's body and was trying to force it into the coffin on top of the old woman. Various limbs protruded as Igor tried different ways to make both corpses fit.

'I've been working on this idea of conducting joint burials,' continued Igor, puffing heavily while trying to interlock the two expired people in the most dignified manner possible. And failing.

'The idea,' he wheezed, 'is to make more efficient use of space and materials.' A sudden cracking sound emanated from the coffin as Igor twisted a limb into a small available crevice. He continued talking loudly to mask any further embarrassing noises. 'Sustainability is the watch word. It'll save you resources, it'll save both you and your customers a stack of money, and it'll keep the graveyard from getting filled up too quickly: win, win, win.'

With a final push, Igor managed to get the squire's left foot wedged in beside the old woman's right cheek. Very few body parts now protruded above the rim of the coffin. Igor stood, looking proudly at his efforts.

'I'm not sure the late Goodwife Merrydew would be too happy about having a cold, dead man forced on top of her,' complained Hubert, conscious that all his hard work of laying out her body would have to be redone.

'From what I remember of Goodwife Merrydew,' suggested Esme, 'she was never that upset about having stiff men on top of her when she was alive.'

The old undertaker nodded.

'So, money saving you say?' he mused. 'So, who is this other sti… er, I mean, dearly departed gentleman? And who will be paying me?'

Igor removed Helsing's stolen purse from his waistband and gave it a tantalising jiggle, the coins ringing tunefully from within.

'Why, I will.'

'You?' exclaimed the undertaker. 'But what is your relation to the deceased?'

'Cousin,' replied Igor.

'Brother,' replied Esme simultaneously.

'Cousin's brother,' continued Igor. 'Stepbrother actually. Adopted. On his father's second wife's side. Basically, a foundling but we were very fond of him.'

'But the service,' asked the undertaker. 'What about the rest of the family? Not to mention Goodwife Merrydew's family?'

'No problem,' said Igor, reassuring the old man. 'Cousin Kolch… er, *Hermann* has no other family left alive. Besides, he wouldn't have wanted to be mentioned at the funeral. Very shy, you see. Hated being the centre of attention.'

'That's right,' added Esme, smiling reassuringly at the old undertaker. 'You could simply treat the funeral as if it is purely for Goodwife Merrydew and pretend cousin… Hermann… isn't even in the coffin. It's what he would have wanted.'

'Well, it's all highly unorthodox,' said Hubert thoughtfully, still not certain about these new arrangements.

'Two fees, no extra work,' replied Igor, gently jingling the purse.

'Twice the weight to carry,' suggested Hubert.

'Not now you have an assistant,' said Igor with a triumphant flourish.

Hubert Plank thought about all he had seen and heard. Mostly, he thought about the richly jangling purse.

'Very well,' he said at last. 'Be here at 5am tomorrow. I'll let you have a lie-in as it's your first day.'

IGOR'S UNDERTAKING

*

Shortly after Igor and Esmerelda had left the funeral parlour, Hubert Plank sat at his desk, thinking. He was an old man, but not a stupid one. There was more to this whole idea of joint burials than met the eye, he was sure of that. Who was this newcomer? What were those two really up to?

He took a quill and scribbled a short note on a scrap of parchment, blotted it and then folded and sealed it with a drop of wax.

He picked up a small bell from next to his writing box and rang it, its soft tinkling tones barely audible.

Presently, there was a gentle knock at the door.

'Come,' called the old undertaker.

A slight, demure young woman in maid's attire entered and curtseyed to her master.

'You rang, sir?' she enquired gently.

'Yes, how is your work coming along?'

'I've finished scrubbing the mortuary floor, sir, and the kitchen, and the backyard.'

'Good work, Polly,' replied the old man warmly. He considered making a joke about her being the best scrubber he'd ever employed, but pondered her delicate sensibilities and thought better of it. 'Now, I want you to take this message to Master Hopkins forthwith, and with all haste. Stop for no one, do you understand me? This is very important.'

'Yes, sir, certainly sir,' replied the young maid, demurely.

'Good, how are those coffins looking?'

'Very shiny, sir.'

'Excellent, well, off you go and hurry about your business.

No need to return tonight.' He thought about making another improper joke about having something else that needed polishing but he imagined the look of shock on her innocent face and couldn't bring himself to say it. Instead, he sent her away with a dismissive wave of his hand.

As the girl departed, Hubert selected a decanter from his drinks cabinet and poured himself a brandy.

'We'll see what the authorities have to say about your deceased relative, Mister Igor,' he mused to himself. 'I've got a feeling this will be a very lucrative day for me indeed. Oh, yes, *dead* lucrative.'

*

Polly donned her warmest and most modest shawl and went out into the night, the undertaker's note clasped in her small, delicate hand. She had gone barely a few paces when a noise from the shadows startled her.

A dark figure emerged from a shadowy corner of the courtyard, leading a large brown-and-white gypsy cob by the halter.

'Oh, it's you,' gasped Polly, relieved at recognising the hearse driver who was putting the horses away for the night.

'It's dark,' noted the hearse driver, his eyes swivelling nervously. 'Where are you off to on this cursed evening, young Polly?'

Polly showed him the note. 'I've got to deliver this message for the master, it's to go to Mr Hopkins,' she said nervously. 'But it's late and I'm exhausted. He's had me on my hands and knees all day.'

IGOR'S UNDERTAKING

The hearse driver considered making a joke about doggies but the look in her delicate, demure eyes was sufficient for him to decide it would be wholly improper.

'You get yourself back inside, Miss Polly,' he said instead. 'I'll deliver this for you. I've still got one of the horses hitched up. It'll be quicker, and I can be back to deliver Mister Fisher to the undertaker before midnight.'

'Mister Fisher?' enquired the young girl.

'In the back of the wagon. Passed away this morning. Very popular chap in the village, so the inn will be packed with mourners tonight. Anyway, I want you to go upstairs and get those feet up.'

'I bet you do,' she said lustily before scurrying away with a bawdy laugh. 'Gimme sixpence and I might let you join me.'

No sooner had she gone than the hearse driver took out the note, sliced open the seal and read the contents. He took a gulp of something strong and warming from a silver hip flask and with a look of determination set off at speed to deliver the message.

*

As the midday rush at the Cadaver's Arms began to subside, Esmerelda made her way across the village towards the funeral parlour, to see how Igor had been faring in his new position as Hubert Plank's under-plank.

She had been worrying all morning about him and his ideas for disposing of the murder victims' remains by surreptitiously burying them in close confines with other, more legally dead people, but had so far not found a chance to leave the inn.

At the graveyard, she saw Father Price studying the ground around the walls of the church. He seemed to be looking for something. Every now and then he would pace out several long steps, then turn and shake his head and go back to looking at the ground.

'Afternoon, Father,' she called to him cheerily.

'Oh, good afternoon, miss,' he replied seemingly still distracted.

'Esmerelda,' said Esmerelda. 'You can call me Esme if you like.'

'What? Oh, yes, of course. Good afternoon, Miss Esmerelda. I hope the day finds you well.'

'Indeed, it does,' she replied smiling. 'Have you lost something?'

'Eh? Umm, no, not lost exactly. More looking for… it's nothing, really. Just a fancy. And what brings you out this fine day?'

'Just off to see my friend. He's got a job with Mr Plank at the funeral parlour.'

'Oh, is that so?' replied the priest. 'What an excellent idea. Mr Plank always seems so overworked. I've never known a village with so many deaths to contend with. At least, not one that doesn't have an overflowing plague pit or one of those new Happy Chef drive-through coach stops. This friend of yours – do I know him?'

'He's new in town,' replied Esme. 'His name's Igor.'

'Igor?' said the priest. 'Yes, I've heard a few of the villagers tell of him. From what I gather he managed to draw the attentions of our noble law enforcement officers within moments of his arrival in town. Please be cautious, Miss Esme, and forgive me for being presumptuous, but he may appear charming and exciting on the outside but underneath Igor may be more of a dangerous rascal than he first appears.'

'Well, let's hope so,' replied Esmerelda cheerily, leaving the priest looking on with a puzzled expression as she walked towards the funeral parlour.

Esme had surprised herself a little, too, with the way she had put so much faith in this mysterious Igor quite so quickly. Yes, he was scruffy and not the best-looking man she had seen by a long way, but there was definitely something in his easy charm, his devilish spirit and what she had seen under the hem of his frayed smock after she had coshed him over the head the night before that gave her a tingle of excitement that she hadn't felt for a very long time. Besides, if he turned out to be a psycho nutter bent on her destruction after all, then her short steel blade would sort that little problem out quickly enough. Sweet and demure as she often chose to appear, Esme had a hard streak inside her that could quickly surface in an act of cold violence when the need arose. She was definitely not the sort of girl to be trifled with.

Trifle!

A sudden flash of images shot unbidden through Esme's mind, that of Igor's rumpled smock and a bowl of trifle. For some strange reason, Esme felt herself blushing as she tried unsuccessfully to force the fluttery feeling that had entered her chest and those slippery images of cream and jelly out of her mind.

By the time Esme arrived at the funeral parlour, she had managed to pull herself together sufficiently to concentrate on the job in hand and knocked gently on the glass pane as she had the night before. There was no answer so she quietly opened the door and entered the reception room. She could see nobody about, but the distinct sound of two people panting breathlessly could be heard from behind the long dark curtains that hid the entrance to the workshop.

Esme cleared her throat noisily. The sounds stopped and the petite maid Polly emerged, red-faced, from behind the curtains.

'Oh, Miss Esme,' puffed the flushed maid. 'You'll excuse me, I'm sure. Master Igor and I have been screwing all morning round the back. He had me sitting on it while he pushed and twisted. It was exhausting. Please, come, I'm sure he'd be really happy for you to join us.'

Wide-eyed with expectation, Esme followed the girl through the curtains to where Igor was fighting with the lid of a coffin. Although the coffin itself seemed to be ever so slightly too tall, the occupant was sitting quite proud at the rim, making it difficult to get the lid to sit flush.

'Esme,' cried Igor. 'Just in time. Give me a hand getting this lid on, will you? Polly is very sweet and all, but she's far too slight for the heavy humping.'

Esme, choking back tears of laughter, clambered up on top of the coffin, which enabled Igor to get the six screws lined up and finally fixed down.

'Well, that was a struggle,' said Igor in a sweat. 'Bloody stiffs. How was your morning?'

'Fine,' replied Esme, 'I was frantically worried about you,

though. Thank God you had Polly to keep your spirits up. Where's old Plank by the way?'

'Ermmm, said he had to pop out for a bit, left me running the shop.'

'Well, that's encouraging,' replied Esme hopefully. 'You never know, this plan of yours might just work. We may get away with it all yet.'

*

The door to the funeral parlour burst open as Hopkins and a band of enraged pitchfork-wielding villagers poured in, shouting and calling for Igor to come forward.

Igor came forward.

'What's all this about, Hopkins? I'm busy here.'

'Nefarious goings-on, that's what! The devil's work,' cried Hopkins frothily.

'Oh, put a cock in it,' replied Igor. 'We haven't all got time to go poncing around the countryside mugging garden gnomes and pulling the wings off fairies. Some of us have got proper work to do.'

'And what kind of filthy work is that then, eh? Murder? Disposal of evidence?' The crowd behind Hopkins murmured angrily in Igor's direction.

'What are you blathering about, you misguided pillock?'

'Misguided, eh? What do you make of this then?' Hopkins produced the tattered note that Hubert Plank had written the night before.

'A scrap of parchment?' scoffed Igor.

'Hardly,' Hopkins retorted. 'Let me read it to you, and to

you all.' Hopkins directed this last remark to the menacing crowd that had gathered inside the small funeral parlour. 'It reads: "Hopkins, you must come quickly. I know who is behind the murders. They will be in my shop tomorrow after the noon. Bring reinforcements. HP".'

'So?' mocked Igor. 'That could refer to any one of you lot.'

The crowd murmured and looked at each other suspiciously.

'Yes, but none of us would be here but for the note. Except you!' accused Hopkins sensibly pointing a shaky finger in Igor's direction.

'Hmmm, yeah, I can see why you might think that,' admitted Igor reluctantly.

'Enough games,' insisted the witchfinder's assistant. 'I must insist you open that coffin. Gentlemen!' This last word he directed to the watching crowd. 'You must all bear witness to this. Inside that coffin is none other than the late Squire Kolchak, who was murdered in his room at the Cadaver's Arms, just two days ago. Exactly at the moment this Igor appeared in Castlemaine.'

The crowd buzzed and murmured loudly. Some called for crowbars to force open the coffin, and others to send for the carpenters to build a scaffold in the village square. There was to be a hanging tonight!

'Now, just you wait one matriarchal fornicating minute,' cried Igor, desperately thinking on his feet. 'You can't just go opening coffins willy-nilly.'

'Why not?' called one of the villagers.

'Yes, why not?' repeated Igor thinking furiously.

'I'll tell you why not,' shouted Esme from behind Igor. 'Because... because... it's a mortal sin.'

'Exactly,' added Igor. 'It's a mortal sin to open a sealed coffin, and anyone who does it is going straight to Hell.'

The superstitious, God-fearing villagers baulked at the idea of going straight to Hell. That didn't sound very nice at all.

'So, what do we do?' shouted another villager.

Lots of head-scratching and mumbling ensued before one bright spark called out the solution. 'Get the priest. He can say an incantation or something that'll make it OK to open the coffin. That's his job, it's what he does.'

Puffing like a petulant toddler, Hopkins couldn't think of any way to avoid the inevitable delay while Father Price was found. He didn't fancy the idea of going to Hell any more than the rest of them, and besides, what if his information was wrong? Reluctantly, Hopkins acquiesced and gave instructions that the priest should be found so they could get on with the job of sorting out this mess and preparing for a damned good lynching.

Several of the rearmost villagers squeezed back out of the building and went in search of Father Price. Everyone stood around inside the workshop quietly tapping their feet, picking at fingernails, furtively comparing the length of their pitchfork handles with those of their neighbours and silently avoiding eye contact with each other while they waited for the priest to arrive. Several minutes later a hubbub arose as the priest was thrust roughly through the throng in the entrance hall and into the workshop where Hopkins and Igor stood facing each other across the sealed coffin.

'Father Price,' sneered Hopkins. 'I need you to say… a poem to God or something so we can get this coffin opened and finally have an answer to all these murders. Will you do it?'

The young priest trembled. None of his lessons in ecclesiastical college had prepared him for dealing with pitchfork-wielding mobs. Burials and baptisms he could handle, but being party to unrighteous and morally debateable vigilante justice was not something he felt ready for. He'd happily leave that kind of thing to the Puritans. He closed his eyes, thought carefully and prayed silently for guidance. Finally, he came to a decision. He would pass the buck.

'Well, yes, I can offer up an exhumation prayer,' he exclaimed loudly to the expectant crowd, 'but without the correct legal authorisation I'm afraid we could all be imprisoned, or worse, and be held liable for grave-robbing.'

'WHAT?' cried Hopkins, incensed.

'I'm sorry,' continued the priest, 'I can't do it without the proper paperwork.'

'Oh for f…' Hopkins looked ready to burst a blood vessel. 'How do we get the proper authorisation?'

'You need a magistrate,' offered Igor, blatantly making shit up as he went along.

'Someone call for Helsing!' cried a villager. Then more and more villagers took up the cry.

'Wait, no!' insisted Hopkins, fully aware that his thunder in single-handedly solving the mystery of the murders would be well and truly stolen as soon as the bumbling, puffed-up loon he was forced to work for arrived. One day, Hopkins would be in charge. He just had to bide his time and wait for his boss to retire or die or get carried off by a horde of Iron Fisted Fire Badgers. But, alas, Helsing was bound to take all the glory for himself and leave Hopkins smouldering in the shadows once more, always bound to play second fiddle to that preening idiot.

The crowd muttered angrily among themselves as it seemed their desire for a nice, relaxed afternoon's lynching looked like dragging on into a long drawn-out palaver. Some sat down as best they could in the confined space, others went outside and started drifting back towards the inn for a restorative flagon or two of Abbott Athelstan's Flatulent Lurcher.

Igor cast a glance towards Esmerelda. She looked as composed as a piano concerto and as cool as a week-old corpse. He felt more strongly the unexpected tug of desire that this beautiful, mysterious, dangerous girl had inspired in him the night before. Their eyes met momentarily. Igor smiled a mischievous smile at her and Esme's heart fluttered again as the thought of blancmange and peach slices flashed unbidden into her head. *What's gotten into me?* she wondered, amazed at her apparent lack of self-control. She tried to force herself to think of her father's victims, all mushed up and bloodied, scattered about the town in torn pieces, but that instinctively pushed her thoughts back to their current predicament and the strength she found in Igor's easy confidence and willingness to get his hands very dirty on their behalf. She began to wonder what his motives were and smiled to herself as she realised that what she was really hoping was that his motives were thoroughly impure and involved Esmerelda herself and a bowlful of whipped cream and sponge fingers.

It was quite some time before rumours started to filter through that Helsing would be arriving in the funeral parlour at any moment.

Igor and Esme instinctively joined hands in mutual support as the moment of their discovery seemed to be approaching.

Hopkins paced, nervously awaiting his boss's arrival.

All of a sudden, a gap opened in the crowd as Helsing, local magistrate, chief of police and witchfinder general, strode forth into the room.

'So, Hopkins, what is all this? Why have you dragged me away from my vital work tracking down the vampiric perpetrators of these most horrific crimes to some seedy little undertaker's shop? What is so complicated here that you can't work it out for yourself? Are you totally incompetent?'

Hopkins bristled at the barbs. Still, he bit back all the vitriol he wanted to throw at his obnoxious superior and through gritted teeth explained briefly what had transpired.

'So, you're telling me,' sneered Helsing, 'that inside this coffin are the mortal remains of Squire Kolchak, and that his corpse hasn't been spirited away to be used as sustenance for the last children of the great vampire hordes of the Carpathians?'

'Yes, pretty much,' replied Hopkins levelly.

'Well, OK then, on your head be it. Father Price, the exhumation prayer if you please.'

Reluctantly, Father Price took out his prayer book and a vial of holy water, crossed himself several times, silently apologised to the Lord for allowing himself to get dragged into this unholy kerfuffle, and proceeded to utter a jumble of words that he truly hoped would absolve all present of the sin of disturbing the blessed rest of those deceased. The prayer done, Helsing gave the instruction to open the casket.

Two villagers picked up screwdrivers and began to undo the screws holding down the coffin lid. There was a palpable silence in the room as one by one, the screws came loose and dropped to the floor.

Esme's grip on Igor's hand tightened. They barely dared to breathe.

As the final screw fell, Hopkins stepped forward and with a flourish, cast the lid from the coffin.

'Gentlemen, I give you...'

*

There was a stunned silence.

'Arse!' muttered Hopkins as the face of the recently departed Mister Fisher presented its pale and lifeless self to the watching crowd.

'This can't be right,' cried Hopkins as he cast himself around the room looking for any other filled casket, of which there were none.

'Where is he?' Hopkins grabbed Igor by the lapels and was shaking him from side to side. Igor, who had been shaken by the best in the business, merely winked at Hopkins before crying to the surrounding crowd, 'Help, help me, he's gone mad, Help!'

Several villagers succeeded in pulling Hopkins away as Helsing rounded on his hapless assistant.

'So, you drag me away from important work for this pathetic charade. I will see you in my office first thing tomorrow morning. Now, I must get back and see if I can salvage the efforts of the real investigators. Come along, back to the mountains!'

As the crowd was starting to file out, Eric the coachman came hurrying in, his mud-spattered cloak showing all the signs of a mad chase through rough forest and wilderness. He sank to his knees, barely able to breathe following his exertions.

'Master Helsing,' he cried, wheezing, and staggering painfully as he spoke. 'Master Helsing, you must hurry. While you've been away from your rightful duties, the vampires have been led away by their villainous leader, none other than Hubert Plank, much loved and trusted undertaker of this parish for many years. He was seen carting off the bodies of the murder victims and all their precious belongings, down by the river and off to the mountain pass. If you're quick, you may catch him yet.' Exhausted, the coachman fell into a dead faint at the witchfinder's feet. Igor squeezed Esme's hand ever so slightly, as her lips curled into a very slight smile.

'You see?' cried Helsing at his miserable assistant. 'This is what your incompetent meddling has cost us. And to think, Hubert Plank was among us all these years. Come, we must try to repair the damage your foolishness has caused us.'

With that, Helsing pushed the deflated Hopkins out of the way and left, followed by the enthralled villagers, who hadn't experienced such drama in several days. This would keep the beer flowing in the Cadaver's Arms for many a long night to come.

*

Igor, Esme and Eric were left alone in the mortuary. Polly had gone to lock the door at Igor's instruction, then off to tidy the mess left by the tramping horde of villagers.

'Well, that was close,' said Esme, collapsing into a soft armchair.

'Bloody good job Eric drives the hearse as well or we'd never have got the tip-off,' replied Igor, smiling.

'I could do with a brandy after that performance,' suggested Eric.

'Ah, none left I'm afraid,' reported Igor. 'Seems our beloved undertaker Plank took rather a lot of it last night. He appears to have tripped and fallen down the cellar stairs in his befuddled state. Dead, alas.'

Esme cast a suspicious eye at Igor who smiled innocently back with just a hint of a wink. 'So, not gone off with all the money then? Where is he now?' she asked.

'Ah, yes, let me introduce you to my new invention: the double-decker.' Igor pointed to the coffin on the table from which the late Mister Fisher's rather bent and battered extremities were now poking above the rim.

'You see, the reason we had so much trouble getting the roof on this bad boy is because below old Fisher face here lies the late Hubert Plank. Helsing and his ego warriors will spend a good deal of time fruitlessly searching for our miscreant undertaker, by which time he'll be snugly interred beneath six feet of soil and one decomposing local. Shame about the old boy really, I'd only planned to get the assistant gig and diddle about with the murder victims when he was out of the office. But then again, he was ready to set the law onto us, so tough titty on him. All we need to do now is hope that whoever is taking over as undertaker is corrupt enough to let us slip the odd extra stiffy in for a few gold schillings on the side.'

'About that,' suggested Esme, thoughtfully. 'You know, you could always stick around and manage the business. You'd make a good undertaker. You can handle a corpse and you look bloody miserable, you're the perfect fit.'

'Well, it's certainly a thought,' replied Igor, flashing Esme a dirty smile.

*

That night, Eric, Esme and Igor celebrated their day's work at the Cadaver's Arms. Igor used up the last of the money he'd filched from Victor buying drinks for everyone. The villagers excitedly recounted tales of vampires and murderous undertakers. Esme served behind the bar as the evening grew into one of the busiest they could remember. Eric sat slumped in his usual seat, murmuring sleepily to himself, 'Mfrmff, snfrlll… not after dark!'

'Why does he say that?' asked Igor; his curiosity about the paradoxical coachman had finally caught up with him.

'Say what?' replied Esme, distractedly spitting onto a beer mug and rubbing vigorously at a stubborn encrusted bloodstain that had somehow got there.

'All that "not taking them after dark" stuff?' replied Igor, staring at the dozing coach driver. 'I mean, he's clearly not afraid of the dark. I imagine that Eric can look after himself well enough, even against the sort of supernatural ghoulies that a full moon in Castlemaine would throw up.'

'Oh, no, nothing like that.' Esme gave up trying to remove the bloodstain and put the grubby flagon back on the shelf, ready for the next unsuspecting customer. She smiled warmly towards the stool that Eric was slowly sliding down. 'No, he just hates to be away from the bar for too long.'

A sudden shrill scream pierced the air and the maid Valerie stumbled, shocked and dazed, into the room.

'Oh no, not another one,' cried Esme, fully expecting to have yet more blood and entrails to deal with. Everyone in the bar stopped still and stared at the poor, quivering chambermaid.

A moment's grim, terrified silence passed before heavy, slapping footsteps were heard coming from the kitchen corridor.

Breaths were held, gasps were gasped and a feeling of imminent panic swept the assembled masses.

With a tremendous crash, the door flew open and old Clam came bursting into the bar, tying his britches back around his huge, voluminous belly.

'Bloody girl,' he cried. 'How many times must I tell you to knock when I'm taking a dump.'

BODY PART II

THE NUN, THE SAINT AND THE CRYPT O' ZOOLOGY

Igor had found it surprisingly easy to inveigle his way into the now vacant role of village undertaker. Hubert Plank had no relatives to assume the business and besides, as a criminal convicted *in absentia*, all his assets were forfeit. It only took a few gold schillings in the right greasy palms before Igor had his hands on the keys to the funeral parlour.

Had Helsing known about Igor's plans to embed himself deeper into the village fabric, then he might have done something to prevent it. But Helsing himself, having at last given up as futile the search for Hubert Plank, was off in the forests searching for his new quarry, a brood of seven-headed, soul-drinking, scaly death raptors, and was thus far too preoccupied.

As it transpired, almost everyone who worked in the magistrates' office hated Helsing as much as the rest of the village, and they were only too happy to accept a handful of gold coins and promote Igor's installation as the new village undertaker, if it meant sticking one up their boss.

Some Castlemanians had speculated that the sightings of seven-headed, soul-drinking, scaly death raptors were merely invented as a prank by Helsing's underlings, to get him out of the office more. Since this notion was utterly rejected by the staff as wholly unacceptable and based on wild accusations, no hard evidence and with absolutely zero foundation in fact at all, there was probably more than a grain of truth in it.

Igor was delighted with his new job. It would make use of his skills, bring in an income, and would allow him to start a whole new life away from all the ghoulish goings-on he'd been party to at Castle Frankenstein. It was time to give up all the nefarious activities of his past and settle down to a peaceful life rebuilding tattered corpses ready for a respectable, and hopefully permanent, burial.

Except, of course, for the fact that he still had to dispose of the bodies that had been piling up courtesy of the inn's somnomicidal landlord. This was a little something he was happy to do on the side, as it meant he got to see Esmerelda on a regular basis.

On the day he got the keys to the parlour, Igor set about his new position with a professional vigour. He made a full inventory of the funeral parlour's assets, checked over the paperwork, ordered new headed stationery, visited Herr Kwaak, the village's apothecary, to obtain fresh embalming chemicals, polished up his tools and thoroughly rifled through old Plank's belongings in search of any leftover valuables.

This last activity proved to be highly beneficial as the old man was as crooked as a second-hand cart dealer and had clearly been pilfering the corpses for many years. With his financial situation now comfortably secure, Igor could relax and settle down to read something from the former undertaker's extensive library. With a glass of port in one hand and a copy of *How to Embalm Friends and Eviscerate People* in the other, Igor drifted off into his first proper night's sleep in many, many years.

*

The next morning, feeling fully refreshed and settled in, Igor decided to have a proper look around the village and then stop by the church to see how much burial space he had to play with.

Castlemaine was a fairly unremarkable village on the face of it. It had the usual array of shops and businesses, along with a traditional marketplace with stalls selling livestock, tools, fabrics, vegetables, cheeses and meats, some cured and some still quite evidently sickly. The people were pleasant enough. Their demeanour was much more attractive in the daytime, even if their looks weren't.

He strolled among the buildings as the sun glowed weakly overhead. He purchased some provisions and several new sets of clothes. His old rags had given up the ghost and he was now wearing items he'd taken from the two corpses currently lying semi-naked in his mortuary. The shirt that he'd 'borrowed' from the late Mister Grimwood was a bit snug, but the long calico skirt Missus Grimwood had been wearing when their carriage fell into the ravine was actually quite liberating. He bought some casual smocks for his days off and a very nice heavy black suit for work.

Munching on a meat pie he'd bought at Gristle, the village butcher's, Igor made his way to the Cadaver's Arms. He was gagging for a swift glass of something antiseptic to wash away the taste of the pie, whose meaty provenance even Igor's broadly experienced palate couldn't discern.

'So, how's our new undertaker getting on?' asked Esme as Igor rested his purchases on the bar.

'Very good,' replied Igor smiling. 'All settled in, I think. Got a couple of clients laid out ready to go.'

'Ah, yes, the Grimwoods. Terrible what happened to them. They'd only just got that carriage last week from Honest Vlad's Used Cart Emporium over in Lower Flinching. To have a spoke blow out like that on such a narrow track… devastating.'

'Hmmm,' hummed Igor. 'Still, looking on the bright side, it's work for me.'

'Absolutely,' agreed Esme with an appraising eye. 'And that skirt looks great on you.'

'Ha-ha!' replied Igor with a smile. 'I've been shopping and bought myself some new clobber. From now on I shall be the respectable man about town.'

'Quite right too,' smiled Esme. 'So, when can we move the next body? We've still got a dozen or so down in the cellar.'

'It'll have to be after dark, which means getting any help from Eric is out of the question, he'll not take 'em. I'm off to visit the priest and suss out the burial plots, see what we can get away with. I'll be back this evening and we can work something out.'

'Great, I appreciate it,' said Esme in a relieved tone.

'I'd like to ask a favour in return,' said Igor, coyly.

'Of course, anything.'

'Come and work with me.'

Esme looked down at the dirty floor. 'No, I can't,' she protested. 'I have to work here, Dad needs me. Especially when he's had one of his "night-time adventures".'

'I understand that,' replied Igor. 'I'm not talking about working at the morgue all the time, just on busy days. You know when the body count goes up. Full moons, local football matches, WI bake-offs, that kind of thing.'

'Well…' mused Esme, sheepishly glancing at Igor through her hair that had fallen attractively across her brow, 'I suppose I could get away occasionally. And you are helping us with our little… problem.' Esme's uncontrollably lustful feelings for the new rogue in town had grown stronger in recent days and she was secretly delighted that she now had an excuse to see him more often.

Igor, equally enthused, grinned like a rigid corpse. 'Great! That's settled then.'

His stomach growled menacingly, 'Now, how about a glass of that carbolic brandy of yours,' he asked with a grimace. 'I thought the pies in Castlemaine were supposed to be good. I'm not sure what meat was in that one I just had, but to suggest it's disagreeing with me is an understatement. It's past the aggressive finger-pointing stage and has started calling me outside for a punch-up.'

*

Three glasses of brandy had proved sufficient to finally defeat the pie that was now cursing quietly to itself and skulking in Igor's upper intestine.

He gathered up his shopping and wound his way back through the village towards the churchyard.

The sun was starting to warm the air so it was no surprise to find Father Price out and about, working away quietly among the graves. What was a surprise, though, was finding him nailing garlic tresses to the churchyard gates.

'Afternoon, Father,' Igor called cheerily across to the priest who was looking around nervously.

'Ah, Igor, good afternoon,' he replied, distractedly.

'Um, might be a silly question, Father, but why are you nailing garlic tresses to the churchyard gates?'

'Ay, yes, why?' repeated the priest, looking nervous.

Igor spotted a heavy bag lying on the ground with several more garlic bulbs dangling out from the opening. He went across and peeked inside.

'Seriously, Father, I didn't take you for a superstitious man,' remarked Igor in a concerned voice. 'What is all this? Wooden stakes, a mallet, tons of garlic.' Igor rifled through the bag as Father Price looked on with a hint of embarrassment. 'Holy water,' continued Igor, 'there must be a dozen crucifixes in here. And what's this?' Igor pulled a large book out of the bag and read the title. '*Ye Olde Booke of Protective Charmes and Counter Curses to Defend Ye Against the Hellish and Diabolic Manifestations of the Nefarious Underworld, for Dummies.*'

'Yes,' stuttered the priest. 'It's supposed to be the leading authority on the subject.'

'I thought that was the Bible?' suggested Igor.

'Oh, yes,' giggled Father Price nervously, 'that too.'

Bewildered, Igor suddenly remembered something that Esme had told him the night before.

'Father, Esmerelda said she saw you pacing the churchyard the other day, looking at the ground as if you were searching for something. What were you looking for? Signs of the undead having risen? Graves being exhumed?'

'Oh, no,' replied the priest. 'That was nothing to do with all this. Well, not directly. You see, apparently, somewhere hereabouts there's a tunnel.'

'A tunnel?' repeated Igor, suddenly very interested.

'Yes. Apparently several hundred years ago, during the plague, a tunnel was dug between the church and one of the buildings in the village. A means for the local dignitaries to get to church without having to walk the infested streets. Long since lost, I'm afraid. There's no sign of it anywhere in the church. I was hoping to see if there was anything on the surface to hint where it might have been.'

'Now that's interesting,' mused Igor. 'Very interesting indeed.'

'Absolutely,' replied the priest. 'If I could find the tunnel, I could do like the ancients and travel to town without having to risk the... err... evils of the night.'

'Seriously, Father,' replied Igor. 'I'm not sure all this stuff about monsters and suchlike is healthy, these things don't really exist, you know.' Of course, Igor knew only too well that all these nightmarish creatures did indeed exist, and in spades. Frankenstein would often perform autopsies on all manner of strange creatures of legend and myth at the castle, in the hope that their bodies had medicinal or magical properties. Igor also understood that what the terrified priest needed right at this moment was a bit of calming reassurance, or else he'd more likely be in need of a clean set of undercassocks.

However, Igor's good intentions were seemingly for naught, for as he spoke, Father Price suddenly stiffened and a look of terror twisted his face.

'Look!' he croaked, fear in his wavering voice. He was pointing at a tall, fearsome-looking figure dressed all in black that suddenly emerged at the church gate.

The dark figure grabbed the garlic tress and ripped it to shreds before their eyes. The priest fled screaming towards the church. Igor stood watching as the figure began to approach. Bravely, he moved towards it and shouted a defiant, 'Oi! What are you playing at, bollockchops?'

Behind him, the priest let out a shriek. Igor turned briefly to see him fumbling with his keys, desperate to get into the holy sanctuary. When he turned back towards the gate, the figure had gone. Vanished into the afternoon as if it had never existed. Only the tattered remains of the garlic showed that it wasn't merely imagination.

Pondering these events deeply, Igor gathered up all the bags and followed the panicked priest into the vestry.

*

Father Price sat at his desk looking very pale. Igor decided to check in cupboards for the Communion wine. Having found a bottle, he poured two large helpings into some silver goblets and handed one to the priest, who drained it in one and handed it back to Igor for a refill.

Two goblets later, the colour was starting to return to the priest's face and he seemed to relax a little.

'Now, what's all this about, Father?' asked Igor gently.

'I'm sorry,' replied the priest. 'I'm usually stronger than this.'

Igor waited while he gathered his thoughts.

'You know, for a man of God you seem to be very susceptible to superstitious beliefs. All that garlic, wooden stakes, and whatnot. What's got you spooked, Father?'

A look of fear returned to the priest's eyes as he thought about his response.

'It's this place,' he murmured, a haunted look in his eye. 'That figure in black. This whole town is cursed.'

'Cursed? What makes you say that?'

'Cursed by the forces of evil,' continued the priest, passion suddenly entering in his voice. 'The dead walk in the night, ghouls haunt my footsteps, succubi tempt me with promises of filthy pleasures.'

Igor studied the wine bottle looking to see the alcohol content.

'Really, Father, you don't need to worry about all that ooky-spooky stuff you know. You've got that... God bloke looking out for you, eh?' Igor was still fighting uphill to quell the terrified priest's wholly rational and perfectly understandable fears. He was failing miserably.

'I know, I know,' whimpered the priest wringing his trembling hands frantically. 'I know this is holy ground, but... you saw that thing, too... I know you did.'

Igor couldn't deny it. He had seen the dark figure, all too large and lifelike. He thought about what to say next and decided to change tack to try and restore some courage and faith into the beleaguered cleric.

'Surely, you, a man of the cloth, were sent here to thwart such evils.'

'Hardly,' replied the priest harshly. 'I thought I was chosen by the bishop because of my devotion and my people skills, but it turns out I was sent here because nobody else would accept the job. That and because of what I saw him up to with the abbot in the monastery bath house last Michaelmas. He wants me out of the way, and somewhere... dangerous.'

'Come now,' reassured Igor emptying the last of the wine into the priest's glass, 'I'm sure it's not all that bad. I can't believe the bishop would want you to come to any harm.'

'Oh really?' sputtered Price angrily, quaffing down a large glugful. 'So what do you make of that?' He handed Igor a document.

'*The Martyr's Charter*,' read Igor. '*1001 ways to die in the service of the Lord.*'

'He keeps sending me things like that. Taunting me.' Father Price broke down, sobbing.

'Yes, but is this place really that bad?' asked Igor, attempting a final run at the comfort angle.

'Do you know what happened to my predecessor, Father Trivett?' replied the priest in-between sobs. 'He was abducted, tied to a cross, ravaged for three days and nights by a coven of sex-crazed witches, then left pale and exhausted with a sign hanging off his... you know what, which read, "How's that for a second coming?" As soon as the villagers found and untied him he ran off screaming into the forest and hasn't been seen since.'

Igor found another bottle of wine and refilled the priest's goblet.

'Well, look, Father, I happen to be something of an expert on the supernatural,' he lied, spotting his chance to gain trust and favour. 'And I'll be more than happy to assist you with any exorcisms or suchlike that need handling.'

The priest's head was spinning with the emotion, and the wine.

'Yes, thank you, Igor,' he replied weakly. 'It would be good to have someone nearby that I can rely on.'

'Well, I'm only a few dozen yards away at the funeral parlour. You can find me there when needed.'

Igor left Father Price trembling in his vestry with a full cup of wine and made his way thoughtfully back to his shop. He wasn't afraid of monsters, vampires, ghosts or witches; he'd seen worse things prowling the dungeons of Castle Frankenstein. But that dark figure disturbed him. There was something unsettling about such an obviously demonic presence sauntering into a sunlit churchyard in the middle of a warm afternoon, and tearing up one of the most ancient, powerful charms against evil, without so much as a 'kiss my foot' or 'have an apple'.

But more significant still was the idea that an ancient and as yet undiscovered tunnel joined the church with another building somewhere in the village. That was something he'd certainly have to investigate further.

*

Hopkins was alone in his office. Helsing was out in the forest again with a party of pitchfork-wielding villagers, searching for a nest of the fabled seven-headed, soul-drinking, scaly death raptors.

Hopkins had avoided going this time by pretending he was dead. He'd have to make up an excuse later for still being alive, but that was easier than traipsing through the woods yet again on another wild raptor chase.

For the moment he was just happy to be alone in the peace and quiet of his office, where he could get on with various snooping tasks he'd been meaning to get back to.

Although normally very keen-eared and alert, Hopkins entirely failed to sense the approach of the tall, fearsome-looking figure dressed all in black as it appeared in the doorway to his office.

For a few seconds, Hopkins continued to scratch away at his parchment without noticing the figure bearing down on him. Then suddenly, with a scream, he leapt back out of his seat and onto the third shelf up of his filing cabinet.

The menacing figure stood slightly inside the room's only doorway, making a swift exit impossible. He was trapped and with nobody else in the building and no weapons to hand, he did what any self-respecting witchfinder's assistant would do: he started crying and grovelling to be allowed to live.

The figure appeared unmoved by his pleadings and silently glided towards him.

Quaking, Hopkins scrambled to his knees and reached up to his desk for the letter opener. The dark figure batted the sharp instrument away easily, then turned, sat down in the visitor's chair and started thumbing through his paperwork.

Bemused by this turn of events, and the creature's apparent disinclination to murder him straight away, Hopkins found sufficient courage to whimper at the daunting apparition, 'Who are you? What do you want with me?'

'I am looking for Helsing,' replied the figure in a deep but clearly feminine voice.

Hopkins was initially stunned to hear the thing speak, but suddenly relieved that it was his useless boss it wanted, and not himself, he revived somewhat and shuffled his way into his chair.

'I'm afraid the m... m... magistrate isn't here at the m... m... moment,' he managed to squeeze out. 'P... p... perhaps you could c... come back tomorrow?'

'NO!' shouted the figure forcefully. 'I must see him today. Who are you, you snivelling little man?'

'Nobody!' cried Hopkins. 'Err, Hopkins... assistant...' he trailed off weakly.

'Hopkins, yes, I've heard of you,' said the figure. 'You will do.'

Do? thought Hopkins. *Do for what?*

The figure stood again and, throwing off a large, hooded cloak, revealed herself to be a tall, fearsome-looking nun with a shock of grey hair and a vicious scar that divided her face horizontally.

'My name is Sister Vigilanta,' exclaimed the nun as if it was supposed to mean something to the trembling little man. 'I have been sent here on papal authority to assess your witch-finding results.'

How did I miss that memo? thought Hopkins.

'We were not made aware of your coming,' he said, relaxing slightly.

'Of course not!' exclaimed the scary nun. 'What's the point of a surprise inspection if you know we're coming?'

Hopkins couldn't fault that logic.

'But that's not the main point of my visit. I'm also here to investigate the disappearance of one of his Holiness's key advisors who was last seen entering Castlemaine en route to an important meeting with the local bishop. He never arrived for that meeting and hasn't been heard of since. I need to speak to your magistrate as soon as possible.'

'Well, I'm afraid that Magistrate Helsing is away on business at the moment, out in the forest, hunting down a pack of vicious seven-headed, soul-drinking, scaly death raptors. I'd be there myself but—'

'Seven-headed, soul-drinking, scaly death raptors?' repeated the nun scornfully. 'What rubbish is this? There are no such things.'

'Yes, that's what I said—' began Hopkins but the nun cut him off.

'I was warned that Helsing was an idiot,' said the nun. 'But you...' She looked Hopkins up and down carefully. 'You look like a man I can work with.'

Unsure whether this was a good or a bad thing, Hopkins merely smiled weakly. 'Thank you.'

'I saw your priest this afternoon in the churchyard. He was nailing pagan talismans about the place and talking to an odd fellow in a calico skirt.'

'Yes,' said Hopkins. 'That would be the new undertaker, a man called Igor. He's new in town and very suspicious if you ask me.'

'They appeared to be plotting something,' exclaimed the nun.

'Doesn't surprise me at all. He's got something to do with all the recent murders, I'll wager, or my name's not Heinrich Rasputin Genghis Osama Hopkins.'

'Murders, you say?'

'Yes, so many of late that we've almost lost count of them. There's been...' Hopkins studied his hands with a befuddled look, before holding up an unconvincing number of fingers, 'must be about eleventy-nine. I suppose this missing papal emissary of yours could be among them.'

'We shall have to investigate that,' stated the nun with a steely look in her eye. 'And why would a priest be using old magic?' she spat, her disdain for such heathen nonsense clear to see. 'The power of the Lord should be enough for a man of the cloth.'

'Yes, well, after what happened to his predecessor and the witchy sisterhood of carnal pleasures, I suspect he's just being cautious...' Hopkins continued carelessly.

'So, you admit it! The Devil's playthings walk among you. You who are appointed protector should be ashamed of yourself for allowing this to happen.'

'Be fair,' snivelled Hopkins as he sank back into his chair. 'We've been really busy what with the murders and scaly soul whatsits.'

'And that is why I am needed, to sort out your shortcomings and purge these lands of all evil as per his Holiness's commands!' cried Sister Vigilanta, striking a statuesque and heroic power stance.

'Well, I'd love to help but I've got quite a backlog...'

'Excellent, we should start straight away and stop at

nothing. We must delve deep into the very cesspits of this miserable little town to find the answers.'

Hopkins felt a little queasy; he wasn't sure that sounded very hygienic at all.

'We need to draw up a plan and observe their movements,' continued the nun.

'Urgh, do we have to?' exclaimed Hopkins, his face pale with the prospect.

'I mean, secrete ourselves and watch all their comings and goings.'

'This really doesn't sound very tasteful at all,' replied Hopkins turning green at the thought of all those movements and secretions.

'I mean *spy* on them,' shouted the nun, exasperated.

'Oh, that,' replied Hopkins. 'Why didn't you just say so?'

*

Later that evening, Igor and Esme sat by the fire in the funeral parlour kitchen, deep in discussion.

'That tunnel would be an amazing find,' enthused Esmerelda, the wine glass in her hand swinging wildly and threatening the soft furnishings with a good staining. 'I can't imagine a better way to sneak the bodies over to the funeral parlour without being seen.'

'Yes, but how do we find it?' enquired Igor, picking at a small tick that had embedded itself in his knee pit. 'Price said he's studied the whole church and grounds thoroughly but came up with nothing. If he can't find it, what hope have we got?'

'We need to get access to the church somehow,' replied Esme.

'But what good will that do if we don't know where to begin looking?' Igor scratched the back of his head thoughtfully. 'I don't suppose there are any old documents that might give us a clue,' he mused.

'If there are then they'd be kept in the magistrates' office. I can't see Helsing and Hopkins letting us nose about their files, and we definitely don't need them getting suspicious.'

'Hmmm... true enough. Any old duffers in the village that might know something?' Igor was trying to find straws to clutch at.

'I doubt it. Sounds like the tunnel has been lost for generations,' replied Esme. 'And, besides, if we start asking questions it'll soon be all around the village. Folk 'round 'ere love a good bit of gossip.'

'Buggeration,' cussed Igor. 'Got any dowsing rods? Crystal pendulums? Special glasses that help you see through solid objects?'

'Not exactly,' replied Esme. 'But I have an idea. Old Mother Demdike who lives out in the forest has always had a reputation as a bit of a scryer. She's helped a few people find missing items. Lost jewellery, wandering pets, the occasional errant husband. Might be worth giving her a try-out. Nothing to lose.'

Igor thought about it for a while and finally agreed that anything was worth a try. 'Well, it's a long shot, my dear Esme, but it might just work. I shall head out there in the morning.'

'Great,' replied Esme. 'Take a weapon. She's old and frail but mad as a bag of badgers and can be quite dangerous when she chooses.'

'Wonderful,' replied Igor. 'Just what I wanted, a day out granny-bashing.'

*

The following morning, Igor armed himself with a heavy cudgel and hired Eric to take him out into the forest to find Old Mother Demdike's hovel. Esme had excused herself from the trip, insisting that it was vital that she kept an eye on old Clam to help minimise his opportunities for having forty winks and a cheeky disembowelling. Igor suspected that Esme's reluctance to go had more to do with Old Mother Demdike's reputation for carrying out acts of random violence of her own.

It was a fine morning and the sunlight glowed a beautiful pale green through the leafy canopy overhead as the small cart wound its way along the ancient forest track. Here and there, small clearings could be seen where villagers had been gathering wood. The occasional woodman's cottage sat back from the track and woodpiles were scattered randomly where workmen had left them.

As they drove deeper into the forest, the undergrowth became much denser. The light began to dim as the trees bunched up closer and the overhanging foliage reached out its woody fingers at them in sinister fashion. Eric began to whimper nervously and was all for turning back or letting Igor walk the rest of the way, but Igor had foreseen this problem and produced a large bottle of brandy from his bag to help steady the coachman's nerves.

With several huge gulps of the strong liquor inside him,

Eric felt able to continue and they wound further and further into the forest.

After what felt like hours, they came at last to a point where the track was too narrow for the horse and cart to carry on. Igor jumped down and left Eric shifting nervously in his seat with just the brandy bottle to keep him company.

Following the track further into the trees, he started to see animal bones tied in bundles dangling from the branches and here and there strange human-shaped effigies nailed to the tree trunks. Realising he must be close, Igor hefted the cudgel in his hand and tucked it under the folds of his cloak.

Rounding a bend in the track, he suddenly came upon a small ramshackle house with a single window and woodsmoke rising silently from the chimney. Igor made his way cautiously towards the door, looking this way and that to ensure nobody was ready to jump out and surprise him.

Cautiously, he raised his hand to knock on the tattered wooden door. As he did so, it swung open inwards with an ominous creaking noise that set his teeth on edge.

Peering into the gloom, he called out, sweetly. 'Yoo-hoo. Mrs Demdike? Are you there?'

'Come in, Igor... *of the castle*.' The crackly old voice sent a chill up Igor's spine.

Gingerly, he entered the tumbledown old cottage. It was very dark inside with only the faintest of light penetrating through the ancient and filth-encrusted window. A strange and unpleasant smell filled his nostrils, like burnt hair mingled with stale sweat and just a soupçon of rotten corpse.

As his eyes got used to the gloom, Igor could start to

make out the shapes of furniture. In a chair by the fireplace sat a pile of old rags which, as he watched, reformed itself into the ancient figure of Old Mother Demdike. The old woman took a taper and lit it from the fire, then applied the flame to a blackened oil lamp, which gave off a sickly yellow glow that barely reached the walls.

The feeble light just about illuminated the crooked and twisted shape of the old woman. Ugly as sin, she was, with four soft black teeth in her wrinkled and gummy mouth, scraggly white hair and a beard that could have fed a family of six for a week.

'You know me?' asked Igor, trying not to retch at the disgusting smells emanating from the old woman.

'I know you… and your *purpose*,' croaked the old witch. 'You seek the dark path.'

Igor was momentarily gobsmacked. How could she know what he was going to ask her? The old woman seemed to read his thoughts.

'I see much that is hidden, young lickspittle.'

Igor felt suddenly uneasy, a chill went through him and the hairs on the back of his neck began to rise. With an effort he shrugged the feeling away and decided to try and get on with it quickly.

'Yes, I want to find the tunnel that lies beneath Castlemaine. Do you know of it?'

'I told you, there is nothing hidden from me,' replied the crone. 'You won't be needing that club,' she pointed a bent and twisted finger at the cudgel underneath his cloak. 'I will do you no harm if you pay me well.'

Igor pulled out Helsing's stolen purse with the last few

remaining coins inside. He carefully dropped it into the old woman's upturned palm.

She chuckled as she squeezed the pouch. Igor pulled up an old stool and sat down. The stool instantly gave way under his weight and he tumbled to the dusty floorboards as it splintered into bits.

The old woman cackled noisily in a paroxysm of dry laughter, before a coughing fit doubled her up, spluttering noisily and spraying Igor with gobbets of sticky phlegm.

The filth and the stench suddenly got to Igor and he also began retching and coughing as he tried to wipe himself down.

Wheezing hard, the old lady reached over to a small table nearby and picked up a clay flask, which held a strange and noxious liquor. Still coughing loudly, she proffered the flask to Igor who, remembering Esme's warnings and not wanting to offend the old woman, sipped as politely as he could manage without inhaling any more of the foul air than was absolutely necessary to maintain the very basics of survival.

A lump of something stringy and unpleasant came away from the volume within the flask and Igor was forced to swallow it whole as the idea of chewing it first almost brought his lower intestines into his mouth. It was a close-run thing, but Igor managed to control his innards sufficiently to avoid a messy explosion. Proud of his inner strength and resolve, Igor gladly handed the flask back.

'Interesting,' muttered the old witch, as she hoiked up an enormous glob of lung butter and spat it into the flask. 'Nobody's ever drunk any before.'

Feeling very green, Igor tried to turn the old woman's

attention back to the point of his visit, so he could get it over with as soon as possible and head back out into the clean air of the forest.

'So, can you find me this tunnel? Please?' he asked, fearing he would faint at any minute.

'I can.'

'Yes?' Igor's patience was running out with the last of the breathable air.

The old witch set her eye firmly on Igor's and she gave out another rasping cackle.

'Hand me that bottle, vermin chaser,' she demanded, pointing to a clear glass phial on a shelf below the window. He went across and retrieved the bottle, handing it over carefully and praying that he wouldn't be required to take any himself.

She grabbed it from him, removed the cork and, throwing her head back, took a huge draught. Not swallowing, she merely held the liquor in her throat. As she did so, she began gargling noisily, forming words with her mouth, apparently having some unfathomable conversation within herself.

Igor couldn't make out anything the mad old woman was saying but there were clearly words bubbling through the liquid in her throat. At times the pitch of her watery conversation changed as if more than one person were speaking. Igor was fascinated and disgusted in equal measure and began to worry about how she was managing to breathe.

Eventually, after several moments of this, she threw her head forward again and spat the liquid across the floor. She sat back, panting heavily. Slowly, her breathing returned to its normal grating rattle.

'The entrance is in the crypt. At the far end is a tomb. Behind the tomb is a wall. Behind the wall is the tunnel. In the tunnel… is a… *curse*.'

She flopped down heavily in her seat and began snoring, clearly exhausted by her efforts. Igor was momentarily stunned. He wasn't sure if what he'd just witnessed was for real or simply the ravings of a crazy old bat. He stood up slowly and started to make his way outside into the fresh air.

'Not even a thank you?' shouted the old woman scornfully.

'Ah, yes, of course, thank you, Mrs Demdike. Most enlightening.'

'Good, eh?' she smirked smugly. As she spoke she reached down beside her chair and picked up a bunch of dried herbs, which she set fire to with the oil lamp.

'Don't mind if I smoke do you?' Shaking out the flames, she inhaled deeply the pungent fug as it threatened to fill up the last of the clear air space between them. 'Takes years of practice,' she went on, 'I don't get to exercise my skills very often these days.'

Igor sensed the old woman wanted a post-oracle conversation.

'Yes, most impressive,' he offered politely, still edging towards the door. 'Don't suppose you're able to give away the secrets of your craft though, eh? The magic triangle being such a closed circle and all.' He wasn't really interested, he just wanted to distract her long enough to make his escape.

Old Mother Demdike grinned her four-toothed smile. 'Oh, I don't mind. Never stood with all this secrecy nonsense. It's easy when you know how. I can tell you if you like.'

Igor couldn't give a flying funt, he just wanted to get out into the fresh air, and besides, he was pretty sure the ancient hag was old enough to have seen the blasted tunnel being dug in the first place. He wasn't at all convinced she had any magical powers beyond the ability to scare off wild animals at a thousand paces with her stench alone. He reached for the door just in time to see the bolt move across of its own accord. The old woman spat and a glob of phlegm landed on the door handle. Igor withdrew his hand.

'Unbeliever, eh?' Mother Demdike's voice was suddenly loud and commanding. Igor turned back towards her and tried to look casual.

'Well, no… but…' he fumbled for a convincing lie, but it was an exercise in futility. The old woman saw all.

'Listen to me, boy, because this knowledge will save your miserable life one day. I won't tell you when, because that would spoil all the fun; but hear ye well, Igor the ignorant. For this alone did ye come here today, though know it did ye not.'

Igor's mouth flapped uselessly as he tried to fathom his way through her last statement. He wasn't sure he liked what the crone had just mentioned about his life needing saving, nor indeed the suggestion that his ultimate survival would be reliant on the ravings of a wizened old hag.

Mother Demdike watched Igor intently, until she detected the precise moment that he finally resigned himself to hearing her out. She allowed herself another smug smirk.

'Inside each one of us,' she went on more gently, 'are links with the dead. Not physical links, astral ones. We are connected through these links to every person who has ever lived and passed over into the nether world.'

Oh great, thought Igor, *that's all I need after my past history.*

'A network of minds, holding all the information ever known by all of mankind. Whatever you're looking for, whatever you want to find, someone, somewhere always knows where whatever it is you're looking for is.' The old woman's eyes glistened in the dim light as she spoke. 'Whether it's a lost cat,' she went on, 'a missing person, a stolen jewel, someone beyond always knows where it can be found. By communicating with these minds, we can discover all things.' The old woman was really getting into her stride. Igor wished she'd get a move on.

'Of course, you need to know how to speak with them. That's what takes the practice. Some folk use herbs, some use smoke,' she waggled her smouldering handful of dried vegetation at him, 'or mushrooms. I use water. By accessing my internal link with the network and allowing the minds of the dead to speak through the water, I can divine their thoughts and find what I seek.'

Mrs Demdike sat back, triumphantly, clearly proud of herself.

Igor was taken aback by this long spiel of complete gibberish.

'So basically,' he summarised, 'what you're saying is...' he paused, 'that you can find out anything by gurgling the inner net?'

'Exactly!' exclaimed the ancient witch, as with a final bout of insane cackling, she vanished back into a crumpled heap of rags on the chair.

*

'So, all we need to do now is work out how to get regular access to the crypt without rousing anyone's suspicions.' Igor had hit the nail on the head.

Esme smiled at Igor with a twinkle in her keen, green eye. 'Leave that one to me.'

*

'Acoustics?' Father Price was struggling to keep up with what Esme was saying.

'Yes, the acoustics in the crypt would be perfect.'

The young priest was still unclear about Esme's sudden desire to run a church choir.

'I'm still unclear about your sudden desire to run a church choir,' he confirmed.

'Oh, it's something I've been thinking about for, ooh, ages and ages.'

Lying to priests came easily to Esme. The last one, Father Trivett, had been a dirty old sod with wandering hands and a nasty habit of fondling bits of the town's churchgoing women at every available opportunity. Esme had taken great pride in winding him up as often as possible, and had grown very good at it. It was because of his lecherous habits that she had finally helped the sex-crazed witches get their insatiable claws into him. Teach him how it feels to be on the receiving end of unwanted physical attention. Esme wasn't sorry to see the filthy old pervert quite literally get his comeuppance. She saw it as her civic duty to deflate anyone who abused their position in such a way and would happily do the same again.

But this new young priest was a lot nicer than the old one, and it did give Esme a very slight twinge of guilt to be telling him porkies, but only very slight, and only for a nanosecond.

Father Price looked at Esme, standing before him in the vestry, and the dozen or so scruffy and ragged-looking locals that crowded in behind her.

'All right,' he agreed wearily, keen to be away and back to the relative sanity of his own fireside. 'Here are the spare keys. Let yourselves out when you've finished.' He handed Esme a huge keyring with several large iron keys dangling from it. Ushering the group out of his office, he locked it and went home for the night. 'I just hope the bishop doesn't get to hear about this.'

*

Igor stole across the churchyard when he saw Father Price leave. He headed into the church and down the stone stairs that led into the crypt. Inside was Esme and her gang of fake choristers.

'Blimey, how did you rope this lot in?' asked Igor, impressed at Esme's industry.

'Oh, that was easy. I just threatened to buy them all dinner at the inn if they refused.'

'Genius.'

'Right, you lot, back upstairs and start singing. Igor and I need some privacy. And sing loudly, I don't want anyone outside hearing us banging down here.'

THE NUN, THE SAINT AND THE CRYPT O' ZOOLOGY

Several of the villagers winked and made leering remarks as they filed back up the staircase. Among the group were Eric, Polly and Valerie plus several others that Igor and Esme knew they could trust to keep their real activities secret. They were needed for two reasons, firstly to give credence to Esme's story of running a church choir, and secondly to sing loudly enough to drown out the noise of the crypt wall being dismantled.

Esme and Igor looked about. Clearly it wasn't a room the priest visited very often, which was good news. Several tombs and grave markers were set into the walls and floor. These marked the final resting places for a number of Castlemaine's historic great and good, as well as a few more mild and mediocre ones.

At the far end, opposite the stairway stood a very large and impressive tomb. Carved in exquisite marble, brought in at great expense from the renowned marble quarries of Eastern Persia, and carved by master stonemasons, hired at huge expense from the workshops of the Sultan of Agra, it depicted scenes from the great and heroic life of its occupant. This impressive and elaborate tomb had been built to house the mortal remains of the renowned warrior bishop, and local boy, Saint Victus, who, legend had it, had killed the last ancient vampire Queen Keg'dranod and so, apparently, had rid the world of a great and terrible scourge.

What Saint Victus failed to consider, however, was that vampires have a nasty habit of coming back to bite you; especially when you kill the queen but fail to deal with the offspring. Queen Keg'dranod had indeed been defeated but due to a rather important oversight, her daughters had survived, disappearing into their hidden mountain strongholds, there to nurture their hatred of all things human, especially puffed-up warrior bishops with their crucifixes, their holy water, and their nasty mallets and pointy sticks.

Locals feared, with good reason, that the vampire princesses would one day return to wreak a terrible, violent and messy vengeance on the honest people of Castlemaine.

Victus chided the simple folk for their unfounded fears. He always maintained publicly that his heroic actions had put an end to the nefarious activities of Keg'dranod and her kind. Of course, his fame, wealth and reputation depended on the whole 'ridding the world of a great and terrible scourge' story holding together. It wouldn't do his reputation any good to have his version of events undermined by a bunch of scaredy-cat peasants. He'd been shamelessly bigging himself up to Pope Lionel IV and was now fairly certain he was in line for sainthood and a bit of eternal fame and glory, plus a seat at God's right hand and all that caper.

So it came as a bit of a disappointment to him when he was visited in the depths of a harsh winter's night by Keg'dranod's youngest daughter, Agrapina, who took great pleasure in avenging her mother's destruction by sucking the good bishop to death on his own altar.

When news of this got back to the pope, he was incensed. The Protestant heresy was still sweeping like wildfire across the known world, and he'd spent a huge amount of time, money and effort on a massive recruitment drive, promoting Victus as the action man poster boy for the modern, forthright and thrusting Catholic Church. Lionel's credibility, and that of his marketing campaign, would be left in tatters if it came out that Victus was a lying, cheating, corner-cutting fraud.

So the whole thing was hushed up. Victus was given a spectacular burial in his home town and fast-tracked to sainthood in the hope that that would help salvage the ad campaign and brush the whole sorry mess under the carpet.

Igor and Esme knew none of this and just stood staring at the overt display of power and opulence before them.

'How the other half die, eh?' muttered Esme, running her hands over the beautifully carved stonework.

Saint Victus's tomb was reputed to contain the perfectly preserved remains of the holy warrior dressed in dazzlingly beautiful battle armour and with his emerald-encrusted sword and mighty golden shield rested proudly on his chest. It had in fact been plundered long ago and actually contained a broken wooden bucket, two chicken leg bones, a mummified mouse and a small scrap of parchment left by one of the last people to break into the grave with a scrawled note that read simply, 'Is nothing sacred?'.

Sadly, all that now remained of Saint Victus's glory was the magnificent and priceless stone edifice.

'We'll have to smash that out,' said Igor.

'I think someone might notice if we removed Saint Victus's tomb,' replied a concerned Esme.

'Really? Oh, OK, so we'll have to work around it then. It's going to take quite a while to knock all that down and clear away the debris.'

Esme shuffled her feet nervously. 'What do you think the old woman meant about a curse?'

'Ah, probably just some old nonsense.' Igor didn't sound

as if he'd even convinced himself with that statement. 'Anyway, what's the worst that can happen?'

He ran back upstairs to fetch the tools. In the church, the makeshift choir was lounging on pews, smoking, and playing cards.

'Oi, you lot, make some noise,' demanded Igor as he ran back downstairs with a pickaxe and sledgehammer in his arms.

Squeezing behind the tomb of Saint Victus, Igor and Esme studied the wall.

'Not much room back here,' she noted.

'Well, let's create some then,' replied Igor. As a screaming array of voices from upstairs began to assault their ears, he swung his hammer.

*

Two shadowy figures crouched behind a large headstone as a cacophony of growls and squeals from within the church pierced the night air. A barn owl took flight from the oak tree above them, clearly upset at having its local screeching monopoly abused so dreadfully.

Sister Vigilanta had been making enquiries, well, threats of physical violence in the village. She was particularly keen to hear more about Igor, the recently arrived newcomer, and his all-too-convenient inheritance of the local undertaker's business. She'd heard that he and the innkeeper's daughter were rapidly becoming as thick as thieves, and this roused Sister Vigilanta's uncanny sixth sense for all things nefarious. She was starting to suspect there was a link between these two miscreants and her missing papal emissary. The tired traveller would naturally have made for the inn, where he would have been easy prey for the innkeeper's daughter and her undertaker boyfriend. Sister Vigilanta was very good at making connections. Not for naught was she Pope Gordon IX's top, secret agent.

'Church choir, my arse,' growled the nun with a tone of utter contempt. 'There's more to this than bloody singing lessons.'

Hopkins shuffled nervously, not daring to say anything that might upset the looming presence beside him.

Sister Vigilanta was not in a procrastinating mood. 'We need to find out what's going on in there. Come on.'

She strode across the churchyard, dragging Hopkins by the sleeve like a naughty schoolboy. As they neared the porch the nun stopped suddenly and thought. *We need to disguise ourselves. All the better to sneak among them and detect their plans.*

Scouting around, she found a pile of steaming fresh horse manure, grabbed a handful and shoved it into Hopkins' face.

'What the f...' he protested as she smeared the foul-smelling muck over his cheeks.

'Stop being such a baby, it'll wash off.'

'Wash?' Hopkins was aghast.

'Now,' continued the nun as she rubbed warm manure across her forehead, 'wrap your cloak about you and pretend to be a hunchback or something. You'll fit right in with the rest of these filthy locals.'

Hopkins did as he was told, spitting out bits of straw as he pulled his cloak about himself and tried his best to look inconspicuous.

Sister Vigilanta put her hand on the old iron ring that would unlatch the door, only to have it yanked away from her as Eric opened it forcefully from the inside and the villagers started to pour forth, their work for the night done.

Thinking fast, she stooped low, and in a scratchy crone's voice started demanding alms from the passing villagers. Hopkins stood dumbly for a second, not knowing what to do. The nun quickly jabbed an elbow into his gut making him double over and moan pitifully. The villagers completely ignored the two smelly vagrants as they filed past and off to their homes.

'Same time tomorrow then?' called Eric to the disappearing locals.

Last out were Igor and Esme, talking quietly together as they locked the church door behind them. Hopkins and the nun leaned in closer to try and overhear their discussion.

Igor turned to see the two figures looming uncomfortably close by.

'Urgh, get away, you stinky tramps,' he demanded.

'Alms for the poor, sir?' croaked the nun, her hand outstretched.

'What? No, bugger off.' Igor was in no mood to hand out any more coins to smelly old women.

He pushed past the pair, gently pulling Esme along by the hand. Esme cast a sideways glance at the two beggars as she passed.

Hopkins seethed behind his cakey mask of poo, their plans for a bit of espionage thwarted for now. 'I'm watching you,' he muttered, his teeth glowing brown in the moonlight.

*

'We're nearly through, I'm sure,' said Igor sipping on a lukewarm ale. They were back at the Cadaver's Arms discussing their night's work.

'It's quite a sturdy wall,' agreed Esme, downing half of her beer in one gulp. 'Whoever sealed up the tunnel definitely didn't want it found again.'

'Or perhaps they didn't want whatever's behind it getting out?' Igor was struggling to completely dismiss the old witch's words about the curse. What if there really was something in there?

He remembered a lesson he'd once had at Lickspittle College about the dangers of underestimating threats, particularly those made by the teachers at Lickspittle College themselves. The boy who sat next to him in third year grovelling class had once snorted derisively at his lecturer's threat to rip his spine out if he failed to simper correctly a second time and ended up not only having his spine torn out but also his lungs extracted via his nostrils and was ordered to attend detention in the college's cesspit for the rest of the term.

Igor and Esme sipped their ales pensively and slipped into a brooding silence, each one thinking how they could get the work complete without unleashing some ancient horror upon themselves.

Clam brought them each a plate of bread, cheese and cold meats.

'That slimy toad Hopkins was in here earlier asking questions about you two.' The old innkeeper sat down on a stool and looked from Esme to Igor, then back again. 'Had some vicious-looking nun with him. Tall with a huge scar right across her face.' He traced a line across his own face with the back of the bread knife to illustrate his point.

'What did they want?'

'Wanted to know where you were, what you were up to. Nobody said nothing of course, 'cept that snivelling little twerp Gougeweevil, the blacksmith's boy. He told them about the choir right enough. He'd sell his own leg for a silver piece that one.'

'Yes, didn't he actually do that once?' remembered Esme.

'Aye, he did indeed,' chuckled Clam. 'Cost the blacksmith two months' income to buy it back. Course it was no use by then, well rotted after several weeks in the butcher's shop window.'

A thoughtful silence descended over their table once more as Igor and Esme munched ponderously on the suspicious-looking meat slices. Igor was well used to the internal anatomy of most of the region's fauna, both wild and farmed, but the texture of this stuff was quite unique. He thought of young Gougeweevil's festering member and decided that perhaps the local butcher was being inventive with his stock again. He picked up a bit of cheese and sniffed it carefully.

'Local delicacy that,' offered Clam as he shuffled over to a nearby table to clear up the half-empty plates that had been left.

'What is it? Sheep? Goat? Not one I'm familiar with.' Igor nibbled a corner of the cheese and immediately wished he hadn't. It tasted far too much of fish for his liking.

'Blue vein cat!' shouted Clam over his shoulder as he carried the crockery back towards the kitchen.

Igor placed the cheese carefully back on his plate and swallowed the rest of his ale in three large gulps, the mild briny taste of Old Seaman's Best entirely failing to wash away the fishy flavour of the cat cheese.

'This is all very interesting,' said Igor with a shudder, noticing for the first time that Esme had completely cleared her plate and was picking at his leftovers, 'but what are we going to do about Hopkins and this nun sniffing about? We can't have them linking the murders back here.'

'Absolutely,' replied Esme, popping the last of the blue vein cat into her mouth. 'I really don't fancy ending my days being impaled and sliding slowly down the executioner's thick, splintery shaft.'

'Ooh, I don't know…' mused Igor, the hint of a cheeky smile playing on his lips, 'I can think of worse ways to go.'

'Yes, well, maybe you can, but I can't see my dad taking too kindly to such an unwarranted penetration. He's very sensitive.'

'All the more reason to throw our inquisitive friends off the scent,' concluded Igor as he refilled his beer flagon from the jug. 'As soon as they find out what we're doing in there then the game's up for sure.'

*

'As soon as we find out what they're doing in there then the game's up for sure.' Sister Vigilanta and Hopkins had returned to his small dwelling in a dark side street not far from the magistrates' office.

Hopkins had been reluctant to take her to his home, but she'd demanded that he put her up for the night while they planned their next move. At the nun's insistence, he had filled a bowl with hot water so she could wash off the dried horse manure. Hopkins was very sceptical about washing, especially when in the presence of a female. There was something not quite decent about the whole affair.

The nun had stripped off her wimple and her outer habit and was scrubbing at her grimy face and limbs.

'This is bliss,' she said, dabbing the warm wet cloth over her face. 'Four weeks on the road from Rome without so much as a moist hanky.'

Before he could do anything about it, Sister Vigilanta grabbed Hopkins' collar and pulled him close. She gazed into his eyes, his face within inches of her own. He feared she was going to bite him, or worse, kiss him. Instead, she pushed him back, took the wet cloth and began to wash away the encrusted horse turds from his cheeks.

'There now,' whispered the nun suggestively, 'isn't that… better?'

He had to admit that, despite the washing, the fact that he was no longer in such close proximity to the nun's mouth did indeed feel much better.

She smirked, a mischievous look in her eye, then went back to washing her own parts.

Hopkins was beginning to feel very uncomfortable. As well as the large scar on her face, she sported many signs of battles, some long healed, others still fresh and festering.

'You, err, you fight a lot of evil things?' he enquired

nervously, desperately trying to divert events away from the direction in which he feared they were headed.

A proud and fearsome glaze entered the nun's eyes as she revelled in the memories of her past glories. 'Oh, yes. I've defeated many of Satan's cohorts. I've travelled the world in the Lord's service.'

She pointed to a large burn scar on her right forearm. 'See this? I got this scar battling the Japanese Basan. A chicken of immense proportions that lives in the Iyo mountains and breathes cold blue fire.' Hitching up her under-habit, she pointed out a large dent in her calf muscle that looked like a huge bite had been taken out of it. 'I got this fighting the Carbunclo, a fearsome, luminous mollusc that steals children from villages by the Chilean coast. And this,' she showed off her crooked left arm that had clearly been badly broken and never properly set, 'this I got after being run down by an English Shug Monkey. I was lucky to survive that one. My assistant was grabbed by the creature as it rushed past and was never seen again, although it is said that his screams can still be heard when the wind is from the north.'

Hopkins was in awe. 'And that?' he pointed to the large ugly scar that crossed her face halfway down her nose. 'I bet that was a werewolf, or a Valkyrie, or a…?'

'No, neither,' interrupted the nun, a look of pained embarrassment in her eye. 'I got that at the convent school when I was ten. The Reverend Mother was a vicious cow.'

Hopkins looked a bit deflated.

'Well,' said the nun sliding close to him. 'I've shown you mine, now why don't you… show me yours?'

'Mine?' Hopkins was suddenly very nervous again. 'I... I... don't have...'

'Nonsense,' purred the big scary nun while running her hand up his leg. 'Big strong boy like you must have some interesting war stories to tell.'

'N... n... no, nothing at all.' Hopkins tried to push the nun's hand away from the sensitive areas it had invaded.

Sister Vigilanta was not to be deterred. 'Don't be modest. I bet you've had lots of... *conquests*...'

'Really, I...' Hopkins protested as firmly as he could but he wasn't nearly firm enough yet for the nun's liking.

'Come now,' she picked him up as easily as a baby and flung him onto his straw mattress. 'You wouldn't want to UPSET ME NOW, WOULD YOU?'

The big woman flopped down on top of him, forcing his arms up as she planted kisses on his neatly scrubbed face and with her free hand, began wrestling with his breeches.

Moments later, several neighbouring villagers heard shrieks and screams coming from Hopkins' house. They chuckled to themselves and left it at that.

*

Late the next morning, Sister Vigilanta slipped out of Hopkins' house with a mind to have a good snoop around. Her long years of guerrilla warfare against the servants of Satan had honed her surveillance skills to a sharp point. If she could fathom the deepest plans of the Prince of Darkness himself, then discovering who was behind the nefarious activities going on in Castlemaine should be a cakewalk.

She attempted to rouse Hopkins and encourage him to come on the expedition, but he merely whimpered and started crying.

'Come on, man, the game's afoot.'

She had tried to drag him out of bed but he just lay there and mumbled.

'Can't... too... sore.' He then rolled over and curled himself into a foetal position. She shrugged and went off without him.

Throughout the day, the big sister haunted the residents of Castlemaine like a giant, ghostly, nun-shaped apparition. She flitted like an ominous shadow between houses, listening to the chatter of the women at work in their kitchens and gardens, the peasants toiling in their barns and workshops, and any of the other local low folk, in a bid to glean some clues about the disappearance of the papal emissary.

Try as she might, with whatever wiles she could devise, Sister Vigilanta heard nothing from the townspeople of Castlemaine that shed any kind of light on her papally appointed mission.

In desperation, Sister Vigilanta offered up a silent prayer, but even God wasn't in a talkative mood that day. Finally, as darkness fell, she made her miserable and defeated way back to Hopkins' home.

Hopkins started violently as she opened his front door, her dark form filling the opening like a huge, black-clad void.

'Right, jumpy, time to don some disguises and head over to the church. Once we're inside we shall see what they're really up to.'

During her tour of the village, Sister Vigilanta had gathered a collection of old ragged clothes from various washing lines. She divided them up between herself and Hopkins. It wasn't easy to work out whether they were men's clothes or women's. They were mainly shapeless bags of rough cloth with holes in for various limbs to poke through.

They kitted themselves out as best they could. As Hopkins was about to open the front door the nun called him back, 'Wait. Finishing touches.'

From within an old sack she grabbed a handful of stinking, wet manure.

'Oh, no, please, not again!' cried Hopkins helplessly as the big nun mushed the squishy gloop into his face and down his shirt.

Spitting bits of straw, Hopkins rubbed as much of the muck from his watering eyes as he could, cursing her under his breath and hoping beyond hope that she wouldn't try to wash him again later.

Satisfied that their disguises were convincing, the nun pushed Hopkins out the door and down the side streets towards the church.

*

At the Cadaver's Arms, Esme entered the bar from the kitchen corridor carrying a large cauldron of something watery with lumps in it and set it over the fire. As she passed back towards the bar, Clam gripped her arm.

'That nun's been snooping about again,' he confided. 'Young Polly told me that old Mister Wetlock the fishmonger told her, that Missus Maggle's cook told him, that the greengrocer's boy told her, that Farmer Plapp let him know, that young Polly had informed him she'd seen a huge, spooky-looking woman dressed all in black, earwigging about outside the wash house this afternoon. Gave her the creeps by all accounts.'

'That is a lot of accounts,' agreed Esme.

'Anyway, as soon as I heard, I told Eric to go out and take a look, and sure enough there she was, still lurking about the market square, picking up whatever nuggets of information she could. As well as nuggets of horse dung it seems, strange woman. Eric followed her at a distance until she slipped back down one of the dark alleys behind the magistrates' courthouse, down near where that slimebag Hopkins lives.'

'Thanks, Dad, I'll warn Igor to be on the lookout.'

'Just you be careful my girl,' said the old innkeeper, concern clear in his voice. 'You're all I've got.'

'You don't need to worry,' replied Esme warmly. 'I've got you to look out for me.'

'And I'm not the only one now, eh?' her father replied with a half-smile.

Esme blushed, uncharacteristically. 'I don't know what you mean,' she said, and went back to the steaming cauldron to see if the lumps had stopped trying to climb out yet.

*

The night was dark and overcast as Igor and Esme arrived back at the church. Carefully, they descended the stairs and unlocked the door to the crypt. Esme scanned the brick dust for any footprints that would show if someone else had been down there since the previous night. There were no other prints but their own. Relieved, they looked about the crypt and found it exactly as they had left it.

*

Hopkins and the nun watched from across the dark graveyard as the would-be choir members arrived and assembled, coughing, smoking, and swigging from hip flasks, outside the church door.

'Right, this time, we get it right,' warned the nun. 'We have to join the group before they enter and make like we're just another couple of peasants come to abuse hymns.'

They began to move stealthily between the gravestones towards the church. When they were almost halfway, there came a loud 'pssssttt' sound from behind them.

'Was that you?' sneered the nun at Hopkins in disgust.

'What? No, I...' Hopkins was cut off as another persistent 'pssssttt' pierced the air.

They both looked around and saw a young boy standing by the churchyard gate, waving, and going 'pssssttt'.

'Go away,' hissed Hopkins, picking up a sizeable cobble from one of the graves and throwing it at the boy.

'Mr Hopkins!' called the boy, unperturbed by the heavy missile, which flew several feet to his left and hit a bewildered cat.

'He's not here,' whispered Hopkins loudly. 'Go away.'

'But I've got a message for you, sir. It's from Master Helsing.'

Hopkins looked helplessly at the looming nun.

'Go on,' she growled. 'Find out what he wants.'

Hopkins scuttled back towards the boy who stood waiting by the gate, digging around in his left nostril for something green and interesting.

'How did you know I was here?' demanded Hopkins angrily.

'Followed you, sir,' answered the boy innocently. 'Besides, you're not a hard fellow to mistake, even in the dark, if you'll pardon me saying so, sir.'

'What? I'm dressed in grotty rags, stooping like an aged hag and with my face smothered in shi… in something smelly and unpleasant.'

The boy stared blankly over Hopkins' right shoulder and merely blinked.

Hopkins gave up. 'Well, what's this message then, boy?'

'Ahem.' The boy cleared his throat and spat a glob of goo onto an ornately carved gravestone. 'Mr Helsing says he's found the lair of the seven-headed, soul-drinking, scaly death raptors, and you're to go to him in the forest right away, sir. You're to bring with you a mob of angry villagers, sporting pitchforks and flaming brands, sir. And if you pretend to be dead again, sir, he said he'll have you busted down to junior cesspit attendant and toilet scrubber second class, and he'll make sure you're on duty every Tuesday morning, after the fresh deliveries of Old Stinking Finger at the inn, sir.' The boy counted the points of his message on his fingers as he recounted them. When he'd finished, he stood staring over Hopkins' right shoulder again with a vacant expression failing to animate any of his facial features.

'Buggering damn and... and... festering arseflaps,' cursed Hopkins as he looked towards the ominous shape of the nun who was still darkly dogging the nearby trees. He went across and explained what the boy had said.

Sister Vigilanta shrugged and told him he'd better run along to his master. She would handle things this end.

Grumbling, Hopkins sidled off to round up a mob of pitchfork and flaming-brand-wielding villagers to make angry.

Scheming, Sister Vigilanta scurried across the graveyard to join the group of peasants who had by now begun entering the church.

Whistling tunelessly, the messenger boy disappeared into the darkness, presumably to do whatever grubby little urchins do once their messaging duties are complete.

*

'OK, sing loud and clear please,' commanded Esme to the group of willing choristers as she and Igor once again descended into the crypt.

Eric took up his position as conductor and encouraged the misshapen group to start the evening's warbling and screeching. Sister Vigilanta staggered momentarily as the noise assaulted her eardrums. Then, gathering herself carefully, she started to move around the back of the group towards the crypt stairs.

Eric, who had pre-lined his ear canals with pieces of cloth soaked in a thick, sound-absorbing gravy from the kitchen at the Cadaver's Arms, stood with his eyes closed in feigned concentration as he waved his arms wildly about.

Nothing could be heard from the crypt as she stood at the top of the stairs, but as she descended, the nun could make out the dull ringing of hammer on stone through the caterwauling of the choir above.

Igor and Esme failed to notice the eerie presence of the warrior nun as they hammered away behind the tomb of Saint Victus.

Suddenly, Esme swung a blow that failed to stop at the wall but went crashing through into a dark empty space beyond. They both stopped and stared through the dust cloud at the black hole that had appeared. With renewed energy and vigour, they swiftly set to again and soon had the hole up to a size that they could both easily fit through.

In a moment of sudden joy, they embraced each other, laughing gayly at their achievement before they remembered themselves and both coughed and looked away from each other as modesty and embarrassment pushed their way in.

They gazed into the dark nothing beyond the crypt wall. The cloud of brick dust slowly settling, Igor held up his lamp and stared into the blackness. They could see nothing beyond a few feet.

'Ladies first?' suggested Igor.

'In your dreams,' Esme retaliated with a wink.

'OK, well we should go together then.' Igor grabbed another lamp, lit it, and prepared to enter the tunnel. As his foot crossed the pile of rubble, a low grumbling sound echoed from deep within the darkness ahead.

Before either of them could react properly to whatever had made that noise, another, more immediate sound drew their attention back into the crypt. They couldn't be certain but it sounded very much like the noise a heavy and well-honed gilded carbon steel broadsword makes as it's drawn slowly and menacingly from its scabbard.

Looking around each side of the tomb of Saint Victus, they were met with the huge shape of the tall black-clad warrior nun, Sister Vigilanta, who stood blocking any chance of exit through the doorway to the crypt. She was holding a heavy and well-honed gilded carbon steel broadsword menacingly in her right hand, its empty scabbard hanging at her hip.

A look of triumph and extreme hatred was only interrupted, but not in a good way, by a large, ugly scar running east to west across the middle of her face.

'Well, well, what have we got here?' demanded the nun in her best righteous, holy-vengeance-of-God type voice.

Igor and Esme were too taken aback to think straight and merely burbled incompetently as the intimidating sword gleamed in the lamplight.

'A secret tunnel is it? So, everything begins to fall into place. I knew you two were up to no good.' Sister Vigilanta stepped forward a pace and waggled her weapon at them.

'Let me tell you what I think has been going on in this filthy little village, shall I?' She was gathering her full power and confidence now that she believed her hunt was over and the welcome return to civilisation was in sight.

'Esmerelda here has been doing away with guests at the inn, to gather their riches, I suppose is the obvious reason. You have been hiding the bodies somewhere. Oh, I don't know, perhaps in barrels in the cellar maybe. How am I doing so far?'

The sound of singing from above drowned out the nervous denials Esme tried to make but the nun was in her stride and continued unabated.

'Igor here has been called in from whatever grubby hole he inhabited before to help you get rid of the dead. But, you need an easier way to move the corpses around the village and when you heard about this ancient tunnel, you thought all your Christmases had come at once and decided to open it up. Am I wrong?'

Igor hefted the large hammer and eyed the sharp-looking sword with dismay.

'Well, actually—' began Esme, but the nun cut her off.

'I'll hear no denials from you, witch. You made a huge mistake when you murdered a messenger from His Holiness the Pope. That was your undoing. Because now I am here and all your evil schemes are undone. There will be hangings in this town before long and you're both going to be central to that entertainment.'

The singing overhead reached another crescendo as a particularly painful note was not quite reached by one of the more adventurous choristers.

Another low rumbling growl emanated from the dark tunnel behind them, this one sounding much closer than the first.

The nun either ignored the sound or failed to notice it; she was revelling in her moment of glory.

Igor finally found his wits and began trying to explain their real reason for being there, or at least, their absolutely not real reason for being there, the nun having got it almost bang on straight off the bat.

'Look, this isn't what it looks like,' he explained, thinking fast. 'We're actually... err...' His brain failed to help him and he dried.

'We're archaeologists,' blurted Esme, the words coming from nowhere.

'Archaeologists?' The nun let out a huge laugh at the suggestion. 'Oh, please, give me some credit.'

'Yes, that's right, archaeologists,' added Igor. 'There's a legend of a lost treasure under the streets of Castlemaine,' he continued, playing for time, then he thought suddenly, 'but it's protected by an ancient curse...'

'You expect me to believe...' said the nun, incredulous.

Another burst of screeching song filtered through to them from the choir above. Another bellowing growl assaulted them from the tunnel; this time, whatever made it was evidently very close and much more energetic than it had been before. This time the nun heard the sound clearly and her eyes refocused behind her two captives to where the beautifully carved tomb of Saint Victus stood, briefly, before it shattered into a blinding cloud of rubble and marble dust.

As the tomb exploded behind them, Igor and Esme bolted for the door but the big nun was still standing steadfastly in their way, sword in hand, blocking the exit.

Another huge roar filled the room as the enormous bulk of a seven-headed, soul-drinking scaly death raptor heaved itself up onto the remains of the tomb.

Two of its heads glared, one each at Igor and Esmerelda who had tumbled to the floor by the nun's feet, not knowing really what else to do under the circumstances. The other five heads glared with piercing yellow eyes at the warrior nun and her dangerous-looking sword.

Without a second thought, Sister Vigilanta bravely sprang forward and set about the raptor with scything blows which, despite their ferocity, totally failed to make any discernible impact on the creature's hide.

The monster's heads gnashed and bit at the striking nun, but she managed to parry away each bite with a vicious sweep of the sharp steel. Her arms were a blur as she put everything she had into each stroke.

Coming to their senses at last, Igor and Esme rushed towards the flailing beast and set about it with their heavy sledgehammers, thwacking its toes and managing to break off several of its claws.

The creature bellowed with renewed rage, which allowed the nun to stab deep into one of its open mouths and through the soft inner lining of its exposed throat. The head in question suddenly lolled forwards, inert.

'Great, only six more to go,' yelled Esmerelda. 'But we're rapidly running out of toes.'

The raptor's rage redoubled and it spread its great leathery wings as wide as it could in the confined space of the crypt.

The nun slashed away at the beast but it was made of very strong stuff and the sword failed each time to pierce the thick, tough skin.

Igor observed, quite rightly in fact, that they were all now standing between the creature and the exit, and he made a spur-of-the-moment decision that it was probably in their best interests right about this point to get the hell out of there as quickly as possible.

He grabbed Esme with one hand and dropped his hammer; he took hold of the flailing nun's outer habit with his other and dragged them both forcefully towards the stairwell.

Sister Vigilanta continued swinging wildly in the monster's direction even while Igor was dragging her backwards up the stairs.

The bewildered villagers stopped singing as they saw the state of the three blood-and-dust-covered people coming up from the crypt. None of the villagers could remember them looking like that when they went down, so heads were scratched and murmurs were murmured.

A fearsome bellow from the creature below sent them all instantly scurrying for the door.

'I don't think it can get through the doorway,' panted Esme optimistically, just before the first of the creature's heads made its presence loudly known at the top of the crypt stairs.

Sister Vigilanta valiantly put herself in-between the raptor and her hitherto hated captives. 'Get out, you can't defeat this thing,' she ordered.

Igor ran up to the altar and grabbed a huge brass cross to use as a club.

Esme found a very sharp pike that was being used as part of a tableau depicting the defeat of Keg'dranod by the mighty Saint Victus.

The three stood side by side as a second, then a third hideous reptilian head squeezed up and out of the crypt stairwell.

At last, the six surviving heads were tearing away at

everything within range. Slowly, the enormous blubbery body had extricated itself from the narrow doorway and the creature stood full height in front of them. It spread its vast wings the full length of the church and began approaching the three defenders.

A deep blackness, darker than shadow, spread out from under the raptor's wings. Igor and Esme unconsciously edged backwards as the monster approached.

Sister Vigilanta stood her ground. The unearthly animal towered above her, poised to make the final, fatal strike.

Suddenly, in a mighty thrust, she stabbed upwards towards the place where she believed the raptor's vile black heart must surely lie. The point of the sword failed to make the slightest dent and she fell backwards in defeat.

All eighteen of the raptor's remaining eyes glared at the prostrate nun. It threw back several of its heads and let out a hideous, bellowing laugh that shook the church violently and made the bells sway and jangle in the tower above.

Sister Vigilanta had never been beaten before. She had fought in every corner of the world, from the mysterious mountains of the east to the verdant forests of Africa, every exotic place that the dark one had ever thrown his evil creations at her. She would be buggered if she was going down in this backwater dump.

In frustration, the brave warrior nun jumped to her feet and, with a prayer on her lips, she screamed and ran towards the braying monster with the sword, point first, above her.

*

Esme and Igor staggered through the battered doors of the church into the cold night air. A few of the braver villagers went to them and helped tend their injuries. Thankfully, neither was badly hurt, but they couldn't say that with any certainty for the unfortunate nun.

Her last charge was something beautiful to behold. All that blazing steel, steadfast valour, stretched sinew and righteous zeal focused into the point of a sword aimed firmly at the creature's soft, delicate nether regions.

The strike, when it came, failed to come anywhere close to killing the beast, but that wasn't its aim. The fact that every eye in that creature's heads had watered simultaneously, and the pitiful squeal the raptor produced when bright sword met reptilian danglies, were all Sister Vigilanta could have wished for. The look of triumph in her eyes was magical as the creature picked her up in his great claw and burst out from the church to fly away over the fields and out towards the dark forested mountains beyond.

They had been completely powerless to save her.

*

Hopkins and his baying mob of followers arrived at Helsing's campsite in the forest just before midnight. After a curt tongue-lashing from his boss, Hopkins deployed the villagers around the mouth of the cavern that Helsing now insisted was the home of a brood of raptors.

At Helsing's command, the villagers angrily brandished their pitchforks and waggled their flaming brands towards the cave. Not a peep could be heard from within.

They shouted angry taunts, as instructed, questioning the raptors' parentage, and besmirching their soul-drinking capabilities. Still no sounds came back in reply.

'Perhaps they're not in,' suggested Hopkins hopefully.

At that moment, a huge, dark shape passed overhead. The small amount of light reflected from the clouds above was cut off and the flaming brands were immediately extinguished by the monster's breath stench as it gave out a tremendous cry, which, if they could have understood it, was the most evil and foul-mouthed sweary insult a seven-headed, soul-drinking scaly death raptor can utter towards a living human.

Fortunately for them, the people below only had to contend with the terror of the creature's passing and didn't have to endure being called rude names as well.

The last raptor ever to be seen in the world of mortal men swept past the cowering group and flew up and over the cold, snow-capped mountains to disappear forever, the small, dark-clad figure of a screaming nun clasped in its talons.

'I have done it!' cried Helsing, an authoritative air of victory in his bearing. 'I have single-handedly defeated the last of that evil race of beings and banished them forever from this earth.'

'Steady on, sir, we did help a little bit,' replied Hopkins curtly.

'Nonsense!' spat Helsing. 'It was I that was here, flushing it out from its lair while you were at home, cowering in your jim-jams.'

Hopkins gave up. He would never win that argument. He took one last look over the mountains to where the creature had flown, taking Sister Vigilanta with it.

He felt sorry for her. She was a good woman. A woman of the cloth. A dedicated soldier in the service of the Lord. A fearsome warrior.

He felt a little bit relieved as well. She was a naughty woman. A sexual deviant with unusual tastes and a horrible set of pointy instruments to use in the bedroom department.

His feelings and his conscience battled with his mixed emotions on the subject. He rubbed his aching midriff. On balance, he decided he could live without her.

*

When Igor and Esme made their way back down into the crypt the next morning to explore the tunnel, they found Father Price already there, nervously examining the destruction.

'The bishop is going to want to know what happened here,' he moaned. 'And it's me he'll blame. All this mess. The tomb of Saint Victus, gone.'

Igor had been thinking about how to explain things to the priest all night. He decided that, as usual, lying was the best policy.

'Look, you said to me that this town is cursed. I didn't believe you at first, but now, this.' Igor swept his hand around to indicate all the mess. It didn't need a lot of indication really; the priest had already seen it.

'Clearly, this is the centre of all the… curse-ness… and as I said, I know a thing or two about this sort of thing. Just leave it all to us. Esme and I will tidy up down here. We'll fix up the tomb; the bishop need never know. Then, with your help, we'll get to work banishing whatever evil has been laid upon this land in days past.'

'Really? Thank you, Igor… and you too, Esme. I don't know what I'd do without friends like you, really, thank you.'

The grateful priest sprinted back up the stairs.

'You'd probably do a lot better, poor sod,' muttered Esme.

Alone again in the crypt, Igor closed and locked the door. They went back to the mouth of the tunnel, which smelled like a thousand pustulating haddock were decaying sourly in the darkness.

'Well, I just hope there aren't any more of them lurking in here,' said Igor cheerfully as they lit some torches and made their way into the stinky inky depths.

The tunnel disappeared into the black distance in the general direction of the centre of town. It was straight, as far as they could tell. No obvious turns, at least, although it was so dark they couldn't really tell if it was gently curving one way or another.

The ground underfoot was damp; here and there the occasional bones of some poor unfortunate creature were stepped upon and smashed.

'Must be what it ate?' Esme surmised. 'Can't have had a lot of food though. I wonder how long it was down here, and how it got in.'

'Maybe it was walled in when they sealed the tunnel.'

'Perhaps.' Esme mused the idea but wasn't convinced. How could such a large creature survive walled up for hundreds of years? It made no sense.

After shuffling through the darkness for what felt like twenty minutes but was, in fact, only nineteen minutes and twelve seconds, they were suddenly brought to a halt by a solid rock wall.

'This can't be right,' exclaimed Igor. 'This is the natural bedrock. No exit this end. I don't get it.'

'I didn't see any side chambers or corridors,' said Esme.

'No, there weren't any,' confirmed Igor, bemused at why the tunnel ended so abruptly.

'But there must have been another opening. Father Price said the tunnel was originally used for local bigwigs to get through the town without having to rub anything against plague-riddled villagers.'

He shone his flaming torch around the walls but found no sign of any openings or doorways.

For several minutes he and Esme scouted the tunnel back for a few yards before returning to the end wall. As he examined the left-hand wall, his foot squelched into something wet and rotten. Igor shone his lamp on the ground and found, quite unexpectedly, the festering remains of a small deer. Its head was intact but the rest of it was a tattered mess. Entrails oozed in all directions.

'How the f...' Igor was stunned. 'Esme, how would a small forest deer get into a sealed tunnel?'

They studied the floor and the walls. Igor stretched up with his torch to examine the tunnel roof. 'Hello, hello, hello, what's all this then?'

As he peered upwards, Igor spotted a small trapdoor in the roof above them. The muck and detritus of a few hundred years had discoloured the ancient wooden hatch so it looked no different to the rock around it. Igor reached up and felt around the hatch. On one side was an old iron ring, heavily rusted, but with a bit of jiggling Igor managed to work it loose.

He pulled on the ring but the hatch wouldn't budge. He hung onto it with his full weight but still it refused to open. He swung himself around and as he twisted, the ring turned ninety degrees and the hatch fell open with a thud and Igor fell down into the slushy muck of the tunnel floor.

Esme looked up and saw that above the door was a metal grate, and above that were the clouds that sulked perpetually over the skies of Castlemaine.

The top of the wooden hatch door was leaded to make it look like any other part of the basic sewer system of the town, but it also had another metal ring so it could be opened from above.

'You know what?' suggested Esme, surprise in her voice. 'I reckon someone's been using this to drop food down to the raptor.'

'What? Why? Who?' Igor always did have a questioning mind.

'It makes sense,' replied Esme, lines of deep thought across her brow. 'It must have got down here somehow. And how do you think that deer got in here? What else could it have eaten? How could it have survived otherwise?' Esme gave Igor a good run for his money in the questioning mind department.

'OK, well, we won't find that out from down here,' replied Igor practically. 'We need to find out where in the town that grate is. Can you see anything up there?'

'Only clouds and rain. Could be anywhere.'

'Bumflaps,' suggested Igor. 'There must be a hundred

of those grates around the town. It'll take us ages to find it from above. Not to mention all the curious looks we'll get pretending to be drain inspectors.'

Esme thought for a moment then with a theatrical 'a-ha!' produced a length of green ribbon from inside her blouse.

'Here, lift me up so I can reach the grate.'

Igor picked Esme up by the waist and held her up so she could tie the ribbon around the metal grate. As he gently lowered her to the ground their faces came tantalisingly close to each other. For a moment they stared into each other's eyes.

Esme was first to break the spell.

'All we need to do now is take a wander about town and glance hither and thither until we spot a green ribbon stuck on a drain grate.'

'Brilliant!' enthused Igor, a warm fuzzy feeling fluttered momentarily in his chest, before fluttering off to another part of the cave on business of its own.

*

Back up in the fresh air above ground, Igor and Esme sauntered, arm in arm, slowly around the market square. They skipped together up Butcher's Row, perambulated down Fishmonger's Terrace, strode along Greengrocer's Crescent, marched into Baker's Walk, trudged out of Tinker's Avenue, and galumphed between Milliner's Way and Tailor's Passage.

Nothing.

Disheartened, they slowly made their way back towards

the Cadaver's Arms. As they crossed the town square, Hopkins appeared out of nowhere and accosted them face to face.

'It was you, wasn't it? You set that creature loose last night. I saw it. It took Sister Vigilanta. She was onto you. I left her safe and well by the church. You did something and now she's dead. You'll pay for this or my name's not—'

Esme interrupted the angry little man before he could get any further.

'We saw her,' she admitted. 'We saw how brave she was. If it wasn't for Sister Vigilanta we wouldn't be here now. When that creature landed in the churchyard and scared off the choir we were left all alone, facing certain death. Sister Vigilanta saved us. She stood between us and the monster and fought heroically until it threw her down and carried her away as a trophy. Or dinner. Or whatever.'

Tears filled Esme's eyes as she recounted the brave fall of the fearsome nun.

Hopkins, clearly moved by the tale, softened and allowed his own feelings of guilt and loss to surface briefly.

'Yes, well…' he mumbled; a look of sadness crossed his face. 'Be that as it may,' he continued, 'remember this. I'm watching you.' And with that he strode away towards the magistrates' office.

Esme's eyes followed the little weasel as he went away. Suddenly, she dashed off in the same direction, pulling Igor after her.

Igor stood next to Esme at the foot of the steps that led into the witchfinder's courthouse. By their feet was a metal grate covering one of the town's drain culverts. Attached to the grate, fluttering gently in the light breeze, was a length of green ribbon.

'Oh, well,' said Igor with a smile. 'It'll be some kind of fun bundling bodies around right under Helsing's nose.'

THE MIDRIFF

'Hold up, I need a wee.' The starey-eyed barrel-shaped woman jumped from her seat and ran outside to relieve her swollen bladder.

'Wait for me, Grizelda,' cried an equally rotund little man who'd been sitting, unseen, behind her, 'I'm coming with you.'

'All right, Norris, if you must.'

Norris grabbed his empty flagon and chuckled enthusiastically as he ran after Grizelda and out into the night.

While they were gone, Basil and the servants set about clearing back some of the empty plates and brought fresh jugs of ale.

Esmerelda sat with her head bowed. Father Price, his eyes moist from all the memories, sat across from her and held onto her hands.

'You don't need to do this, you know,' he said warmly, stroking her gnarled and twisted fingers with his own hard, calloused ones. 'You have nothing to prove to anybody.' Esme sat silently, the images of Igor – happy, young, full of life – still played before her eyes. She smiled to herself as she remembered him in that calico skirt. He'd worn it again a few times after, but only when they were alone together in his dark room at the funeral parlour playing 'guess the body part'.

'So, who was it then?' said Grizelda as she returned to her seat, poking Esmerelda's thin arm to grab her attention as she passed by.

Norris followed close by, trying desperately not to slop his now full, frothing flagon. Several of the other villagers shrank away from him as he regained his seat.

Esme was startled out of her memories and back into the present, her keen, green eyes returning to large black holes.

'I'm sorry? What?' Esme's thought processes were not as sharp as they had been when she was young, so the question took her off guard.

'Who was it?' persisted Grizelda, puffing away frantically on her long bone pipe.

'Who was what?'

'Who left the seven-headed, scaly whatnot thing in the tunnel? Who was feeding it all that time? You must have found out.'

'Oh, yes, we did find that out,' Esme's thoughts were still lost in the past as she replied absently.

'So, who was it?' Grizelda's eyes bulged dangerously out of her face like a constipated toad.

Before Esme could answer, she was interrupted by a thin bald man with eyebrows that looked like a couple of fighting squirrels.

'No, hang on, hang on,' he demanded, forcefully, 'what about Clam's murdering spree? Did he ever get caught?'

A few of the other villagers mumbled their agreement.

'Your stories leave too many questions unanswered.' This from a squeaky-voiced woman who was poking at the dying embers of the fire, trying to stab some life back into it.

'She's right,' shouted another voice. 'Did the nun ever get found?'

'Aye,' came a third, dripping with excited bloodlust and far too many flagons of ale. 'Was she ripped to bits and eaten? Did they find her tattered remains in the death raptor's festering stools?'

'I want to know what you did with the tunnel,' said Squirrel Brows.

'I reckon she's making it all up,' sneered the squeaky-voiced woman by the fireplace, as she bent down and dropped a fresh log on the glowing ashes. 'This Igor sounds a right criminal, not a hero at all.'

Esmerelda stood up suddenly; her fists slammed into the table in front of her, making the jugs and plates jump noisily.

'You have no idea, do you?' she spat angrily at the now silent crowd. Her short steel blade was in her hand.

Nobody dared move.

'Bugger!' exclaimed Norris, breaking the silence. His empty flagon and its former contents were in his lap. 'You made me wet myself.'

'We're sorry, Miss Esme,' soothed Grizelda as she placed a chubby hand on Esme's shoulder. 'We really do want to know more. Your tales are a wonder to us, ain't they?'

The other villagers mumbled their contrite agreement. Esme sat down wearily, her anger spent.

'You don't need to go on, Esme.' Father Price's old, lined face showed nothing but love and concern for his dear friend.

'It's fine, really,' smiled Esme. 'Igor deserves to have his story told.'

'So, tell us more about your dad.' Grizelda had retaken her seat and was sponging Norris down with a bar towel. 'He sounds like a lovely chap... aside from the violent bloody murdering, of course. Did he ever get cured? Did you manage to lift that gypsy curse?'

'We tried.' Esme's eyes focused on a point in the far distance as she recalled the events of that time long ago. 'It was about the time one of Igor's old acquaintances came to town.'

The crowd settled back into their seats, and a respectful hush descended once more as Esme continued her long tale.

*

Nobody in the bar noticed as the side door opened and two shadowy figures crept into the room. Maurice Flatweight and Percival Stoat had waited for the right moment to reappear, when they knew that everyone's attention would be elsewhere.

Cautiously, they stole across the room to the corner where their comrade, Hector Smallfoot, remained impaled on the jagged coat hook. Gingerly, they carefully lifted their injured friend and shuffled back across the bar towards the side door.

Stoat slapped a hand across Smallfoot's mouth as his agonised groan threatened to alert the crowd to their presence.

But the villagers were too intent on the ravings of that crazy old woman in the centre of the room, confessing her youthful crimes to everyone as if she was in court.

Well, we'll see you in court, you old witch, thought Flatweight as they manoeuvred Smallfoot out through the door and into the black, brooding night.

BODY PART III

THE HYDE ENTITY CRISIS

As day once again prepared to fulfil its bargain and make way for its counterpart, night, to temporarily hold sway upon the earth, Igor issued a sigh of what he could only assume, due to its unfamiliarity, was contentment.

It had, he thought, been a perfect day. He and Esme had arranged for Esme's innkeeper father, Clam, to visit the sanatorium of the renowned Dr Seward in England for a few months in an effort to treat his unfortunate sleep-murdering condition, giving them both a break from trying to prevent and, where failing, covering up his deadly nocturnal activity.

Old Clam himself was under the impression, thanks to the gentle deceit of Esme and Seward, that he was merely having a brief holiday in England to visit his cousin Renfield, who had also recently become a guest of the doctor, in what he believed to be fully portered accommodation as opposed to a period of observation in a secure facility for the criminally insane and chronically homicidal.

Once they had bade the innkeeper bon voyage and his carriage had borne him on his long journey to the nearest port, Esme wiping a tear, tinged with sadness but infused with hope as they waved him off, the pair had made plans. Deciding they needed some quality time to themselves, Igor and Esme had left Valerie, the head serving girl, to oversee the Cadaver's Arms while they treated themselves to a brief break.

Free of duty for a while, they had finally managed to snatch a few precious hours together far from the hurly-burly of Castlemaine, their only thoughts being those of each other.

Together, amidst the rolling countryside that bordered the village, they had happily enjoyed a picnic comprised of a hearty, crusty loaf, spirited from the oven of the Cadaver's Arms before it could touch anything, a delicious hunk of locally sourced goat shank, provided by Four-Fingered Franz, formerly known as Five-Fingered Franz, their favourite local butcher, and to top it off, a Castlemaine delicacy – a jug of pickled voles lovingly prepared by Esme herself.

The fledgling couple revelled in a brief period of carefree abandonment, liberated from the day-to-day pressures of running the thriving undertaker business; the emotional demands of shepherding the ageing and unconsciously lethal innkeeper; and the cloying atmosphere produced by the varied malignant odours of the village peasants as they thronged together at the inn.

In addition to the usual rigours of their lives, Igor and Esme had endured a particularly busy and stressful time recently, ensuring their new subsurface body disposal system, aka the hidden tunnel under the churchyard, was fully disguised and operational in the event Clam's treatment overseas proved unsuccessful.

They had installed iron torch holders along the tunnel's dampened walls, placing them strategically throughout its length to ensure bodies could be transported, should the need arise, without one tripping over one's feet in the dark, and thoroughly swept the tunnel path clear of bones to aid easy and crunch-free progress.

All this under the very noses of Helsing and Hopkins, the stern-faced representatives of officialdom in the area who, it had to be said, really had it in for them. Today had indeed been a merciful oasis of peace for them both.

It had been with a wistful sigh that they had eventually resigned themselves to the fact their idyll must end, and it was time to head back to the village and the responsibilities it represented.

Nonetheless, they had ambled contentedly arm in arm back to Castlemaine, their hearts singing, their souls alive with the anticipation of the possibilities that a new infatuation will bring and both semi-plastered from imbibing the flask of thistle vodka that Igor had distilled in the cellar of the funeral parlour for just such a special occasion.

As Igor and Esme arrived with the gathering shadows of late afternoon at the edge of the village, their attention was commandeered by a flurry of activity outside the local apothecary.

'The new owners must be moving in!' exclaimed Esme as she observed a couple of raggedly attired villagers groaning and wheezing under the weight of huge crates of chemicals and medical equipment, which they were unloading from a cart stationed outside the shop.

The premises had remained vacant for several weeks following the untimely passing of the previous tenant, Herr Kwaak. The unfortunate former proprietor of the business had been found slumped across the counter with multiple knife wounds peppering his back. The local coroner, one Otto Kronenbourg, the notoriously corrupt and eminently bribable nephew of the Burgermeister, who also happened to be Kwaak's landlord, had ruled that the ill-starred apothecary had accidentally fallen backwards on an eight-inch blade. Several times. Finally, Otto adjudged that Kwaak, in a last violent death spasm, had propelled himself across the counter.

No explanation was given for the lack of an actual knife being present post-mortem, but Otto had swatted away any further questioning of his judgement by darkly murmuring something about not wanting any more such 'accidents' in the village. No mention was made of the recent dispute Kwaak had been embroiled in with his avaricious landlord over a proposed rent increase.

As the pair stood and watched the to-ing and fro-ing of the hired peasants, a tall, thin, and decidedly austere-looking gentleman, swathed in grey, emerged from the shop entrance. A seemingly fixed sneer of superiority leant an ugly aspect to his somewhat blanched features.

'I don't believe it!' gasped Igor. 'Henry? Henry Jekyll?'

The tall man stopped in his tracks as if slapped by an invisible assailant. He slowly turned to face Igor and regarded him with the same expression he might have assumed had he been examining something that had fallen from his nostril.

'Well, well. It's Igor, isn't it? Victor Frankenstein's lickspittle.'

Igor bristled at this unwelcome reminder of his former station. 'How's Edward these days?'

Jekyll's face flushed an angry purple. It could not have been any angrier or more purple if it had been a plum that had just received an insult about its mother.

Making a visible effort to control his rising temper, Jekyll coldly replied, 'My nephew, Mr Hyde, is currently... away.'

'I can see that,' smirked Igor. 'Will he be joining us anytime soon?'

'I sincerely hope not,' responded Jekyll curtly. 'I intend to make a new start here. This is a village crying out for purity and moral direction and I have every intention of doing my bit to raise standards accordingly. Now, I am very busy and must bid you good evening.' With that he turned and retreated into the shop.

'Who...' questioned Esme, '...was that?'

'An old acquaintance, Dr Henry Jekyll. A complete git.'

'Well, I could see there was no love lost between you,' Esme replied. 'He seemed like a real barrel of laughs,' she added sarcastically. 'He's hardly going to liven things up around here is he?'

'Oh, don't worry,' smiled Igor knowingly. 'Things are going to liven up all right!'

*

THE HYDE ENTITY CRISIS

A mere couple of months had passed since Jekyll's arrival in Castlemaine and he had wasted no time in carving out a name for himself as a fierce puritan dispensing both medicines and admonishments in equal measure.

In Jekyll's first week of trading, poor Frau Blooter had initially been pleased to be issued with a foot salve to ease the discomfort of her chronic bunion, only to be subsequently lectured on the moral decay inherent in the wearing of frivolously attractive footwear.

The bunion, she was informed as she was handed the foul-smelling medicinal paste, was the physical manifestation of the evils of ardour-inflaming cordwainery. Frau Blooter, a frail septuagenarian with sixteen grandchildren and owner of a moustache that could not unreasonably be described as 'walrus-like', was both simultaneously ashamed and curiously titillated by this revelation.

Things did not improve from there. Young Pietro Greeve, a mere adolescent, was provided with a vial of eye drops to ease his hayfever-inflamed pupils, only to suffer a twenty-minute lecture on the repercussions of staring inappropriately at the opposite sex.

His equally pollen-afflicted father, on receipt of his drops, was dealt a stinging blow to the knuckles with a bamboo cane as he claimed his change and was informed in no uncertain terms he should never be allowed to tend sheep.

Jekyll's pharmacy quickly garnered an unwanted reputation as a place where, whilst one could seek relief for one's ailments, one had to be prepared to have one's moral character torn to shreds, and possibly face a direct physical assault while doing so.

To compound matters, Jekyll had managed to further alienate himself from the inhabitants of Castlemaine by spending his free time poised behind a home-made lectern positioned in the village square vociferously attempting to dissuade the villagers from their dissolute lifestyles.

Jekyll's attempts at public sermonising had proved a spectacular failure. On his first appearance a mildly curious crowd had gathered. However, it had quickly dispersed, grumbling unhappily, when it became apparent that what the villagers had hoped would be a new form of street entertainment was merely a monotonous drone on morality and, worse, seemed deliberately designed to make them feel bad about themselves.

Jekyll had endeavoured to take heart from the fact that one villager had lingered, his face taut with concentration as if attempting to digest and savour each word that Jekyll delivered. His heart had quickly sunk when he realised the villager was one Maximilian Hoff whom he was currently treating for a severe case of excessive earwax accumulation.

Further public sermons had resulted in, at best, utter apathy and, at worst, his becoming the target for various hand-launched items of rotting vegetation.

Now, after two months of residing in Castlemaine, Jekyll was awash with feelings of despondency and desperation. Unbeknownst to him, this length of time to reach despondency and/or desperation was actually a fairly decent record for Castlemaine but, even if Jekyll had been aware of this fact, it would have offered him scant comfort.

*

Jekyll sat in the rear parlour of the apothecary shop, slumped in his armchair as an angry storm raged outside. A long wooden bench stood behind him, cluttered with his collection of test tubes and chemicals in the otherwise sparsely furnished room. A crackling fire, by which he sat adrift in thought, was his only companion. As he gazed into the dancing flames Jekyll fancied he could visualise a familiar face beginning to form amongst them.

'No!' he barked aloud despite his solitude. 'Not you!'

Jekyll buried his face in his waxen hands, the beginnings of a sob emanating from a place deep within himself. What was he to do? He could cope with the unwashed ingrates of the village ignoring his sage moral advice but, despite his own self-loathing on the subject, he needed their custom to survive. For some reason, trade appeared to be rapidly petering out and his savings, a large chunk of which had been donated to Otto Kronenbourg as an advance on his rent, as well as an admin fee to ensure the speedy wrapping-up of the inquest on the previous proprietor, thereby facilitating Jekyll's tenancy of the premises, were dwindling rapidly.

'You know what to do!' came a sudden voice from behind him.

'Leave me alone,' pleaded Jekyll. 'I don't need you. I don't want you.'

'Oh, stop moaning,' came the voice again. 'You need customers and you know very well only I can bring them in. Face it, you're about as popular here as an infestation of fleas in the britches of a man with no arms.'

Jekyll expelled a shuddering sigh and heaved himself from his chair.

'All right! You win, damn you!' he exclaimed as he lurched across the room coming to a halt in front of a mirror hanging by the parlour door. 'You win. For now!' he spat at his reflection, which stared maniacally back at him.

Turning away from the mirror, Jekyll crossed hurriedly to his workbench. Crouching to the floor behind the bench he reached down and flicked back a reed mat that lay there, revealing a wrought-iron handle. He yanked the handle back and reached inside the hidden compartment. He withdrew his hand, carefully cradling in his palm the stoppered glass vial he had removed from its hiding place.

Jekyll walked slowly back towards the mirror and stared again at his reflection.

'For now,' he repeated quietly and, in one fluid motion, he flipped the stopper away from the neck of the vial with his thumb and took a deep draught of the liquid within.

As the chemical burnt its way down his throat in its all-too-familiar manner, Jekyll thought he heard a peal of laughter in the distance.

Laughter that grew louder and louder until it was everywhere.

*

The Cadaver's Arms was experiencing a slow night. The weather, foul even by Castlemaine's less than lofty standards, had played its part in keeping many patrons away but even those hardy regulars who had braved the storm and sat sipping from their flagons of foaming ale seemed unusually subdued and uncommunicative.

THE HYDE ENTITY CRISIS

Esme observed the paltry number of patrons from behind the bar as they sullenly imbibed their beer, barely making conversation with their fellows but, rather, staring into their drinks and generally looking miserable.

She sighed deeply. She knew exactly what the problem was. The villagers were bored. There had been nothing to amuse them or galvanise their gossip-loving tongues into action for weeks. She could barely remember the last time even a common-or-garden murder had been committed in the vicinity to pique their interest, let alone the thrill of a mysterious one.

No corpses had turned up drained of blood, no one had spotted any unholy-looking creatures stalking the countryside and Helsing and Hopkins had accused no one of witchcraft for days. Trade at the inn always suffered when torch-bearing mob activity was at a low point.

Even the Burgermeister, Randolph Epstein Van Kronenbourg III, had failed to implement any new laws designed to fatten his wallet, which the villagers could have communally moaned about over a drink or ten.

Esme watched as one of the regulars attempted to fend off his growing boredom by beginning to count the warts on the back of his hand.

She sighed again and considered calling Valerie down from her room. Perhaps if she asked the lithesome serving wench to try and enliven the atmosphere by flaunting her renowned feminine charms, some modicum of excitement may be generated in the otherwise listless ambience of the inn.

However, Esme recalled, the poor girl had spent the previous evening posing for local artist, old Hugo Heiffner, who needed a lot of assistance with his brushstrokes these days, and she had appeared exhausted on her return.

Just as Esme was considering instigating a bar brawl to relieve the tedium, the inn door swung inwards and a booming voice declared, 'Drinks for everyone. On me!'

A cheer reverberated around the previously silent interior of the inn. All eyes turned to the strikingly handsome young stranger at the inn's entrance, a tousle-maned vision clad in a dandyish suit of scarlet velvet, a frilled silk shirt unbuttoned to the navel and a flowing black cape, which he threw rakishly over his shoulder to reveal a bulging purse at his hip.

The stranger plucked the purse from his belt, juggled it in his palm a couple of times, each movement issuing forth an enticing clinking of coins, and then hurled it towards Esme, who caught it with cat-like reactions.

'Hyde's the name, my friends. Now, drink!'

The patrons needed no further inducement. They rushed the bar, thrusting their empty receptacles towards Esme who filled each as quickly as she could pour while Hyde clapped each of them jovially on the shoulder and encouraged them to down their ale as swiftly as possible so they could have another. And another.

Soon, laughter began to echo around the inn. Someone amongst the throng produced a fiddle, another a whistle and singing and dancing ensued. Hyde led the way, snatching up a clearly smitten maiden and whisking her around the room in a frenetic two-step. He ended the dance by kissing her passionately on the lips and depositing her in a semi-swoon back on her bar stool.

Song had followed song and Hyde stood for a moment conducting the makeshift band, grinning with delight. The number of patrons at the inn had begun to swell considerably, inquisitive villagers having been attracted by the sound of music emanating from the Cadaver's Arms. A rapidly circulating rumour that a stranger was providing free drinks had also contributed to the increase in attendance.

'More drinks!' he declared and wheeled his way to the bar where Esme waited with a fresh jug in her hand.

'Well, you've made quite an impression, Mr Hyde,' she smiled.

'Oh, call me Teddy,' he purred. 'And have one for yourself, my dear.'

'Don't mind if I do,' replied Esme breathily before suddenly becoming aware of the fact she had been unconsciously twirling a strand of her lustrous hair between her fingers as she conversed with the good-looking stranger.

She silently chided herself for her foolishness and added, 'But not whilst I'm working.'

'Well, maybe later. After work.' Hyde winked.

'Yes, that would be lovely. Perhaps you could also buy one for my gentleman friend, Igor, as he will be joining me before the end of the evening.'

A look of what may have been disappointment began to form on Hyde's features but almost immediately faded, replaced by a deeply thoughtful expression as if he were striving to recall an elusive memory.

'Yes,' he said to himself quietly. 'You did see him, didn't you?'

'I'm sorry?' said Esme.

Hyde snapped back into his previous jolly state and drained his drink in one gulp.

'Igor, eh? Good old Igor. Lovely chap. We're friends from way back, you know. My Uncle Henry mentioned he'd seen him in the village.'

'Uncle Hen...' began Esme. 'You mean Henry *Jekyll*? He's your uncle?' she spluttered incredulously trying to mentally reconcile the image of the ugly and downright boring Jekyll with the hedonistic young rake before her.

'I'm afraid so!' laughed Hyde, noting Esme's expression of disbelief. 'But don't worry, I can't stand him either. I'm just here to help bail out his failing business. He is family after all.'

*

Igor trudged his way towards the Cadaver's Arms. The anger of the storm had subsided and now only a thin curtain of persistent drizzle accompanied his progress to the inn.

As always, Igor couldn't wait to see Esme. Unpleasant weather would not dissuade him from his journey. In fact, it would have taken nothing less than a hurricane tearing through Castlemaine to prevent him from walking to the inn to meet her, such was the strength of his feelings towards her.

The recent spell of quiet that had settled upon the village lately had frankly been a relief.

Helsing had received no cause to pry into Igor's business of late, and all trade at the undertaker's had been legitimately obtained for the last few weeks, his customers, other than the recently expired Kwaak, comprising of the terminally aged, the fatally clumsy and the usual intake of suicides that Castlemaine tended to regularly throw up.

It was a welcome bonus to Igor that he had not been forced to cover up, or indeed partake in, any murders or misdemeanours in recent days and, of course, he had Esme's company to savour.

With a smile, Igor decided he could happily accept a boring evening or two as he traversed the path to the entrance of the Cadaver's Arms. As he walked, he caught a glimpse of his grinning reflection in a moonlit puddle. He paused for a moment and regarded the image of this new Igor before him. Mere months previously he had been a contorted version of his true self, an obsequious lickspittle cowering and crawling at Victor Frankenstein's bequest. Now, here he stood, a free man and business owner. He had friends and maybe, if he truly dared to believe it, love in his life. He walked on, his step lightening as he went.

Igor hesitated at the inn's heavy wooden door. Something seemed amiss. He had fully expected the premises to be as quiet as the interior of one of his freshly constructed coffins, yet there were strange sounds emanating from within.

He pressed his ear to the door. Surely that was fiddle music he could hear? The music was somewhat out of tune, admittedly, but it was certainly being raucously bashed out by the fiddler in a display of enthusiasm that more than compensated for his less-than-polished bowmanship.

Furthermore, Igor could hear the shrill accompaniment of a whistle, which closely followed the same tune the fiddler was attempting. *Could that be old Herr Hamlyn playing the whistle?* Igor wondered.

Hamlyn was well known for attempting to play his instrument at any opportunity, appropriate or otherwise, and had once been threatened with an unauthorised medical procedure involving said whistle and a vulnerable part of his anatomy by members of the deceased's family at a village funeral service, when he had whipped it out and offered to play a tune 'to lighten the mood'.

The patrons must be in fine spirits indeed to not only tolerate, but encourage, a performance from perhaps the least popular whistle-blower in the area.

But it was not just the music that had surprised Igor. The inn seemed to be alive with laughter, a situation that had not occurred since the day a stray ember from a public witch-burning practice run had taken hold of Hopkins' coat-tail and sent the witchfinder's brutish cohort diving headlong into the nearest horse trough to the delight of all present.

Igor pushed his way through the swell of inebriated revellers and, upon spying the colourful figure of Hyde atop one of the tables, attempting what appeared to be a drunken version of the can-can with a comely maiden attached to each arm and an upturned breadbasket perched on his head, immediately understood the dramatic change in the mood of the inn and its previously jaded patrons.

'Edward!' he bellowed in greeting to the cavorting Hyde.

'Igor!' reciprocated Hyde heartily and, pausing only to kiss each of his beautiful companions in turn, hopped down to the floor and embraced his old friend in an affectionate bear hug.

'Come and have a drink, you old scoundrel,' Hyde laughed and steered Igor to the bar where Esme awaited, two flagons of ale already drawn for them.

The two old friends clinked tankards, commenced the downing of their drinks, and began to catch up.

'I was hoping you would put in an appearance when I saw old Henry a couple of months back,' said Igor. 'What kept you?'

Hyde sighed. 'Well, the boring old duffer has been keeping me under wraps for a while. It's not fair, you know, we had an agreement. Equal shares and all that.'

'So, what happened?' questioned Igor.

'Apparently, he was a little upset about having to leave our last place of residence, the village of Staid Virtue, under something of a cloud,' explained Hyde.

'Staid Virtue?' repeated Igor. 'Doesn't exactly sound like your kind of place, Edward.'

'It wasn't,' agreed Hyde. 'Terrible village, the whole council was comprised of puritans. Jekyll loved it, of course. But we had to leave eventually. We always do.'

'I assume the vacation of the vicinity had something to do with your behaviour?' said Igor knowingly.

Hyde did his best to assume an expression of offended innocence. 'Moi?' he began, then, remembering precisely who he was talking to, conceded, 'Oh, all right, there was a slight indiscretion with our then landlady's daughter.'

'Why is it always landladies and their daughters with you?' asked Igor.

'I suppose they're just convenient,' shrugged Hyde. 'Plus, they're usually bored and I help bring a little sparkle into their lives. It's not entirely my fault you know. It's Jekyll and his repressed urges that are the root of the trouble. He just lets me out to enact the life he dare not live. I relieve his frustrations, so to speak. If he had just been more honest with himself, he would never have needed me in the first place.'

'So, Jekyll took a fancy to this young girl?'

'Of course he did, the hypocritical old hound, although he'd never admit it. I just acted on his impure thoughts. Unfortunately, the situation became a little awkward when her father surprised us, *in flagrante* in the barn, whilst in possession of a blunderbuss.'

'Same old Edward,' said Igor shaking his head. 'Still, it's good to see you again and you've certainly improved the spirit of this place tonight.'

'Here's to many more nights!' exclaimed Hyde raising his tankard. 'And to hell with Uncle Henry,' he added with a conspiratorial wink.

The rest of the evening was whiled away in a blur of drunken frivolity. The villagers, newly invigorated by the arrival of the handsome visitor, danced. Some sang, many fell over and vomited.

Igor, delighted to be reacquainted with the only real friend he had ever had – Simon the dead rat's company somewhat paling in comparison to Hyde's – found himself swept up in the moment.

No slouch when it came to alcoholic intake, Igor did his best to match his friend drink for drink but Hyde's capacity for liquor knew no peer.

Eventually, Igor slid unconscious from his bar stool, his fall broken by Eric, the coachman, whom Igor had formally introduced to Hyde a few hours earlier. Eric had happily partaken of Hyde's hospitality only to be the first to unceremoniously pass out and swap his stool for the floor.

Hyde had assisted Esme in dragging the comatose duo through to the backroom of the inn to sleep it off before deciding to retire for the night himself and offering to escort home his two earlier can-can partners.

'Tell me, my dears,' he was heard to say to the giggling pair as they headed for the door entwined, 'are there any comfortable barns on the way home?' before waving a cheerful farewell over his shoulder to those patrons who were still in a fit enough state to acknowledge him.

*

Igor awoke the following morning deciding death would be a blissful release from his current state of being. The throbbing agony he was experiencing in his head made him feel as if, during the course of the night, his cranium had been prised open by a maniacal midget with a chisel who had proceeded to clamber into his skull and knock seven bells out of his brain matter.

In addition to this, his throat felt as if it had been scoured with a portion of hot gravel wrapped in a vagrant's sock. He was also less than happy to arrive at the conclusion that the uncomfortable moistness in the general vicinity of his britches was unlikely to have been the result of someone spilling soup down his trousers.

'Good morning,' came the somewhat frosty greeting from Esme who was staring down at him with a disapproving glare. 'And how are we today?'

'Uurrghh,' was the best that Igor could manage in response, a thin ribbon of spittle looping from the corner of his otherwise parched mouth as he made his first faltering attempt at coherent conversation that morning. The very sound of his own incomprehensible gargle sent fresh splinters of pain radiating throughout his cranial cavity.

'I thought you might say that,' retorted Esme coolly and handed him a tumbler of water. 'Drink this and take these,' she added as she offered him her outstretched palm on which rested two pills, roughly the size of a pair of marbles.

'Whaa?' was the best response Igor could muster but he reached out for the pills and water, nonetheless.

'Your friend Teddy, I mean Edward, left these for you. They're from his uncle's pharmacy. He said you would need them.' With that, Esme abruptly turned away and headed back to the kitchen where a fresh batch of voles awaited pickling.

Igor downed the pills without hesitation. Edward had provided him with these hangover remedies following previous evenings of carousal and he was certainly grateful for his friend's thoughtfulness now. He gulped the water down to ease the passage of the weighty pellets and waited.

A few painful minutes later, Igor began to feel a gurgling build-up of pressure in the lower recesses of his stomach. A wave of biliousness began to swell and expand in his insides as if a bile-filled balloon were being inflated amongst his innards until, finally, he emitted an enormous belch.

He immediately blacked out only to awaken a few seconds later feeling almost his old self. A faint headache nibbled at the edges of his consciousness, but it was barely noticeable. He leapt to his feet, renewed.

Igor had asked Hyde years ago why Jekyll hadn't marketed these miraculous hangover cures and made them both a fortune, but Edward had informed him that Jekyll had wanted nothing to do with anything that would encourage the consumption of the demon drink. In fact, Jekyll regretted ever creating this chemical compound in the first place and had instead decided to work on a cure for evil itself as an aid to the soul rather than just attempt to heal the punishing effects that the assuaging of its unhealthy appetites had on the body.

After apologising to Esme and, of course, nipping back home to the funeral parlour to change into a fresh pair of britches, Igor had spent the rest of the morning, as a somewhat placatory measure, assisting her with various chores about the Cadaver's Arms.

Esme, being a reasonable woman, had not remained in a sour mood with Igor for long and whilst enjoying a spot of lunch together, the subject of Edward had arisen. Esme had again expressed her disbelief that Jekyll and Hyde were related.

'Listen,' said Igor leaning forward in a conspiratorial manner. 'There's more to it than that. You see… Jekyll… and Hyde… are one and the same.'

'What do you mean?' questioned Esme, her tone of voice one of puzzlement rather than disbelief. 'You mean one is in disguise? How can that be? For a start Jekyll is taller than Hyde.'

'Oh no, it's far more complicated and unusual than that,' replied Igor. 'You see Jekyll literally *becomes* Hyde and vice versa. They are two different personalities sharing the same existence. You've heard what a puritan Jekyll is? Well, he strove for years to obtain the means to separate the baser side of his nature, as he would have it, from his own moralistic self. He reasoned he could get on with his good works uninterrupted and never yielding to the temptations of the flesh if he could somehow physically separate the two sides of his personality. He may be a miserable old goat but he's a brilliant chemist and he eventually managed it. The result was Edward.'

Esme weighed this information thoughtfully. Frankly, it wasn't the strangest situation she had encountered in her years of living in Castlemaine.

'So how do you know him, I mean them, no, I mean him?' she asked.

'Henry was an associate of Victor Frankenstein during my period of employment with Victor,' explained Igor. 'They communicated regularly, compared notes, then finally began to meet up. Supposedly, they intended to encourage each other and offer assistance where they could but it soon became obvious they both just wanted someone to boast to. Victor was full of himself showing off that great cretin of a monster of his but you should have seen his face drop when Jekyll downed his transformation elixir and turned into Hyde right in front of him.'

Igor paused, smiling to himself as he recollected Frankenstein's furious countenance.

'Anyway,' he continued, 'Edward and I hit it off. We got chatting after Victor demanded I escort him from the premises. He seemed to recognise there was more to me than the craven toady I had to portray to keep my job.'

Igor took a deep breath as memories of his previous life at Castle Frankenstein flooded back.

'I suppose it was the duality of his own nature that enabled Edward to see there was another side to me. He took me out for a few nights on the town, while he and Jekyll were staying in the area, and on those rare occasions when Victor had no need of my grave-robbing services as he was too busy sulking about Jekyll's success. The sleeping powder he gave me to stir into Victor's cocoa also helped matters of course.' Igor shook his head. 'I could never keep up with Edward on a session though. Luckily, he sorted out my hangovers as he did today or I would never have been able to get up at 4am to start my lab-cleaning duties. Thankfully, sedated as he was, Victor was none the wiser to my new-found social activity.'

'What happened then?' asked Esme, entranced.

'They fell out over a gambling debt. Edward had got himself involved with their landlady's daughter. That was bad enough in itself but he was also involved with the landlady at the time too. Anyway, he had come narrowly close to being caught in the daughter's chamber when the mother had brought her up some cocoa and he had been forced to leap from her window to avoid being caught in the act, so to speak.

'Unfortunately, he had landed feet first on their beloved cat, Wellington, and killed the poor feline outright. Edward saw a way out in the form of Victor so, playing on his vanity, he visited him, told him he believed his reanimation experiments were faked and bet him a purse of gold he couldn't bring Wellington back from the great scratching post beyond.

'Victor couldn't resist of course and immediately set to galvanising the expired Wellington. Which he did, for a time.'

'For a time?' asked Esme.

'Yes, that was the problem,' sighed Igor. 'Victor was at the start of a bit of a slump on the work front. He'd never really managed to repeat the success, if you can call it that, of his creature and whilst Wellington had indeed been reactivated for a while, unbeknownst to Edward, he'd expired again in his bag while Edward was transporting him back to the lodging house. Edward arrived at the lodgings during a furious family argument where the daughter was informing her parents she was in love with Edward and would be marrying him at the earliest opportunity.'

Igor rolled his eyes as he recalled his friend's amorous misadventures.

'Edward, attempting to calm the jealous mother and furious father, informed them he had been out searching for their lost cat and they could now rejoice at his safe return. He tipped up the bag expecting Wellington to land, well, cat-like, on his feet, only for the feline carcass to land with a dull thump on its back. They had all stared at Wellington, speechless for a few seconds, until, sensing the further increased hostility in the room, Edward had again leapt from the window shouting that his Uncle Henry would settle the bill. He was never seen in the area again.'

'I can see why they... *he*, had to leave,' said Esme.

'Exactly,' nodded Igor. 'But not only that, Victor was livid. Edward never paid him for losing the bet on the reanimation.'

*

The following weeks saw Hyde's popularity spread amongst the villagers at a quicker rate than the last outbreak of pox.

The inn heaved with customers every night and he was always the natural centre of attention, leading the merriment with his drinking, gaming, and all-round carousing. It had become a generally accepted idiom about Castlemaine that 'Hyde always brings the party with him.'

Edward's natural charisma and bacchanalian ways had not only won over the fluttering hearts of the local maidens, as well as one or two of the gentlemen, but also ensured a steadily increasing stream of customers to the pharmacy once the people had realised he was a partner in Jekyll's business. Between the takings of the shop and his success at cards, Hyde had soon swelled his and Jekyll's coffers to the point of obesity.

But, despite all his financial, not to mention carnal, success, Hyde was not a happy man. Away from the nightly drunken festivities of the Cadaver's Arms, and the welcoming, often hay-ridden, embraces of the village girls, he could not escape the nagging subconscious voice of Jekyll insinuating itself into his thoughts. He knew that soon his cursed alter ego would once again demand his time in the saddle and, frankly, Hyde had not the slightest intention of being replaced again. Who knows when Jekyll would once more allow him his freedom, if indeed he ever did, now that he had fulfilled his purpose? No, enough was enough. He would be doing the world a favour if he were to ensure the permanent absence of the terminally boring Jekyll.

Hyde sat, lost in thought by the fire in much the same way that Jekyll had those many weeks ago prior to him succumbing to Hyde's demand to be returned to the world. A plot began to form in his devious mind. Yes, Jekyll had had his day and now it was Hyde's turn.

A Machiavellian smile stretched across Hyde's face. Yes, he decided, Jekyll had to die and he was confident his good friend Igor would assist.

*

The following evening, Igor was pleasantly surprised to receive a visit from Hyde as he was closing the undertaker's shop for the day.

'Edward!' he exclaimed, checking his pocket watch. 'Shouldn't you be at the inn by now?'

'All in good time, Igor, my dear fellow. But first, I have a little proposition for you.'

Igor felt a sudden shiver of trepidation. Hyde was the best company a chap could have on a night out but his plans often veered to the side of recklessness.

*

'So, let me get this straight,' said Igor handing Hyde a tumbler of his home-distilled thistle vodka as the pair sat in the living quarters of the undertaker's parlour. 'You want my help to blow up the apothecary and fake your, or rather Jekyll's, death?'

'Not exactly,' replied Hyde as he took another swig of his hooch, noting the pleasing prickly aftertaste the liquor provided. 'I want *you* to blow it up!'

Hyde had expounded his plan as they sat and drank. It all sounded so simple. Hyde would entertain the villagers at the inn while Igor laid a trail of gunpowder to the apothecary which, once lit, would burn its fiery course to Jekyll's collection of highly flammable chemicals. The latter included a sealed jar of Jekyll's self-synthesised, magnesium-based wart-removal tonic, Epidermal Flare, designed to blast unsightly and unwelcome growths from the surface of the patient's skin by means of a small explosion incurred by contact with living tissue. Unfortunately, Jekyll had been forced to preclude the tonic from sale at the apothecary shop due to an unfortunate rash of injuries incurred by volunteer patients in the testing stage of the treatment. Whilst the potion was undoubtably effective in the removal of warts, skin tags and other unwanted protrusions, it proved dangerously unstable and the explosions possessed a tendency to remove entire limbs and other essential body parts on detonation. It would, however, be ideal for Hyde's current scheme.

Once contact was made, the deadly combination of chemicals and explosive would blow the shop, and the last of Jekyll's transformation serum, to smithereens. Hyde would proclaim Jekyll blown to atoms and be free to move on with his life as permanent occupier of his and Jekyll's previously shared existence.

Igor had listened without interruption. He understood the level of animosity between Jekyll and Hyde and had always suspected one half of their shared existence would eventually make a decisive move against the other in their struggle for dominance. The prospect of seeing an end to the dreadful Jekyll, and securing the future of his friend Edward in the process, appealed to him greatly but he could not shake a sense of doubt over the level of risk involved. Those officious snoops, Helsing and Hopkins, were never far away and he had no desire to attract their attention.

'So...' asked Igor, 'when do you intend to put the plan in motion?'

'Tomorrow night,' answered Hyde. 'It's my birthday, after all. Well, I say birthday, you know what I mean,' he added, miming the act of drinking down a chemical, holding his throat for a few seconds and then pointing to his chest as if to announce his own arrival.

Igor rubbed his temples where a dull ache had begun to make its presence felt. He was beginning to have a bad feeling about this.

'There is one more thing,' added Hyde. Igor's temples began to throb. 'I don't suppose I could impose on you to supply a body?'

'A body?!' spluttered Igor, coughing back up his last mouthful of thistle vodka.

'Well, it would provide evidence of poor Uncle Henry's passing...' reasoned Hyde then, gesturing at their surroundings. 'And, it is somewhat in your line of work.'

Igor's mind raced. It was one thing to blow up the shop with the villagers distracted at the inn but he was the only undertaker in Castlemaine and, while he had no major qualms when it came to utilising lifeless bodies for his own purposes, any unscheduled relocation of corpses would immediately be traced back to him.

'I can't just let you have any old body I may have lying around, you know!' exclaimed Igor. 'People at funerals take a dim view if the dearly departed fails to make an appearance at their own burial!'

'Relax, Igor,' soothed Hyde. 'I've already thought of that.'

'I'm sure,' replied Igor sullenly, his headache now at full force.

'Yes, simple,' reassured Hyde. 'We merely exhume the last body you buried, place them in the shop and let the explosion and resulting fire do the rest. A few charred remains will add weight to the story.'

'Oh, hell,' groaned Igor.

'Relax Igor,' repeated Hyde. 'I have every confidence in you. Besides, I will, of course, be compensating you for your efforts with a sizeable contribution from the apothecary's coffers. Once I have full control of the purse strings, of course.'

'How sizeable?' replied Igor, suddenly more enthused.

'Very,' grinned Hyde. 'Enough to see you comfortable for a while, old friend.'

Igor nodded to himself. He could certainly use more funds. Frankenstein's stolen purse had long since been depleted and, while the undertaker business provided a steady income, especially in Castlemaine, the prospect of a lump sum was an attractive one. He smiled as he realised he would be able to treat Esme to something special, perhaps a trip away. Or even something sentimental, such as a new dagger.

And so, the two friends had sat and schemed. It was agreed Hyde would entertain the villagers in the Cadaver's Arms celebrating his 'birthday' while Igor, with the assistance of Eric, would retrieve the recently interred body of poor old Herr Hamlyn whose sudden demand for regular whistle recitals after years of rebuttal, combined with his feeling the need to add a series of frenetic dance steps to freshen up his performances, had proved a fatal exertion for a man of his advanced years.

Once the body, freshly planted only a couple of days prior, had been successfully placed in the apothecary, Igor would set the explosion while Eric joined the revellers at the inn.

Once the shop had been obliterated it would then be a simple matter of Hyde announcing Jekyll's unfortunate demise convincingly, availing himself of their joint funds and taking sole occupancy of their formerly shared existence on a permanent basis.

*

Elsewhere, as Hyde and Igor drew their plans, a complication had already arisen. In fact, this particular complication had already found its way to the Cadaver's Arms, had taken possession of a jug of ale from Esme and was currently considering whether to sample one of the salted meat lumps of indeterminate origin which sat sweating inside a suspiciously opaque terrine jar lurking on top of the bar.

'Well, deary,' asked Esme, assuming her well-practised comely serving wench persona as she tended to do when trying to assess a stranger to the inn. 'What brings an 'andsome gentleman like you to these parts?'

The stranger, a rodent-faced fellow possessed of a thinning pate, protuberant nose, and a distinctly shifty gaze, offered a leering grin in return.

'Sadly, madam, I am here on business,' he replied.

'Really, sir?' asked Esme leaning forward to reveal a tantalising glimpse of cleavage. 'And what sort of business are you here for?'

The man swallowed, his mouth having suddenly dried, then composed himself. He offered Esme a battered sketch from his inside pocket. The picture revealed Hyde, his handsome face rendered extremely accurately by the artist and lit with a familiar mischievous smile.

'I'm looking for someone. A gentleman, and I use the term in its loosest possible sense, by the name of… Edward Hyde.' Esme's face revealed nothing.

'Edward… *Hyde*, did you say?'

'That's right, madam. Do you perhaps know the fellow?'

Esme pretended to wrack her memory then shrugged noncommittally. 'We do get a lot of gentlemen here,' she offered vaguely.

'Do you recognise *this* gentleman, madam?'

The stranger tapped his index finger on the drawing of Edward's face.

'It's Teddy!' yelled one of the patrons who had been attempting to manoeuvre his way to the bar but had paused long enough to peer inquisitively over the stranger's shoulder. A huge cheer went up around the inn at the mention of Hyde's name.

'Well, he *may* have been here a few weeks ago,' said Esme as she contemplated slipping a knife into the nosey customer.

The stranger's hand once again returned to the dark folds of his coat. This time he produced a printed card which he brandished under Esme's nose.

'Horatio Doggett,' announced the stranger, mirroring the words inscribed on the card, 'investigator.'

Esme feigned an expression of wide-eyed respect. 'So, why are you looking for this Hyde character?' she asked.

Doggett stared at her gravely then, drawing himself up to his full height of five foot eight, adopted a more authoritarian tone of voice. 'I have been charged by the authorities of the village of Staid Virtue to arrest this man Hyde and bring him back to face his responsibilities. Namely, he has besmirched the daughter of a local landlord and landlady and left her in a state of double jeopardy.'

'Double jeopardy?' queried Esme.

'Thanks to him, she's had twins,' replied Doggett.

'Surely, that's cause for celebration?' smiled Esme.

Doggett solemnly shook his head and offered her an almost pitying look. 'Madam. This blackguard has damaged the reputation of a respected family and sired a brood outside of wedlock. This does not sit comfortably with the good community of Staid Virtue. He must be dragged back to the village where he will be compelled to marry the young lady, whether he likes it or not, provide financially for her and her children and take a damn good horse-whipping from her father as punishment for his misdeeds.'

Esme's mind raced. Hyde could arrive at the inn at any moment and would likely walk straight into his pursuer.

'Now that you mention it, deary,' she bluffed. 'This man does look familiar. I'm sure he said he was just passing through on his way to, where was it now? Yes, that's it, Devil's End.'

'Devil's End?' said Doggett thoughtfully. 'Hmm, that certainly sounds like the kind of vice-riddled dung-hole he would make himself at home in. I must ride tonight!'

'Oh no,' simpered Esme as best she could. 'Must you really leave us so soon?'

Doggett took one last, lingering gaze at Esme's bountiful cleavage then drained the foamy remnants of his ale. He shook his head regretfully. 'I'm sorry, young lady, but duty calls,' he uttered and, with that, turned sharply on his heel and headed for the exit having developed what appeared to be a slight encumbrance to his normal gait. Esme reached over the bar counter where Eric lay snoozing in his usual position, his head surrounded by a collection of empty bottles and a scattering of discarded peanut shells. She shook him violently awake.

'I'll not take 'em. Not after dark!' barked Eric, clearly startled by his sudden forced awakening and taking a moment to recall exactly where he was, what day it was and, indeed, who he was.

'There's trouble, Eric,' whispered Esme urgently. 'We need to warn Edward that this Doggett character is looking for him.'

Esme had grown fond of Edward. It was clear he meant a great deal to Igor, which had naturally inclined her to warm to him. Besides which, he had proved to be exceptionally good for business. The arrival of Doggett was therefore as welcome as a bout of chronic flatulence inside a suit of armour.

At that moment, Esme breathed a sigh of relief as she heard the familiar roar of welcome that greeted Edward Hyde as he entered the inn, his arm wrapped fraternally around Igor's shoulders.

As the two men made their way through the smoke and noise of the inn, Hyde enduring a series of friendly pats on the back as he approached the bar; their jovial expressions vanished as they spied the look of concern etched on Esme's face. She gestured urgently to them to follow her and bundled them into the back room of the inn where they were joined by Eric who still wore an air of inebriated confusion about him.

Esme called for Valerie to relieve her behind the bar. She had been busy relieving one of the inn's guests earlier in the evening but now, having only time on her hands, took up her position without complaint.

Esme recounted her conversation with Doggett to Edward and Igor. Edward merely laughed off the encounter and congratulated Esme on ridding him of his pursuer. He gleefully outlined his plan for the following evening to her.

'Surely, this is a time for caution, Edward!' extolled Igor, once again feeling the familiar nagging of a tension headache making its presence felt behind his eyes.

'Nonsense, old chap!' laughed Hyde. 'The fool has been diverted and we go ahead tomorrow night as planned,' he continued, oblivious to the concerned looks swapped amongst his companions.

*

The next day was spent in preparation. Igor stowed a brace of shovels in Eric's coach along with a pouch of gunpowder drawn from a barrel that Esme kept secreted in the cellar 'for emergencies'. Esme had noted Igor's questioning look when she had revealed the existence of her gunpowder stash, but she had been in no mood to proffer further explanation. Maybe one day she would make him privy to the story of her past but for now, she had decided, she need not reopen the wounds that were memories of her beloved mother and the explosive revenge she had once planned for the man she held responsible for her fate. Instead, with a growing sense of worry over Igor's involvement in the scheme, she decided to concentrate on running the inn as usual that night with the added responsibility of deflecting any queries that may arise from curious patrons concerning Igor and Eric's whereabouts during the execution of the plan.

Hyde had attended the apothecary where he served potions and invitations to his birthday celebrations simultaneously.

Word spread swiftly amongst the villagers that the Cadaver's Arms was the only place in Castlemaine to be that night and, by the time Edward had arrived at the inn to a cacophony of welcoming cheers, the bar was swollen with seemingly the entire adult population of the village.

Soon, the building was alive with laughter and non-whistle-based music as Hyde danced and drank, ordering round after round for the villagers and generally displaying even greater exuberance than he had managed on any of his previous bouts of hedonism. The more Hyde cavorted, the more the villagers responded as the party spirit took hold of them.

Igor had waited, biding his time until the festivities were in full swing before taking the opportunity to slip away, unnoticed by the revellers. He clambered up beside Eric who was waiting with his coach in the shadowy rear yard of the inn. Each took a fiery belt from the coachman's hipflask, both to ward off the chilly embrace of the night air and to soothe any unsteadiness of nerve that may assail them on their nocturnal endeavours.

Grimly, they set off for the local graveyard.

*

With a ragged sigh of exhaustion, Igor dropped onto his haunches. The flickering glow of the oil lamp he had positioned beside the newly opened grave of Herr Hamlyn betrayed rivulets of perspiration trickling freely from his brow. Igor dabbed his face dry with a grubby pocket handkerchief that had seen better days.

'My back is killing me!' he groaned in the general direction of Herr Hamlyn's recently exhumed corpse. 'If I'd known I'd be digging you up again, I wouldn't have bothered burying you in the first place,' he added testily. Hamlyn maintained his silence.

'Come on then, Eric,' Igor huffed, addressing the coachman who was seated on a freshly excavated pile of soil on the other side of the grave, breathing laboriously and struggling unsuccessfully to light his pipe against the blustery night wind. 'Let's get the body into the coach and go and blow up the shop.'

Igor ruefully shook his head at the sound of his own words and cursed his predicament. He had truly believed his grave-robbing days were behind him after he had left

Victor Frankenstein's employment but here he was, stuck in a cemetery in the dead of night.

He was supposed to be interring corpses these days, not uprooting them but, once again, he was disturbing the rest of a poor unfortunate rather than setting them at peace, as was the usual requirement of his chosen profession. On top of everything else, grave-robbing was a young man's game and his body ached at the demands of his recent rigorous activity. Getting too blasted old for such corpse-snatching shenanigans, Igor reflected grimly, had been a further reason he had been glad to vacate his position at Castle Frankenstein. Still, he consoled himself, at least this time he would be getting paid for his toil. Well paid.

After shovelling the soil back into the now vacant grave, the two men heaved the freshly retrieved body from the muddy ground. Eric grasped Hamlyn's feet, Igor clamped his hands under the corpse's armpits, and together they began to stagger and wheeze their way back to the coach.

After every few steps, Igor would hiss a warning and the men would freeze, their senses scanning the night for any signs they might be under observation. Igor would spend a few seconds silently evaluating their surroundings before deciding it was safe to continue their journey. He was well-practised in the art of sifting through and identifying the myriad sounds of night: the flutter of a circling bat's wings, the eerie sigh of the wind as it rustled the thick clumps of bushes bordering the graveyard and the creaking of the skeletal branches of the cemetery trees as the night breeze played amongst them.

However, this did not prevent the sudden screech of a recalcitrant owl, hunting in the darkness, very nearly causing him to soil himself with shock. Clearly, his nerves were not what they used to be since adopting his new, more settled, lifestyle in Castlemaine.

'Sod this!' he exclaimed as they arrived at the waiting coach. 'Sling him in the back and let's get out of here!'

*

Edward Hyde reeled drunkenly against the bar and slammed down the latest in a succession of empty tankards onto the wooden surface.

'Another!' he demanded of Valerie who was busy handling a large order on the other side of the bar.

'Edward,' interjected Esme. 'Don't you think you've had enough?'

Hyde's features creased into a lopsided grin as he staggered slightly, wrapping his arm around the slender waist of a female patron for support. The woman, a village girl named Zena whom Hyde had entertained several times since his arrival in Castlemaine, was perfectly receptive to his embrace.

'You do look a touch worse for wear, Teddy,' said Zena with a suggestive wink. 'Perhaps you should have a little liedown.'

Esme raised her eyes to the ceiling. The atmosphere of the Cadaver's Arms was becoming ever more riotous thanks to Hyde's exuberant celebrations and encouragement, with several tables already destroyed thanks to various patrons deciding they made excellent stages on which to display their alcohol-enhanced dancing skills.

Perhaps a brief break from Edward's influence may save some of the inn's furniture from harm as well as provide her and Valerie with an opportunity to replenish the rapidly dwindling ale supplies from the stock in the cellar.

'Take him upstairs,' Esme said to Zena. 'Valerie's busy down here so the Sweetheart Suite is empty.'

Hyde's grin grew wider. He turned dramatically to face his fellow drinkers, extending his arms as if embracing the whole room as he addressed them.

'Ladies and gentlemen. I must take my leave for a few moments,' he announced to a chorus of disappointed groans. He gestured for silence. 'Fear not, friends. I will return shortly. In the meantime, have another drink on me!'

The patrons' groans became a uniform cheer and they once again flocked in number to the bar as Zena led Hyde through the back of the inn and up the stairs.

Esme and Valerie filled flagons and broke open bottles as the customers continued to drink and sing. As she tended to the customers, Esme found her thoughts drifting towards Igor and she wondered how the plan was unfolding. He should have retrieved the body from the cemetery by now and, according to the schedule, was due at the apothecary imminently. Even though Igor was to be rewarded with a handsome sum for his efforts, and the village would be free of the tedious moraliser Jekyll, she was experiencing a growing feeling of concern as the night wore on and decided she would not rest easily until he had returned safely to the sanctuary of the Cadaver's Arms.

Esme glanced up hopefully as the inn door swung inwards. Her heart immediately sank as she saw it was not

Igor who had entered the establishment but rather the rat-like figure of Horatio Doggett.

Doggett was throwing questing glances about the premises, his eyes narrow and hungry. Esme grabbed Valerie by the shoulder and whispered urgently to her. Valerie nodded, acknowledging her instructions, and stole away from the bar.

Doggett elbowed his way through the throng of customers and approached Esme, his demeanour full of purpose.

'Oh, hello, deary, so good to see you again,' cooed Esme as convincingly as she could manage. 'I thought you were in Devil's End.'

'Madam,' began Doggett in a clipped tone. 'I have reason to believe Edward Hyde is on these premises.'

'Edward!' cheered one of the customers at the sound of the name and raised his tankard as if proposing a toast. He received an appreciative 'hoorah!' from the assembled drinkers in response.

Doggett glared accusingly at Esme. Esme leaned forward in her practised manner. 'Well, he *was* here but he left a while ago,' she offered.

Doggett glared. A swollen vein pulsated visibly on his temple. 'And where did he go?' he demanded.

Esme was formulating a response when she paused, her attention caught by the looming figures of Helsing and his appendage-like assistant, Hopkins. The pair had run into a dead end in their hunt for the perpetrator of the Castlemaine murders of several months ago, little realising the killings had been committed by the somnomicidal Clam, and the extent of their investigations had lately been reduced to loitering at the inn of an evening in the hope they may overhear some incriminating gossip.

On this particular night the two of them had been lurking sullenly at a corner table but now appeared at each of Doggett's shoulders. Esme groaned internally. The situation had just grown exponentially worse.

'Good evening, Master Doggett,' proffered Helsing. 'My name is Helsing, magistrate, constable and…' he paused to place a restraining finger on Hopkins' lips, '…witchfinder.'

Doggett surveyed the gaunt figure of Helsing and was immediately impressed with the high-quality polish of the witchfinder's buttons and the general air of pompous officialdom he exuded. The two men shook hands.

Hopkins also extended his meaty paw in greeting but Doggett failed to notice the gesture. After a few seconds, Hopkins, silently seething, returned his arm to his side. His formerly outstretched hand was now clamped into a tense fist.

'I see you are interested in one Edward Hyde,' stated Helsing. 'I am more than happy to offer my assistance in your locating this individual,' he continued, wondering if it was his imagination that a few of the inn's customers appeared to have just booed him. He noticed Hopkins had removed a cudgel from his belt and was casting accusing glances to all and sundry whilst tapping the weapon menacingly against his fleshy palm. He concluded the sound of discord had indeed been genuine.

At the sight of Hopkins' aggressive demeanour, the villagers turned away, murmuring discontentedly amongst themselves. Helsing and Doggett resumed their conversation.

'Hyde has indeed been seen at this establishment,' confirmed Helsing. 'I had a feeling he was trouble although he seems to have made himself extremely popular with the villagers. I, on the other hand, do not like him!'

'What makes you say that?' enquired Doggett.

'Because no one likes us!' interjected Hopkins, drawing a stern look of rebuke from his superior.

Resisting the urge to issue a sharp blow to Hopkins' simian head, Helsing turned his attention back to Doggett. 'I suggest you direct your enquiries to his uncle Henry Jekyll's apothecary. I believe that is where the villain resides,' Helsing advised. Doggett's weasel-like face broke into a triumphant smile.

'So, he's here too?' Doggett exclaimed excitedly, raising one eyebrow much higher than the other. 'Find one, find the other. Pray tell, Master Helsing, can you direct me to this establishment?'

Helsing's chest swelled with pride. Not only did he find himself in the presence of someone who seemed to respect his position for once, but it appeared he may finally have the opportunity to be involved in a successful arrest.

'More than that, friend Doggett, I can escort you there myself. It would be a pleasure to see you arrest this reprobate!'

With that, the two men barged their way through, and out of, the Cadaver's Arms. Hopkins trailed sulkily in their wake, his mood only tempered by the possibility of indulging in a spot of legally sanctioned violence once they located their quarry.

Esme watched them leave. The matter was rapidly careering out of control. She had been swayed by Edward's promise of cash, and Igor's keenness to help his friend gain his freedom from Jekyll, but now her mounting concern for Igor threatened to overwhelm her.

*

A few minutes earlier, Valerie had burst into the Sweetheart Suite, a room in which she had helped boost the Cadaver's Arms' customer approval rating on many occasions, to find Hyde and Zena laying entwined amidst tangled sheets. Hyde's smile, summoned by the prospect of Valerie joining the party, had swiftly dissipated as she had informed him of Doggett's unwelcome arrival at the inn.

He sprang to his feet and hurriedly gathered his discarded garments. Hastily buttoning his shirt, Hyde glanced towards the window. It appeared he would once again be employing his habitual escape route.

He turned, blew a kiss towards the concerned figure of Zena, who lay covering her modesty with a bed sheet drawn up to her chin, bowed courteously to Valerie and, without further delay, vaulted through the open window.

Hyde felt a familiar rush of air about him as he plummeted towards the ground below and prepared for impact. As he thudded heavily into the muddy earth, a sharp pain flared through his left leg. He stifled a cry and began to limp as quickly as he could in the direction of his apothecary.

Cursing his predicament, Hyde decided his only course of action was to retrieve the transformation elixir and allow Jekyll to take over for a while after all. Doggett had no reason to hold Jekyll and he, Hyde, could not be arrested if he did not physically exist.

He was unsure how or when he would be able to wrestle back control from Jekyll but, he reasoned, at least the old goat would surely possess enough wit to concoct a cover story for his 'nephew' and throw Doggett off the scent for good.

Gritting his teeth against the regular bursts of fiery pain in his leg, Hyde pressed on.

*

In the shadowy recesses of the apothecary, Igor surveyed his handiwork by the sickly yellow glow of his gas lamp. He had hurriedly stacked Jekyll's medical equipment, including a multitude of test tubes and vials filled with various mysterious chemicals, onto the floor of the parlour. He had carefully crowned the pile with the jar of the highly volatile Epidermal Flare, as instructed by Edward.

After Eric had helped him carry the cumbersome corpse of the unfortunate Herr Hamlyn into the shop, and positioned him in a somewhat rigid sitting position in Jekyll and Hyde's favourite chair, he had sent the coach driver on his way, back to the Cadaver's Arms.

Igor retrieved the sack of gunpowder he and Eric had brought with them from Hamlyn's lap where they had placed it for safekeeping. He poured the explosive in a rough circle around the base of the glass pile.

He had considered tipping the powder over the bottles themselves but, as he had no idea what the chemicals in the containers were and no desire to blow himself to pieces should the gunpowder react with the liquids they held, decided against that particular course of action.

Walking slowly backwards, Igor began to pour more gunpowder from the sack, laying a trail from the pile of chemical containers, through the interior of the shop, and out into the deserted alleyway at the rear of the premises.

Once he had extended the trail a safe distance from the property, Igor patted the pockets of his jerkin and located a match. Using the worn heel of his boot, he struck the match into flickering life then dropped it onto his end of the gunpowder trail.

The powder flared and began to slowly burn a sputtering path towards the apothecary's entrance.

*

Hyde, grimacing in pain with each step, halted in his tracks as Eric's coach emerged from the darkness before him like a phantom materialising in the moonlight. The strident pounding of his own heart as he drove himself desperately along had prevented him from hearing the clattering of the approaching horse's hooves. Eric, spying Hyde in his path, drew up sharply.

'The shop!' panted Hyde raggedly. 'The potion!'

'Igor's set the fuse!' exclaimed Eric.

With a cry of despair, Hyde resumed his painful, limping run. Eric contemplated going after him. Hyde would make far better time in the coach but, as he prepared to manoeuvre the vehicle around, he spotted the figures of Helsing, Hopkins and Doggett brandishing oil lamps and striding purposefully in their direction.

'You there!' shouted Helsing in his most officious tone

whilst raising a gauntleted hand. 'We have need of your coach!'

'I'll not take you. Not after dark!' exclaimed Eric and whipped his faithful steed into motion. He steered the coach deliberately in the direction of the three men, causing them to scatter and fling themselves wildly from his path, with Helsing emitting a very un-officious, high-pitched squeal as he dived for safety.

As he sheepishly dragged himself to a standing position, Helsing attempted to claw back some semblance of authority in the eyes of his companions by shaking an angry fist after the fleeing vehicle as it rattled away into the darkness.

*

Igor instinctively dropped to a crouch behind a festering pile of discarded rubbish as he heard frantic footsteps pounding towards him. Wrinkling his nose with displeasure, he peered over the detritus which, judging by the offensive odour it generated, was comprised mostly of rotting vegetables discarded by the adjacent greengrocer.

As he narrowed his eyes and attempted to penetrate the gloom, he was stunned to observe Edward Hyde running as fast as his damaged leg would allow towards the apothecary.

'Edward!' bellowed Igor and scrambled over the decomposing mound of garbage in pursuit of his friend. He quickly caught up with the limping figure and urgently clamped a hand on his shoulder. 'What the hell are you doing?! I've lit the fuse!'

Hyde stared at him wild-eyed and rapidly mumbled something barely comprehensible about Doggett, the shop, and the transformation elixir.

Before Igor could calm him down Hyde shoved him unceremoniously away causing him to lose his footing on some of the slippery vegetable matter he had disturbed and unwittingly trailed from the rubbish heap. Hyde resumed his frantic journey.

'Sorry!' floated across the night from the receding figure as Igor picked himself up.

He was about to start after Hyde once again when the familiar voice of Helsing broke the air.

'This way!' came the excited cry of his nemesis.

Igor was disturbed to see Helsing, Hopkins and a third party, who he guessed by Esme's description must be Doggett, breaking into a run and heading rapidly towards him. Igor stepped deliberately into their path.

'Good evening gentlemen,' he offered with a doff of a pretend hat.

'You!' sneered Helsing. 'I might have known you were involved!'

'Involved?' asked Igor in the most innocent-sounding voice he could conjure. 'Involved in what?'

'Hyde!' snapped Doggett. 'Where is he?'

'I've not seen him, sir,' replied Igor.

Helsing glared at Igor for a moment, his eyes alight with hostility. Deciding, quite rightly, this was most likely some form of delaying tactic on the part of Igor, he turned back to his fellows.

'Come on!' he shouted. 'The apothecary is around this

corner. The three men ran on and, after a second's pause, Igor followed them.

*

Hyde, desperation blinding him to all about him, overtook the slow-burning gunpowder fuse as he rushed into the shop, failing to register the progress the spark was making in its journey towards the makeshift bomb prepared by Igor.

Frantically, he tore through the interior of the apothecary as fast as he could limp, the arrows of pain that shot through his leg no match for his determination. Panting, he dropped to his knees at the location of the secret floor compartment and wrenched open the cover.

Scrabbling in the darkness, his trembling fingers located the familiar shape of the vial containing the transformation fluid and closed gratefully around it.

Hyde felt a surge of triumph rush through him as he held the bottle aloft. At that moment, he noticed a sudden flare of brightness partially illuminating the formerly darkened room. The fuse had burned as far as the parlour. Hyde muttered an obscenity.

*

The ear-rattling explosion lit the night sky like a fiery rose blooming in the darkness. Helsing and his companions, as well as their pursuer, Igor, were blown forcibly backwards by the power of the blast and landed stunned and winded on their respective backs.

Orange tongues of flame extended from the ruined shop and lapped hungrily at the sky. As he pulled himself upright, Igor felt a tremendous wave of grief wash over him. Poor Edward.

The four men gingerly approached the burning building, the intense heat keeping them at a healthy distance.

As they stared, transfixed by the conflagration, they were soon joined by a crowd of villagers, roused by the sound of the blast and the sight of the flames painted on the canvas of the night.

Many had rushed from the inn and Igor was pleased to see Esme amongst their number. They locked eyes and Igor sadly shook his head in answer to her questioning gaze.

'Look!' came a cry from one the villagers pointing towards the blaze.

Impossibly, a figure had appeared, seemingly from the heart of the shop, and was staggering out into the street, its head and upper body covered by a large blanket. The figure unsteadily traversed a few steps forward before collapsing in a smouldering heap. Igor and a small number of villagers rushed towards it.

Igor tore the blanket from the figure's head to reveal the pale face of Henry Jekyll. Jekyll's eyes fluttered open and recognition instantly flickered across them.

'Igor,' he murmured weakly. 'Help me up.'

Igor supported Jekyll as he painfully regained his feet. Igor noticed he had in fact also gained someone else's foot and was clutching the severed body part to his pigeon-like chest.

Of course, thought Igor to himself. *Hamlyn*. He surmised that, having downed the transformation elixir, Hyde, or

Jekyll, must have employed the musician's corpse for use as a human shield against the blast.

The villagers crowded around the pair, sharing excited whispers.

Having attempted to approach the fiery ruin of the apothecary, still focused on his pursuit of Hyde but beaten back by the intense heat, Doggett, followed closely by Helsing and Hopkins, barged through them and rounded on Jekyll.

'Where is your nephew, Edward Hyde?' demanded Doggett. Helsing and Hopkins materialised at each shoulder, glowering accusingly. Jekyll raised the dismembered foot for the crowd to observe.

'My dear nephew, Edward Hyde, has been blown to pieces whilst assisting me with my work,' announced Jekyll. A gasp of horror erupted from the crowd and the sobbing of several ladies could be clearly heard amongst their number.

Doggett glared at Jekyll, seething with fury at the knowledge his prey had eluded him. The fact Hyde had been killed seemed to be of scant comfort. Doggett turned sharply on his heel.

'Come friend, Doggett,' offered Helsing. 'Let us repair to the inn and share an ale, to celebrate the death of this villain.'

Doggett subjected Helsing to a withering stare.

'I must report to the elders of Staid Virtue forthwith and, frankly, I have no wish to linger in this debauched cesspit for a moment longer. Goodnight.'

With that, he took his leave.

'Ladies and gentlemen,' said Jekyll, addressing the villagers. 'Although Edward is dead, I intend to rebuild my business and redouble my efforts in curing you of your physical and spiritual ills. I intend to work even harder to provide good, solid moral direction for you all.'

The crowd groaned, seemingly as one, and slowly began to disperse, the majority heading in the direction of the Cadaver's Arms.

Igor, who had been joined by Esme, turned to Jekyll. He nodded towards Hamlyn's toasted foot.

'I suppose you will have to hold a funeral for Edward,' he said.

'Hmm,' said Jekyll. 'I suppose so.'

'Well, I *am* in the undertaker business,' replied Igor. 'Of course, I will have to charge full price, even though there's not much of him.'

Jekyll's face flushed the familiar angry purple. He raised his hand as if to remonstrate, but Igor cut him off.

'It's a fair price considering the circumstances,' replied Igor. 'After all, you wouldn't want people to know exactly what those *circumstances* are, would you?'

Jekyll stood for a moment shaking with silent anger. Finally, he sighed.

'Fine,' he said through tight lips.

Esme glared with hostility at Jekyll. She could scarcely believe Castlemaine had lost the larger-than-life Edward Hyde for good and now the village found itself permanently saddled with this puritanical nuisance.

'Oh, and one more thing,' she added to both Igor and Jekyll's surprise. 'I think it's best you took yourself away from Castlemaine after the funeral and set up shop elsewhere. We really don't want your sort bringing the place down.'

Jekyll did not answer. Instead, he simply swallowed and walked away, his lanky form an ill fit for the singed, yet still flamboyant, clothes of Edward Hyde.

BODY PART IV

MEDIUM AT LARGE

As the mournful chime of his grandfather clock dolefully announced the arrival of midnight and echoed throughout the darkened interior of his well-appointed residence, Marius Belrott contemplated a hanging.

As Chief Justice of Castlemaine, it was his usual habit to consider any defendant placed before him to be deserving of the rope. Belrott prided himself that such decisive judgement was a mark of strength on his part as well as being wonderfully time-saving when there were plenty of other things he could be getting on with. For example, he was damned if he was going to let a decent lunch be delayed by having to waste precious hours listening to the pathetic lies and snivelling excuses of common criminals. Besides, it was well established that a good hanging provided a lovely day out for everyone.

As he sat alone in his four-poster bed, propped up by a sextet of goose-feather-stuffed pillows, Belrott pored over the notes pertaining to the case he was to preside over in court the following morning by the glow of a guttering candle. The matter looked extremely straightforward as far as he could see. The defendant, one Herbert Crocklegg, had been accused of stealing a loaf of bread from a Castlemaine bakery. There were no witnesses and no evidence had been found on Crocklegg but it was common knowledge the defendant was currently cohabiting with the baker's estranged wife, which clearly illustrated the low character of the blackguard. *Yes*, thought Belrott, *guilty as sin*.

Having decided he had put in enough legal work for the night, Belrott placed his papers to one side. He glanced at the small bell sitting atop his bedside cabinet and briefly thought of summoning his young maid, Justine, to help go over his particulars before recalling the lass was away for the night visiting her ailing aunt in the village of Leper's Cleft. Belrott sighed wistfully. Justine had proven to be a marvellous asset around his home and he certainly missed that asset when she was not there.

Belrott reached across to the bedside cabinet. He deftly ran his fingers down its back and located the button discreetly positioned there. He pressed the switch and grinned lasciviously as a lacquered wooden panel in the cabinet swung smoothly open. Reaching into the camouflaged compartment, Belrott withdrew a pile of documents bound loosely together by a silk ribbon. He shuffled through the pile before selecting one of the well-thumbed sheets and extracting it from its fellows.

'Ah, Wanda, you wicked woman,' he breathed heavily in appreciation as he drank in the image of the shapely female form displayed on the calotype he held in his trembling hands. 'It's time to pass sentence.'

A loud crashing sound from downstairs shattered the silence of the night as well as Belrott's concentration. He started violently at the noise, inadvertently flinging the picture of Wanda into the air in a paroxysm of shock. Panic seized him for an instant. Had someone, or some*thing* invaded his home? This was Castlemaine, after all. One could never truly feel safe in this village. Especially after dark.

After a few breathless seconds, Belrott composed himself. A ray of hope had penetrated his fog of panic. Perhaps Justine had abandoned her trip and returned early. *Yes*, he thought, maybe the obliging maid had decided his needs were more pressing than those of her aunt. *Still*, he told himself, *one must be careful and always have protection at hand.* Belrott swung his legs out of bed, scooped up the candleholder and headed for the fireplace. The hearth was barely visible in the midnight darkness with only a faint glow of nearly expired embers and the feeble light of his candle betraying its presence in the room. Belrott tried to ignore the jagged shadows thrown by the candlelight, which seemed poised to strike at him as he gathered a poker from its resting place beside the hearth.

Belrott began to pad stealthily towards his bedroom door but froze once again, icy tendrils of fear gripping him as the thump of what appeared to be footsteps sounded through the otherwise silent household. Someone was climbing the stairs.

'Who's there?' shouted Belrott in a voice far higher and less commanding than he had intended it to sound. The footsteps did not falter at his challenge. Instead, they seemed to quicken their pace and, to his alarm, were clearly heading in the direction of his bedchamber. Belrott swallowed hard and raised the poker above his head with a quivering arm. Despite himself, he let out a squeal of terror as the door handle first shook, then turned from the outside. Finally, torturously slowly, the bedchamber door opened inwards accompanied by the eerie squeaking of rusty hinges. That was one thing Justine had failed to oil up properly. Although the doorway appeared to yawn emptily before him, Belrott was acutely aware there was a presence with him in the room.

'Who's there?' repeated Belrott, his voice breaking into a near sob. He gasped in horror as the discarded picture of Wanda began to float upwards from the floor where it had fallen. It hung impossibly in mid-air for a couple of seconds before crumpling into a ball as if squashed by a ghostly hand. He flinched as the ball of paper struck him between the eyes, hurled by an unseen force.

'Spirit,' wailed Belrott in despair as he sunk to his knees, 'what do you want of me?' No voice answered him, a sinister silence was his only reply. After a heartbeat, Belrott's eyes widened as he became conscious of a scraping sound emanating from the direction of his recently vacated bed. His hands were shaking so forcefully he had to employ both of them in order to hold the candle steady. Belrott fearfully directed the flame towards the sound. In the flickering half-light he could see an object slowly moving across the floor, away from the shadowy area beneath his bed, and in his general direction. Unbelievably, his chamber pot was travelling towards him across the bedroom floor, seemingly of its own volition.

Belrott watched in slack-jawed awe, no longer capable of vocalising, as the chamber pot slowly levitated from the floorboards and paused, floating at eye level directly in front of him. The pot was so close to him he could make out the intricate pattern on the china even in the shadowy darkness. He winced again as the pot was dashed to the floor by the unseen power that manipulated it and shattered loudly into pieces about him. In his terror, he felt an all-consuming need to make use of the pot but he knew it was now hopelessly beyond repair.

Belrott wrapped himself into a foetal position on the floor, sobbing hysterically as a wave of destruction swept through the room. The bedside cabinet was raised and hurled across the bedchamber by invisible hands, books were thrown from their shelves and Belrott's wardrobe door was wrenched open, his clothing violently expelled from inside and strewn throughout the room. Then, as suddenly as the assault had commenced, the activity ceased. A pall of silence settled over the previously chaotic bedchamber. Still, Belrott dared not raise his head. He continued to shake and weep in fear, barely registering the sound of footsteps vacating the bedchamber and hurriedly receding down the stairs. He did not venture from his position until the first rays of morning sunlight had appeared in his room.

*

Esmerelda watched with affection as her father, old Clam, busied himself about the Cadaver's Arms. She had watched him grow noticeably older these last few months, but he was still the same man she had grown up loving and respecting. She admired the way he had run the inn all these years, becoming a pillar of Castlemaine society whilst raising her at the same time. Nowadays, her father's back was a little more bowed with the weight of passing time, his formerly dark hair now a shade of winter and his movements a little less easy, at least judging by the sounds that emanated from the privy when he was in occupation. But, she smiled to herself, he was still the first man she had loved and always would. If only the mad old bugger would stop murdering people in his sleep.

His recent trip to England to stay at Dr Seward's sanatorium did appear to have done the landlord some good. Of course, he had not been aware that she and Igor had sent him for a medical assessment of his homicidal somnomicidalism. Rather, he had been under the illusion they were treating him to a nice holiday abroad to visit his cousin Renfield. Sadly, his condition prevailed but, on a positive note, he did seem to have returned with a ruddier complexion following his rest, so the fog had obviously agreed with him. Perhaps she and Igor could get away one day too, she thought wistfully, but not, she sighed, while her father still needed her.

It was early evening at the Cadaver's Arms. Trade had died down considerably now the much-missed Edward Hyde was no longer a customer but, financially, the inn was ticking over nicely, thanks to a recent sales convention in the area. Several of the visiting traders had taken rooms at the inn and, although most of them seemed to be purveyors of questionable wares such as werewolf training whistles, vampire-friendly shampoo (Neck and Shoulders), anti-zombie air fresheners and vegetarian sausages, the villagers of Castlemaine were a generally gullible bunch and would pretty much buy any old tat if it came in a nice box. For Esme, this meant fully let and paid-for rooms and a healthy flow of cash over the bar where the traders spent most of their free time. So far, thanks to powerful sedatives and Valerie's expertise in tying people up in their beds, her father had not added to his unconscious kill tally with any of their number which, she reflected, was an added bonus.

Esme's musings were interrupted as one of their guests, Cornelius Padd, a freelance exorcist, medium ('removals a specialty', according to his business card), and demonic infestation consultant, swept into the room. Esme had found Padd to be a smarmy yet polite enough customer during her dealings with him. He did, however, seem to stand somewhat apart from the other traders staying at the inn. Whilst the others generally socialised together, Padd remained aloof, spending much of his spare time in his room. Still, Esme thought to herself, at least he was not causing any drunken trouble on the premises and, more importantly, he paid on time. The fact he seemed to have quite an appetite, often ordering two meals during an evening, both of which he ate alone upstairs, all helped swell the inn's coffers.

Padd removed his top hat to reveal his oil-coated, slicked-back hair. He bowed politely to Esme. 'A small cognac, dear lady,' he purred through thin lips crowned by a well-groomed moustache.

'Busy day, deary?' asked Esme, not particularly interested in a reply but making small talk out of professional politeness.

'Indeed,' confirmed Padd. 'I have today expunged a troublesome spirit from the home of Chief Justice Belrott. Nasty business, but all in a day's work for a fighter of dark forces such as myself,' he boasted, puffing out his chest.

'Another haunting?' asked Esme, her curiosity piqued. 'That's the third in Castlemaine this week!'

'You are quite correct,' agreed Padd. 'Thankfully, for the sake of your fine village, I appear to have arrived in the nick of time. Dark entities have taken a fancy to Castlemaine and they must be stopped!'

'Yes,' nodded Esme. 'It's lucky you are here.'

Cornelius Padd bowed once again, ordered a double portion of toad stew for a late supper, and retired to his room. Esme watched him go, an uneasy feeling playing inside her. It seemed her powerful feminine intuition, a gift inherited from her beloved mother, was trying to tell her something.

*

Later that night, Baroness Agnes Wildflower sat alone, perched on the chaise longue of her plush drawing room. As was her usual nightly habit, she poured herself a sweet sherry from a crystal decanter and raised a toast to the portrait of her long-deceased husband, Cedric, whose likeness stared back at her just as it always had these long years since his passing. She sipped demurely at the sherry, a classical tune crackling away on her gramophone in the background. Dear Cedric, he had gone so early, she mused to herself. She wondered what he would say to her now, were it possible for them to commune. What happy reminiscences would they share she wondered, what sweet words of regret over the limited time they had been granted together would he offer? And, of course, would he forgive her for the way she was carrying on with the stable boy?

Baroness Agnes grinned contentedly to herself at the thought. Yes, the strapping young Hans certainly gave her a spring in her step in her twilight years. She was sure her dearly departed Cedric would not begrudge her a few fleeting moments of pleasure to ease her loneliness and Hans's heart was far stronger, and his constitution more robust, than poor old Cedric's had ever been. She further consoled herself with the thought that, despite her husband's early demise, he had at least departed this mortal realm whilst wrapped in the loving arms of his wife and with a smile on his face.

Agnes started abruptly from her reverie. Was it her imagination or had a sudden draught just rippled the pages of the periodical that lay on the occasional table beside her? It was almost as if some unseen entity had brushed its way swiftly past her, disturbing the newspaper with its passage. She felt a knot of dread begin to tighten in the pit of her stomach. Earlier that very day she had overheard some of the servants gossiping amongst themselves about the rash of supposed hauntings in the village. She had chastised them for their foolishness in no uncertain terms and sent them about their duties. At this moment, however, their simple-minded talk suddenly seemed distinctly less foolish.

Agnes screamed as a silver candleholder flew from its former position on the mantlepiece to crash violently against the wall behind her. She stared wildly about her until her crazed eyes alighted on Cedric's portrait.

'Oh, Cedric!' she wailed. 'Is it you? Are you angry with me? I was only having a bit of fun. I get… *urges*, you know!'

At that moment, Agnes thought she had detected the sound of what could have been an embarrassed cough in the otherwise silent drawing room, but this fancy was driven swiftly from her mind as she observed Cedric's painting seemingly detach itself from its hook and begin to float through the air towards her.

Agnes jumped to her feet, her whitened knuckles pressed against her gaping mouth as Cedric's picture made its impossible journey towards her. She watched, transfixed in horror, as the portrait lurched suddenly downwards just as the footstool which lay between her and the hovering painting was shunted violently to one side as if it had been kicked.

'Arse!' barked a gruff disembodied voice from the general direction of the painting, which had now righted itself in the air and was once again heading for her. That was not Cedric's sweet tone, thought Agnes immediately. Surely, that obscenity could only have been uttered by nothing less than… she shuddered at the very thought: a demon! Agnes let out a blood-curdling scream of primal terror and dropped into a dead faint onto the chaise longue, her sherry glass slipping from her bony fingers and rolling away across the floor.

A rumble of urgent footsteps rapidly approached the drawing room and culminated in the portly form of Agnes's butler, Grabbitt, having been alerted by the sound of his mistress's ghastly scream, bursting through the door. Grabbitt was swiftly followed by the doughy figure of his wife, Lotte, the housekeeper, who rushed to the stricken baroness.

Grabbitt glanced nervously around the room, crossing

himself at the sight of Master Cedric's portrait upturned on the floor by the chaise longue. Lotte gently patted the baroness's cheek in an attempt to revive her. Seeing no result from this course of action, she tried her face instead.

'That scream,' she uttered fearfully. 'I mean, it wasn't like the others, you know, when Hans is up here.'

'Quiet, woman!' hissed her husband. 'There's something unnatural going on up here...'

'There's something unnatural going on when Hans is up here,' began Lotte, but Grabbitt's stern look silenced any further such talk.

'I'll fetch the smelling salts,' said Lotte decisively and hurried from the room. Grabbitt swallowed nervously. He too had heard a multitude of rumours pertaining to foul deeds and hauntings in Castlemaine. This was a cursed village, he told himself. They should never have taken their positions here, but job opportunities were few and far between in these parts, especially when one's main skills were limited to cooking, cleaning, and knowing one's place.

Grabbitt was thrown out of his own thoughts when a whirling and swishing sound appeared to emanate from a movement behind him. He felt his stomach begin to churn as his bowels threatened to betray him.

'Wh... who's there?' he stammered fearfully before doubling over with an agonised gasp as the force of a tremendous blow thundered into his testicles. He collapsed to the ground, his hands clamped over his injured genitals. He lay there shuddering with pain. He did not register the retreating footsteps that slapped their way swiftly from the room.

A few seconds later, Lotte returned to the drawing room, clasping a small glass bottle of smelling salts in her pudgy hand. Her eyes widened at the sight of her husband rolling on the floor, cradling his private area and moaning softly to himself.

'Oh, she woke up then,' began Lotte before spotting the baroness's unconscious figure in the same position as she had left her. Lotte was undecided as to who she should attend to first, her husband or her employer. She finally decided on the baroness as she was, after all, the one who paid her wages. Besides, poor old Grabbitt rarely proved any use to her these days as far as that particular part of his anatomy was concerned, so he could wait.

Lotte removed the stopper from the bottle of smelling salts and gently waved the foul-fragranced receptacle in the general vicinity of the baroness's nostrils. After a few moments, her mistress came to, a grimace of revulsion contorting her features. She pushed away her servant's hand, attempting to escape the unpleasant odour.

'Madam, are you all right?' asked Lotte, her tone one of grave concern.

'Terrible, it was terrible,' whispered the baroness weakly.

'But, my lady, what happened?' questioned the housekeeper.

'A demon, Lotte. I was attacked by a demon!'

Lotte gasped in shock and clapped her palm over her mouth in horror while the baroness, her nerves shot, slumped back into her seat. For some while, the only sound in the drawing room came from Grabbitt who remained on the floor, a pained keening issuing from his lips as he massaged his stricken manhood.

MEDIUM AT LARGE

*

By the time the first rays of morning sun had penetrated the grime-smeared windows of his undertaker's emporium, Igor had already been out of bed and active for a couple of hours. He had still not managed to shake the habit of waking in the early hours after his many years of slaving for Victor Frankenstein.

His former employer had always insisted Igor thoroughly clean the laboratory each day before he had breakfast. That is to say, before Frankenstein had breakfast. Igor himself had been assigned a packed itinerary of daily chores that simply left no time to indulge in such frivolities. Victor, of course, had sat down to a luxurious spread each morning, prepared by the castle's resident cooks and fetched from the kitchen by Igor as part of said itinerary. But, as he had once explained to his hapless servant, this was not breakfast per se, this was in fact, work. Victor had stated that consuming a morning meal merely assisted his thought process and claimed to have had some of his most profound thoughts whilst ladling down a full Transylvanian. He had further opined this was something only a genius such as himself could fully comprehend and was nothing that could be appreciated by a servile clod with the brain capacity of a cold sore.

Igor shook his head ruefully as these unhappy memories flitted through his mind. He asked himself for the hundredth time, why had he not struck out on his own long before he had finally done so? Ah, well, he reflected, having survived the grimness of his early years, life now was good. He had freedom, he was making a semi-legal living and, most importantly, he had Esme. If only he could have told his younger self, as he cowered under the cruel tongue and indiscriminate blows of his psychotic employer, that the future would be brighter.

Igor's musings were interrupted as his attention was caught by the sight of a figure moving slowly past his parlour. He rubbed his elbow against the dirty windowpane in order to create a small patch of clear glass through which he could better see. He was surprised to spy old Grabbitt, Baroness Wildflower's butler, painfully limping his way towards the nearby church. As he watched, Igor noted the butler seemed to be pausing every few steps and rubbing his groin. But not in a good way. Igor had heard some scurrilous tittle-tattle concerning the baroness and her male servants but surely, she wasn't so hard up she had resorted to Grabbitt? Not at his age! His curiosity aroused, Igor stepped out into the dawn sunshine.

'Morning, Mr Grabbitt,' greeted Igor cheerily. 'What brings you out so early?'

The butler turned slowly to face him, and Igor detected a wince of pain crease his features as he raised an arm in an acknowledging wave.

'Morning, Master Igor. I have urgent business with Father Price,' he replied in a register Igor was certain was slightly higher than that in which he usually spoke.

Igor frowned. It was unusual for anyone to have need of Father Price in Castlemaine, let alone an urgent one. With a twinge of panic, Igor's thoughts strayed to the recently discovered tunnel behind the demolished tomb of Saint Victus. Surely, his and Esme's secret passage hadn't been discovered? The last thing the couple needed was their handy subterranean corpse transportation route being cut off, especially now the unconsciously homicidal innkeeper had returned to Castlemaine. These days they relied on the underground. However, Igor swiftly batted away this fearful notion. No, Baroness Wildflower could not possibly have located the tunnel as she rarely ventured from her mansion. In fact, she rarely even went downstairs from her bedroom. Still, something was amiss, and Igor's natural inquisitiveness, no longer suppressed since freedom from the employ of Victor Frankenstein, had been awakened by Grabbitt and the quest on which he limped with such determination.

'My dear fellow, you can hardly walk. At least allow me to give you some support and assist you on your journey,' offered Igor. This seemed an ideal opportunity to discover for himself the details of this mysterious errand.

Grabbitt smiled in gratitude as Igor placed a supportive arm around his shoulder and took some of his not inconsiderable weight. They began to slowly make their way towards the vestry to find Father Price. The pair made slow progress as they shuffled through the churchyard, Igor hampered by the burden of the butler's excess poundage and Grabbitt encumbered by the painful swelling in his undergarments.

Finally, the shuffling pair arrived at the church. Igor carefully released his hold on Grabbitt and rapped on the wooden door. After a few moments, the sound of an iron key turning in its lock could be heard from the other side. The nervous features of Father Price appeared at a crack in the door.

'Igor!' exclaimed the young priest, his relief evident. 'Come in, come in.'

As Igor and Grabbitt entered the building, Price's agitation increased. He ushered them into wooden chairs.

'Oh no, what's happened now?' he asked, shaking his head. 'This place, this cursed place.'

'Calm down, Father,' replied Igor in as soothing a manner as he could manage. 'Mr Grabbitt here has a message from the baroness.'

Price brightened somewhat. 'A confession?' he asked hopefully. 'It may take a while from what I understand. Still, my diary is quite empty so I'm sure I can fit her in.'

'No, sir,' replied Grabbitt gravely. 'Evil business is afoot. The Devil's work, no less!'

Father Price groaned and rubbed his temple. He slumped into a vacant seat and sighed resignedly. 'Oh, well,' he uttered weakly. 'I suppose you'd better tell me about it.'

*

A few hours later, Igor mounted his usual stool at the Cadaver's Arms and, over a warm tankard of Old Claggy's Warthog Pizzle, one of the guest beers Old Clam had brought back with him from England, he appraised Esme and her father of Grabbitt's visit to Father Price and his mistress's plea to the priest to carry out an exorcism.

'I can't believe there's been yet another haunting. I mean, so soon,' said Esme in disbelief.

'A demonic manifestation, according to Grabbitt,' replied Igor.

'Strange business,' muttered the innkeeper darkly, as if anyone really needed telling.

Esme nodded in the direction of Cornelius Padd who was making his way towards the bar. 'Someone's done all right out of it,' she said. 'Still, it looks like he won't be profiting from this one, not if the baroness wants Father Price to handle the matter,' she noted as the dapperly attired medium approached.

'Please!' retorted Igor. 'Can you really see Price going toe to toe with the powers of darkness? He's so scared he's asked me to go with him to see the baroness.'

'You? But, why?' laughed Esme as Igor swallowed more Warthog Pizzle.

'Don't forget, he thinks we cleansed the crypt of evil forces after that whole Sister Vigilanta incident,' Igor reminded her before raising a finger to his lips to request silence.

The three immediately ceased their conversation as Padd arrived within earshot. He dramatically swept off his topper and bowed in greeting before ordering a double portion of braised cow cheeks, served on a bed of fungi of the forest, for luncheon.

'Extra helpings again, deary?' smiled Esme. 'I don't know where you put it all.' Not for the first time Esme noted that, for one with such a prodigious appetite, Padd really was a rather small medium.

Padd presented her with a smile as oily as his hair and stroked one curled end of his carefully waxed moustache with a well-manicured finger.

'I do so enjoy the excellent cuisine served in your fine establishment,' he purred smarmily. 'Besides, duelling with the unspeakable shades of the netherworld is hungry work,' he added whilst theatrically patting his stomach and winking.

'I suppose it must be,' nodded Esme, her previous feeling of unease again making its presence felt.

'As a matter of fact,' continued Padd. 'I believe my services will be called upon again today if I hear correctly.'

'Really?' interjected Igor. 'How so?'

Padd shot him a glance so sharp that, if it had been a stick, it could have taken his eye out.

'I hear Baroness Wildflower was disturbed by an unearthly incursion in her private quarters last night,' he responded.

'Interesting,' replied Igor. 'As far as I understood, that's not common knowledge outside of the Wildflower Estate. I thought only myself and Father Price knew anything about it.'

Cornelius Padd paused, his mind racing for a second. 'Ah. Yes, well,' he began uncertainly before composing himself and continuing in a tone one might adopt if one was addressing a simpleton. 'I know it is probably hard for you to understand but I am a medium. The spirit world tells me everything.'

Igor glared hotly at Padd for a moment and wondered how far his tankard would bounce if he dashed it against the top of the medium's head. He caught Esme's cautionary expression as he contemplated this action and desisted. 'I'm surprised the spirits didn't tell you it was your night off then,' he said through taut lips.

'What do you mean?' snapped Padd.

'The Baroness has requested Father Price, priest of Castlemaine, to expel this troublesome entity,' smiled Igor smugly.

Padd stood silent for a moment clenching and unclenching his fists, his face and neck flushed a vivid shade of scarlet.

'I wish the good Father well,' he said eventually and in an entirely unconvincing manner. He returned his attention to Esme and ordered a brandy, which he drained in one long pull.

'I shall take my luncheon in my room as usual,' he stated curtly and headed for the stairs. Igor and Esme swapped questioning glances as he left.

*

An hour later, Valerie rushed along the inn's upstairs corridor. Her shift was due to commence in five minutes and she was running late having overslept thanks to her exertions during a busy session the previous night. Despite her hurry, Valerie found herself pausing outside one of the guest bedrooms as her attention was diverted by the sound of what appeared to be a heated discussion emanating from within. She immediately thought this strange as she knew this to be the room rented by Cornelius Padd, the medium and exorcist but, according to the register, he was the sole occupant. Valerie pressed herself tightly against the door and strained her ears in an attempt to better hear the conversation.

'...stubbed my bloody toe!' came an angry male voice that Valerie did not recognise. 'And for what?'

'It's not my fault,' came an almost pleading response in a voice that Valerie did recognise: it belonged to Padd. 'How was I to know she'd call the priest. She's hardly devout by reputation.'

'It's all right for you!' accused the other man. 'All you have to do is prance about trying to look mystical and count the money. I'm the one doing all the hard graft, not to mention freezing off his boll—'

'Wait!' hissed Padd urgently. Valerie stepped back from the door instinctively, recoiling at the sound of footsteps approaching the door on the inside. Padd wrenched the door open and stood on the threshold glowering down at her. 'Well?' he demanded icily.

'Sorry, sir,' replied Valerie hurriedly. 'I just wanted to make sure you were all right. I heard voices, you see.'

'I am fine, girl,' snapped Padd. 'I was simply thinking aloud. Now kindly leave me in peace and ensure I am not disturbed again until my meal is ready to be delivered.' With that he slammed the door shut without awaiting a reply. Valerie muttered a colourful adjective under her breath and resumed her journey to the bar. Padd leaned back on the bedroom door, listening to Valerie retreat into the distance. He cringed as a hostile voice whispered menacingly into his ear.

'You'd better sort this out quickly, Padd. Or… you'll have me to answer to.'

*

As evening wrapped its shadowy embrace around the village of Castlemaine, Father Price sat in the comforting surrounds of the Cadaver's Arms. He drained the remaining dregs from the glass of brandy Esme had provided in an effort to help stiffen his resolve. Igor laid a reassuring hand on his shoulder.

'Come on then, Father, time to get to the bottom of this business,' he said gently.

'Strange business,' reiterated Old Clam, again, unnecessarily.

The young priest nodded resolutely and girded himself. He reminded himself he was here to do a job and the people of Castlemaine were relying on him. That in itself was a scary thought, but, he supposed, it did make a nice change. Price got to his feet, jutting out his chin in a determined fashion. He resolved he would stand tall against whatever malevolent creature had insinuated itself into the baroness's private chambers and face it down.

'You are still coming with me, aren't you?' he asked Igor.

Igor nodded his confirmation. In truth, he did not particularly relish the prospect of tackling a demonic entity, especially after witnessing the state Grabbitt had ended up in. The very thought brought a tear to his eye. However, after the way he and Esme had pulled the wool over Father Price's eyes concerning the tunnel in the church, he felt he owed the priest and just could not find it within himself to let the poor lad go up to the mansion, to face whatever was lurking there, alone. Not only that but, despite the adverse effect such a quality was widely believed to have on felines, his curiosity would simply not be satisfied until he had witnessed for himself exactly what was going on at the Wildflower Estate.

As Igor and Price donned their overcoats, they were approached by the predatory form of Cornelius Padd who had been hovering nearby awaiting the moment of their departure.

'Father,' greeted Padd in his familiar honeyed tone, extending a hand to the priest whilst completely ignoring Igor. 'May I wish you every success in your righteous endeavour.'

'Why, thank you Mr, err...' began Price, not entirely sure who the moustachioed stranger addressing him was.

'Padd. Cornelius Padd,' Padd announced solemnly with a small bow. 'Medium, exorcist and fellow combater of evil. You are a very brave man, Father,' he added.

'I am?' gulped Price, his eyes widening in surprise. Since taking up his post in the village, the priest had found compliments to be so rare as to be bordering on extinction.

'Indeed, Father,' purred Padd. 'I know of few mortal men who would risk their lives, nay, their very souls, facing a demon in the dangerous heat of an unholy battle.'

'Yes, w... well,' stammered Price uncertainly, tugging nervously at his collar. 'All part of the job you see. Erm, *dangerous*, you say?'

'Of course!' exclaimed Padd heartily. 'To be bested in such a confrontation would surely result in the agonising shredding of one's very being! But I have no doubt you will emerge triumphant from your mission for I see lights of bravery shining in your steely eyes.'

Price's heart sank. He had rather hoped no one had noticed he had tears forming. 'Um, yes, thank you,' he murmured, suddenly feeling distinctly queasy about the aforementioned mission.

'I wonder, Father,' began Padd before seeming to check himself.

'Wonder, yes?' replied Price eagerly, happy to delay their departure.

Padd waved his hand as if shooing away a fanciful notion. He tutted loudly and shook his head as if chiding himself for his own foolishness.

'What?!' Price very nearly screamed.

'I just wondered, and I apologise for my impudence, whether you would deem to allow me to assist you in this encounter?' asked Padd. 'You see, I would be honoured to witness a puritan warrior such as yourself earn a famous victory at close quarters,' he fawned. 'And, of course, if I could play some small part...'

'Really?' asked Price, a note of pleading evident in the question.

'I have had some measure of success in these matters, Father,' boasted Padd. 'Since my arrival I have already successfully banished three troublesome spirits from Castlemaine so I'm sure I could be of some use to you. I promise I won't get in your way during the fight.'

'You can do it if you like!' spluttered Price, then realising he had spoken aloud, hastily added, 'with my guidance, of course.'

'Splendid!' beamed Padd. 'Then let us away to rid the baroness of this... evil.'

Igor's eyes narrowed in suspicion. Price may have been only too happy to accept Padd's offer of assistance, but it seemed clear to him there was more to Padd's enthusiasm to join the mission than he had revealed. Igor silently questioned the nature of the exorcist's true motives. As well as any potential demonic adversary, he found himself wondering if he would also find himself having to protect the young priest from Cornelius Padd.

As Father Price, Cornelius Padd and Igor headed for the inn door, their progress was arrested by the arrival of Helsing and his ubiquitous henchman, Hopkins. They halted deliberately in their path.

'Gorblimey, it's getting like Piccadilly Circus around 'ere,' said Old Clam employing a colloquialism he had picked up on his trip to England that was completely lost on everyone present.

'Gentlemen,' began Helsing. 'And Igor,' he added pointedly. 'I take it you are on your way to the home of Baroness Wildflower.'

'News travels quickly,' said Igor.

'I am the magistrate, chief of police and...' Helsing said haughtily before shooting a warning stare at Hopkins, '... witchfinder of Castlemaine. It is my duty to know when the residents of my village are threatened.'

'Especially the rich ones,' clarified Hopkins.

'Quite!' nodded Helsing. 'Father, I understand you have been summoned by the baroness to eradicate the evil presence that molested her last night. As witchfinder, I am here to assist, for I will brook no devilry in my territory.'

'Thank you, Master Helsing,' replied Price, scarcely believing his luck. 'However, Igor and Master Padd here have also agreed to lend their services.'

Helsing had already been made aware of Padd's presence in Castlemaine and news of his recent successes in the field of exorcism had not gone unnoticed by the village's witchfinder. Finally, he had thought, here was the calibre of visitor the village needed. He directed a courteous bow towards Padd. 'Master Padd, it is an honour to meet another soldier in the service of light, another warrior of righteousness in the ongoing battle against the forces of darkness,' he offered grandiosely.

Padd looked confused. 'Another? Who was the first one?'

Helsing shifted uncomfortably and coughed a nervous cough. 'Why, I mean myself, of course. I am a witchfinder of some renown in these parts.' He tried to ignore the sound of sniggering that rippled through the inn.

'Oh. Right,' said Padd, clearly unimpressed. He turned to Price. 'Father, time wastes and darkness descends. I am sure you and I will be more than sufficient to battle this hellish scourge.'

'The more the merrier!' replied Price quickly, realising he now had four people to hide behind if things went badly up at the mansion. He failed to notice the flash of anger that momentarily crossed Padd's features at this declaration. Igor, however, did not miss this change in Padd's expression and rubbed his chin thoughtfully. Why, he wondered, was Padd so unhappy at the prospect of further additions to their party? His suspicion of the exorcist was increasing by the minute.

As the five men left the inn and set off on their mission, Igor determined to keep a close watch on Cornelius Padd during the evening's demon battling, providing of course, he did not find himself too busy running away should events take a downwards turn.

*

In the chill of the Castlemaine night, beneath a sickly yellow moon, Father Price and his four companions were met by Grabbitt at the tradesman's entrance of the rambling Wildflower mansion. Igor noticed the butler appeared to be moving a little more comfortably than he had when the two had met that morning. Igor had recommended to Grabbitt the prolonged application of an ice pack to his injury. Although he had personally never had his vitals battered by an unholy imp, Igor had discovered the healing properties of ice for himself during his days at Castle Frankenstein. Many were the times he had taken down various swellings and brought out bruises, developed following his ill treatment at the hands of his quick-tempered employer, with the help of ice chunks procured from the body parts preservation tank hidden in the depths of the castle.

Grabbitt ushered them sombrely into the mansion, Helsing and Hopkins leading the way with Price following closely behind. There was no way he was going to be left alone, not with a diabolical entity rampaging about the place. Igor noted that Padd was the last to enter the building but, once inside, swiftly pushed his way to the front of the party as the butler led them hurriedly through the kitchen then up the servants' stairway to the baroness's private chamber. Grabbitt tapped lightly on the door of the drawing room and, following his mistress's call to enter, announced the five men.

Baroness Agatha Wildflower greeted the group sat in her favoured position on the chaise longue, her face anxious and pale in the lamplight.

'Father Price,' she said with a sigh of relief, 'I'm so glad you're here.' Price took her hand and respectfully kissed the back of it.

The men listened attentively as the baroness recounted the details of her harrowing experience the previous evening. Father Price glanced nervously around the drawing room as the baroness talked until, finally, she addressed him directly.

'Well, Father, what are you going to do about this… *demon*?' she asked with a shudder.

Price swallowed. 'Madam, are you absolutely certain this visitation wasn't the shade of your much-missed husband come to commune with you rather than the appearance of an evil being? Perhaps he simply had a message for you?' he asked hopefully.

The baroness shook her head. 'No, I'm certain. Dear Cedric lived a good, happy life and would never have barked an obscenity at me the way that, *thing*, did!'

'Obscenity?' queried Igor. 'What did it say?'

The baroness raised the back of her hand dramatically to her forehead and shuddered.

'I couldn't possibly repeat it.'

'Madam,' said Padd raising his palms, 'do not distress yourself. The mouthing of foul oaths is a known characteristic of unholy entities, an infernal tactic employed to upset the pure of heart such as yourself.'

Agnes nodded. 'Well, I am absolutely certain it was not my dear Cedric. I know he rests in peace.'

Helsing and Hopkins exchanged awkward glances. They well recalled the night Baron Cedric had died those long years ago. Hubert Plank, the village undertaker at the time, had been so shocked by the drained and ravaged appearance of the corpse he had naturally suspected vampirism. Once he had removed the baron from the marital bed, where he had expired, and had him ensconced at the funeral parlour, he had summoned Helsing who insisted he bang a wooden stake into the heart just to be on the safe side.

This course of action, whilst taken in the best interests of the village, had proved somewhat problematic when the baroness had informed Plank her husband must lie in state for a week at the mansion. The undertaker had carefully sawn away the protruding end of the stake, buttoned the baron's ceremonial jacket, in which he was to be buried, over the site of the post-mortem injury and hoped for the best. Fortunately, the grief-stricken baroness had been too busy being consoled by her gamekeeper to notice anything was awry. Helsing wondered if the baron's spirit, angry at the treatment of his corpse, had returned to complain. But, if so, why now after all this time?

Perhaps then, it was indeed a demon they were contending with, thought Helsing. The notion had originally seemed quite exciting when first mooted but, now they were here at the scene of the manifestation, Helsing nervously wondered what exactly they would do if the priest was unable to banish the fiend. He could hardly burn it at the stake. For a start, he thought despairingly, how would he arrest it? Besides, even if the unholy villain did respect his authority and come quietly, didn't these sorts of things actually quite like a bit of fire? He was beginning to wonder if they should have just left this matter to Price and Padd after all.

A sudden crash directed all of their attentions to the centre of the drawing room. One of the baroness's sherry glasses lay smashed on the floor. Price crossed himself and Grabbitt crossed his legs.

'It's here, Father!' shrieked the baroness.

The group flocked into the drawing room.

'Um, yes,' mumbled Father Price, fighting to keep any trace of panic from his voice, and rummaging in his bag for the bottle of holy water he had packed for the occasion. He began splashing the liquid wildly about the drawing room, and shouted, as authoritatively as he could, 'Get out of it, you!'

Without warning, Price found himself shoved by powerful unseen hands and flew face first into the chest of Hopkins, sending the two men toppling awkwardly to the floor in an ungainly tangle of thrashing limbs. Igor rushed to help Price back to his feet but reeled backwards under the impact of what felt like a punch that caught him squarely on the chin. Another glass smashed, the baroness screamed and Helsing ran for the door.

'Stop!' came the commanding voice of Cornelius Padd, defiant against the chaos.

'I was just off to get help!' whimpered Helsing in a somewhat pitiful defence of his own cowardice before realising the exorcist was not actually addressing him. Rather, Padd had strolled boldly into the middle of the drawing room and raised his arms aloft. Another glass had floated into the air and, incredibly, hung motionless directly in front of the defiant Cornelius Padd.

'Evil spirit!' Padd shouted in the general direction of the levitating receptacle. 'You have no right to be here!'

Padd paused dramatically for a moment, his eyes closed as if listening for an otherworldly response, then continued in clipped tones. 'You will leave this place immediately and never return, at my command!' his voice grew louder. 'At the command of Cornelius Padd!'

At that, the glass dropped, without breaking, to the floor. Padd pointed theatrically towards the door of the drawing room. A haunting scream split the air. It quickly tailed off and the room fell silent. 'The demon has departed!' announced Padd melodramatically.

Igor, still crouched on the floor and rubbing his painful jaw, was certain he could detect faint footsteps heading in the direction of the doorway. Scrambling to his feet, he snatched up the fallen sherry glass, and followed after the sound as the others began to slowly regain their composure and gathered around Padd offering words of congratulations.

Igor sprinted to the top of the stairs. Yes, he was absolutely sure now he could hear rapid footsteps descending the staircase. He hurled the sherry glass in their general direction and gasped as the glass travelled a few feet before spinning away in a drastic change of direction as if bouncing off something unseen but very solid.

'Oww!' came a disembodied voice echoing up the staircase.

Igor paused thoughtfully for a moment then headed back to rejoin the others. As he returned to the drawing room he could see Padd remained the centre of the group's attention.

'Amazing, amazing!' gushed Helsing. 'We won't see that fiend around here again!'

'We didn't actually *see* him this time, did we?' answered Igor, staring pointedly at Padd.

'Quiet, fool,' hissed Helsing. 'We all saw what happened, that's the main thing.' Then, he turned to Padd. 'You are a hero, sir!'

The others, except Igor, nodded and closed around the exorcist, patting him on the back and continuing to offer their congratulations. Padd raised his hands as if modestly trying to deflect their admiration, but in reality, lapped up the praise being lavished upon him. He did so enjoy a bit of sycophancy.

Eventually, Baroness Wildflower beckoned Padd over to her and presented him with a leather purse, bulging with gold coins, which had been passed to her by Grabbitt at her nodded signal. 'Thank you, Master Padd,' she said as she handed him the weighty money bag. Batting her eyelashes, she added suggestively, 'If there is any further reward I could offer you…?'

Padd coughed nervously, then composed himself. 'My dear baroness, your gratitude, and this generous contribution to help fund my fight against evil, are all the reward I require.'

The baroness took this rebuttal in good grace; after all, Hans was an early riser and the stable lad was always ready for an early morning ride. She shrugged. 'As Master Helsing says, Herr Padd, you are a hero!'

'I helped a bit too,' mumbled Father Price to no one in particular. The group all looked at their feet.

Igor stood detached from the group. He surveyed the room, his eyes narrowing in suspicion as his gaze settled on the puffed-up form of Cornelius Padd, who stood soaking up the praise being lavished upon him whilst affecting a rather transparent air of false modesty. Something was very wrong here and Igor was convinced Padd was at the heart of it.

*

Esme crept furtively along the darkened landing of the Cadaver's Arms. She required no candlelight to find her way. Her many years living, and drinking, at the inn had imbued her with the ability to navigate the building's interior purely by memory. Quickly and stealthily, she arrived at her destination, the room rented by Cornelius Padd.

Esme tapped softly on the door. No response was forthcoming. She knocked again, this time much louder. Again, silence was her only reply. Satisfied the room was unoccupied, Esme removed the inn's master key from a hidden pocket on her skirt and slipped it into the lock. She stole into Padd's room and locked the door behind her.

Esme walked slowly towards the bed, her questing hands outstretched in the dark, groping for the bedside cabinet. Once she had located the cabinet, she removed a match from the box she had brought with her and struck it into life. By the match's weak glow, Esme ascertained the whereabouts of the lamp Padd had left beside his bed, positioned beside a half-empty bottle of brandy. Esme touched the flame to the wick and once it had taken hold, she raised the torch aloft and commenced a search of Padd's room guided by the shimmering lamplight.

Earlier that night, Valerie had relayed to Esme details of the mysterious discourse she had overheard emanating from the exorcist's room. Esme, whose feeling of unease regarding the presence of their guest had continued to grow, had paid heed to her trusted female intuition, and resolved to indulge in a spot of detective work while Padd was occupied at the Wildflower mansion.

Esme made her way around the room, examining the fixtures and fittings, alert for anything out of place. Nothing unusual appeared to be lurking in the shadows, which was always a bonus in this vicinity. She crouched beside the bed and flipped back the bottom of the counterpane. The lamplight revealed a bulky suitcase stowed under the bed, which Esme grasped by the handle and dragged from its resting place. A faint clinking sound issued from the case as she manoeuvred it towards her.

Esme popped the catches open and flung back the lid of the case. It was packed with laboratory phials containing unidentifiable liquids of various colours and hues, empty test tubes, and a variety of syringes and other scientific apparatus. Esme secured the case and pushed it back into the dark recess from whence it came.

As Esme shifted her position on the floor, and prepared to stand, the lamplight illuminated another curious discovery lying a few feet away. A pile of sheets and the extra pillows Padd had requested on his arrival at the inn 'for his posture' had been laid out on the floorboards as if to construct a makeshift sleeping area. Why, wondered Esme, would the exorcist pay for a perfectly good bed, only to decide he would sleep on the floor? She fully conceded the Cadaver's Arms could not honestly be described as a 'luxury' establishment, even though it clearly stated that was the case on the new signage they had installed, but she was confident the beds were comfortable enough.

Esme rose and headed for the wardrobe. Maybe Padd held a secret in the closet. She opened the doors to reveal a collection of expensive-looking garments, all of which she recognised as belonging to the exorcist having seen him attired in the various outfits during his stay at the inn.

However, as she thumbed through the items, which hung like sleeping bats from the wardrobe's clothes rail, Esme discovered a series of less familiar apparel. A heavy overcoat, functional rather than flashy as she would have expected from a dandy like Padd, appeared alien to its showier companions. The overcoat also appeared to be cut to a larger size than would be suitable for the exorcist. Esme patted the coat's pockets. One of the outer pockets bulged, clearly stuffed with something bulky, yet soft to the touch.

Esme slipped her hand into the voluminous pocket and withdrew what, on initial inspection, appeared to be a loose bundle of rags. Closer examination revealed the articles to be bandages. Exploration of the second outer pocket allowed Esme to unearth a pair of sunglasses, the lenses so dark Esme wondered how the wearer could possibly see out of them. The impenetrable eyepieces stared sightlessly back at her, revealing nothing.

Esme reached up into the wardrobe and ran her hand along the shelf installed above the clothes rail. She gasped aloud as her exploring fingers met with something lurking unseen on the shelf above her. Something hairy. She jumped backwards instinctively as the object fell to the ground, displaced by her touch.

Esme took a deep breath and directed the lamp to the spot where the bushy article had landed. The wan glow of the lamp disclosed a shaggy mound lying motionless at her feet. Esme tentatively extended the pointed toe of her boot to the object and nudged it gently. There was no reaction to the contact made by her probing foot, so she crouched down and decisively grabbed hold of the mysterious item. She stifled a laugh of relief as she realised she was holding a gentleman's hairpiece. Esme was puzzled. Padd's well-oiled mane was clearly his own, so to whom did this wig belong?

Esme was startled from her thoughts. She had heard what sounded like someone moving on the landing a few doors down. Judging by the creak of the floorboards – described as 'original features' as opposed to 'rotting', in the latest fake review Igor had written for inclusion in the Transylvanian tourist board advertising literature – they were heading in her direction. Esme cursed under her breath. She was trapped. Thinking fast, she gathered up the wig and hurled it back onto the top shelf of the wardrobe then swiftly moved beside the bed and placed the lamp back on the cabinet, blowing the flame into oblivion. She crossed back across the now dark room and climbed into the wardrobe, pulling the doors almost closed, leaving a narrow gap through which she could see the bed area, or would have been able to if there had been any light left in the room to see by.

Esme held her breath as she heard the sound of the door being unlocked. Soft footsteps slapped across the floorboards and Esme realised the perpetrator must be barefoot. She had only been able to detect the approach of the unknown party along the landing due to her ability to recognise the squeak of each individual floorboard of the inn and pinpoint its exact position in the Cadaver's Arms.

The mysterious arrival uttered a grunt as it scrabbled for the lamp on the bedside cabinet. Esme heard a drawer being pulled open and the sound of rummaging within, followed by the harsh strike of a match. Her eyes widened in disbelief as the lamplight illuminated the area by the bed. The match appeared to be hovering in mid-air. There was no one holding it. Esme watched in amazement as the match swiftly shook from side to side, the flame extinguishing, and was then flicked away by an unseen hand. The bottle of brandy was borne aloft by the same force that had struck and put out the match. The bottle seemingly tipped itself up at a steep angle, the dark liquor within running down the inside of the bottleneck and vanishing into thin air once it reached the opening, accompanied by a loud gulping sound.

'Threw a bloody glass at me!' grumbled a deep voice from nowhere. 'Me, the greatest scientist of this generation!' The bottle tipped and poured again. 'It's bloody freezing in here.'

Esme observed in disbelief as a robe levitated from the bed. The sleeves raised one at a time as if unseen arms were threading themselves through. Then the sash at the front of the robe rose in the air and seemed to tie itself at the opening of the garment, holding it in place. The robe sat there, fully filled out by the shape of a man. An invisible man.

Esme shrank back into the wardrobe, scarcely daring to breathe. Tense minutes seemed to crawl by tortuously slowly as she waited, dreading discovery by the creature in the room. Eventually, after what seemed an eternity, she watched the robe lean back onto the bed, the mattress depressing as it did so to create a human-shaped indentation on its surface. She did not move until the sound of a rasping snore began to fill the bedroom. She carefully extricated herself from the wardrobe and slipped silently out of the room and onto the landing without disturbing the slumbering, impossible, being within.

*

Esme had returned to the bar and was in the process of downing a nerve-calming shot of her father's special house vodka, when Igor, Padd, Price, Helsing and Hopkins finally returned. Under normal circumstances, the inn would have been closed to the public at this hour, but Esme had remained open as she knew the party would require a stiff drink after their supernatural encounter. If they managed to survive it, that is, she thought darkly, deep concern over Igor's safety tormenting her. Whoever, or whatever, was asleep in Padd's room had clearly returned unscathed so she could not help but fear the worst.

A huge feeling of relief swept over her as the inn door swung open and Igor and the others, all apparently still in one piece, entered the building. Her happiness at seeing Igor was safe was so great it even assuaged the sense of disappointment she felt at seeing Helsing and Hopkins were also unharmed.

'A drink for the hero!' proclaimed Helsing boisterously clapping Padd on the back. Esme poured a flagon of ale for each of the five men.

Igor smiled warmly at her and it was all she could do to restrain herself from rushing to the other side of the bar and hugging him passionately. She was perturbed to note the angry-looking bruise flowering on his chin.

'What happened?' she asked gently.

'What happened?' interrupted Helsing. He drained his drink and wiped the back of his gauntleted hand across his mouth. 'We defeated a demon! A violent, murderous demon!

IGOR AND THE TWISTED TALES OF CASTLEMAINE

Padd here commanded it begone in the manner of a true holy warrior.'

'I helped a bit,' mumbled Price sulkily.

Helsing downed another ale. 'A battle against darkness!' he rambled drunkenly. 'Fought and won in Castlemaine!' He threw his arm around Padd's shoulder who shifted uncomfortably at his sweaty embrace.

'Well, the battle is over, but the war against evil continues,' said Padd, attempting to push Helsing's arm away from his person. 'I must have sleep to refresh myself and gather my energies for the next encounter. Evil can strike at any time...'

'You'll need your energy to count your money!' slurred Helsing, as he started on another drink. 'Why, you'll be as rich as the Burgermeister himself at this rate!'

Padd looked thoughtful. 'Hmm, yes, the Burgermeister,' he nodded. 'Gentlemen, I must bid you goodnight. Sapping the demon of its power has sapped me of mine.'

'No, no!' implored Helsing. 'Stay and celebrate. We have claimed a famous victory over the forces of darkness together.' He swayed unsteadily on his feet. Hopkins moved to catch him, but he was too slow and Helsing stumbled awkwardly into Padd, inadvertently emptying the contents of his tankard onto the exorcist's hand-tailored jacket.

'You cretin!' snapped Padd. 'This jacket cost a fortune.'

Helsing waved at Esme to provide another drink. 'Come friend, Padd,' he pleaded. 'We are bothers in arms, are we not?'

'Brothers in arms?' retorted Padd angrily. 'It was I who dealt with this devil. You tried to flee like a quivering coward.'

'C... coward?!' blustered Helsing, rapidly trying to sober

up and acutely aware of the others staring at him. 'I... I am the witchfinder!'

Padd laughed cruelly. 'Witchfinder? You couldn't find a witch if your life depended on it! I doubt you could find your own backside with both hands!'

Helsing flushed a shade of deep crimson as hot needles of embarrassment lanced through him. Hopkins briefly considered giving Padd a taste of his cudgel in a show of support for his superior, but decided he was enjoying the situation far too much to interfere.

A moment of tense silence followed. Padd and Helsing glared furiously at each other whilst their companions exchanged uncomfortable glances amongst themselves. Finally, Padd announced, 'My jacket needs changing,' and, turning sharply on his heels, headed for the stairs, his coin-purse clutched tightly to his chest.

Helsing, pausing long enough for Padd to travel out of earshot, slammed his right fist into his left palm. 'Lucky for him he backed down. I had a mind to thrash him where he stood!'

Igor felt his eyes roll skywards at this ridiculous show of bravado. He also experienced a profound sense of disappointment that the stand-off between Padd and Helsing had not resulted in at least one of the two participants receiving a hefty blow to the face. He rubbed his own facial contusion ruefully.

Helsing gestured to Hopkins and the two officials made their exit. Helsing nodded to Father Price as they left but made no acknowledgement of Igor. The priest followed shortly after, although not without bidding Igor and Esme goodnight and thanking the former for his companionship on the night's adventures.

Esme poured Igor a frothy tankard of Skankie's Festering Goat, another acquisition from her father's trip to England. Having listened attentively to Igor's account of the visit to the Wildflower mansion, in hushed tones Esme appraised him of her own exploits that night including her chilling encounter with the unseen visitor slumbering in Padd's rented room.

'Griffin!' exclaimed Igor. 'I should have realised as much but I thought he was dead.'

'Well, that never stopped anyone around here did it?' responded Esme. 'Who, or what, is Griffin?'

Igor took another swig of his ale. 'Professor Claude Westin Vincent Griffin. I've never actually met him, but I've heard stories. He's an eccentric chemist who discovered the means to actually turn himself invisible. Goodness knows why, I suppose he must have been bored!' He took another deep swallow of his beer.

'Anyway, he clearly wasn't as clever as he thought he was as he didn't think to create a cure before injecting himself with his invisibility serum. He ended up stuck like that! Had to bandage up his invisible face and hide his missing eyes and hair so that he could travel in public. It was either that or walk around in his birthday suit. Not much fun in the winter.'

Esme shook her head in disbelief. 'First Jekyll, now this Griffin. Why are all these scientists such lunatics?'

Igor shrugged and sighed. 'The more brilliant they are, the crazier they are. Frankenstein was the same. I expect breathing in all those chemicals in confined spaces doesn't help matters.' He fished inside one of the inn's snack jars, extracted a gelatinous lump of cooked meat, and held it to the light. Once he had satisfied himself it contained no hair, eyes, or visible parasites, he popped it into his mouth and continued to talk between chews. 'It was actually Edward who told me about Griffin,' he continued. 'Apparently, Jekyll had studied the case and, according to the story, Griffin went increasingly bonkers. He came up with some hare-brained notion he was going to rule the world with an army of invisible soldiers! I'm not quite sure how that was going to work, they wouldn't even have been able to see each other to march in the same direction.'

Esme refreshed Igor's tankard and helped herself to another vodka. 'Obviously, he didn't carry out his plan.'

Igor shook his head. 'Edward claimed Griffin eventually went full-on homicidal in some village outside of London. The locals didn't take too kindly to his behaviour and expressed their displeasure by beating him to death. Supposedly, the serum also increased his strength, so I assume he survived, recovered, and fled the country. Now he's upstairs!'

Esme tipped back the last of her vodka. 'So that explains the sudden rash of hauntings. Obviously, he's working with Padd.' A note of admiration crept into her voice. 'It's actually a decent scam. Griffin scares the pants off them, ironically while his pants are off, then Padd "exorcises" him for a fat fee.'

Igor nodded. 'It sounds good, but Griffin is a psychopath. As soon as he's collected enough gold, what's to stop him disposing of Padd?' he asked, drawing a finger across his throat to illustrate his point.

'What's to stop him disposing of any of us?' replied Esme solemnly. She lifted a large, serrated kitchen knife from the counter. 'Perhaps we should take matters into our own hands while we have the chance?'

Igor considered for a moment. 'No, too much of a risk,' he eventually answered. 'Padd is up there as well. We'd have to deal with him too and if Griffin wakes up while we're...' he mimed a stabbing action, '...then we've had it. We'd literally never see him coming.'

Esme plunged the knife downwards in frustration. The tip of the blade thudded into the wooden surface of the counter and stuck there, vibrating from the force of the impact.

'You're right,' she said. 'So, what do we do?'

Igor pondered briefly before replying. 'Padd's *customers* have all been rich, otherwise there would be no point in targeting them. We need to keep our ears open. Now that he's helped one of the most pre-eminent women in Castlemaine, word will spread amongst the village elite who will no doubt soon experience "hauntings" of their own. We need to find out who the next victim is going to be and I'm fairly sure I already know the answer to that question.'

'I thought Padd was the psychic around here,' teased Esme.

Igor grinned. 'Did you see how Padd's eyes lit up when Helsing mentioned the Burgermeister?' he asked. 'He has to be the prime candidate for the next scam.'

'So, what do *we* do?' repeated Esme.

As much as I hate to say this,' began Igor, then pausing for an instant as if suddenly experiencing a foul taste in his mouth, worse even than the spongy bar snack currently agitating his gag reflex, 'warn Helsing.'

'Warn Helsing?' spat Esme, her face contorting into the

type of hate-filled expression one might reserve for a flesh-eating virus.

'I know, I know,' soothed Igor, his hands raised in mock surrender, 'but better he deals with a naked invisible maniac than we do!'

*

Two days later, Randolph Epstein Van Kronenbourg III, Burgermeister of Castlemaine and the surrounding provinces, contentedly patted his boulder-shaped stomach. As he pushed away his empty breakfast plate, having devoured the last of his usual seven courses, he reflected happily on his current circumstances.

Here he sat, the most senior official in the land, reclining comfortably in the opulent surroundings of his luxurious chateau and rich beyond the wildest dreams of the Castlemaine peasants who dwelt far from his walls thanks to a combination of hard work, driving ambition, and an utter lack of any moralistic hindrance when it came to partaking in a spot of bribery and corruption.

Having completed his meal, he gestured to his manservant, Boris, to fetch him his smoking tackle. Boris duly presented the Burgermeister with his favourite pipe and silk tobacco pouch as was their morning ritual. The Burgermeister packed the funnel of his Calabash with a generous helping of the finest Castlemaine shag, struck a lucifer and began to carefully char the top of the tobacco. A series of steady puffs soon brought his post-breakfast pipe into pungent life.

A sudden bout of fierce coughing seized Kronenbourg and, as he hawked loudly and lobbed an unattractive lump of brown phlegm into a waiting china bowl positioned in readiness on the breakfast table, he congratulated himself on having excellent lungs. The way his system could handle an influx of smoke so efficiently illustrated just how strong his constitution was. His mighty stomach and the constant flush of healthy scarlet that coloured his facial features bore testament to his claim that he was the fittest Burgermeister in the history of Castlemaine.

Wheezing healthily, he hauled himself from his chair and waddled his way to the castle ballroom, his pipe produced a steady flow of smoke as he went giving him the aspect of a human steam engine as he trundled through his home.

The Burgermeister paused at the entrance to the ballroom. The ornately carved double doors yawned open to reveal the interior of the vast chamber, which was alive with activity. A team of workmen were busying themselves within, applying the contents of large containers of paint to the walls with horsehair brushes whilst balancing atop a series of wooden ladders and platforms.

At the heart of the ballroom stood the radiant vision that was Inga, the Burgermeister's third, and youngest (so far), wife who was currently directing operations within. Kronenbourg smiled warmly at the sight of her beauty and his heart fluttered with a feeling he was certain was far more than his usual indigestion. Tall as an Amazon, with a toned dancer's figure and the face of a classical goddess, he really had hit the jackpot with this particular wife, he thought smugly to himself. Their path to happiness had not been an entirely smooth one, however. The two had met whilst the Burgermeister was still married to his second wife, Freda, an old maid of thirty-two. Freda, ever suspicious of her husband's philandering nature, had discovered their dalliance and, in an entirely unreasonable fit of temper, had attempted to divorce him with an eye on half of his vast fortune. The Burgermeister shook his head at the memory. If it had not been for her mysterious coach accident, he would be half the man he was today.

But, he decided, this was not a day for unhappy recollections. Next week would see his and Inga's first wedding anniversary. His young wife had insisted on redecorating the ballroom ready for a celebratory party to be attended by the upper strata of Castlemaine society and he wished no dark shadows from the past to spoil her happiness. He had willingly agreed to the soiree as the date of their anniversary coincided with the annual tax increase he would soon be imposing on the Castlemaine residents, so the occasion would be something of a double celebration.

Yes, he thought, life was good.

Inga moved through the ballroom in the same manner she moved through life, with complete determination. As she strode, the diminutive figure of Alonso Ravielli, Castlemaine's foremost, or rather only, events planner, struggled to keep pace with her. As Inga reeled out her litany of requirements for next week's anniversary party to Alonso, who frantically attempted to scrawl down the ever-increasing series of decorations, musicians, and exotic finger foods as they went, she regularly stopped to berate any of the painters who appeared to be slacking on the job. Inga was a woman who knew exactly what she wanted in life, from a place at the top table of Castlemaine society to the origami swans and gilt-edged place name settings on that very table. What she wanted at this particular moment was to ensure the ballroom would look perfect for the forthcoming anniversary dance. This was to be the most lavish, exclusive social event Castlemaine had seen since, well, her wedding.

She glanced over at her husband who, she noted, was staring at her with his usual combination of lust and self-satisfaction. She sighed. She had achieved her objective to depose her rival, Freda, as well as see off the various other mistresses the Burgermeister had accumulated, and marry the richest, most powerful man in Castlemaine and its neighbouring territories. But, she wondered, how long could she realistically cope with being the trophy wife of this bloated sack of blubber? Not only did she constantly have to assume the guise of a brainless bimbo so as to not intellectually intimidate him, but there were also the wifely duties he demanded. She knew her current position depended on her assuming lots of other ones, but surely, she would not have to endure many years of this career marriage judging by the perilous appearance of her husband's physical condition. She consoled herself with the thought that, by the time his corpulent carcass had finally caved in under the effects of the years of excess he had subjected himself to, she would have cemented her place amongst the Castlemaine elite and be a very rich young widow with her whole life ahead of her.

Inga turned from the displeasing sight of her husband and redirected her attention to Alonso. 'Now, did you get the silk collars for the ceremonial swans written down?' she demanded.

Alonso, normally an excitable, highly talkative individual, said nothing. He merely stared in wide-eyed horror.

Inga eyed him questioningly. Surely, Alonso was not going to argue with this crucial party detail? She quickly realised that the event planner's horrified expression was not caused by the latest of her exigencies, but rather he was staring beyond her. Inga followed Alonso's gaze, anxious to discover the cause of his distraction. She felt her mouth gape open at the sight of a paintbrush hovering in the air behind her. She gave a small cry and dodged from its path as the brush seemed to thrust itself in her direction. Alonso took the full force of the paint-laden bristles directly in his face and fell to the floor in a swoon, his complexion now a tasteful shade of china blue.

'Ghost!' shouted one of the painters and he and his fellows began to stampede in terror from the ballroom. Kronenbourg, scarcely believing the evidence of his own eyes, strode furiously into the ballroom.

'Get back to work!' he bellowed, only to be roundly ignored, and narrowly avoiding being trampled by the terrified workers as they fled. The Burgermeister crossed the room to his wife's side. 'Are you all right, my dear?'

'All right?' shrieked Inga. 'My event planner has just been attacked by a… a… ghost!' she exclaimed in disbelief.

The Burgermeister cleared his throat as if addressing a crowd and loudly exclaimed to the empty room, 'Nonsense! There are no such things as ghosts! I mean, werewolves and vampires, obviously, but ghosts? That's just ridiculous!'

Before he could add any further statements to this speech, the front of the Burgermeister's shirt was grasped by a powerful, invisible hand and he felt himself being hauled forcibly upwards onto his tiptoes. His head snapped violently first to his left, then to his right side, as the unseen hand slapped him back and forth across the face before dumping him in a heap of gasping flesh onto the ballroom floor. An eerie peal of guttural laughter echoed around the ballroom, thanks in no small part to the wonderful acoustics the room offered. The Burgermeister lay huddled on the floor, his cheeks stinging and his heart thumping at a rapidly accelerated rate. Inga stood, shocked into immobility, tears of anger and fear prickling in her eyes. Silence settled over the room.

Inga was the first to pull herself together. She had no doubt they had been assaulted by a ghost. She had no idea why that would be the case, only that it had happened. However, Inga had dealt with many rivals in her relatively short life in order to attain her current status and she was not about to allow the small matter of this particular rival being dead to stand in her way on this occasion.

'Randy!' she said in her best concerned voice. 'My poor husband. Are you all right?'

Kronenbourg opened his eyes and glanced about wildly. 'Has it gone?' he asked nervously.

'I think so, Randy,' replied Inga. 'But, now the chateau is haunted, we'll have to do something.'

'Do? Do what?' implored the Burgermeister.

'That man Baroness Wildflower raved about yesterday, Cornelius Padd. He's the answer!' replied Inga.

'He was quite expensive,' said the Burgermeister cautiously.

Inga tried not to let her impatience show. She ran a slender finger down his cheek and allowed it to linger on his lips. She gazed into his eyes and pressed herself against his bulk.

'But Randy, I would be so sad if we can't have our anniversary party.'

The Burgermeister gently kissed, then squeezed, her hand. 'Then my dear, I shall send for Padd.'

*

That night in the Cadaver's Arms, Igor and Esme received the news they had been waiting for. Cornelius Padd strutted into the inn clothed in a new frockcoat and cape combination acquired from Castlemaine's finest tailor, Bruno Morse.

'Nice outfit,' Esme had commented, not wishing to antagonise Padd whilst his invisible accomplice was still at large. 'Must have cost a fair penny?'

'Oh, this little thing?' Padd preened. 'Well, yes, it wasn't cheap I must admit. Still, I have an engagement tomorrow evening with the Burgermeister himself, so funds are not an issue.'

'Oh yes?' replied Esme, making eye contact with Igor, who sat at the bar nursing a murky tankard of Father Shawshank's Crotch Gristle.

'Yes indeed,' crowed Padd. 'It seems the Burgermeister has also been targeted by a restless spirit and has sent for me to exorcise the troublesome spook from his chateau.'

Igor set his tankard down upon the bar and, nodding subtly to Eric, exited the inn. Once Padd left to make his way back to his room, Eric too headed out of the Cadaver's Arms. He walked to the rear of the inn where his tethered horse and coach were waiting in the yard, as was Igor, who had positioned himself on one of the passenger seats inside.

'Take me to Helsing, Eric,' whispered Igor.

*

The following evening, Padd stood staring thoughtfully out of his bedroom window at the dreary Castlemaine streets below.

'This is the big one, Griffin,' he said to a seemingly empty room. 'The Burgermeister will pay anything to exorcise his chateau and save his anniversary party.'

'Especially if I rough him up a bit more,' came the cruel tones of the Invisible Man beside him.

'What then?' asked Padd, not without a note of trepidation in his voice. 'Do we move on?'

'Move on?!' exclaimed Griffin. 'Certainly not!'

'But why?' asked Padd. 'We never stay anywhere this long.'

Padd felt an invisible hand clamp on his shoulder. Even after all these months, any physical contact from his unseen associate sent a chill coursing through his blood. There were times when Padd cursed the day he had first encountered Griffin.

The two had met some eighteen months earlier. Unbeknownst to Padd, the Invisible Man had been in the process of robbing a house where the exorcist/medium was performing a fake seance, as was his then stock-in-trade.

Whilst silently observing Padd's con act, Griffin had spotted an opportunity. He had abandoned his robbery attempt and followed Padd out of the house before making contact with him in the gaslit street outside, nearly causing Padd to have a heart attack as he introduced himself. Once the terrified Padd had realised he had not somehow caused a real spirit to manifest itself during his routine, he had begun to listen to, and warm to, Griffin's proposed money-making scheme. It seemed so simple: Griffin would terrify the life out of rich people and Padd would claim to banish the supposed ghosts and demons for a sizeable purse. They would split the takings. Griffin would fund his work on a cure that would allow him to turn invisible and visible at will. Padd would establish the life of luxury he had always desired.

Gradually, however, the unpleasant reality of having an unseen partner had become painfully apparent. Not only could he never be certain Griffin was not standing somewhere near him, spying on his every move, but the Invisible Man's psychotic side had grown to terrify him. It had become apparent after a couple of beatings at Griffin's invisible hands that this was no partnership, and Padd was merely a subordinate. How he wished he could exorcise his unseen associate the way he pretended to banish the spirits he portrayed.

'Once we have fleeced the Burgermeister, we can work through the rest of the monied guests at his anniversary ball,' came Griffin's sinister voice, rasping uncomfortably close to Padd's ear, causing the exorcist to recoil. 'Besides, I like it here. This inn could be a good base. Why, you could even become the new landlord, Padd, once I've disposed of that bungling oaf of an innkeeper and his slutty daughter. Now, go and get the horse, I'm not walking barefoot all the way to that blasted chateau.'

Padd swallowed hard and did as his unseen master bade him.

*

Boris, the Burgermeister's manservant, met Padd at the main entrance to the chateau, nestled amongst the picturesque, heavily wooded hills that surrounded Castlemaine. Padd, and the invisible Griffin, who had been riding pillion, dismounted and a stableman led the horse away to be fed and watered. Boris led Padd, and unwittingly Griffin, through the sweeping hallway of the chateau to the doors of the ballroom where they were greeted by Randolph.

'Thank you for coming, Master Padd,' he said warmly, extending his hand in greeting. 'I thought it best you conduct the exorcism in the ballroom as that is where we experienced the haunting.'

'Quite so,' nodded Padd as they entered the vast room within. Padd glanced about the ballroom. The heavy velvet curtains were drawn closed and the room was dimly lit. Ghostly shapes of assorted items of furniture draped in dustsheets adorned the room and the skeletal forms of wooden painting rigs stood abandoned along the walls. Padd nodded towards the containers of paint scattered about the room. 'A work in progress,' he announced to no one in particular.

Kronenbourg replied, 'Yes, indeed. We just can't get the workmen to finish the job. Not while they believe the ballroom to be haunted,' he explained.

Padd smiled knowingly. 'I can indeed feel a supernatural presence in this room, Burgermeister. But never fear for I, Cornelius Padd, will remove it… for a fee… forever!'

Padd strode purposefully to the centre of the ballroom and extended his arms. He closed his eyes, theatrically tipped back his head and drew a series of deep breaths before announcing in a booming voice, 'Spirit, I feel your presence. Reveal yourself!'

Griffin, who had been lurking unseen at the far end of the ballroom, having run past Padd and the Burgermeister once the double doors of the ballroom had been opened, grabbed one of the discarded paintbrushes and slowly raised it. He waved it in what he judged to be a suitably spooky manner and slowly advanced towards his accomplice.

'Now!' shouted Kronenbourg.

The room exploded into motion.

Griffin, still clutching the paintbrush, stared in disbelief as the dustsheets around the room were thrown back and a large group of the Burgermeister's servants emerged from their hiding places beneath and formed a living circle. They began to advance on his position. The velvet curtains, too, were pulled aside and Helsing and Inga, who had insisted on being present, stepped into sight.

Cornelius Padd whirled around in alarm only to witness the large double doors to the ballroom being pushed closed by Hopkins and Igor who had been hiding each side of the entrance. Hopkins swiftly turned the huge iron key in the lock, sealing them in. He pocketed the key in his tunic, withdrew his favourite cudgel and raised it menacingly as he took up his position as sentry to the ballroom's only exit route.

Igor stared at the centre of the room where the Invisible Man still held the paintbrush, seemingly shocked into a state of inaction. Igor knew this situation would not last and was quickly proved correct as Griffin suddenly hurled the brush at one of the oncoming men. The circle of servants was broken as one of their number was bent double by an invisible fist to his stomach. Several of his fellows leapt in the general direction of their stricken comrade, only to grasp at thin air.

One of the windowpanes began to shake violently as Griffin attempted to wrench open the locked window and effect his escape. Igor dashed to where one of the large abandoned paint containers stood. He wrenched off the lid, snatched up the container in both hands and ran towards the next window Griffin was attempting to open. With all the might he could muster, Igor swung the paint container, like someone hurling water onto a fire, sending a wave of brightly coloured blue paint crashing over the Invisible Man. Griffin howled in rage as the back of his head, upper body and a pair of distinctly pimply bare buttocks were revealed thanks to the thick paint oozing down his person.

'More paint!' shouted Igor at the group of servants. The men reacted swiftly, grabbing the containers, and splashing their contents over the cornered Griffin. Soon, his entire outline was cast in blue paint. Cursing, Griffin rubbed furiously at his stinging eyes as the servants moved closer.

'Padd! Padd, you fool, help me!' screamed Griffin.

Padd, gripped by blind panic, bolted towards the ballroom doors. His progress was violently interrupted by the impact of Hopkins' cudgel swiping across his forehead. He crashed onto his back, a galaxy of bright stars bursting in front of his eyes.

Griffin roared in anger and launched himself at Igor. Igor collapsed under the weight of Griffin's assault and, as they both thudded to the floor, he felt powerful fingers wrap around his throat as the paint-splashed maniac straddled his chest. He gripped Griffin's wrists and attempted to prise himself from the now quite visible man's murderous grasp. It was no use. Griffin's homicidal strength was too great for Igor and he began to feel himself slipping into blackness.

'I'll kill you! I'll kill you all!' screamed Griffin as he continued to choke Igor. His partially revealed face, now a combination of ghoulish blue mask and missing facial features, appeared far more terrifying than any of his attempts to play the role of malicious spectre had been, as it bore down on him.

Just as Igor felt the life beginning to ebb from him, he heard a sudden whooshing sound followed by a sickening thud. Griffin instantly released his grip and slumped over him.

'No one ruins my party!' came a shrill female cry. With a grunt of effort, Igor painfully rolled the unconscious figure of Griffin from him and climbed to his feet, gingerly rubbing his bruised windpipe. Inga stood triumphantly before him. She still clasped the punch ladle she had used to send Griffin into oblivion. Igor noted the heavy ladle had been bent backwards at a forty-five-degree angle, such had been the force of the impact on Griffin's skull. Igor looked down at the lifeless form of the Invisible Man. A crimson flow of blood seeped from his head and pooled onto the ballroom floor where it mixed freely with the spilled blue paint. Inga wondered why she had never previously considered a shade of purple for the walls.

Across the ballroom, where he too lay stunned, Cornelius Padd was vaguely aware of a fuzzy black-clad shape entering his field of vision as it leaned over his prostrate form. Through a hazy curtain of pain, Padd groaned as the shape shimmered into clear relief and solidified into the sneering face of Helsing.

'Well, well,' came the witchfinder's mocking voice. 'It appears you have come undone while attempting to flee like a, what was it now?' he asked. 'Yes, that's it,' he continued. 'A quivering coward!'

Even Hopkins smiled at that one as he bound Padd's hands behind his back.

*

Later, shortly after the chime of the clock had ushered in the witching hour, Igor was back on his familiar stool in the Cadaver's Arms easing his injured throat with a soothing tankard of Squire Belch's Mange. They could all breathe a collective sigh of relief now that Griffin and Padd were safely locked up. The Burgermeister and Inga could have their anniversary ball in safety and, more importantly, at Inga's insistence, the Burgermeister had grumblingly agreed to provide Igor with a modest purse of gold coins for his plan to capture the Invisible Man and his cohort.

Even Helsing had seemed happy. He had taken a little convincing when Igor had first warned him of Griffin and the threat he posed. However, Helsing, slow-witted as he was, and despite his usual habit of immediately ascribing a supernatural cause to every mystery, could see Igor's story made far more sense than a sudden rash of hauntings, at least one that only affected the rich inhabitants of the village, occurring in Castlemaine. The opportunity to take revenge on Padd after he had insulted him so publicly was also far too much of an incentive for him to refuse and so the trap had been planned and set with the collusion of the Burgermeister and his staff.

Once Igor had learned that Griffin's initial attack had taken place in the partially decorated ballroom, he had suggested to Helsing and Kronenbourg this was the ideal place to ensnare the Invisible Man. The room could be locked and sealed completely, and there was space for a large number of servants to secrete themselves in preparation for tackling Griffin en masse. Igor had also pointed out the ballroom's proliferation of paint-filled containers offered them the means with which to reveal the presence of their unseen foe.

Helsing had, however, maintained his natural suspicion of Igor and had insisted he also attend the arrest in order to ensure he could keep an eye on him for any duplicitous behaviour. Now it was all over, Igor hoped the successful conclusion to this evening's adventure might buy him a little good grace from the witchfinder and perhaps keep him away from his and Esme's affairs for a while. Whilst it was true the pair were not currently involved in any nefarious activity of note, Igor despised Helsing's constant lurking presence in their lives. He grimaced as another mouthful of Mange travelled down his sore throat and shook his head. Painful though drinking the ale was, he still found it easier to swallow than the idea that Helsing might let up on him.

Igor's train of thought was interrupted as a large object was thumped down on the bar in front of him by a grinning Esme. An object that issued a familiar and welcome clinking sound.

Igor returned Esme's smile. 'You found it then?'

'Under the floorboards,' replied Esme. 'As you said, Griffin really wasn't the genius he thought he was!' She unbuckled the large saddlebag she had placed on the bar and pulled it open. She and Igor leaned over from their respective sides of the bar and peered into the bag. They were greeted by a shining mound of gold coins. 'I nearly put my shoulder out carrying it down here,' laughed Esme.

'Griffin and Padd's haul,' breathed Igor. 'It's no use to either of them now.'

'Never mind,' said Esme. 'We'll give it a good home.'

The two of them stared at the gold for a moment, then their gaze turned to each other, their eyes locking over the open saddlebag. A moment, full of unspoken meaning, passed between them. They leaned further over the bag, towards each other. Igor closed his eyes and pursed his lips.

'It's a pea-souper out there and no mistake,' announced Old Clam as he struggled into the bar dragging a barrel of ale he had retrieved from the yard. Igor and Esme sprang apart as the moment was broken. Esme swiftly buckled the saddlebag.

'I've just thought of something,' she said. 'If Griffin was naked, where did he keep the key to the room? I heard him unlock the door while I was hiding.'

Igor frowned. 'Put it this way, I've got an idea as to why he was so bad-tempered most of the time.'

*

Elsewhere, in the Subotsky Asylum for the criminally insane, far from the village of Castlemaine, a bandaged figure sat sullenly on the damp straw that lined the cold floor of his dingy cell. One ankle, which like the rest of the prisoner's body had been hastily wrapped by the asylum guards, was manacled firmly to a large iron ring solidly embedded in the stone floor. The figure muttered to himself.

'They'll be sorry, all of them. Padd, Igor, Helsing, the whole blasted village of Castlemaine,' he ranted. His voice began to build in volume. 'No one can hold me. No one can hold Griffin, the Invisible Man!' He burst into a peal of insane laughter that would have chilled the soul of anyone who could have heard him. But no one did. His cell was a subterranean dungeon reserved for only the most dangerous of inmates. Griffin's fate was to be that he remain both unseen, and unheard, forever.

BODY PART V
THE GRAVEYARD SHIFT

Igor and Esme lay together in a warm, sunlit glade in the forest. Above them, the dark coniferous trees rose high up the sides of the mountains to be lost in the snow-covered peaks above. A soft, bubbling stream gurgled its leisurely way past them as flies flitted and danced in the air above the waters. The first of the early evening bats flip-flapped silently overhead, gathering up the oblivious bugs.

'I love this spot, it's one of my favourites.' Esmerelda was gently stroking Igor's face with her long, delicate fingers.

'Do you really?' replied Igor lazily. 'I was going to give it a squeeze but if you like it so much I might let it fester a bit longer.'

Esmerelda giggled easily, her auburn hair falling prettily across her face, with just a sparkle from her keen, green eyes glinting within.

'I suppose we should be thinking of heading back,' she sighed. 'Although I could happily stay here with you forever.'

Esme's eyes locked onto Igor's and for a breathless moment, the world stopped.

'Esme,' said Igor tentatively. 'There's something I want to ask you.' He paused, trying to formulate his next words carefully.

'Yes, my dear Igor?' she smiled sweetly, guessing, and hoping she knew what he was going to say next.

He fumbled clumsily for the right words. 'Esme,' he began again, but a noise from the nearby greenery startled them.

'Wait, what was that?' Esme sat up suddenly and peered into the trees. 'Did you hear it?'

'Yes, what was it?' replied Igor, blinking through the hazy sunlight, and straining to hear anything that wasn't part of the ordinary woodland noises.

'It sounded like someone...' Esme's voice trailed off and there was a long silence as they sat listening and scanning the treeline.

The sound of cracking twigs and a rustling from the undergrowth drew them both to their feet. Igor grabbed a large stick and Esme drew the short blade of steel that she kept in her sleeve for special occasions such as this. They stood poised, ready to defend themselves from whoever or whatever was approaching.

Suddenly, a figure appeared from the treeline, heading uncertainly towards the river. It was staggering slightly and seemed not to be paying any attention to them at all, but was focused on something away to their left.

'That's old Mister Fudgegusset,' said Igor, a strong tone of surprise in his voice.

Esme squinted through the sunshine. 'Is it?' She couldn't

quite see the man's face, partly due to the dappled light, but mainly because large bits of his skull were flopped forward covering most of the important features.

'I do believe it is,' replied Igor, somewhat taken aback. 'I'm somewhat taken aback however by the fact that I distinctly remember burying him not two weeks ago.'

'Oh, that Mister Fudgegusset,' said Esme in surprise. 'That is odd.'

'Yes,' pondered Igor. 'He was killed when that gargoyle fell off the church and landed on top of him. What a mess that was. Funny to see him wandering about now though.'

'I wonder what he's doing out here,' mused Esmerelda.

'Let's find out, shall we? Oi, Fudgegusset,' Igor bellowed across the clearing at the dead man.

The corpse stopped, turned its head slightly then began staggering towards the river again.

'Over here!' shouted Igor.

Again, the late Mister Fudgegusset paused, this time altering his direction slightly, apparently adjusting his movement towards the sound of Igor's voice.

'Yoohoo, that's it,' continued Igor encouragingly. 'Left a bit. Yes, that's right. No, not right, I said *that's* right. No, left a bit. LEFT! LEEEFFFTTT!!! Oh, bugger it.' Igor strode across to where the body of Fudgegusset was now stuck on a large rock, and in danger of slipping into the turbulent waters.

Igor grabbed Fudgegusset's arm to help steady him as he slid off the boulder. The shattered remains of the dead man's skull hung in ribbons, with bits of bone and flesh dangling over his scrawny, narrow shoulders. Only the lower part of his face remained intact. One eye was completely gone, the other dangled below his chin by its thin, sinewy optic nerve. The eyeball was blue and bruised, but it swung and twisted this way and that, apparently straining to see who it was that had grabbed his arm.

Esme moved across and stood beside Igor. 'I will say it again for clarity. That is odd.'

'Hmmm…' pondered Igor with a worried look suddenly etched on his face. 'I do hope Missus Fudgegusset isn't going to ask for a refund.'

The corpse seemed to be listening to them and started to flap his mouth as if it wanted to say something.

'What's that Mister Fudgegusset?' shouted Igor, noticing how both of his ears were dangling at armpit level.

'Grnmerrrww mmwwe gneerrfm,' replied Fudgegusset rather unhelpfully.

'No, not getting that,' cried Igor towards the gently swinging earlobes.

'Gerrinng mrrss gnrrsng.'

Several days in a dark box underground had clearly done nothing for Fudgegusset's communication skills. Neither had the half ton of grotesquely carved sandstone which had embedded itself into his cranium beforehand.

Igor and Esme were at a loss what to do with their undead interloper.

'I suppose we could take him back to the village and see if Missus Fudgegusset wants him back.' Igor sighed heavily, resigning himself to the probability of making a sizeable reimbursement to the grieving widow.

Mister Fudgegusset, however, seemed to have other ideas. Although where he was having them wasn't quite so obvious, since much of his brain matter was smeared down his jacket and shirt front.

At the mention of Missus Fudgegusset, he wrenched his arm free from Igor's grip, turned, lost his footing, and stumbled into the rapidly bubbling waters of the stream.

The inner ear is the centre of balance in humans, and unfortunately Fudgegusset's were at present bobbing around on fleshy strips somewhere close to nipple height, so he found standing on the slick stones in the churning waters something of a challenge.

The foaming river quickly swept his feet from under him, and with a final, 'Gwmeerrgnul,' he floated downstream and was quickly lost among the weeds as he was swept around a bend and deeper into the forest.

The pair stood, staring mutely as the body of Fudgegusset disappeared out of sight.

Esme shrugged. 'Oh well, best get back,' and she sang cheerily to herself as she began gathering up their picnic things.

Igor was in a world of his own, wondering how on earth one of his burials could be up and walking about again, just two weeks after being firmly planted beneath six feet of good Transylvanian topsoil. Not to mention the added inconvenience of having had a sizeable piece of ecclesiastical architecture pass through a vital part of his anatomy.

Something was not sitting right in Igor's mind. Fortunately, in his case, it wasn't a half ton piece of medieval masonry. The episode had raised troubling old feelings.

It wasn't just the decaying Mister Fudgegusset that Igor wished would stay buried.

*

Dusky darkness had fallen by the time Igor and Esme found themselves back in Castlemaine. They wound their way through the maze of small streets towards the Cadaver's Arms.

As they approached, they could hear a hubbub of voices ahead. One or two villagers ran past them carrying flaming torches, and others followed with sharp, dangerous-looking garden implements.

When they arrived at the central square, they found a large throng of villagers crowded near the steps to the magistrates' office. Igor and Esme elbowed their way through the crowd. In a circle of firelight stood four tattered-looking individuals, cowering, and confused by the flaming torches and baying mob.

On the steps of the magistrates' office was a group of very angry, red-faced people carrying banners and pointing, shouting, and jeering at the four terrified figures.

'Go back to where you came from,' yelled one of the banner-waving individuals.

'We don't want your kind here,' cried another.

The small, ragged group huddled together ever more tightly as the crowd closed in.

Esme instinctively sprang forward and stood between the poor tormented figures and the banner-waving mob. The sweet, cloying smell of decayed flesh made her gag slightly and she turned to look more closely at the people she had stood to defend. They were all quite clearly dead, but showed no signs of behaving like it.

'Someone needs to take back control!' yelled a well-dressed, portly gentleman carrying a painted banner which read, 'Transylvania First'.

The crowd cheered in agreement. Various cries erupted from the watching supporters. 'Transylvania for Transylvanians!'

'Make Carpathia Great Again!'

'Go back to Deadland!'

Among the group of well-wishers (i.e. people who wanted to throw others down a well), Igor recognised the portly, well-dressed gentleman as Thaddeus Slenderman, the owner of the newly opened smock factory, which was doing brisk business making the huge quantities of low-cost garments that had recently started to flood the local markets.

Thaddeus Slenderman may have been a new arrival in town, but his money and strong business acumen meant he was already well on his way to becoming one of the leading citizens, one of the wealthy elite, and he appeared to be leading this rabble-rousing chorus of angry villagers.

Clearly his political views were proving popular with the townsfolk, many of whom were struggling to make ends meet now that their own smock-weaving services were no longer in demand.

But as Slenderman explained so convincingly, it was these existentially challenged intruders and other such undesirables that were ruining the country's traditional way of life. Someone had to make a stand. Transylvania First was the only political organisation in the country to be a fully paid-up member of the Magic Triangle, with a particular specialism in sleight of hand.

THE GRAVEYARD SHIFT

Despite a sudden uncertainty about the people she had rushed to defend, Esme stood her ground. She was damned if a bunch of bullying bigots was going to scare her off from protecting the four bewildered people behind her, living or not.

Igor bundled his way forward and stood beside her, hefting the stick he'd brought from the woodland glade.

Someone behind them threw a chilled milk-based beverage, which sailed over their heads and hit one of the Transylvania First mob full in the face. Enraged, the hardliners began advancing towards the defenders, wielding ugly-looking clubs and swinging their banners about like badly spelled weapons.

Igor and Esme stood their ground, ready for the inevitable attack. There was a sudden uproar to their left and the crowd bulged in towards them. In an instant the people flew apart as two horses, followed by a heavy coach, cleared a swathe through the mob. Eric sat atop the coach, grimacing madly and setting about the nearby thugs with his horsewhip.

Igor and Esme hurled the four dead people into the coach and grabbed on themselves as Eric whipped up the horses to push his way forwards and out to safety.

But the crowd were not giving up so easily and they pressed inwards, clutching at the horses' bridles. Things were looking quite bad as the mob surged, growing ever more fierce, angry, and purple.

A loud bang echoed around the square. The crowd fell silent. The smell of gun smoke drifted across on the light breeze.

Helsing, witchfinder, magistrate and chief of police, stood at the top of the steps with his smoking pistol raised in the air.

Another, unused, was in his left hand and was pointed at the crowd. Suddenly, and in a dominant voice that for once seemed to grab people's attention, he bellowed across the scene.

'Away! All of you. Go home! Now! The next shot will be terminal.'

The sound of marching feet could be heard from across the square as the local military guard advanced on the rioters, expertly sharpened pikes poised and ready to do some serious poking. In typical fashion, they only ever seemed to turn up at the end when all the fighting was over, just too late to be of any practical use.

Mumbling and muttering, the villagers wisely began to disperse. Within moments, only the coach with the four reanimated corpses and their staunch, if somewhat shaken, defenders remained. Nearby lurked the hardcore of the Transylvania First supporters.

Helsing surveyed the scene with a satisfied 'harrumph!'. He clicked his fingers and his underling Hopkins stepped forward to take over. Helsing pirouetted on the spot, his cape swirling out magnificently in a well-rehearsed manner, and went back to his office to repolish his medals, already thinking about the new one he would award himself for his brave, riot-quelling heroism.

Hopkins, short, stocky and with a face like a pinched pitbull, paced between the two opposing groups. On one side, Slenderman and the Transylvania First supporters muttered obscenities and threats at Igor, Esme, Eric and the four living corpses on the other.

Hopkins hated Igor with a passion, but he was no fan of the hardliners either.

'You,' he shouted, pointing a stumpy finger at Igor. 'Get these things away from here. The dead have no business being alive – and they have no place in our town. Go away and bury them properly this time. I shall be over to your funeral parlour in the morning to make sure you do it right.'

Hopkins turned his attention to the other group. 'And you,' he sneered at Slenderman, 'I don't want to see your lot demonstrating here again without a proper permit. Do you understand me?'

Thaddeus Slenderman was unimpressed. 'You don't scare me, sonny,' he replied sneeringly. 'I know who the real power is in these parts, and it ain't you, and it ain't that prat Helsing either. We'll see you again real soon.' He signalled to his followers and they marched off, swearing loudly, and shouting catchy three-word slogans.

*

A stiff brandy soon helped Igor and his companions regain their composure as they slumped gratefully into the funeral parlour's soft furnishings. The four moving corpses they'd rescued were bumbling around, knocking into the half-finished coffins, and threatening to overturn the furniture.

They had once been two women and a man, plus the remnants of someone who'd spent too long in the ground to be entirely sure. Each was in a different state of decay so they had clearly not all died at the same time.

Igor tried his best to examine them, but his traditional skills were more in the dismemberment line. What they needed was a proper physician to work out what was going on.

Unfortunately, Castlemaine hadn't had a trained doctor in town since the departure of that pompous oaf, Henry Jekyll.

'I could go over to Dead Man's End for the barber surgeon,' suggested Eric, before hastily adding, 'in the morning.'

'No good,' replied Esme, shouting over a sudden clap of thunder. 'It's market day tomorrow, he'll be up to his ears in pie filling. He'll never come.'

'Is there a vet in town?' asked Igor, desperate to find anyone with a hint of anatomical expertise, whatever the species.

'No, but there is a midwife,' suggested Esme. 'They're almost the same thing in these parts. Old Gretchen Hornbuckle has been delivering children, lambs, and the occasional litter of three-headed puppies in the village for, well, must be more than eighty years. She's a miserable old battleaxe but there's not much she hasn't seen in her time.'

'Perfect,' cried Igor. 'Where do we find her?'

'Probably elbows deep in some poor creature,' suggested Eric. 'You just have to follow the screams.'

*

It didn't take long to track down Old Gretchen Hornbuckle, Castlemaine's aged midwife. Much as Eric had suggested, she was discovered fists first inside a pregnant horse, heaving away at the reluctant colt who seemed quite unwilling to leave the warm, amniotic comfort of its mother's interior.

All the while she was pulling, the old woman's teeth remained firmly clenched on a foul-smelling pipe, which was smoking and sparking away furiously with each tug. The floating embers threatening to burn down the entire stable.

'Good evening, Missus—' Igor got no further as the aged midwife stuck out a hobnailed boot and silenced him with a sharp kick to the shinbone.

'Shut it, sonny, I'm working here.' The old woman was concentrating on the job in hand, or rather fist, and would brook no interruption.

'Apologies, madam...' Another hard-booted kick reminded Igor that he was on dangerous ground. He decided it was probably safest to limp back to the doorway, well out of hobnail range, and wait. He sat down by the door and massaged his bruised leg bone.

After a lot of heaving, and a fair amount of grunting, and two or three large showers of glowing tobacco embers, the reluctant equine infant was finally deposited, shocked and bewildered, onto the thick straw.

Old Hornbuckle wiped her arms on the flowing folds of her favourite midwifing skirt, rolled down her sleeves and set about an enormous herring and onion sandwich.

'Hungry work,' she spattered through great mouthfuls of the pungent comestible. 'Now, what do you want, you scrawny little turd?'

Igor gave his bruised limb another rub and cautiously explained his reason for calling on her.

'This is a wind-up, isn't it?' Missus Hornbuckle's scepticism was evident in her tone and the thick spray of wet herring flakes that accompanied it.

'I assure you it's real, madam, if you'd only come and look.'

'I will,' said the elderly midwife. 'But only because Miss Esmerelda is there. I brought her into this world as I did her fat old father. I trust them. You, on the other hand, I don't know. If this is some idiotic prank, I'll remove your kidneys the same way I removed that foal, so be warned!'

Igor clenched his buttocks involuntarily.

'No problem,' he squeaked in a quiet, trembling voice.

As they walked back towards the funeral parlour, Igor had terrible visions of Esme having let the corpses run wild, and feared not so much for his internal organs as for the orifice through which they were threatened. He relaxed audibly as they entered the workshop to find the walking corpses safely corralled behind a makeshift barrier of coffin lids.

At 106 years old, Gretchen Hornbuckle had seen pretty much everything in her time. But the sight that confronted her at the funeral parlour was entirely new. She was clearly fascinated by the reanimated corpses tramping about inside Igor's workshop.

'Well, bugger me!' she said by means of confirmation to the fact.

'Quite so,' replied Igor. 'Any ideas as to what might be causing it?'

Hornbuckle studied each of the dead people in turn. She watched how their bodies moved. She followed their eyes as they stumbled around in the confined space. She noted how they interacted with each other and the furniture around them. She flicked and poked at them to see how they responded.

She then examined each of their bodies in closer detail, lifting bits of skin here, sniffing at pustulating fragments of bone there, scratching away at scabby lumps and even once biting into a rancid bony member before spitting out some green goo into a nearby flask and swirling it around in the candle flame.

'Hmmmm,' she hummed thoughtfully, relighting her stinking pipe, and taking a huge, black lungful.

Igor and Esme watched her work and tried unsuccessfully to divine her thoughts. The old woman had been around long enough to know when a good show was as important as the final revelation, and she was milking it like a prize cow.

Igor was still having troublesome thoughts about his days back at the castle and the reanimation experiments he used to be part of. The days when his whole life revolved around Victor Frankenstein's efforts to bring the dead back from the dark beyond. All that seemed a lifetime ago and involved such a difficult and mysterious process, which Igor had never really understood. And yet here were four very mobile and clearly deceased individuals with no signs of electric probe marks or reconstructive surgery to be seen. Victor Frankenstein would have been beside himself, his life's work apparently meaningless in the face of some other force which was at work in the world.

'Ox pox!' exclaimed the old woman suddenly, loud enough to startle Igor out of his idle thoughts and make Esme's hand twitch towards the blade hidden in her sleeve.

'Ah, so you don't know either then?' exclaimed Igor, grinning. He'd grown to dislike the crabby old bag very quickly after her threats to his rear doors and took delight in her apparent uselessness.

'What are you saying, simpleton?' cried the old woman giving him a withering look.

'Oh, nothing. Just interesting to hear you cussing and admitting defeat.' Igor smiled his least sincere smile.

'I said it looks like Ox pox,' she spat back, sneering up at Igor and trying to work out if he was as dim-witted as he appeared. 'You don't know what that is, do you?'

Igor detected the slight sigh in the old woman's voice. The sound that only old people can make. The sound which perfectly conveys the highest levels of disdain for someone several generations less intelligent.

'Afraid to say, I don't,' he admitted, then in a deliberate attempt to wind her up further he added, 'something to do with oxes, perhaps?'

'It's oxen, not oxes, you uneducated oaf. It's as if they don't bother teaching young people to speak proper Transylvanian anymore.'

Hornbuckle creaked her weary bones onto a tall stool beside the embalming table and began to explain, as if to a small slug with learning difficulties.

'Ox pox isn't a pox, and it doesn't infect oxes, I mean oxen.'

'Ha-ha, bit of an obvious misnomer then, no?' Igor was clearly in no mood to be civil.

'Do you want to hear this or not?' demanded the old woman, her boot shooting out and catching Igor just below the kneecap.

'Absolutely, yes we do,' encouraged Esme warmly. 'Don't we Igor?' She said the last bit not so much as a question, more a command.

THE GRAVEYARD SHIFT

'Mrmmmn s'pose so,' mumbled Igor through the tears.

'Well, then,' continued the elderly midwife. 'Ox pox isn't a pox, and it doesn't infect... ox... oxen.'

Igor winked at Esmerelda, who stung his earlobe with a sharp flick.

'It is actually pronounced Ogs'pogs. It's a potion that was used by African shaman to help them communicate with their ancestors. When used properly it sends the shaman into a trance that allows them to see through the veils of death and ask their departed relatives important questions. Questions like, will the crops be fruitful this season, or when will the herd migrations begin, or where did you bury all your money, you spiteful old sod?'

Igor placed his hands on the table and leant closer to the old hag.

'The trouble with Ogs'pogs,' Hornbuckle continued, 'is that even a small overdose can kill. Too many shamans died using it, so it fell out of fashion and people had to rely on simple prayers and meditation instead. Of course, the dead refused to answer. Why should they expend all their energy breaking through the mysterious wall of death while all the shaman could be bothered to do was sit there, mumbling nonsense to themselves? It wasn't the dead that wanted answers, they already had them.' Mrs Hornbuckle drew a long ponderous drag on her pipe, sending clouds of filth billowing out towards the stumbling stiffs.

'Then one bright spark realised that if Ogs'pogs is so powerful in clearing a path between the mortal world and the spiritual, and if a little bit can kill the living, then perhaps a lot can, temporarily at least, bring the dead back across the divide. So, they tried it. Gave ever-increasing doses to the recently deceased until, eventually, one woke up.'

Igor was stunned. All Victor's work was based on research he'd carried out in his own lab and with ancient texts from the Far and Middle East. He'd never thought to look into the ancient wisdom of Africa.

In his mind, he saw Victor curled up in a ball on his laboratory floor, weeping, while Igor danced around wildly flicking enormous Vs and singing, 'I know something you don't know, I know something you don't know.'

He allowed himself a moment's hysterical laughter.

Esme flicked his earlobe again. 'How do you know all this?' she asked, turning her attention back to Hornbuckle.

'Ah, well, you can thank the late Mister Hornbuckle for that.' The old woman's eyes glazed over as she reminisced warmly. 'My husband, Typhus, was the first mate on a merchant vessel that sailed the dark waters off the coast of Africa and around the cape to the east. He always came back with such stories. Brought me presents, too, oftentimes. Beautiful snake-tooth bracelets, exotic vampire rodents, feathers from the great fire-breathing devil birds of Madagascar. That's how I found out about Ogs'pogs, or Ox pox, as he used to call it, the simple fool.'

It was hard to tell if the old woman's rheumy eyes were watering through the sadness of her recollections or because of the greasy smoke that puffed in great clouds from her unfeasibly hairy nostrils.

'One time,' she continued more softly, 'he brought me a romantic gift – the head of an old cackling doomsayer in a beautifully inlaid ebony box. Every time you opened the box the head would cackle and then shout out prophecies of the end of the world. Nothing too clever really, just the usual tourist tat. Anyway, the locals who made these things used to steal heads from the burial grounds and pump them full of Ogs'pogs to reanimate them. But the potent drug not only brought life, it also made the dead highly suggestible, so they could be easily taught some simple repetitive task, like cackling and spouting nonsense prophecies every time the lid of their box was opened. Of course, the potion wears off over time and the things stop working without fresh doses being applied. And besides, they continue to rot even with the potion so the smell when you open the box becomes unbearable. I stopped using mine years ago. I only keep it now to scare the grandchildren when they really annoy me.'

The old woman sat silently for several moments while Igor and Esme tried to reconcile her fantastical stories with the very real presence of the cadavers that were still bumbling about the room. Mrs Hornbuckle stood up and stretched her back.

'And you think someone's been using this Ogs'pogs potion on the local dead people?' asked Esme, bewildered and yet fascinated by the idea in equal measures.

'I have no idea, sweetie,' replied the old woman as she shuffled towards the door. 'I mean, who could get hold of Ogs'pogs here? And what would be the point? Probably just kids messing about, you know how bored they get. I expect one of them accidentally stumbled upon the recipe in alchemy class and has been trying to impress the girls with his superpowers or something. Anyway, I ought to go. Old

Mister Slackfinger's prolapse must need poking up again by now. Regular as clockwork that one. Bye-bye, deary.'

Hornbuckle cast a final scornful glance at Igor as she left the funeral parlour trailing clouds of noxious smoke from her filthy pipe.

Igor raised his foot with the intention of giving her a parting gift, but the reproachful look on Esmerelda's face stopped him in mid-swing.

'Well, what do you make of all that?' he asked Esme, looking thoughtfully at the slowly pacing corpses.

'I don't know,' she replied, pondering the old woman's tale. 'I don't think it's kids. You know what they're like around here, they'd bring them to life just so they can kill them again. No, there's a deeper purpose here. Someone's definitely up to no good.'

'There's another problem too,' suggested Igor, a worried look furrowing its way across his brow. 'What if whoever is behind all this manages to reanimate one of your father's late-night subjects? If they somehow identified him as their killer then we'd all be in the shi—'

Esme cut him off sharply. 'Oh, Hell's tits, you're right. We'd better get this fixed before Helsing wises up and starts snooping about.'

'...fting sands of disaster,' concluded Igor. 'And what do we do with these?' he asked, pointing at the four perambulating corpses cluttering up his workshop.

'You heard Hopkins,' replied Esme. 'Bury 'em. If what the old lady said is true, the potion will wear off soon anyway and they'll go back to being regular stiffs again. Might as well get them ready. Then, I think, we need to visit Father Price.'

THE GRAVEYARD SHIFT

*

Later that afternoon, Igor and Esme nailed the last of the four coffin lids down on the poor unfortunate corpses, who still wriggled and rifled about. While they waited for the kicking and banging to die down, they went the short distance across to the church to see Father Price.

They found him pacing angrily around the graveyard, followed by two tired-looking gravediggers, whose job it was to fill in any opened graves, of which there seemed to be plenty.

'Good afternoon, Father,' called Esme sweetly as they approached. 'You look... busy.'

'Good afternoon, Miss Esmerelda, Igor, yes, no rest for the wicked – or dead – it would seem.'

'What's going on?'

'Grave robbers, I'm sorry to say. There's been a real spate of them lately.'

Esme did her best to sound surprised and sympathised, 'Oh, that's terrible.'

'It's the poor families I feel sorry for,' continued the priest, 'seeing their loved ones' rest disturbed in such a way. I can't understand who would do such a hideous, uncaring thing.'

Igor flushed slightly, remembering his past life in the castle and his nightly jaunts to the local churchyards looking for suitable specimens. He'd never really given any thought to the families of the dead. It was all about spare parts to him then.

'I've informed Magistrate Helsing, of course. He says it's certain to be the work of the giant carnivorous mole men and that there's nothing us simple mortals can do to prevent it except pray. But I can't help thinking there's a slightly more… earthly… explanation.'

Father Price called across to his two gravediggers. 'Mister Hare, you and Mister Burke can finish for the day now. I'll see you tomorrow.'

The two men shouldered their spades and trudged wearily away, tipping their hats to the priest and his companions as they passed.

'Those poor chaps,' continued Price. 'I'm afraid I've kept them rather busy since breakfast. They looked so tired when they arrived as well. As if they'd already done a full day's work.'

Igor passed Esme a knowing glance. He felt sure he'd seen the two men somewhere before but couldn't quite place them.

'Sorry, where are my manners? Please, come into the vestry and have a glass of holy wine.'

The priest led his guests into his office and offered them each a chair while he went to find some clean goblets and a fresh bottle of Communion wine.

Igor took a seat and picked up a Bible from the desk. He opened it at a random page and read the first verse he saw: *Revelations*, chapter 21, verses 3 and 4.

'And I heard a loud voice from the throne saying, "Look! God's dwelling place is now among the people, and he will dwell with them. They will be his people, and God himself will be with them and be their God. He will wipe every tear from their eyes. There will be no more death, or mourning or crying or pain, for the old order of things has passed away."'

'No more death, eh? Looks like I'm out of a job then,' Igor said scornfully and threw the book back on the desk. As he did so, a piece of paper blew onto the floor. He picked it up and showed it to Esmerelda. It was a printed pamphlet detailing the manifesto of the Transylvania First group.

'Hello, what's this? Seems our beloved priest is a hard-line Trannys First nutter.'

'I most certainly am not!' cried the disgruntled priest as he entered carrying the wine.

Igor flushed slightly. 'Sorry, Father, but what is this odious rag doing here then?'

'That? I had a visit yesterday from the charming Thaddeus Slenderman. He wanted to sign me up to his "patriotic organisation". He told me it was the duty of every high-standing person in the area to speak out against the influx of unwanted "others", as he called them, swarming into the area, and taking up the scant resources from hard-working Transylvanians. I told him I couldn't in all good conscience shun anyone in need, wherever they came from or whatever their background. And that the Lord would provide for the righteous. He just laughed at me and poked around the churchyard for a while before stopping to chat with those two gravediggers you saw earlier. He left that pamphlet and I hadn't got around to lighting the candles with it yet.'

'I knew I'd seen those two somewhere,' exclaimed Igor. 'They were on the steps of the magistrates' office last night when we were being harangued by the crowd. So, they're in with Slenderman are they? Now, that is interesting.'

'What are you thinking?' asked Esmerelda, her curiosity piqued by Igor's conspiratorial tone.

'I'm thinking that we need to go and say a proper "howdy" to our good Mr Slenderman,' replied Igor. 'I'm beginning to suspect he's not all he claims to be.'

*

It was quite a way from the church to Slenderman's smock factory and the afternoon was growing old before they arrived at the imposing entrance gate. The building was ancient and had been empty for many years prior to Slenderman's arrival. It sat in a large patch of woodland on a steep mountainous outcrop, high above Castlemaine at the end of what must have once been a wide and well-trodden road. The road was now overgrown and blocked in many places by fallen branches and the encroaching woodland.

The gates were tall and wrought from thick, black iron. Welded into the intricate bars were two cast-iron figures facing each other, as if ready for battle. They looked like normal people except for the great bat-like wings which spread out wide on either side. Each figure carried a sword in their right hand and a shield bearing the image of a dragon in their left. Around them were the tormented shapes of human bodies impaled on long, very sharp-looking pikes. Beneath their feet were the trampled remains of their agonised enemies.

'Nice imagery,' suggested Igor. 'Old convent, do you think?'

'This was the ancient seat of the De'Ath family,' replied Esme studying the old and worn gate with its imposing imagery. 'A rich, powerful, unpleasant bunch so the stories go. The last of them died more than a century ago. This place has been abandoned ever since.'

'And now Slenderman has moved in.' Igor peered between the bars into the tangled and overgrown gardens beyond. 'Fancy a look about?'

The gates were far too high and difficult to climb and had a nasty-looking row of barbed spikes at the top, which resembled upturned fangs.

Esme rattled the gates but they were firmly bound with a heavy old lock and chain. 'The place still looks deserted.'

Igor examined the area around the gates. 'There are definite signs of recent use on this chain; see the shine where the rust has been rubbed away? And there are lots of fresh footprints in the mud beyond. Someone's been through here, and not too long ago. Let's go around and see if there's another way in.'

They followed the old perimeter wall to their right, which disappeared into the trees and thick scratchy undergrowth.

Their going was slow and the wall long, high and impenetrable. Igor considered climbing one of the trees to see if he could get over that way, but the tall conifers offered no suitable branches at lower levels, and he had forgotten to bring his twenty-foot ladder and climbing spurs. He cursed himself angrily for his lack of foresight and looked around in case anybody had dropped an axe or two-man saw nearby. By this time, Esme had disappeared further into the trees, so he gave up his search and followed on despondently.

After an hour, scratched and raw, they had chased the wall around four left-hand corners and realised that they must soon arrive back at the gate where they'd started. There had been no other roads or gates into or out of the property.

'Whoever built this place really didn't want to be disturbed,' observed Esme, wearily.

Igor rubbed his sore legs and grunted miserably. 'Although, judging by the pictures on those gates, they clearly were.'

About thirty-five feet ahead, Esme could just see the treeline where the road to the gate cut through the forest. About ten feet closer was a tall old conifer that had lost its rooting in one of the recent storms, and was tilted towards the wall at a conveniently shallow and perfectly climbable angle.

'Brilliant,' scoffed Igor. 'Next time, I decide the direction, OK?'

'You did!' snapped Esme, a fiery look in her eye.

'Well, next time, make sure you disagree with me properly or I won't come out and play with you anymore.'

The fallen tree was propped on the wall and they scurried up it with ease. The drop on the other side was quite far, so they walked back along the top of the wall until they came to a large pile of firewood stacked inside the grounds, which halved the distance they needed to drop. It would also make a convenient place to climb back out in a hurry should they need to.

Finally inside, they made their cautious way through the overgrown gardens towards the main building. It was an ancient stone pile of a house, almost castle-like in its construction, with thick, heavy walls and high, narrow windows. Here and there, circular towers rose up and were capped with tall, pointy spires. Fearsome-looking stone creatures gazed down at them contemptuously from on high.

'Enough to put the willies up anyone,' mocked Igor, thinking back to the truly terrifying scale of Castle Frankenstein.

'Not now, dear, we've got a job to do,' replied Esme with a cheeky wink.

The large house seemed empty. No lights or sounds anywhere. They walked around towards the back of the building and stopped suddenly when they heard the sound of someone whistling a merry work tune in the nearby trees.

They both crouched low in the tall weeds as whoever it was that was so cheery in their work came closer. They held their breaths and waited.

Suddenly, and without warning, an old man burst through the undergrowth and tripped over the crouching forms of Igor and Esmerelda.

All three of them rolled about, cursing, swearing and trying to be the first to regain their feet.

Esme sprang to her feet and quickly pulled Igor up before unsheathing her short steel blade in a cold flash and pointing it menacingly at the writhing jumble of limbs that represented the dazed, elderly intruder.

'Wha… who the buggering twatflaps… my gammy foot…' the old man let out a stream of course language before he was finally able to sit upright and look properly at his captors.

'Who the fank-wungling ballscrotes are you? And what are you doing… here?' he demanded, looking warily at Esme's sharp blade.

'Exactly the questions we were going to ask you,' replied Igor in a dominant tone. 'And more to the point, what's going on in this fank-wungling factory, my old ballscrote?'

'They make clothes, is all. I'm the caretaker here,' admitted the old man. 'Wassit to you?'

'Well, we'd just like a look around and to question some of the workforce, make sure everything's in order.' Esme stood up very straight and put on her best official tone.

'Oh, you would, would you? Under whose authority?'

'We're, err, here on behalf of the, err, Smock Makers' Unified Guild, doing research into the General Industrial Trading Standards within the sector,' advised Igor. 'It's called the S.M.U.G. G.I.T.S initiative.' He gave the old caretaker a quick flash of his battered and very expired Lickspittle College library card.

'Sounds plausible enough,' admitted the old man, failing entirely to read the proffered identification. 'What's the knife for?'

'Oh, yes, sorry about that,' Esme smiled sweetly as she sheathed her blade. 'I used to be a schools' inspector. Old habits...'

The old man grunted and held up his hands for them to pull him to his feet. 'Well, I suppose you'd better come inside.'

Igor and Esme shared a silent high five as the old man led the way towards the servants' entrance at the back of the huge stone building.

After a few minutes of scrambling through the overgrown undergrowth, they reached an old iron-bound oak door set into the stonework of the ancient house. From above the door a large, hideous gargoyle stared down at them. It had the same huge batlike wings they had seen on the gates earlier.

'Blimey!' exclaimed Igor staring up at the grotesque stone carving that was staring back down at him. 'That's not the face you want to see when you're being taken in the tradesman's.'

Esme shivered as the cold, blank eyes seemed to bore into her skull.

The caretaker made a healthy meal out of finding the right rusty brown key on a ring full of other identical-looking rusty brown keys. Several more minutes passed while he cussed, scraped and clanged with the lock, before the door eventually groaned inwards and they entered a dark bare stone passage.

The air inside was chill, and laced with the stale, damp smell of mould and decay. The caretaker lit a match and put it to the wick of a blackened oil lamp that hung just inside the door.

'Follow me,' he instructed and led them deep into the dark, silent building.

Igor and Esme followed willingly, glad at last to be out of sight of that nasty piece of stonework.

The flame of the lamp flickered and shadows danced as they shuffled carefully after the old man along the dark, uneven passageways and down several flights of worn steps.

He stopped in front of another heavy wooden door and fumbled with his keys. Another few moments of mumbled swearing passed until again, the lock screeched and the door complained loudly as it swung reluctantly open on old, stiff hinges.

'Here, hold this.' The caretaker handed the oil lamp to Esme as they passed inside, then turned to close the door behind them.

Igor and Esme peered into the darkness ahead. Neither

of them could see beyond a few feet. They had evidently entered a large chamber of some sort, the yawning blackness stretching out ahead of them.

The door shut with a dull wooden thud, and they heard the turn of key in lock before either had noticed that the old man was now on the other side, grinning through a small metal grate in the wood.

'You can wait here until the master returns. He'll know what's best to do with you.'

A wooden shutter slammed shut over the metal grate, and as they rushed to the door, all Igor and Esme could do was shout impotently through the thick wood as he whistled his jaunty work tune and shuffled carefully back up the dark corridor.

*

'Balls,' Igor swore as they turned away from the door. 'I suppose we should have seen that coming.'

Esme took the lamp and lengthened the wick, making the flame glow fiercely behind the smoke-blackened glass. With it, she carefully examined the room they had been trapped inside. It was tall and round with only the single door through which they had entered and a small trapdoor, high above, well out of reach in the centre of the concave roof. The floor, too, was slightly concave, with a small hole in the centre, presumably for drainage.

'Looks like an old icehouse,' she surmised disinterestedly. 'Bloody cold, for sure. I hope we're not stuck in here too long.'

Igor wasn't listening, he was busy running as high up the curved walls as he could, before sliding down again on his back. 'This is great!' he exclaimed with a delighted grin.

Esme sighed and sat down on the cold stone.

Hours passed. It was impossible to tell in the cold, dark underground room just how long they had been there, but eventually the oil lamp started to spit and gutter. Esme did her best to trim the wick, but its reservoir of fish oil was running low and they were soon faced with the probability of a long dark wait ahead.

Just as the flame began sputtering out its death rattle, the hatch in the door opened and the old caretaker's face grimaced through at them.

Keys rattled and the lock mechanism ground unwillingly. The door opened.

'Come on,' barked the old man. 'Master's back and he wants to see you.'

The caretaker was holding a fresh lamp and behind him were two gaunt-looking individuals carrying staves and staring blankly into the room.

'Oh, and don't try any funny business or my friends here will take great pleasure in caving in your skulls without a second's thought.'

The old man led the way, Igor followed and Esme fell in behind him, the two silent heavies bringing up the rear.

Esme stole a glance over her shoulder and whispered to Igor in the gloom ahead, 'They're dead.'

'Bloody will be by the time I've finished with them,' he hissed, glancing daggers over his shoulder at the two men following.

'No, I mean they're actually dead. Like the others we found.'

Igor looked back and saw that the two thugs with the heavy batons were, indeed, very much of the next world.

'What was it that gave it away?' he asked Esme quietly. 'Was it the green pallor of the one on the right, or the fact the one on the left is missing his jaw?'

'Neither,' she replied. 'I stuck my blade through green boy's jugular when we left the ice room and he still hasn't fallen over yet.'

They wound their way back up through the old building, through a confusing series of empty rooms and corridors. The quality of the archaic decorations improved noticeably as they made their way up from the lower servants' areas into what must have been the part of the building formerly inhabited by the De'Ath family themselves.

Here and there, reminders of the gruesome winged creatures they had seen earlier glowered at them from the carved wood panelling, faded frescoes and ornate plasterwork ceilings.

After a few too many minutes, the old caretaker finally led them into a large, cavernous open space, which had clearly served as some kind of feasting hall in days gone by.

The tall windows were mostly shuttered with only a few panels open to allow a view of the once magnificently manicured gardens, now choked with thorny scrub and dead, twisted trees. Several lighted torches dotted along the walls made up for the lack of natural light but added to the gloomy atmosphere with their greasy smoke.

THE GRAVEYARD SHIFT

At the far end of the great hall, a vast stone fireplace, twice the height of Esmerelda, yawned darkly back at them. No embers were now permitted to warm the stale, cold air inside that dark, forbidding chamber.

Above the fireplace and dominating the room was the life-sized portrait of a tall, elegant woman, dressed in dark purple and wearing a thin, gold coronet. The painting was old and filthy from the hundreds of fires that must have burned in the ancient hearth below over the years. As Esmerelda looked, the dim quavering light from the torches made it seem as though the background of the painting was swirling behind the woman, almost like a pair of gigantic, dark wings were gently beating and waving in the shadows, while her eyes glistened and held Esmerelda in a cold, hypnotic gaze.

Igor touched Esmerelda's hand and the spell was broken. With a force of will she withdrew her eyes from the painting and read the title which was written in black scripted letters below, 'Madame Agrapina De'Ath – Heir of Keg'dranod'.

The old caretaker cleared his throat and brought their attention back from the almost irresistible attraction of the painting.

'The master will be along shortly,' he announced and shuffled off to the side of the room, leaving them to finally take in their wider surroundings.

How they failed to notice it when they entered the chamber they could not say, but the hall was populated on all sides by at least a dozen rows of workbenches. At each workbench sat a corpse, busily working away. Men, women, children, and others unidentifiable, working tirelessly cutting, sewing, ironing and embroidering a vast number of smocks in linen, cotton and silk.

The dead workers were all in different states of decay. Some had bits missing, others had bits hanging off. Bits of some littered the workshop floor. A purply-green-looking child with one arm swept up the loose bits and scooped them into a large bucket.

The old caretaker went across to a particularly sluggish-looking wretch and injected something into the side of its face. The creature immediately began to sew at such a speed that several of its fingers found they could hold on no longer, and spun off across the room, the purply-green child and her broom in hot pursuit.

'Impressive, isn't it?' A loud, deep voice resonated around the draughty chamber.

Igor and Esme turned to see the portly figure of Thaddeus Slenderman filling the doorway at the end of the room. He paced slowly towards them, his arms spread wide.

'This is progress, my friends,' he said, puffing out his chest and smiling proudly. 'The future of manufacturing.'

The old caretaker cleared his throat and addressed his master, 'If I may make so bold, master, I think we'll be needing a few fresh ones soon. Several of these have been out of the ground for a number of weeks, and their production levels are dropping significantly.'

'Thank you, Typhus, that will be all for now.' Slenderman waved his servant away.

Igor and Esmerelda stared at each other, then at the old man who had brought them into the castle. 'Wait!' Esme called after the old man. 'Your name's Typhus? Not Typhus

Hornbuckle by any chance? Husband to Old Gretchen Hornbuckle, the midwife?'

'Curse that evil harpy's name, the vicious old hag,' Mister Hornbuckle spat, bitterly. 'I knew we shouldn't have come this close to Castlemaine.'

'Relax, old friend.' Slenderman tried to comfort his aged servant. 'Nobody knows you're here. These two won't be around long enough to tell anyone. And besides, we've just about cleared out all the useful workers in this area. I'll need you to move onto the next village and dig up some new recruits soon enough.'

'So, that's your game,' Igor was beginning to see the light in the situation. 'You're the one behind all the grave-robbing, using the dead to make your cheap clothes. Slave labour!'

'Of course, who's going to complain?'

'Well, they might for a start.' Igor waved his hands to imply the vast swathes of undead workers busy sewing and stitching.

Slenderman stepped in behind one of his deceased workers and began massaging her shoulders, his large hands grinding the bones together with a sickening rasp. 'They have no thoughts, no feelings. What's the point of leaving them mouldering away in a box when they can still make a useful contribution to society?'

'Master, if you don't mind,' began Typhus, looking for a means to leave the uncomfortable conversation.

'Not so fast, my salty old seaman!' Igor rounded on the old man and pointed an accusing finger that he'd just picked up from one of the work benches. 'You're supposed to be dead too, but I somehow doubt it's Ogs'pogs that's keeping you going.'

'Ah, you know about that, do you?' said Typhus.

'Yes, we had a rather interesting conversation with your wife this morning, albeit peppered with intermittent bouts of physical violence.'

'Ah, she hasn't changed then,' sighed the old sailor.

'Indeed, but she's very much of the opinion that she's a widow.'

'Yeah, well I had to. She was a bloody awful woman. Kept beating and kicking me whenever I said a wrong word or put the knife and fork arse about on the table. It's why I went to sea so much. Couldn't abide being near the old witch.'

'But all the gifts you brought her,' added Esme, casting her eyes about the room, looking to find anything that might be useful as a distraction or to aid their escape. She decided to try and keep them talking and buy some time. 'You must have loved her once.'

'Nah, those gifts were meant to get rid of her. Venomous snake-tooth bracelet, still full of venom. She never bloody wore it. The vampire rodents were meant to get her while she was sleeping. When they didn't work I brought the devil bird feathers to try and burn her out. Nothing worked. In the end I had to pretend to be lost at sea and try to start again, somewhere new. She made my life a living hell.'

'And the cackling head?' asked Igor as he wandered over to one of the dead workers whose severed arm was now rotating rapidly and drawing large wet circles in the air, having been grabbed by the spinning wheel he was continuing to operate.

'Wasn't meant for her. I brought that back as a sample for Mister Slenderman but the wife got her hands on it first.

THE GRAVEYARD SHIFT

'So, you've known each other a long time then?' Esme was starting to see the bigger picture emerging.

'Long enough for me to make my fortune, Miss Esmerelda.' Thaddeus Slenderman took Esme's hand and kissed it, his pendulous lips leaving a warm wet ring on her crawling skin. She snatched back her hand and wiped it on her shirt sleeve.

'I met Mister Hornbuckle in a tavern on the Italian coast,' he explained. 'Must be twenty years ago now. I was visiting the local merchants looking for new and exotic materials for my garments and he was on shore leave. We fell into talking and he relayed many of his fascinating stories from all his travels around the dark continent. When I heard tell of this "Ox pox" potion everything became crystal clear to me. Suddenly I had a way to reduce all of my staffing costs to virtually nothing. All we had to do was find out how to make sufficient potion to reanimate a few dozen corpses and keep them dosed up to run the production line.'

For all his growing distaste of the obnoxious Slenderman, Igor had to admit a certain ingenuity in the businessman's thinking. Then he decided that actually, no, he was a total git and deserved no such admiration. Igor tried to grab the spinning arm with the thought of striking Slenderman firmly about the chops with it.

'I paid for my old friend Typhus here to ship back to Africa where he mastered the art of brewing the potion, and now he keeps me well stocked. He organises the exhumations and administers the potion to the workforce. A lovely, simple, efficient and cost-effective business model, I'm sure you'll agree.'

'And now you travel around the country, going from town to town, exploit the recently deceased population, kill off the local economy, then up sticks and start again a few miles up the road?' exclaimed Igor.

'In a nutshell, yes,' replied Slenderman with a smug look on his jowly visage. 'Although, I have to say,' he continued rather mysteriously as if talking more to himself, 'I've definitely landed on my feet in Castlemaine.'

'So, what's all this Transylvania First stuff about?' Igor was getting riled up and decided he disliked Thaddeus Slenderman even more than he disliked aubergines, and that was really saying something.

'Oh, just a bit of a diversion really. We inevitably have a few escapees, usually after they've had their first dose. They can get a bit lively to start with. To stop the locals sniffing about too much we blame all the downturn in their own financial situation on the outsiders, the dead.'

'Yes, but everyone knows it's you that's making all these cheap garments and flooding the market. You're the one to blame for their loss of earnings, I mean, your name's even embroidered on them. It's blindingly obvious,' said Esme.

'Ah, not so,' smirked Slenderman, pulling a small jewelled pendant from inside his shirt. 'This is a smoke and mirrors charm. It helps to, how can I put it, twist the reality of a situation slightly. If you're brash enough to face down an obvious truth with a big enough lie, then the smoke and mirrors charm amplifies the effect and you can pretty much get people to believe whatever the devil you want.'

'So, you exploit the dead for financial gain, destroy hard-working people's lives, and to top it off you breed division and hatred among otherwise peace-loving people and call it progress?' Esmerelda was spitting feathers at the businessman's complete lack of morality and blatant utter gittishness.

'Erm, yes,' Slenderman laughed long and hard at the brilliance of his own genius. Igor and Esmerelda fumed.

'I've met some lowlifes in my time, fat boy, but you take the biscuit. In fact, I'd go as far as to say you take the whole packet, smash it up and spit all the crumbs into someone else's cup of tea. You're despicable.'

'Well, thank you for your kind assessment, Igor, but I don't need any lessons in human rights from a man with your background. You see, not all my digging has been in the graveyard. I've been digging up the dirt on you. I know who you really are.'

'We all do,' mocked Esmerelda. 'He's Igor from Castle Frankenstein, former lab rat to a mad scientist. That's no great secret, you psychopathic, bigoted, cruel, demented, industrialist… twat!'

'Of course, that's the bit he likes everyone to hear, isn't it, Igor? But that's only part of the story. We know the whole dirty truth of it.'

Esme looked at Igor who looked at anything but Esmerelda.

'Igor?' A pained look crossed Esmerelda's face as Igor still refused to meet her eye.

Igor decided to change the subject before things got any weirder.

'Of course, you'll never get away with it, Slenderman. Even as we speak there's a timid Catholic priest rounding up a posse of pike-wielding psychopaths who'll come riding to our rescue any minute. Did you think we'd come here without arranging a rescue plan should we fail to reappear by teatime?'

Slenderman threw back his head and laughed loudly. The laugh echoed around the large room.

'You are pathetic, you and all your grubby little gap-toothed village friends. You have no idea what Castlemaine really is do you? You and your Catholic priest and your pike-wielding guards. Hah!'

'Give up now, Slenderman!' cried Esmerelda who was clutching the purply-green sweeping girl to her side in an attempt to give her a last taste of human comfort. 'Stop this and we can give these people back their dignity and let them rest peacefully.' A tear of sadness mixed with anger and frustration ran down Esme's cheek as she spoke.

'Give up now?' mocked Slenderman callously. 'Just as my mistress is getting started? I think... no.' Slenderman bellowed in great raucous, almost insane laughter.

'Your mistress?' spat Igor, the exasperation clear in his voice. 'What's this now, your girlfriend the boss in your relationship, eh?' He glanced at Esme who was standing beside him still hugging the little dead girl protectively. 'OK, so mine is too, but you can still put an end to all this nonsense. Turn yourself in, let these people rest in peace.'

'You fools,' mocked Slenderman. 'You poor, weak fools. You stand at the brink, at the very edge of magnificence and still you fail to see what's coming.'

The room had grown significantly darker in the preceding minutes; a mist-like blackness was slowly crawling through the space around them. Igor and Esme shivered as an icy chill breezed past them.

'You're bigging yourself up just a tad too bigly there I think, Slenders.' Igor had seen a rather sharp pair of scissors lying on one of the workbenches and was quite obviously and visibly doing a bad job of sidling nonchalantly towards them.

Typhus Hornbuckle quickly moved to the workbench, picked up the scissors and wagged his finger at Igor.

Rats! thought Igor as he looked about for any other sharp objects he could use to prick Slenderman's pomposity.

'This venture of yours isn't sustainable. Soon, word of your vile practice will spread and you'll have nowhere to go. Face it, Largechap, you're finished.'

The cold, dark air was becoming quite oppressive. Esme and Igor huddled close together.

'Oh, I'm not going anywhere.' Slenderman grinned widely, his flabby jowls flapping vigorously as his sense of victory grew. 'Didn't you know?' he roared towards Igor and Esme as they stood confused and uncertain in the middle of the chamber. 'I told you, I've landed on my feet in Castlemaine. I have a permanent home now, thanks to my new mistress. Have you met the lady of the house?'

Slenderman swept his arm back towards the painting which now stood empty and black above the great stone fireplace.

In the hearth, huge swirling clouds of dark nothingness were expanding slowly towards them. Moments passed as they stood, frozen to the spot. Suddenly, the blackness before them opened up and outwards, revealing the shape of the tall, beautiful, terrible and all-too-real figure of Agrapina

De'Ath, last surviving daughter of the ancient vampire Queen Keg'dranod. Her long purple dress flowed in waves towards the floor; the blackness that had been swirling around her flew suddenly upwards into the form of a pair of huge wings, filling the room and cutting out all but the dazzling light from her own eyes, which burned with a fierce intensity. Her thin gold coronet glistened and shone like fire.

Igor and Esmerelda felt a cold grip on their hearts under that fearsome gaze. Neither could move. They knew for certain that this was their last moment, that they had completely failed to comprehend the full extent of the powers that were ranged against them and the poor, simple folk of Castlemaine.

The terrifying form of Madame De'Ath loomed hugely above them and they knew this was the end. Instinctively Esmerelda and Igor reached for each other's hand and as their fingers intertwined for the last time, their eyes met and Igor managed a weak smile at his recently discovered love as the darkness enveloped them completely.

*

There was a terrible scream.

There was a terrible silence.

There was a terrible cry of, 'Oh, balls!'

Igor carefully opened one eye, and when that seemed to work, he opened another one just to make sure. He was still crouched on the floor next to Esmerelda who was similarly daring a peek at the changed surroundings. That black shadow with the fearsome eyes was gone. They were back in the middle of the room with all the noise and bustle of the industrious corpses carrying on about them.

Slenderman and Typhus Hornbuckle stood open-mouthed beside the fireplace with stunned and worried looks on their faces.

Beside them, with just the hint of a smile, was the small purply-green dead child. In her hand was the severed arm which she had wrestled from the spinning wheel and in a deft manoeuvre had proceeded to ignite the rancid flesh from a flaming torch before throwing it with supernatural skill right between the glowing eyes in the now burning portrait of Madame Agrapina De'Ath, while all their attentions were elsewhere. The girl had retrieved the flaming member and was now waggling it defiantly towards the rotund figure of her tormentor.

'Oh, you clever girl!' cried Esme as she hugged Igor in a tearful, fierce embrace.

'Well, doesn't that just seem a bit too easy?' suggested Igor, disappointed at the rather speedy and anticlimactic end to such a powerful and ancient vampire queen. 'I mean, after all that dramatic build-up. I somehow doubt that's the last we'll be seeing of her, Esmerelda!'

Esme nodded in agreement. 'I believe you might be right, Igor. We'll see her again in the future, or my name's not Esmerelda Maggie Lucrezia Eva Braun Bathory.'

Slenderman sagged visibly. His powerful backer was, for the time being at least, ashes on the floor and his future was looking bleak.

The sudden sound of many rapidly approaching heavy boots grabbed their attention.

'Ah, the cavalry,' grinned Igor, springing up and pulling Esme gently to her feet. 'Unless I'm very much mistaken, that is the sound of our good friend Father Price bringing rescue. You villains do jabber on, so wrapped up in your own cleverness.'

Slenderman ran to the window and saw the shiny tips of a bristling hedge of very sharp pikes crossing the grounds and heading towards them.

'Typhus, time to go!' he called as he ran for the door.

The old man grabbed his medicine bag and ran as fast as his gammy foot would allow after his master. He pulled a small whistle from his pocket and blew a short piercing blast.

The effect on the dead workers was instant. As one, they dropped their work and began stumbling towards Igor and Esmerelda.

There was no real force in their attack, but their clumsy presence was sufficient to slow down the chase.

Igor picked up one of the smaller corpses and hurled it at the rest. They all tumbled over in a heap at his feet. 'Strike!' yelled Igor and sprinted after the escaping bad guys.

He made a flying grab for Slenderman and Esmerelda threw a disembodied head, which arced through the air and floored Hornbuckle; his medicine bag was sent spinning into a dark corner of the room, spilling out all its contents as it went. As she pulled out her blade, the two corpse heavies grabbed her from behind and carried her forcibly towards the far end of the room.

Igor had a hand on Slenderman's throat but the larger man managed to push him away and onto the stone floor.

Immediately, several corpses lumbered across and sat on Igor as Slenderman made another dash for the door.

Igor managed to throw off the slow-witted stiffs and made a grab for a pair of scissors that had fallen from one of the workbenches. Instinctively, he threw them and they spun end over end through the air to land with an ugly red squelch, point first, in Slenderman's plump thigh. He fell with a yelp and Igor was on him in a moment. Hornbuckle had been frantically gathering up his scattered belongings but now turned and saw his master being throttled by the raging Igor.

From her lofty position across the room, Esmerelda watched as events seemed to take on a surreal slowness. Her frantic efforts to free herself from the grasp of the two bodyguard bodies ceased as she watched Hornbuckle raise a long, thin wooden pipe to his lips.

Igor was on top of Slenderman, his hands grabbing at the larger man's throat. Hornbuckle gave a mighty blow and a feathered dart, three inches long and dripping with enough Ogs'pogs potion to kill an army of shaman, flew with infinite slowness towards the unsuspecting Igor.

Seconds turned to minutes turned to hours as the death-dealing dart flew inexorably on.

With all her remaining strength, Esmerelda let out an enormous cry, 'IGOR!' as the dart embedded itself firmly into his chest, injecting its poisonous cargo instantly and causing him to tumble backwards off the prone figure of Thaddeus Slenderman, and back onto the hard stone floor.

Esmerelda fought her captors like a wounded Valkyrie, slashing with her blade at their arms and faces.

Hornbuckle helped Slenderman to his feet and, limping together, they fled the building, even as Father Price and the Castlemaine Military Guard burst in, just in the nick of too late, but bristling heroically with razor-sharp pikes and a fiercely wielded Bible.

With a final desperate slash of her blade, Esmerelda broke free from her captors and sprinted across the room to where Igor lay. She fell to her knees beside his prone body, tears welling up in her keen, green eyes.

Father Price ran across and knelt beside Esme. Together they wept for their fallen love, friend, companion.

*

As the minutes passed, Esmerelda squeezed her eyes tightly shut and fought back her grief. Only one thing mattered now: Kill Slenderman.

She gently laid Igor's head on the cold stone floor and resolved herself to her task. With her bright steel blade in hand, she made off to follow Igor's killers. Whatever happened after that didn't matter. Her life was over anyway, and she knew it. The light that had so recently entered her heart had been extinguished forever.

Slowly, numbly, she paced across the room. Father Price called to her, an unexpected sound of hope in his trembling voice. 'Esmerelda, look!'

Igor's eyes flickered open and he sat bolt upright. 'FRRREEEOOOWWWNNGGG!!! Wowee the wee wee!!' He fell back down again in a dead faint, then sat up again and started barking.

Esmerelda ran across to him and, crying openly, threw her arms around his neck. 'I thought I'd lost you, I thought you were dead.'

Igor struggled to focus; he'd been somewhere very weird and he wasn't really sure if this was normal or even which way was Tuesday. For the moment, he didn't care. He stopped barking and started singing a saucily worded version of 'La Marseillaise'.

Esme stroked his head as he slowly regained his senses.

After a time, his breathing settled and he began to look at the faces around him. He recognised Esme and smiled his broadest smile.

A painful twinge made its unwelcome presence felt, and he looked down towards his chest where the dart had hit. It was still there, and he could feel its sharp point digging into his flesh. He could also feel the silver locket that had slowed the pace of the dart, and which had deflected most of the Ogs'pogs potion. He removed the dart carefully from his shirt and then took out the locket. The locket he had worn every day since his escape from Castle Frankenstein, the locket that he'd had since he was a small boy, the locket he had sort of just owned, without remembering how.

The dart had hit it a hair's width from the edge, passing through the thin metal bracing around the hinge. The corrosive potion had tarnished the silver and when he opened it, Igor could already feel the hinge weakening.

With the small amount of Ogs'pogs potion that he had received, Igor had passed beyond the veil and visited the dead. And the dead were most definitely not happy.

*

Hornbuckle hefted his wounded boss into the cart and together they galloped hurriedly towards Castlemaine. Slenderman had deposited most of his cash at the magistrates' office for safekeeping and he needed to make an immediate withdrawal. They had to move on again and find new, richer pastures.

The cart rolled into the town square where Slenderman, aided by his faithful servant, slowly climbed the steps to the magistrates' office.

A crowd began gathering behind them as they made their way inside. Neither Helsing nor Hopkins were available to open the safe, as they were presently laying traps by the river for a recently sighted herd of giant carnivorous mole men, so the pair had to wait nearly an hour while the deputy keyholder could be found and sobered up.

After all the paperwork was completed, Slenderman picked up his cash and sneered rudely, wishing the good people of Castlemaine a short life, ill health and much misery. The keyholder looked at the two men, coughed, turned a peculiar shade of green, then vomited on Slenderman's shoes.

With a mixture of strong alcohol and stomach acid rapidly eating its way through his shoe leather, Slenderman exited the magistrates' office and stood, cash bags in hand, at the top of the steps, blinking in the horizontal rays of the late evening sun.

A large crowd had gathered and were standing in the square looking up at the two men. Many were holding flaming torches while others carried a varied array of sharp and dangerous-looking garden implements.

'Fear not, Hornbuckle,' smiled Slenderman. 'These are my people.'

Steadying himself carefully, he raised his hands in the air and cried out to his supporters, 'Transylvania for Transylvanians!'

A stony wall of silence greeted him from the blank-faced crowd.

He tried another one, 'Make Carpathia Great Again!'

Nothing.

'Take Back Control?'

The crowd began to shuffle forwards, murmuring menacingly and waggling their tools at him. Slenderman started to look worried.

He reached up for the jewelled pendant around his neck.

'Looking for this, fat boy?' Igor was standing at the front of the crowd; in his hand was Slenderman's smoke and mirrors charm. No longer bound by its effects, the villagers could finally see Slenderman for the lying, cheating fraud he really was.

'Igor, you're alive, how wonderful.' Slenderman picked up his cash bags and began stumbling back up the steps. The crowd shifted forwards, rakes and pitchforks waving ominously in the air.

Hornbuckle felt a strong hand on his shoulder and he winced as the fingers gripped deeply into muscle and bone.

'Hello... *husband.*' Gretchen Hornbuckle stabbed a hobnailed boot into the back of her not-so-late husband's knee and he fell to the ground with a crack.

'Gretchen, I...' he got no further. The horny knuckles of his wife's iron fist hit him square between the eyes and he tumbled to the stones in a messy heap.

Slenderman watched in horror as his only remaining supporter was dragged away by the fearsome centenarian, a trail of noxious pipe smoke trailing greasily behind.

All eyes were now fixed on Thaddeus Slenderman and his bulging cash bags.

'Seems like you owe the people here some compensation,' said Igor, the crowd murmuring their agreement. 'After all, who was it that took their livelihoods?'

'Slenderman!' shouted the crowd angrily.

'And who was it that disturbed the peaceful rest of their dearly departed loved ones?'

'Slenderman!' they cried again.

'And who put the ram in the rama-lama-ding-dong?'

The crowd looked at Igor, bewildered. Clearly, the Ox pox was still playing havoc with Igor's circuitry.

'Slenderman?' the crowd jeered uncertainly.

'Oh, no don't worry, just something I heard in a trance a short while ago,' smiled Igor. 'Which reminds me.'

Igor held up the whistle that had fallen from Typhus's flying medicine bag and put it to his lips. He blew a long blast and a dozen shambling corpses pushed their way to the front of the crowd, followed in their turn by a dozen more, their cold, dead eyes staring menacingly at Slenderman. At their head was the small purply-green child, angrily waving the smoky stump of the severed arm she had used to burn the painting.

'You see, you failed to realise one simple thing in your haste to exploit these poor, voiceless, powerless people.' Igor stared hard at the whimpering industrialist, remembering his own past of being exploited by powerful men with no thought for anything but their own profit.

'And that one simple thing you failed to realise, my old fruitcake, is that inside each one of us are links with the dead. It's a kind of inner net. You can use it to find absolutely anything. Or anyone. It's how the shamen got their answers all those years ago. You can even gurgle it, apparently. So, when I was in my Ogs'pogs trance I made use of the inner net and connected with all of the dead within a fifty-mile radius and I told them who you are and where you could be found. Any corpses that can move, all those that you exploited, all those you used and abused, are on their way here, right now.'

Igor smiled a charming, menacing smile. 'Time to lose a bit of that extra weight there, Slenderman. Time for you to run!'

Thaddeus Slenderman cast a terrified look at the rows of angry faces in the crowd, both living and dead.

'It wasn't my fault, Igor, you must know that. It was Madame De'Ath, she made me do it, all of it, I had no choice, I swear.'

Igor blew the whistle a final time. The dead groaned and began to shuffle forwards.

'On you go, lads,' smiled Igor.

As Esmerelda slipped her arm around Igor's waist and rested her auburn curls on his shoulder, the crowd surged forwards, gathered up Thaddeus Slenderman and his money, and carried him away into the last rays of the evening sun.

THE TALE END

'Well, we still don't know who was feeding that bloody raptor thing do we?' The thin man with the fighting squirrel eyebrows harrumphed as Esmerelda's story came to an end.

Esme smiled a crooked smile. 'Oh, yes, I forgot. It was…'

But just as Esme was about to speak, the space around her table was abuzz with a feast of unfamiliar faces throwing a myriad of questions and observations all at once.

'Who was it put the ram in the rama-lama-thingummybob?'

'What did Fudgegusset smell like?'

'Could I gurgle the inner net?' cried one old man. 'Or should I send a female?'

'Can you really destroy a major descendent of ancient vampire royalty just with a single firearm?'

'Enough for now, I think,' said Father Price firmly, coming to Esme's rescue.

THE TALE END

A groan of disappointment radiated out among the tired but fascinated villagers.

At that moment, Basil appeared through the front door of the bar, a large sack thrashing and screaming in his hand. 'Don't mind me.' He walked through the bar towards the kitchen, the bag making angry noises at his side.

'You look exhausted, Esme. Go to your bed now.' Father Price held his dear friend's wrinkled and bony hand and caressed it warmly.

'I won't sleep,' she replied, a look of deep sadness filling her eyes. She poured herself a glass of the rough gin that Hector Smallfoot and his companions had been drinking earlier. She swallowed the acrid liquid in one then poured herself another.

Basil burst back into the room dragging a dishevelled-looking man behind him by the arm. Esme barely recognised the weathered traveller, particularly as he was newly shaven and was also now naked, except for a very large and angry-looking boar-badger which was roped firmly to his bare backside.

'Right,' shouted Basil. 'You're a man of your word now, aren't you? Off you go. Head south for three days, then turn west for two and then south again for another six days and you should be somewhere near the monastery of Saint Olaf the Salty before Whitsun.' The villagers cheered heartily as Basil pushed the contrite wanderer out through the door and into the first rays of dawn.

'Now then, for the rest of the rubbish.' Basil went across to the coat rack where Smallfoot was last seen, groaning with the pain of having been impaled through the shoulder on a rusty, bent coat hook.

He was nowhere to be found. A trail of dried blood ran from the coat rack to the side door. Clearly, Smallfoot had made his quiet escape much earlier in the night while Esmerelda had been recounting her tales.

Never mind, thought Basil lightly. *He'll be back for more soon enough.*

The villagers began to disperse, some heading back to their homes, but others went straight back to the fields; a fresh new day was beginning and there would be no sleep for many.

Father Price helped Esme to her feet and called over one of the servants. 'Come on, we can talk more tomorrow. You need some rest.'

Her eyes were damp with the tears that all her memories had evoked. She took the servant's arm and allowed him to lead her towards the stairs.

She turned and looked back at her old friend. 'I still can't believe it's you,' she smiled warmly. 'Goodnight. And thank you.'

As she turned to go, Grizelda's voice called nervously across the room. 'Miss Flossie, I mean, Esmerelda. There's people coming.'

Basil and Father Price went to the window to look.

'Smallfoot!' exclaimed the huge landlord, clenching his fists angrily. 'What mischief has he been up to?'

Esmerelda joined them at the window. She looked out at the approaching crowd, shock and fear suddenly draining the blood from her haggard face. Her hand reached out towards Father Price just as he reached out for hers.

Smallfoot was approaching and with him came the Bishop of Saint Augustine and his holy warrior guards.

THE TALE END

There was nowhere to run. They were trapped. Their secret identities, which had remained hidden for so many years, were now known to all, and the bishop, who had his own special reasons for wanting to see them both dead, was staring back at them from outside the filth-encrusted window.

Esme sighed heavily, weariness flooding her old bones. *I really must clean those*, she thought.

POSTFACE

The wind howled, blowing a flurry of snow through the iron grate at the top of the thick stone wall. The chamber was dark except for a short tallow candle, which guttered and spat, giving off a feeble yellow light.

The gaunt old man sat hunched, naked except for a rough sackcloth garment, which can have given scant comfort on such a fiercely cold night.

A flask of clear liquid sat on the floor beside him. Shakily, the old man picked up the flask and, with an effort, removed the leather stopper. He took a short sip then threw back his head and let the warm liquor run slowly down his throat. He coughed gently, the air bubbling up through the liquid.

'I know, I know,' he murmured quietly to himself. 'She mustn't tell them, it's too dangerous.'

Several minutes passed. The old man stared blankly up

POSTFACE

at the iron grate before opening the flask once more to take another short sip. He coughed again.

'Yes, she has the priest now, but that won't be enough. No, never enough.'

He slumped down on the bench, old age and much toil lying heavy on his thin, bony shoulders.

He slept.

A strong gust of wind sent another icy blast slicing through the iron grate and up inside his tattered garment.

The man woke with a start, his weak old eyes struggling to focus on something that lay under a broken chair, which was just within range of the candle's insipid light.

He unstopped the flask once more and sipped. Another cough, then another rattled in his hollow chest.

A look of extreme sadness settled on the old man's thin, sallow face.

'So, it's time then, Simon, old friend,' he muttered, sadness hanging off every syllable. 'De'Ath is coming for us all.'

ACKNOWLEDGEMENTS

Richard would like to thank:

My partner Jenni for putting up with my flights of fancy and generally humouring me. Malcolm Croft for his advice, assistance, and sense of humour. Without Malcolm's encouragement, Ian and I would never have progressed this book to publication, so now you know who to blame! My mum and dad for creating this monster in the first place, providing me with a wonderful childhood and an inherited anarchic streak, both of which I treasure. Great mate and artist par excellence, Simon Pritchard for the terrific imagery that graces this cover. All at Matador for giving our creation a home. Lon, Boris, Bela, Vincent, Christopher, Peter et al for a lifetime of entertainment and inspiration. And of course, Ian J Walls – collaborator, co-conspirator, and dear friend, whose fantastic imagination, Herculean work ethic and all-

ACKNOWLEDGEMENTS

round enthusiasm has rescued me from a seemingly eternal loop of banging on to anyone who will listen about how I intend to write a book one day. It is thanks to Ian agreeing to co-author a project that I can finally give all those around me a rest. It's alive!

Ian would like to thank:

My wife Anne for constantly telling me I had a book in me. I knew her X-ray vision would come in handy one day. My co-author Richard for coming up with the idea for Igor's backstory and for making the whole thing happen. Had Richard not been there to prick my conscience into seeing it through then my debut novel would still be very firmly wedged where only Anne could see it. Malcolm Croft, our editor extraordinaire, for his excellent and very valuable experience and advice, and for insisting that we give our murderous innkeeper a name. So now you know why we called him Clam. Simon Pritchard for an amazing piece of original cover art. The man's a genius! Rob and Martin Walls for being totally brilliant and supportive throughout. My writing buddies at *The Evening Harold*: Jeni Brand, Max Curé-Freeman, Sofie Tayton, David Oliver, Malcolm D Goring, Rick Westwell, Stephen Lukey, Stephen Noonan and Martin Hinchcliffe, for producing some of the best comedy writing I've had the pleasure to read over the years and for allowing me to tag along and hone my scribing skills in a safe, nurturing, but weirdly damp environment; *in Quaz nos confidimus*. John O'Farrell and the team at NewsBiscuit for opening their doors to all and sundry and allowing people to write mad stuff about badgers. The good people at Matador for risking their careers and reputation by allowing us to publish under their banner. Helena, Dipti, Louise and John for still being good friends forty-odd years later. Finally, the late Audrey Whale and Gerry Anstock for setting the bar high and inspiring us to aim at the stars.